# THE SEDUCTION OF MRS CAINE

### Mary Ryan

**HEADLINE**

First published in1996
by HEADLINE BOOK PUBLISHING

10 9 8 7 6 5 4 3 2 1

British Library Cataloguing in Publication Data

Ryan, Mary, 1945–
The seduction of Mrs Caine
1. English fiction – 20th century – Irish authors
I. Title
823.9'14 [F]

ISBN 0-7472-1534-0

Typeset by
CBS, Felixstowe, Suffolk

Printed in England by
Clays Ltd, St Ives plc

HEADLINE BOOK PUBLISHING
A division of Hodder Headline PLC
338 Euston Road
London NW1 3BH

For Nora

## ACKNOWLEDGEMENTS

With thanks to Johnny for his help and inspiration, to Jean Perrem who provided the story of the woman on the bus, to my sons, John and Pierce, for unwitting advice on background detail.

I would also like to thank my editor Geraldine Cooke for her encouragement, Kirsty Fowkes for her help and copy-editor Helen Norris for her painstaking work.

Mary Ryan
Dublin, March 1996

'Then suddenly the tune went false,
The dancers wearied of the waltz . . .'

Oscar Wilde
*The Harlot's House*

# Prologue

'We'll take a walk on the Common when the rain eases,' Bernard Whiston promised, and Herbie, to whom this comment was addressed, panted enthusiastically and whacked his tail on the floor. Bernard glanced around to satisfy himself that he was alone, before openly studying himself in the mirror above the fireplace, and addressing his reflection in the sardonic tenor which was his wont.

'More and more like a vulture each day, old chap. Still, the story could be worse! Miller is beginning to look like a marmoset, and Warren rather like a weasel.' (He was thinking of two of his cronies, members of the same club.) 'There is a relative nobility in vultures . . . a hauteur. You don't mess with them . . .'

Through the French window he saw his son-in-law Keith in the garden. Keith would garden even in the rain. What age is he now? he wondered. Let's see . . . he was twenty-six when he married Marguerite and that was thirty years ago. He's fifty-six . . . by Jove . . . catching up on me . . . If he's not careful he'll become middle aged, boring . . .

Bernard looked across the room at the portrait of his dead daughter; he thought of his granddaughter Mo, whose real name was Sophie, now working in New York for a law firm he had once had dealings with. He even remembered his wife who had divorced him when she was fifty, only to die (from want of excitement he supposed) the following year. Occasionally his life flashed its way through his head; sometimes it seemed absurdly short: that so little should have happened in real terms . . . Other times it seemed to stretch behind him into a reverse infinity.

'I'm as old as sin,' he conceded to Herbie, with a kind of dog

1

to dog candour. 'But who cares! Time is pure nonsense! The only thing any of us really needs is a bit of excitement.'

He picked up his paper and sat by the fire, but his eyes turned again to the mackintosh-clad figure in the garden. 'All this introversion can't be good for the boy . . . I'll have to think of something . . .'

# Chapter One

The housing estate stretched into the distance and beyond it you could see the mountains. Polly often wondered what it looked like from the air: fairly geometric, she assumed, precise rows of dog-boxes. Sometimes she wished she lived at the edge of the development, with nothing behind her house but the cloud-patterned fields, wished she could see from the kitchen window the long stretch of green to where the mountains rose. Vistas like that made her fantasise about freedom.

If you inspected the names of the roads and cul-de-sacs of the housing estate you would see that they were mostly sylvan. There was The Grove, and The Willows, and The Copse. There was Beeches Road, although it was twenty years since any beech had reared its branches in its vicinity. There was Ashgrove Lawns, where Polly lived, a cul-de-sac of semi-detached houses with small squares of garden, some well tended, some languishing from the combined attentions of pets and children. But they were dwarfed by the presence in their midst of Willow House with its incongruous atmosphere of an age long gone.

At the inner perimeter of this suburban sprawl was the village, a quaint anomaly, which still managed, despite the recent advent of a shopping centre, to preserve its nineteenth-century ambience. The new shopping complex was built on some waste ground adjoining the old workhouse churchyard. The workhouse itself, a derelict shambles from a destitute past, had been cleared to make way for the Pyramid with its high glass dome and automatic doors. This was built on two levels and had a wide variety of retail outlets, as well as a gym called the Health Club and a coffee shop. It was from this building that on a Friday afternoon in February two women emerged,

3

shivered suddenly and adjusted their scarves against the east wind. One was Polly and the other her friend and neighbour Susan O'Brien.

'Poll,' Susie said, as she pushed down the lock of red hair which the wind had taken. 'Did you hear the one about the woman who kidnapped the baby?'

'No?'

'Fifteen years later she brought it back. Ha . . . ha . . . And guess who didn't want it? Ha ha . . .'

Polly, who was no stranger to Susie's immoderate witticisms, laughed, but raised her eyes to the overcast sky.

Polly's real name was Pauline Caine. She and Susie were neighbours, living respectively at Nos 14 and 15 Ashgrove Lawns. Their cul-de-sac contained thirty houses ranged around a turning space and connected to the main estate roadway. Only the presence of Willow House, set apart from the other houses and closeted in its own spacious precincts behind a high railing, took Ashgrove Lawns out of the ordinary.

Willow House had once lorded it over the land the estate was built on, land which had once belonged to the Reeveses. But they had fallen on hard times and the last of the line, Muriel, had sold the land for housing and had spent part of the very considerable proceeds in refurbishing the mansion.

Sometimes Polly thought of her own advent to Ashgrove Lawns, when she had come with diffidence, a full twenty years before, keenly aware of her ambiguous position as replacement to Martha, Rory's first and only legal wife. Sue, having noted her arrival from next door, had given her two hours before arriving on the doorstep.

'Welcome to Shangri-la,' she had said, handing her a pot of home-made marmalade. Later, having partaken of two glasses of sherry, Susie had given Polly some advice about the neighbours: 'Don't take one bit of heed of that Laura Flanagan at the corner, or madam across the road with the manse . . .'

Polly had soon met Laura Flanagan who lived in one of the three detached houses at the end of the cul-de-sac where it merged into the main estate road. Laura was an accountant's widow, a bit longer in the tooth than most of the other women, and laboured under the delusion that she was the fulcrum of the universe. Polly had also met Muriel Reeves, the reserved, enigmatic young woman living across the road in Willow House, last of the old, local, land-owning family. She had been introduced by Susie one day in the village.

'Muriel ... this is Polly Caine. She's living at number fourteen. Polly, this is Muriel Reeves ... she lives in Willow House.'

'Oh yes, Rory's new wife!' Muriel said, in a voice with the startling precision of cut glass. 'I do hope you'll be very happy in Ashgrove Lawns.'

There was something about the chatelaine of Willow House that marked her as different, like a being who had been kidnapped by a time machine and transported from the past. Everything about her spoke of attention to form; her voice, her posture, the severe way she wore her fair hair – pulled back from her face and screwed into a bun – her perfect clothes. Above all, there was her careful social demeanour, too formal in an informal age. Polly was initially intimidated, but she had murmured her thanks and had told her how much she liked looking out of her window at Willow House. 'When I look out in the morning I always think I've been transported back in time ... It gives the whole cul-de-sac such a lovely atmosphere ...'

Polly had blushed then, wondering if she was being too effusive. She hated to gush, but meant what she had said. A country girl, she had been used, in childhood, to unencumbered horizons, and, in her student days, to the ramshackle amplitude of the Georgian house where she had shared a flat; only Rory and Susie and Willow House reconciled her to the cul-de-sac. She had always proclaimed her intent to avoid suburbia: 'No kennel for me, thank you ... A little breathing space, a bit of character, or forget it ...'

That, of course, had been before she had walked into Rory Caine one Monday lunchtime at the delicatessen in Upper Leeson Street, before passion had engulfed her and she had assumed that it would have the same currency for all her tomorrows.

Of course they were only beginning then, those tomorrows, and Muriel, studying her new neighbour, had smiled.

'Why don't you come over ... both of you ... why not come over for a drink this evening!'

\* \* \*

5

'You seem to have made an impression on madam!' Susie had said to her later as they crossed the road to the gates of Willow House. 'Wait till you see her gaff . . . money no object. You know, when the estate was newly built, she used to give a garden party every year – she seemed desperate to get to know everyone – but she hasn't held one for the past two years! She's probably sussed us out . . . knows what she has. Ha!'

But that evening, while entertaining her two neighbours in her drawing room, Muriel had spoken with a curious kind of diffidence, as though seeking some kind of forbearance for the vicissitudes of fortune. 'You see,' she said, 'it was only when I sold the land that I could afford to do up the house. Prior to that we – my mother and I – lived in a kind of sieve, buckets in the landing to catch the drips. We might as well have been in Noah's Ark. We were quite primitive in those days . . . very countrified . . . not a house between us and the village.'

Muriel sipped her drink and looked from one of her guests to the other. 'When she died I made the decision to sell the land . . . but I kept the Ark!'

'Some Ark!' Susie said flatly, looking around at the silk Chinese carpet and the antiques. 'Where did you quarter the animals?' and Muriel laughed suddenly, a genuine peal of mirth which seemed to Polly to be elicited more by Susie's flamboyance than by the small witticism.

Polly, admiring the lovely pieces in Willow House, had shyly confessed her love of antiques, and Susie had said that Polly was an expert – hadn't she worked with them before she got married?

'Really?' Muriel had said. 'So you're some kind of antiquarian?'

'Well . . . I did History of Art in college and after that two years with Adams, an apprenticeship really . . .'

A few days later Muriel had encountered Polly in the village, where she was gazing in the window of the small antique shop with the bemused, famished expression of the lovelorn. Polly was regarding with solemn intensity a fine Italian white marble figure of a young lady, which bore a price tag of fifty pounds.

'What are you staring at with such interest?' Muriel asked.

Polly pointed at the white marble figurine, the little maiden frozen for ever in timeless grace. 'Isn't she gorgeous!'

6

Muriel considered the statuette with interest. 'Yes . . . Are you going to purchase it?'

'Can't afford her!'

'Polly,' Muriel said after a moment, 'would you do an inventory of the stuff in my place . . . for insurance purposes? I meant to ask you—'

'I'd be delighted.'

Polly had spent the following Saturday in the old house, cataloguing the antiques, discussing their fine points with Muriel, losing, in the process, the shyness which sometimes almost strangled her. There were things in Willow House from the eighteenth century, a Sheraton cabinet, early Coalport porcelain, silver bearing early Irish hallmarks. There were portraits of people gazing out gravely across the reach of two hundred years.

'This was worked by my great-great-grandmother,' Muriel said, holding up a fine linen tablecloth, embroidered and edged with lace. There were drawerfuls of old linen, lace table mats, a banquet cloth so beautiful that it would be a sin to use it. But as the day wore on, even more esoteric items surfaced from various cabinets, among them some photographs in silver frames face down in a drawer. Polly exclaimed on the frames, but when she saw not only that the glass in these was broken but that the faces in the photographs had been deliberately obliterated, she had had a strange feeling of unease, as though something dark lay at the heart of Muriel's life which threatened to overtake her, like rot at the core of a shining apple.

Before she left she said, 'What about old books – first editions . . . ?'

They were standing in the hall. Scarlet and amber light from the stained-glass window in the return of the stairs patterned the wall.

Muriel gestured. 'Oh, they're in the study . . .' and she indicated a closed door. 'It's locked . . . I'm afraid the key is lost.'

'Oh . . .' Polly said and then was silent. Muriel asked her what she owed her for her work.

'I couldn't charge a neighbour for something which gave me so much pleasure . . . !'

A few days later a small parcel had arrived at No 14, and in it was the Italian figurine. The accompanying card simply said, 'Dear Polly, A small token of thanks. Muriel.'

That had been twenty years ago. The marble lady had graced Polly's sitting room since, but Muriel had seemed to have become more distant, removed in real time, like the denizen of a bell jar, although she waved whenever she was passing, and offered lifts if she chanced on her neighbour in the village. When Polly tried to find out more about her she was informed that Muriel had been jilted. No one seemed to know very much about the circumstances; it was rumoured that her fiancé had been a doctor. She did not seem to have a current boyfriend. In fact, except for the exotic foreign holiday she took each year (places like Antigua and the Seychelles were mentioned), she seemed something of a recluse, although she did turn up with engraved silver christening mugs when Polly and Sue had babies and made wistful comment on her neighbours' good fortune.

'That one!' Susie said in exasperation. 'All *plamás*! You didn't hear her offering to babysit!'

'It was very nice of her to call and bring a lovely present,' Polly said, uneasy at this acerbity.

'I know . . . but I think she'd buy you if you let her.'

Polly demurred, but the knowledge that Susie disliked Muriel discouraged her from deepening her friendship with her, and the burgeoning entente which had sprung from a shared interest became more or less moribund.

Time passed and everything, quietly, almost imperceptibly, mutated. The wonderful babies became teenagers bearing no resemblance at all to the enchanting infants they once had been. They were loud, aggressive and opinionated, interested in the putting-down of parents, in a variety of zit-banishing unguents, and in various rackets passing for music.

And life had also worked its subtle depredations. Susie's husband Fergus, who worked in computer software, was now about to be made redundant. He had, among other things, developed a program, based on fractal geometry, to compress huge programs into small areas, but because his company were cutting back on R & D staff he was suddenly surplus to requirements.

Polly's husband Rory, who was a teacher of history in the local Community School, had been pipped for the position of department head, and now drowned his sorrows in his computer, hacking away every spare moment, striving to complete a data base which would form the core of a book he intended to write on early European history. He tried to interest Polly in it occasionally, but while the history was interesting, the computer jargon was not. Fergus was a help to him, designing flow-control algorhythms to assist with cross-indexing.

Susie, through all the vicissitudes of motherhood, had kept on her part-time secretarial job for a solicitor, Mr William Penston, who had a thriving practice in the village. The sign on his windows, in bold gold letters, said 'Penston and Company, Solicitors, Commissioners for Oaths'. William Penston had inherited the practice from his late father, but had modernised the outfit, so that the great bundles of deeds and dusty papers, which used to hold up the office walls, were no longer in evidence. He had a small moustache, red-grey, and looked a bit like a terrier. But he was kind, despite occasional forays into pomposity, and because of this and because she was lazy, Susie had stayed with him down the years. She did not suspect that her husband Fergus was jealous of William Penston.

Polly, amenable and diffident, sensible to her duties as mother and wife, feeling virtuous when the local parish priest declaimed on the horrors of 'latch-key kids', glad that no stones, in that context at least, could be thrown at her, did not work outside the home. Rory was dead set against it; 'No wife of mine is going to work . . .' he had said with much bravado when they first set up house together.

At the time this had suited Polly well enough. While the children were babies she loved having the leisure to dote on them, kiss them, nibble their toes, cart them around on her back, talk nonsense to them. Later, when she began to chafe at the restricted tenor of her life, she found that she had lost crucial career-building time, which, in the nature of things, was non-returning and non-renewable.

9

Although she had an honours degree in the History of Art she had never forged a career. Quite apart from the delectable babies, there were reasons why she had so readily accepted domesticity as her role. As Rory's second wife, if wife she could be called because he was still legally married to Martha, she coped with her secret guilt, her sense of having outraged conventional morality, by being the perfect housewife and mother. This was all right while she was still terribly in love, waiting for the touch of Rory's hand, the scent of his breath, the response of his body, the magic of communion.

When other demands had begun to assert themselves she suppressed them. Anyway, she was profoundly shy, as great a handicap as a stutter or partial paralysis. And she was also a devout Catholic, a believer in self-sacrifice and duty and the various other pious imperatives aimed most particularly at women. This belief was a refuge from the increasing unease which bedevilled her. It enabled her to convince herself that her lot was immutable, and absolved her – when the subliminal prompting to alter the status quo became vociferous – from the terrifying prospect of effecting radical change.

Polly stopped at the gate of No 14. Behind her a reluctant spear of February sunlight brightened the walls of Willow House.

'I'd better go in and get on with it,' Polly said. 'Pity you can't come to supper . . . meet Michelle. She sounds really nice!'

She was referring to the visitor coming that evening, her brother Tom's fiancée, who was in Ireland on business and was dropping in to meet her prospective new in-laws. Polly had already asked Susie if she and Fergus would join them for supper, but they had a prior engagement.

'Of course . . . you did mention that your mysterious brother had finally got himself engaged,' Susie said. 'He left it late enough, didn't he?' She chuckled and said suddenly, as she regarded the front of her own home, 'Christ, I'll have to replace those bloody nets. It's that fucking pup—'

Polly, whose head was full of her brother and his fiancée, did not immediately follow her friend's drift. But then she saw the smear on next door's white net curtains, the way the edge of one of them was chewed, and remembered Wags, the twins' new pet.

'My mother wouldn't let them in the house . . . dogs.'

'Damn right,' Susie said. 'I'll wring the little bastard's neck
. . .' She gave a determined heave to her shopping bag and
strode up her short pathway, letting herself in. There was a
joyous yapping, followed by Susie's voice.

'You're a little rat. I'll send you to China where dogs like you
end up in the stew . . . Hey! Stop that . . . OK . . . OK . . . Take
it easy, I love you too . . .'

Polly let herself in to her home, shut the door and put the
polythene shopping bags on the table. Her arms felt as though
they had been dragged from their sockets, so she sat down for
a moment and contemplated the shopping, the table, the clean
floor which she had mopped before she went out, the wall clock
which clicked as the red minute hand twitched sedately around
its face. It was three o'clock. Jason would be home from school
at half past, and Peter would be home from college at six, around
the same time as his father, who liked to stay in school after
hours to mark his pupils' work. This gave him time to spend at
his computer when he came home.

She got out her favourite well-thumbed cookery book, found
the recipe for boeuf bourguignon, and had a cup of instant coffee
while she perused it. Then she got up and started to work,
dicing the beef and bacon and peeling the shallots and garlic.
The family pet, a fat tabby who had no proper name and was
simply called 'Cat', appeared on the windowsill outside. When
she saw Polly she mewed, at first plaintively and then
peremptorily, as became an important cat summoning her
attendant. Polly sighed, but she finished what she was doing,
trying to block out the sounds from the windowsill until she
had added the wine to the casserole and put it in the oven.
Then she opened the back door and Cat, reverting to elegance,
entered sedately, tail held high, and went straight to her bowl
which was in the corner by the sink. The bowl contained a few
scraps of meat which Polly had placed there, and Cat ate them
very quickly and then gave a few gentle n'urps to show that
she had dined insufficiently. Polly sighed, found the new tin of
Miaou, opened it and spooned some of its evil, glutinous contents
into the bowl.

Sixty-five pence! she thought, looking at the sticker on the
tin – (Cat turned her nose up at cheaper brands). One tin lasts

a day. There are three hundred and sixty-five days in the year. That's two hundred and thirty-seven pounds per annum. Multiplied by twelve which is the expected feline life span. Then we had to have her spayed and there was the stay in the Pets' Hospital the time she was knocked down by a car. By the time she croaks that cat is going to have cost in excess of three thousand pounds!

'You're not cheap, Cat,' Polly said. 'This may have escaped your notice, but it has not escaped mine . . .' Then she thought, God, that stuff stinks . . . and she picked up the bowl and put it outside the back door. Cat hurried after, giving piteous cries.

When Polly had wiped up after her cooking she checked the heat in the oven and went upstairs. The children's rooms were in disarray, especially Jason's, whose socks were strewn under the bed. She had recently decided that she would stop picking up after her children, so she resisted the temptation to clean everything up, shut both doors, went into her own bedroom which overlooked the back garden, sat at the dressing table and examined her face. She had caught her reflection earlier in the plate glass of a window full of lingerie displayed for Valentine's Day and had moved quickly away. Now she summoned up the courage to look for lines, angling her face so that the light caught it sideways. Her face was still unlined, but her short hair was mousy and tinged with grey. She stood and took a dispassionate look at her figure, noted with resignation the midriff bulge, the sturdy stance of her matronly shape in the old track suit.

Outside the afternoon was already turning towards dusk. Some youngsters' voices could be heard from the play-area behind her garden. For a moment she thought one of the voices sounded like Jason's. She glanced out of the window, but the leylandii which had grown so tall around the fence blocked her view.

On impulse she went into his room, looked out on the cul-de-sac. The only person she saw was Sharon O'Brien, Susie's teenage daughter, returning home, her canvas satchel over her shoulder. Polly watched Sharon turn in her front gateway, saw her glance at No 14 and look away swiftly when she saw Polly at the upstairs window.

Nice kid, Polly thought. But her mind reverted to Tom's fiancée, wondered what she was like. She hadn't seen her brother for years, hadn't even had a letter from him. But seven weeks ago he had sent a card to say he had got engaged, a laconic typewritten note from London to advise her of this event and to say that Michelle, his fiancée, would shortly visit Ireland on business and would look her and Rory up.

She had been pathetically glad of this small missive. She had always regretted the stupid rift with Tom. He was her kid brother, the beautiful one for whom she had taken the blame for all childhood peccadilloes. His loss had been the sore point of her life, the tender place in the psyche which must not be touched.

'I'll always look after you!' she had told him, when he was four and she was seven and they had gone to live with Aunt Rita in the Tipperary countryside after the terrible accident which killed their parents.

When she had told him she was going to marry Rory, he had said she was flying in the face of common sense.

'How do you think he's going to support you . . . with a wife already in existence? Do you want to spend your days in poverty? And besides, the fellow's a space-cake . . . He's not good enough for you! And you're a bird-brain that you can't see it . . . When you put a space-cake and a bird-brain together what do you get?'

Polly was unreceptive. Part of her realised there was some truth in her brother's invective. Rory did already have a wife, and had no money. But he was not a space-cake; he was quite brilliant. She suspected, however, that she was not overendowed in the quick-wits department herself, that her judgement was contaminated by passion and hope. Besides, Tom was younger and had no business bossing her about. So her response had been angry.

'Mind your own damn business and keep out of my life!'

'All right . . . I'll keep out of it! But don't come crying to me!'

'Oh, just piss off! You're not in any position to give lectures!'

He had 'pissed off'. Their old relationship had fractured, then broken. Initially they had simply tried to teach each other lessons. Polly had wanted recognition for her own space; she wanted respect. She was in the grip of a force that blinded her, but she did not want to hear that she was blind. By the time she did find out, she had made her bed, and every canon of decency and pride dictated that she continue to lie on it.

She had tried to mend the breach with Tom by sending birthday and Christmas cards, but Tom never reciprocated. The knowledge that her beloved brother, the one person she had always counted on, could cut her out, turn on her judgementally and then disappear from her life, had brought with it a lonely re-evaluation of her perspectives and a feeling that personal relationships were a stormy sea with no safe havens. It had, if anything, fused her more deliberately to her hasty 'marriage' on the basis that there was little else to be had anywhere.

But perhaps it was when she had received the card from her brother telling her of his impending marriage, that the discontent had begun; perhaps it had been festering for years. The dynamic still evident at the heart of her brother's existence (was he not still sculpting his life?) rose up to taunt her. Polly found herself looking forward with some delight to the phone call from Michelle, and to the sense it would bring of resuming her place within the wider family. But the phone call had not materialised. Oh Tom, she had thought, why don't you phone and talk to me? She tried British Directory Enquiries to see if she could locate a number for him, but his number was ex-directory. And she did not have his address.

'Nothing exciting ever happens to me,' she complained to God at Mass one Sunday. 'I spend my one and only life as a domestic prop, and You sit up there all smug, in Your little gold tabernacle, and allow me to be wasted!'

Polly gave the impression of being happy; she projected the aura of a woman who was in control of her life; she was always ready to help with any organised activity, the parish fête, the school bazaar. But in the private space where she really lived, a desperation was fermenting which she could barely contain.

The vista stretching ahead seemed bleak. The children would be gone, and she would still be there, fading and vanishing, but still serving. She knew that her visibility, so far as Rory was concerned, was now more or less non-existent, at least as a woman, and because he, the person to whom she had

14

committed her life, did not see her she was having difficulties seeing herself. This, in turn, was undermining her self-esteem to the point of collapse.

Looking at the golden tabernacle door whence help should emanate, she had thought, with something of the panic which consumed her when she dared to contemplate the future, 'What should I do; what can I do?'

Polly needed God but God was not communicative. 'You could send me a Sign,' Polly said silently. 'You were great at that in the good old days . . . or so the Bible would have us believe . . .'

The doubt, which had also begun to burgeon in recent times, that there was really nothing on the altar except some expensive ornaments, prompted a presumptuous addendum: 'Sure, You probably don't exist anyway. I dare You to send me something, some portent, an angel for example, to act as a catalyst on my boring days!'

But no great portent had emerged to excite the tenor of Polly's life and in due course she had more or less forgotten her challenge to the Creator. It seemed very silly in retrospect. Instead of handing out challenges to incorporeal entities, she tried to cultivate resignation and acceptance.

Eventually a phone call had reminded her of the promised visit of her prospective new sister-in-law; a musical American accent said its owner was just dying to meet her and so Polly had immediately invited her for Friday supper to meet the family.

Now staring at her own reflection in her dressing-table mirror, she wondered what Michelle looked like. She didn't know how old she was, or what she did. She reached into her wardrobe, pulled out the new jumper she had bought in the sales, put it on, changed into a straight black skirt, fighting with the button on the waist band.

The back door opened and shut downstairs. Then there was the sound of the fridge door being opened, then the sound of crockery.

'Is that you, Jason? Don't touch the salad in that fridge, or the chocolate mousse . . . !'

She hurried down. Seventeen-year-old Jason was dangerous to leave unsupervised in the kitchen. He had a gargantuan appetite and regarded everything edible as grist to his ever-hungry mill. He turned to his mother when she came in the kitchen door, and then looked lugubriously at the mousse in the glass bowl, which he had taken from the fridge and which was now sporting a dent. Polly saw that an extremely generous spoonful had been abstracted.

'The mousse is for tonight – your uncle Tom's fiancée is coming – you should have asked,' Polly said in dismay, examining the damage. 'I'll have to do a cover-up job with some whipped cream.'

Jason sighed loudly. He was almost six feet tall, incredibly skinny for someone who could pack away more food in a day than she could in a week; his forehead was liberally studded with pimples, and the remains of whatever salve he had anointed them with gave a repulsive yellowish tinge to their perimeters.

'Well, is there *anything* to eat in this house?'

'You can have bread and butter and cheese. There's chocolate spread or some peanut butter . . .'

'I meant *food*, Mum.'

'You'll have to wait for your dinner . . .'

Jason sighed again, more loudly than before. Cat, who had finished her repast, jumped up on the windowsill and stared in at them. The east wind was not to her liking and she suggested, in a slightly threatening tone of voice, that she be admitted forthwith.

'Drop dead, Cat,' Jason said, liberally spreading peanut butter over some sliced bread.

'How was school?' Polly asked.

'Same as usual, boring.'

'How did you do in your French test?'

Jason chewed meditatively. 'Forty per cent . . . At least I passed,' he added, seeing his mother's disappointed face. 'Most of the class failed! It was bitch hard!'

'You'll have to do better than that if you want to go to college . . .'

Jason made a face. 'I'll get the damn points. You worry too much, Mum . . .'

'And you don't worry enough!'

Jason finished his sandwich, washed it down with half a

litre of milk and went upstairs. The cat mewed again, this time urgently and dangerously, indicating that her patience was exhausted and that she wouldn't be a nice cat for much longer. Polly opened the back door and the family pet rushed from her chilly perch on the windowsill, recovering propriety once she was indoors and padding in a mincing fashion to her basket under the kitchen bookcase, where the dictionaries and atlases were kept. She described a few circular movements, kneading her cushion into optimum comfort; then she curled up and pretended to sleep, keeping one eye half open in case something exciting happened. She had a vague memory of the sweeping brush which had swept her out the door one morning after her mistress had found a smelly posset of regurgitated Miaou in the corner of the hall.

Polly cleared away Jason's plate and glass and kitchen knife from the table and then noticed the dirt that he had trailed across the floor. She ran into the hall, saw that the formerly pristine olive green carpet bore small chunks of mud which had escaped from her son's soles, and that these had continued up the stairs like some kind of spoor. In a few seconds he had undone the careful hoovering which had taken up so much of the morning.

'Jason,' she howled, 'get the Hoover and clean up that mess you brought up the stairs after you! But first take off your boots . . .'

Jason appeared in the landing, looking down at her over the banister. 'What mess?' he demanded hotly. Then he saw the mud. 'F—' he muttered, but he came down, dragged the Hoover from its home under the stairs, and began to clean it up.

'And when you've done that,' Polly said, 'you can give your own room a going-over. It's like the city dump! And I'm not a slave!'

'I have work to do,' Jason said. 'I have a history essay . . .'

Polly sighed. This excuse was the well-worn panacea for all maternal demands.

'Well at least liberate your socks,' his mother said acerbically. 'There are so many of them living under your bed that it's a wonder they haven't already made a spontaneous bid for freedom. There is a laundry basket outside your door. What do you think it's there for?'

Jason muttered something which was intended to convey what a poor opinion he had of maternal sarcasm. He returned to his room, gathered up his socks from under his bed and slammed them into the wicker basket on the landing.

Polly felt tired. She felt Jason's angst keenly; she felt how he dismissed her domestic will. It made her wonder whether he was right, whether she was a fussy old mother who made his life a misery. But she had nothing to compare herself against, and did not know what to do about the problem. Her automatic reflex was to force herself to live within the parameters permitted her, the parameters which had come with the air she had breathed all her life, which exalted family values and motherly self-sacrifice. But her reflexes were increasingly at war with the insistent subliminal voice within her which demanded life.

She took refuge in a duster, folding it and carefully wiping every piece of furniture in the dining and sitting rooms, lingering lovingly on the Italian Victorian statuette on the mantelpiece, which Muriel had given her so many years ago, the gilt-framed pier mirror, and the Victorian marquetry snap-top table; these latter items she had bought at an auction some years previously and had cleaned and restored.

She rubbed the cloth with less enthusiasm over Rory's computer which took up the corner of the dining room. It was on its own table, with a bookcase beside it and an angle lamp. The bookcase was filled with history books and small paperback volumes with titles like *Take Word for Windows to the Edge*.

She looked out at the small wintry garden, saw how it was in need of tending, how the snowdrops were tentatively drooping small white heads, how ragged the leylandii were around the fence. In her mind's eye she landscaped this garden, gave it a patio, a crazy-paving pathway to the shed, a lovely small lawn that was not scuffed by teenage feet, a few rose trees that would be allowed to bloom in peace.

Then she got out her damask linen tablecloth and began to set the table. When that was done she returned to the kitchen and began to bake. She had to make a chocolate cake for the parish bring and buy sale.

She was taking the cake out of the oven when Rory came

home. She heard the car in the drive, the sound of the door shutting, his steps on the path to the back door, the thump of the bulging gladstone bag which preceded him into the kitchen. The old relief – that he was home safe, that he had not had an accident, that he had not gone back to Martha – rose in her, despite the fact that twenty years had elapsed and Martha probably wouldn't have him now anyway.

'Hello, darling,' she said.

Rory was forty-six years old, medium height, spare, balding, bespectacled. He was dogmatic in his approach to life; he knew a good deal about history and other things, not least the science of computing, and was quite prepared to give anyone interested the benefit of his expertise. He liked to keep everything in life on a sound basis, where reason and logic ruled. He had no time for silly sentiment. Despite this, however, he sometimes forgot the ordinary parameters of his own life, like which of his children was which, or where he had left his false teeth. They were insignificant compared to the questions he tossed over in his mind, questions concerning historical problems and the ever-growing complexity of computers.

Rory's ears had, in recent years, become hairy. Polly was fond of these hairy ears and when the children called their father 'the Hobbit' in her hearing (but never in his) her reprimand was not full blooded; the name conjured a creature both peaceable and endearing. Rory was certainly peaceable, except when he couldn't find his socks or his keys or his underpants or his new sweater, or when he was disturbed at the computer. On these occasions there were small, albeit intense, explosions, and mutterings about 'those effing children'.

To protect his underwear, he had acquired a heavy leather pilot's bag with a combination lock where he now kept his shorts and his vests and socks. Although under lock these items still mysteriously vanished; Jason had tried all the family birthdays on the combination and, sure enough, one of them had been the magic formula.

Polly did not tell Rory that his missing sweater had disappeared in a nightclub, courtesy of his younger son. It was, Jason had told her defensively, gone when he had turned around. It wasn't his fault. It was the fault of the nightclub

19

for allowing knackers into the place.

'So far that makes one leather jacket, one Dannimac coat, one Levi jacket, and one Tricot Marine sweater gone to clothe greater Dublin. I can't afford to clothe greater Dublin . . . You should look after your clothes, especially your father's clothes . . .'

'It wasn't my fault,' Jason repeated sullenly.

'You could have left your things in the cloakroom.'

'That costs money, Mum. It costs a quid!'

Polly had given up. After that she had bought Jason a twenty-five-pound jacket from Penneys to replace the one that had been purloined in the nightclub.

'I can't wear that!'

'Why not? It's warm, even stylish . . .'

'But everyone will know it only cost twenty-five pounds,' Jason said, eyes wide, pimpled forehead creased in dismay.

'Tough! But I have to operate on the basis that next week, or perhaps the week after, it will have gone AWOL and that I'll have to buy another one.'

'I won't wear it!' Jason growled. 'It's all right, Mum; be as mean as you like . . . I don't mind freezing!'

Now she looked at Rory, measuring how tired he was, longing secretly for a loving word or touch from him. Rory said, 'Hi, Poll . . .' dropped his gladstone bag and made for the downstairs loo. When he came out he went into the dining room and emerged chagrined. 'Why is the dining-room table set? Are we having visitors?'

'Yes . . . Have you forgotten? Michelle is coming for supper—'

'Michelle? Who's she?'

'I have a brother called Tom,' Polly said drily, remembering clearly that she had advised him of Michelle's identity at least twice in the last forty-eight hours. 'He is about to marry. Michelle is his wife-to-be. I told you about this some time ago. And last night I told you we would be having her to supper!'

'What I'd like to know is why he's getting pally now . . . sending his lady to us. He didn't bother us for twenty years!'

'I'm very glad she's coming!' Polly said. 'I don't believe in nursing grievances!'

Rory gave a grunt, drew up a chair to his table, turned on the machine and was immersed in a moment. This immersion was patent; his voice assumed a slow-motion register, rather like that of Hal, the diseased computer in the film *2001*. Polly longed to continue talking, to discuss Tom's fiancée, Susie's pup, Laura Flanagan's narrow escape from being savaged by a Doberman (recounted loudly to her by that lady in the shopping mall), Jason's low marks (always a sore point), and whether they could afford new curtains for the sitting room. But she knew from the set of Rory's head that conversation was pointless. He was immersed. He would respond to anything she said in the same robotic slow motion, the only kind of speech available to someone whose thoughts were centred elsewhere. From the moment he sat at the monitor, the computer owned him.

Peter came home from college just after six. He was very tall, six three, handsome, blue eyed. He wore round spectacles with fine black frames which gave him the air of a nineteenth-century revolutionary.

'How's my favourite Mum?' he asked, bending over his mother.

Polly looked up at him fondly. This was her first born, the seven-pound miracle who had destroyed her belief in natural childbirth, as he tore her savagely in his tormented rush for the light; this was the baby who had howled almost non-stop for three months until she thought she would go out of her mind. But when the colic ended he had given his first smile to her and that smile, luminous with intelligence, had repaid her in full. Sometimes she looked at his large frame and tried to equate it with the helpless mite she had fed at her breast.

'What did you do with my baby?' she had asked him once, when he had come to crow that he had reached six foot.

'But I am your baby, Mum,' he had answered mournfully.

Now he dropped his canvas rucksack full of books on to the floor, glanced into the dining room to ascertain that his father was at his usual post, and said he was starving.

'What's for din . . . Scrumptious smell!'

'Supper's at eight tonight . . . we're having company!'

'Who?'

'Your uncle Tom's fiancée, Michelle. I told you about this yesterday.'

21

'No kidding . . .' His face fell. 'I won't be here!'

'Why not? I asked her to meet the family!'

'I told the crowd I'd meet them at eight . . . But I'll be back before she leaves.' Polly knew the component members of the 'crowd' and also knew that one of their number, a girl by the name of Elsa Rattigan (affectionately known as 'Rats'), was a star attraction.

Polly sighed and said he'd better eat something now in that case, but Peter was already rooting around in the ice box. 'Hamburgers . . . you wouldn't buy them, Mother dear, if you knew what was in them . . .' he intoned. 'Fish fingers . . . food for pouffs . . . ah . . . pizza . . . cheese supreme . . . that'll do.'

'I'll pop it in the oven,' Polly said. 'You'd better have your shower and change . . .' She tore open the pizza carton, put it on a Pyrex plate and placed it on the spare shelf in the oven.

'Is the zit-bag home?' Peter asked.

'Your brother is not a zit-bag!' Polly said reproachfully. 'And take off your boots. Jason has already carried mud around the house.'

'But they're squeaky clean,' Peter said.

'Take them off!'

Peter complied, unlaced his black Doc Martens and put them down beside Cat. He scratched her between the ears and she started purring, raising her head and squeezing smug eyelids. Then he padded into the hall, pausing for a moment at the dining-room door to say, 'Hello, Father. Remember me? This is your son . . .'

Rory frowned at the computer screen. 'I'm trying to concentrate, Jason. Don't interrupt . . .'

'Yes, Papa, I'm very sorry, Papa,' Peter said meekly.

Polly laughed to herself in the kitchen. She sat down and doubled over with sudden, silent mirth. The cat looked up at her conversationally as much as to say that at least *she* knew which of the boys was which and that no computer would ever seduce her away as long as there was a tin of Miaou in the house.

Peter reappeared. 'Did you see my blue shirt, Mum?'

'I ironed it the other day . . . It's in your drawer.'

'No, it isn't,' Peter said in a dangerous voice, rushing back to the stairs and taking them two at a time.

'Jason, you little fart! You took my shirt . . . my good blue one . . .'

'No I didn't,' came Jason's muffled voice.

'What's this then, Greaseball?' came Peter's angry triumphant tones from Jason's room. 'Dumped under your awful jeans. I've a good mind to break your deceitful little head . . .'

'Huh . . . you and what army?'

Polly shouted up the stairs. 'No quarrelling! Peter, your brother is trying to study . . . I'll iron you another shirt!'

She looked at her husband's back through the dining-room door. 'Effing children,' he muttered to forestall any suggestion that he might leave his computer to intervene.

Polly went upstairs and quelled the incipient battle, ordering Peter out of Jason's room, telling Jason he shouldn't take his brother's clothes. Then she got Peter's cream shirt from the hot press and asked him if it would do. When he conceded with a loud sigh that it would probably have to now, she brought it downstairs and took out the ironing board and ironed it. When she had done that she folded the board, but caught her index finger in the underneath catch. She gave a sudden sharp intake of breath; a blood blister welled painfully under the skin. For a moment she wondered if Rory had heard her small cry of pain, but he evidently had not; the clicking of the keyboard continued happily from the dining room. She sucked at the hurt for a moment before remembering that she should set and light the fire in the sitting room. When that was done the scent of cooking cheese reminded her that Peter's supper was ready and she took it from the oven and called him.

He came downstairs in vest and underpants, reeking of aftershave, acknowledged his ironed shirt on the back of a chair with a 'Thanks, Mum' and sat at the table to eat his pizza. Then he said with raised eyebrows, looking diffident and innocent, 'Mum, I . . . ah . . . suppose I couldn't borrow ten quid . . .'

Although money was very tight, Polly did not want to refuse. She did some rapid calculation as to what she could economise on, got her bag, found a ten-pound note in her wallet and handed it to him. 'You can trim the hedge tomorrow. Money doesn't grow on trees!'

'But I thought it did!' He grinned. 'Thanks . . .' He went back upstairs to dress, reappeared in a moment, said, 'Goodbye, Mum,' glanced into the dining room and intoned, 'Farewell, Father . . .'

There was silence for a moment.

'What?' Rory said from the computer without turning around. 'What did you say, Jason?'

Peter winked at his mother and exited through the back door.

When he was gone Polly went to the dining room and informed the back of Rory's head:

'That was your son Peter who spoke to you just now, not Jason!'

'Oh . . .'

'You have two sons. Both of them are living in fourteen Ashgrove Lawns. I presume you know where that is!'

Rory turned his head and looked at her quizzically. He gave a sheepish smile.

'Michelle should be here in fifteen minutes,' she added. 'Why don't you get ready?'

'I am ready . . .'

'You're addicted to that bloody machine!' Polly cried in exasperation when it was clear that he had no intention of moving. 'You should at least change your shirt . . .'

'For Christ's sake . . . ! I'm in the middle of something important . . .'

Polly retreated to the sitting room, found that Jason had got there before her and was watching *Home and Away.*

'I thought you were supposed to be studying.'

'How can anyone study in this house? Just when I was concentrating Peter came in and started pushing me around.'

'You shouldn't have taken his shirt!'

'He takes mine whenever he wants!'

Polly knew that this was true. She looked at her son's pimpled face, saw his anxiety and insecurity and bravado.

'Never mind,' she said, ruffling his hair.

At that moment the doorbell tinkled. She went to answer it. 'Rory,' she hissed, putting her head into the dining room, 'turn off that damn computer. She's here!'

# Chapter Two

The young woman stood at the front door clutching a bottle of wine. Polly drew her in from the sharp east wind, took her hand and greeted her warmly. Michelle looked about thirty. She had a mane of long black hair, with a widow's peak; her perfume wafted in small eddies. She had amber eyes with unblemished whites. She was beautiful, not through symmetry of feature, but through an aura of the exotic.

'Hi,' she said. 'I've been longing to meet you guys. Tom has told me so much about you!'

'Please don't believe a single word of anything he has told you,' Polly said with a sidelong look at her husband and a sudden dart of insecurity. What does a young girl like her see in Tom, she asked herself. And then she wondered, what has he told her about us?

Rory, who had padded silently from the dining room, was suddenly all urbanity and brought his guest into the sitting room where Jason had turned off the TV and was sidling out of the room.

'This is our younger son, Jason,' Polly said. Jason shook hands with Michelle, said something about having to finish an essay and manoeuvred himself bashfully out of the room.

Rory began to pour drinks. Michelle said she'd have a glass of white wine. Polly asked how Tom was, what was he doing, was he keeping well.

Michelle did not reply immediately. 'He's doing very well . . . He's very busy . . .'

'We fell out years ago,' Polly said, sure that her guest must be wondering why she had to plumb her for information. 'It was very silly, but after a while it acquired a

25

momentum – a status quo – of its own . . .'

'These things always do if they're not nipped in the bud!'

Polly was conscious of the way the girl's eyes studied her. Do I look too fat, Polly wondered. Or is there a smut on my face? What has Tom told her . . . that we're not really married . . . that I'm bird-brained?

Rory poured and Polly handed the glass to her guest. When she turned she saw that Rory was looking at Michelle and that there was a light in his eye which she had not seen for years.

A keen needle of pain shot through her. Turning she caught her own reflection in the mirror above the mantelpiece, saw that of Michelle behind her, saw that she was studying her. She excused herself, went to the kitchen, inspected her face carefully in the mirror, found no smut, and took the casserole from the oven. It was nicely cooked. Cat raised her head, jumped out of her basket and mewed hideously, running to Polly and stretching her paws along the pine door of the sink cupboard in supplication.

'Out you go,' Polly said through her teeth, picking Cat up and dumping her outside the back door. Then she lit the candles on the dining-room table and ran upstairs to Jason's room. She would have shouted for him, but, with a guest in the house, she was wary of his response.

'Come down, supper is on the table . . .'

'. . . I'll eat later!'

'Oh, come on!'

'I don't feel like it. I'll eat later. Leave me some. I'm going out now . . .'

'Where?'

'I'm just going to call on Tim. We'll probably go for a game of snooker.'

'What about Michelle? I invited her to meet the family.'

'I have met her! Anyway, she really wants to talk to you and Dad.'

'What about your homework?'

'What about it?'

Polly stifled the sharp retort. The time for confrontation was not now. She accepted defeat, as she always did, with good grace. 'All right! Wrap up well!' There was some comment she didn't quite catch about him not wearing THAT jacket anyway.

She went back downstairs, removed Jason's place setting, readjusted the others and went to tell her guest and Rory that supper was ready.

'This is simply delicious,' Michelle said.

'She was always a great little cook,' Rory responded, looking at his wife affectionately. Whenever anyone paid her a compliment Rory would look at her appraisingly as though her existence, as a separate being, had suddenly occurred to him. 'I fell out of the right side of the bed the day I took her on!'

Michelle frowned. 'Took her on?'

Polly said lightly, although she had been privately piqued, 'Ah, don't mind him. He's adept at impertinent pleasantries!'

Rory looked slightly crestfallen. 'I was going to say "When I married you" but . . .'

'But that wouldn't have been entirely accurate . . . ?' Polly finished. 'Isn't that what you meant?'

Michelle looked puzzled.

'We were married all right,' Polly explained hastily. 'A good Church marriage which, however, is not recognised by the State. Rory, you see, was married before. It lasted a year . . . and then he met me. But there's no divorce in Ireland, so he got a Church annulment. Tom's probably told you all this stuff?'

'What's a Church annulment?'

'An annulment given by the ecclesiastical courts . . . it means the marriage never existed as far as the Catholic Church is concerned, so he was free to re-marry in Church.'

'But bigamously in the eyes of the State,' Rory said with a laugh, reaching over and taking his wife's hand. 'Polly and I are not living in sin, only in bigamy! It's divorce Irish style!' Rory took a gulp of wine. 'There's a divorce referendum promised, and then we'll regularise things . . . and I'll get Martha off my back!'

Michelle raised nicely arched eyebrows. 'I think Tom and I will stay in London,' she said musingly after a moment.

Rory hooted with laughter. 'That way you can keep your options open,' he said. But his laughter upset his dental plate, which had been recently fitted and was still giving problems. It wobbled dangerously, and he closed his mouth hurriedly.

'I didn't mean it quite like that! I just need the buzz of a big city. I come from New York.'

'So tell us all about yourself, Michelle,' Polly said. 'What part of New York do you come from?'

Michelle had a lovely way of wrinkling her nose when she laughed, which reminded Polly of a rabbit. She described Brooklyn and Manhattan and the Bronx. Polly laughed till she cried over a story about a cab driver and a parrot and was sorry when her guest said she would have to go. She wanted to keep her longer, to find out more about her life and Tom's.

'Just what exactly is he doing now?' she had asked and Michelle said he was still self-employed.

'Oh . . . what kind of a business does he have?' Polly persisted. The sense of loss, of life unshared, rose in her. Tom had always been possessed of a fierce ambition; he was like someone forever conscious of the cavern yawning at his feet and that the only way out was up and up. She remembered how, when he was all of eighteen, he had come to tell her he was going to work in London.

'Watch this space my girl!'

'I'm watching!'

'We'll have to make sure you get a good job, somewhere you'll meet the right kind of bloke . . . rich . . . worthy of you. London's the place! London is where the money is!'

She had often wondered if he had married, sure that he had enough charm to keep any woman happy. And now here was his lady, smiling into Rory's eyes.

'And what do you do yourself?' Rory interjected.

'Oh, I'm a kind of public relations executive,' Michelle said smoothly. She then explained that she was staying in the Westbury Hotel, courtesy of her company.

'What company is that?'

'Oh, you probably never heard of them, Hanker Limited.' Polly thought it was a queer name, but Michelle asked Rory a question about teaching before Polly could question her further.

Michelle demurred when she was offered a lift to her hotel and insisted that they phone for a taxi.

While they were waiting for the taxi, Jason (wearing a heavy sweater) came back with one of his friends, David Flanagan, who lived down the road. They said hello, looked sheepish and vanished into the kitchen. Peter arrived hot on their heels and was introduced to Michelle.

'This is my elder son, Peter.'

'You're very big!' she told him.

'I can't help it,' Peter said. 'I always knew I would be the biggest and the strongest. It's a heavy responsibility! Not that it runs in the family or anything,' he added, looking down severely at his father.

'Oh, stop boasting,' Polly said, adding apologetically to Michelle, 'If he doesn't stop growing soon I don't know what we'll do!'

Peter excused himself and said he had an urgent appointment in the kitchen. From those precincts there came, in a moment, the sounds of an altercation revolving around the fact that the mousse was all gone, Jason being informed that he was a little turd.

Polly went to the kitchen and spoke sotto voce to her children. 'Stop this perpetual arguing! I don't want to hear another sound. Peter, come back to the sitting room and talk to Michelle. Seeing as you weren't here for supper you can eat after she's gone!'

Peter directed a look prognosticating doom to his brother, but he complied. He returned to the sitting room, perched his long person on a chair and smiled at Michelle.

'Did anyone,' he asked, filling a pause in the conversation with juvenile aplomb, 'ever hear of a bunch called the Rosicrucians?'

Rory seemed taken aback. 'Yes . . . they were a secret society. Had their origins in the seventeenth to eighteenth century. What put them into your head?'

'Oh just something which turned up in a pub quiz this evening.'

'Yes,' Michelle said in her melodious American accent, 'they were a secret religious organisation who claimed to have magical knowledge.'

Peter stared at her with interest. Jason emerged from the kitchen, David behind him. 'What kind of knowledge is magical knowledge?' he demanded.

'What kind do you think, you little pimple factory?' Peter said in exasperation. 'Magical . . . as in spells and incantations and grown-up people acting the eejit!'

Jason glared at him. 'Huh,' he said. 'That's what I meant!'

'Oh I don't know . . .' Michelle continued. 'I think they believed there were twelve good people in the world, whom they called the Watchers. Some people still believe we have the Watchers in our midst!'

The youngsters were interested. 'Where did you learn about all this stuff?' Jason asked.

'I majored in History,' Michelle said with smile. 'Once I even thought I would like to teach it.'

'What do you do?'

'I work in public relations,' she said, adding very quickly, 'but seriously, it's amazing the things you come across in history. I'm sure Rory will back me up on that.'

Rory looked like a man who would back her up on most things.

They heard the taxi draw up outside. Polly fetched Michelle's cashmere coat and both she and Rory went out with her to the taxi.

'Lovely to have met you, Michelle. Give our love to Tom. Tell him,' and here emotion informed Polly's voice so that it became unsteady, 'that I'm looking forward very much to seeing him again. Will you tell him that?'

Michelle started, looked at Polly with a sudden intent stare in which there dwelt no friendship whatsoever.

'Of course!' Then she added, 'You're not like him, you know, there's no resemblance.'

'I know,' Polly admitted. 'I'm a bit of a dodo. He used to say I was bird-brained. But . . . do you think I could phone him . . . you could give me the number. Or would it be better for me to wait until he phones himself?'

This eager request was greeted with momentary silence. 'Well, he's abroad a lot. It might be as well to wait for him to call you . . .'

Michelle got into the back seat of the taxi and wound down the window.

'It's been awesome meeting you,' she said, looking from one

to the other, but her eyes dwelt particularly on Polly. 'I'll be in touch soon.'

As the taxi moved away, Polly saw the curtains of the big old house across the road stir as though a breeze had moved them and then she saw Muriel's face peer out. Muriel still liked to keep an eye on all the comings and goings in the cul-de-sac. Sometimes Susie joked about her in a staccato mock German accent: 'Gestapo-Gertie-is-vatching-you!' And then she might launch into a limerick she had coined:

'Gestapo Gertie,
Gets up at eight-thirty,
So that she may sit at her wind-ow . . .'

There was more to this indifferent rhyme, and the more Polly tried to get it out of her head, the more it stuck.

Later, in bed, Polly, who was lying on her side thinking, said to Rory, who was reading *Micro Mart*, scanning it for software bargains:

'What did you think of Michelle?'

'Gorgeous!'

'Yes . . . She's a bit young for Tom, isn't she!'

'Oh, a young wife will soon brighten things up for him,' Rory said in a suddenly suggestive voice. 'Nothing better for your health than a young wife!'

'Do you really think so?' Polly said in a small voice, pushing away the hand which had begun to fondle her bottom.

Rory sighed. 'Oh, Poll . . . I like the one I have! Did you think I was making comparisons?'

'Of course not,' Polly said hurriedly. 'Michelle said it was "awesome" meeting us!' she continued, turning to face him, and trying to remember anything she might have said or done which would have warranted so lavish a compliment.

'She was giving vent to a little American hyperbole,' Rory said. 'Did you take her seriously? Oh, Polly . . . What an innocent you are!'

'But,' Polly persisted, aware that she was innocent and disliking it very much, 'you didn't find anything peculiar about her?'

'Peculiar! Unless being very attractive and feminine is peculiar . . .'

He went back to his magazine and Polly lay, thinking of Michelle and Tom, dealing with the hurt she had felt that she still was not to have his phone number, or his address.

Oh, Tom . . . how can you be so unforgiving?

Rory put down his magazine, turned off the light and reached for her. They had not made love for several weeks and now Polly suspected that his ardour had more to do with gorgeous Michelle, who had sat beside him that evening, than with her.

When it was over Rory kissed her earlobe in appreciation, rolled over and immediately fell asleep.

Polly stared into the darkness, smelling the beef casserole which Peter had reheated. She wished he would not cook or reheat food late at night because she always thought it made the house smell unpleasant. She had said it many times, but her children went on doing it all the same. She heard laughter and knew that David was still downstairs. She thought of Michelle back in her hotel, and wondered for a moment if she and Tom made passionate love, the kind that banished loneliness and opened the door to dimensions of wonder and peace.

Next day, Saturday, Polly woke at nine. Rory was already up. She knew he would be at his computer, *hors de* communication, so she lingered in the warm bed, watching the streak of sunlight through the curtains, moving her eyes over the wall, over the ceiling, saw the small recent cobweb in the corner, made a mental note to take the Hoover to it. She ran her mind over the various duties ahead of her for the day – housework, cooking, shopping, icing the cake she had made for the parish bring and buy sale.

She knew her children were still asleep, her husband immersed in his computing. Susie was next door, but although a wonderful friend, she belonged to her own life, particularly on Saturdays, when she and Fergus liked to spend most of the morning in bed. Sometimes Polly could hear them through the wall, the sudden squalls of Susie's laughter, the deeper tones of Fergus, the long intervals of quiet.

It came over her suddenly, the sense of personal silence, its sound, its provenance, an interior void that had nothing whatever to do with peace. This silence was white, pristine, perfect loneliness. It possessed a purity like the glaciers of

Antarctica, where everything was reflected back and only penguins lived.

Frightened by the intensity of the sudden pain, by the desperate need for radical contact, she got out of bed, put on her dressing gown and went downstairs.

Rory, as predicted, was in the dining room, clicking away at his computer, totally concentrated. He was not aware of his wife at the door, and when she stood and stared at him long enough he raised his head in the way people do by instinct when they are being watched.

'Morning!' he said cheerily but with obvious effort, wrenching his thoughts away from the screen. 'And how are we this morning?' Polly saw how his eyes reattached themselves to the monitor.

'Fine,' she said acerbically. '*We* are absolutely fine. But are *you* going to be stuck into that thing all day?'

'I'm not stuck into anything,' Rory said crossly, raising his voice a fraction and speaking with sudden cold precision. Rory was not the kind of husband who would turn and say, 'Darling, is something wrong? Are you upset about something?' Polly saw this as a reflection on herself, as a statement on her unimportance. She knew that the best way of avoiding domestic unpleasantness was never to complain. So she went into the messy kitchen. Although she had cleaned up the night before, the table was now bearing a quota of dirty plates. Peter never cleaned up after himself and charmed his way out of maternal ire. 'Ah, Mummy mine . . . I'm sorry . . . It won't happen again.'

Jason came downstairs wearing an expression of woe.

'What's wrong with you?' Polly demanded on a note of irritation as she put the dirty dishes into the sink. 'You look like a week of wet Sundays!'

'I'm depressed,' Jason said.

'What have you got to be depressed about?'

'I just know I'm going to fail the Leaving!'

Polly felt her heart sink. This was something she was afraid of herself. Jason was no academic, but he was being squeezed through a system which was not interested in anyone who wasn't. She absorbed his angst, contained her own, made comforting noises, assured him that if he worked all would be well.

'I can't stand studying,' Jason said. 'I just want to act, or play in a rock band . . . or something exciting!'

'But no matter what you do, life is predicated on work!' Polly said. 'It's the way things are. It's the way people learn and grow. You'd have to work at acting or rock music too—'

'But I wouldn't mind that!'

'Well, give this year your best shot,' Polly suggested, pouring some tea. 'Will you have toast?'

'Thanks, Mum.' Then he added, 'What do you think of Uncle Tom's new mot?'

'She's not his mot!' Polly said. 'She happens to be his fiancée!'

'She's not just a pretty face either. I always like intelligence in women,' he added with male patronage, putting on the gravitas he sometimes tried out for size. 'Although I did get the feeling that she was on her best behaviour.'

'On her best behaviour?' Polly echoed. 'What do you mean?'

'Just that the butter-wouldn't-melt bit didn't seem to fit.'

Polly sighed and clicked her tongue.

'Yeah,' Jason continued reflectively, 'but she's a babe . . .'

The phone rang. Polly went into the hall and answered it.

'Polly,' the American voice said. 'Thank you for a wonderful evening. I enjoyed myself so much . . . The meal was delicious!'

'Not at all, Michelle. We loved having you. Jason was just saying how . . . pretty you are!'

'That's very nice of him. Polly, what I really phoned to ask is, what are you doing this afternoon?'

'I have to do some shopping.'

'In town?'

'Yes.'

'Why don't you have tea with me here in the Westbury. I'll be all on my little own! My flight isn't till eight this evening.'

'Thanks . . . that would be nice!'

'Around four o'clock?'

'Lovely.'

'See you then!'

At four o'clock Polly entered the foyer of the Westbury, walked upstairs to the spacious lounge and spotted Michelle in an armchair by a window, reading a magazine. She jumped up when Polly approached, calling out, 'Hi there,' and Polly went to her and sat down in the adjoining armchair with a sigh of relief.

'God,' Polly said, 'my feet are killing me!'

It was the boots she had bought in the January sales. The right one pinched and the top of her big toe felt raw. She longed to take it off to inspect the damage, but this was neither the time nor the place.

'How are you, Michelle?' she asked with as much urbanity as she could summon. 'You look lovely. Being engaged to Tom obviously agrees with you!'

'Oh, I always look lovely!' Michelle said airily. She smiled at the expression on Polly's face. 'Well, one might as well . . . It takes a little effort but the effect is well worth it. Power has a terrible effect on people who don't have it – as some Italian or other is reputed to have said. Looking good is the basis of most women's power!'

'It's easy when you're still young,' Polly said with a smile, adding, 'anyway, who wants power based just on looks?'

'It doesn't matter what it's based on,' Michelle intoned. 'So long as you have it! And as for being young – I left my youth behind me more years ago than I care to remember . . .'

The waitress approached and Michelle ordered two afternoon teas. Then she arched her back and pulled down the black sweater, which Polly saw was cinched in at her small waist by a suede belt. Her nails were blood red.

'Michelle . . . can I ask you a personal question?'

'Sure!'

'What age *are* you?'

Michelle laughed. People sitting on the nearby sofa turned to stare for a moment. Michelle leaned towards Polly and confided in a whisper, 'Forty-one!'

Polly leaned back in need of support. 'You're nearly as old as I am!'

'Am I? Well, it's not a hanging offence, is it?'

'But you look so young . . . I don't believe you . . . you're having me on!'

'I'm not. What age did you think I was?'

'About thirty . . . even twenty-eight . . .'

'God bless your innocent heart!'

'Tom is forty-one . . .'

'I know. He thinks I'm thirty-five . . .'

Polly stared. 'You didn't tell him the truth?'

'Of course not. You can't possibly go around telling men the truth!'

She regarded the expression on Polly's face with amusement. 'Men are cupboard revolutionaries; they can't stand women who do what they want! But give them subtle revolution, turn their complacencies upside down . . . and watch them adore you. They should be kept at the edge of their seats as much as possible.'

'It's a pity about them,' Polly said with a sniff. 'Why waste energy?' She knew that the only thing that would keep Rory at the edge of his seat was a new software program. After a moment she added, 'Share the secret of your eternal youth?'

'What a flatterer you are, Polly!'

'I'm serious!'

'If there is a secret it's an open one. Just give yourself permission. Reach for what you want . . .'

'Oh, Michelle . . !'

Michelle sat back and stared at her from amber eyes and then she said so softly that Polly wasn't sure for a moment whether she had heard correctly:

'You know what I think? I think that what you need, Polly Caine, is to be seduced! There are wonders to be learnt from certain kinds of unsolicited experience!'

When this sank home Polly gave a snort of derision. 'I've enough problems, thank you very much. I need seduction like I need a hole in the head! Anyway, who'd bother?'

'Oh, I don't mean sexual seduction with nothing behind it. I mean something much better, something that makes you take stock, stand back, inspect the chains.'

'What chains? If you mean my family, you're mistaken. I love my family!'

'Of course you do!' After a moment Michelle added, 'It's just that I believe in provoking Fate a little. You know . . . ? People who get up and look for the circumstances they want, and if they can't find them, make them!'

'Is that a Michelle original?'

'No, actually, G.B. Shaw . . . but he was no dope either!'

'What makes you think I want any kind of change?' Polly asked a little disingenuously, taken aback by how well this new prospective sister-in-law had read her.

Michelle did not answer, but she raised her hands in acquiescence. Then she said, 'Sorry, Polly, don't take me up wrong. I'm an awful gabbler!'

Polly sipped her tea. She felt a bit like Alice in Wonderland. The woman opposite smiled. Her expression was reassuring; everything she said seemed coined in another mind-set, where you could look twenty years younger if you wanted. All you had to do was give yourself permission, stir things up a little, provoke Fate!

She glanced down at her spare tyre and her sagging figure, at her chubby knees. She tried to readjust her position in the chair to one of grace, but felt this to be unsuccessful. Why shouldn't she look like the glamorous woman opposite? What had happened to her pretty face and body to make her become a frump? She knew the answer; it was not domestic life that had done it. It was herself. She had gone along with it, made it her exclusive focus, out of hope and out of fear and, mostly, out of love.

After a moment Michelle asked tentatively, 'Did you know your husband's first wife?'

Polly thought of Martha, whom Rory sometimes referred to (half admiringly) as 'The Preying Mantis'.

'Oh, Martha . . . well . . .' Polly heard herself talking, telling her prospective sister-in-law things she had never discussed with anyone except Rory.

'But she's still his wife?'

'Well . . . technically.'

'I know. So . . . if anything happened to Rory . . . what position would you be in?'

'Martha would be entitled to one half of his estate!' Polly hated this as a topic of conversation, although it was something which worried her constantly. 'She refused to sign a proper separation agreement waiving her legal succession rights! But there was a written agreement that he would pay off her share in the house by instalments. Trouble is, he's behind with the instalments!'

'Not a good scene?' Michelle said sympathetically, shaking her head.

'No.'

'Well . . . it's best to think positively.'

Polly went home in a foul temper. The euphoric mood which had subsumed her in the Westbury had dissipated and she spent the whole bus journey home evaluating her life, doing a private stock-taking.

Why the hell was she, at forty-four, stuck in a semi-detached dog-box, with a 'husband' who wasn't legally her spouse, an income far too small for family needs, with two youngsters who were still dependent, and with the sword of Damocles – what would happen to the family home if Rory keeled over – perpetually hanging over her head? She didn't even have the comfort of a loving relationship. Rory, the erstwhile insatiable lover, had become the computer addict.

Polly found that Rory was still in front of the computer and that the kitchen was again in disarray. Evidently the children, both of whom were nowhere to be seen, had entertained some friends and they had cooked chips and sausages. The greasy plates were left on the table. The air was filled with the smell of hot fat and burnt chips. She opened the back door and went into the dining room to talk to Rory.

Rory did not turn his head to look at his wife. He said, 'How was town?' and Polly said, 'Fine,' and when he didn't attempt to progress the conversation further she turned away. She had been going to tell him about her tea with Michelle, but she decided there was no point. What was the good of telling a computer junkie anything unless it was some waffle to do with Windows, or E-Mail or the Internet or whatever, about which she knew nothing. Instead, harnessing the patience which she had cultivated down the years as a kind of force, she set about cleaning the kitchen and washing the dishes her children and their friends had left behind for her. But the anger simmered, giving added zest to her efforts. She caught sight of her reflection in the mirror and reached into the fridge for ice cream. Some kind of pleasure was an imperative.

She went upstairs, made beds and began to hoover. It was no use waiting for the children to clean their bedrooms, so, although she had resolved to let them live in a tip if that was what they wanted, her resolution broke and she cleaned their rooms because she could not bear the thought of two pig-sties on the same landing. Then she sorted out clothes for the wash. Her library book was on the bedside table. She picked it up and sat down on the edge of the bed. It occurred to her that most of her life had been lived through books and, restlessly, she put it down again.

She glanced around the room she had slept in for the past twenty years. It hadn't changed, had been painted four times, always the same colour – magnolia.

The thought came unbidden – I must change my life!

When the children came down she told them that she was fed up and was leaving, that she was treated like a servant. She said it in a loud voice and Rory came into the kitchen to listen. He leaned against the door and smiled. Then he laughed.

'God, Poll, you're so funny when you're angry . . .' He went back to his computer and the children, if such they could be called, defended their position vociferously and aggressively, particularly Jason who felt that he was being picked on.

That night Polly had a dream. In the dream she saw herself looking down on the nations of the earth. They were all at her feet. She had power and untold riches. She was beautiful too, sought in marriage by a prince.

'But I'm married to Rory,' she told him and he said he didn't know it was a marriage, that he thought it was some other arrangement and he apologised and went away.

Polly woke when the first light of dawn crept through the curtains. It was Sunday. Rory was lying beside her. He had come to bed very late, something which he now did often, and he lay still deeply asleep. He looked like a boy, innocent, trusting. The old love for him welled up in her. She touched his hand. But although he stirred, he did not wake and she let him sleep, lapsing back herself to slumber, trying without success to recapture the dream and the prince and the sense that she mattered. She had married Rory, in order to have time with him, to be alone with him. That prospect had once seemed to contain all the world held of rapture. But they were never alone together. They were simply alone, each in his and her patch with a wall between them, the wall built of monotony and bills.

When she woke again Rory was up and when she went downstairs in her dressing gown he was sitting at the computer and the keys were clicking with plastic precision under his fingers.

'Good morning,' Polly said.

''Morning,' Rory said, staring at the screen.

Polly went into the kitchen and began to make breakfast. She always made a full breakfast on Sundays, bacon, egg, sausage, tomato. When it was ready she called the boys who came downstairs sleepily, digging each other's ribs en route, ending up in a scuffle in the hall. Then there was a sudden whispered conference.

'. . . No . . . take off your specs . . . he won't know who you are . . . 'specially if you put on a shirt and tie . . . bet you two quid.' It was Jason's voice and Polly knew he was suppressing laughter. She leaned into the hall for a moment to see what was going on, saw both of her sons disappear back upstairs. When she heard suspiciously quiet footfalls she glanced into the hall again. She saw Peter in shirt and tie, his hair slicked, his glasses removed, walk into the dining room beside his younger brother.

'Dad,' Jason said, 'this is my friend Derek.'

Rory turned from the computer with as much grace as he could muster. He was annoyed at being disturbed, and did not really look at the youth 'Derek' who was supposed to be Jason's friend, but he shook his hand with ostensible avuncularity. 'Eh . . . hello, Derek . . . nice to meet you . . .'

Peter stood stockstill and then said, 'Jesus Christ, Dad, it's me . . .'

Jason, unable to contain himself, fell with whoops of laughter against the dining-room door, which, not being fully closed, opened inwards with a crash. It slammed against the flex connecting Rory's computer to its electricity supply and pulled the plug out of the socket. Rory leaped up, caught Jason by the scruff of the neck and heaved him into the hall. Then he turned on Peter.

'Why don't you two shape up? I'm sick to death of you . . . There isn't a moment's peace. I've just lost the program on the computer because of you . . .'

He glared at his elder son, then returned to his post by the computer breathing heavily.

Polly listened with more than her ears. She had heard the genuine frustration, the disappointment in Rory's voice. She put on her coat.

'Do you know who I am, Mum?' Peter asked as he came sheepishly into the kitchen.

'Of course I know who you are!'

'Dad doesn't!'

'Of course he does. But his mind is elsewhere,' Polly said.

'Where are you going, Mum?'

'Your breakfast is ready. Eat it and clean up after you. I'm going to Mass.'

The church had been built about twenty years earlier to serve the estate, an edifice in stained glass, pine pews, quarry-tiled floor, and was devoid of the dark recesses and ponderous atmosphere of old churches.

Polly sat in a pew to one side of the altar and listened, saw Father Brennan in his gold and white surplice do things with the chalice, waited for the consecration. All the while the strange discontents and angers of the last two days boiled in her.

Life, she thought, is an illusion-stripping process, where our projections perish on the rocks of reality.

It's a mug's game, she told the statue of Our Lady standing on a side plinth. There you are, looking up to heaven to the Lads. There's the father, the son and the bird. But what about you? Are we all crazy or what!

But Our Lady's pious demeanour was unruffled.

When the priest raised the host at the consecration Polly did not bow her head. She stared at the white, round wafer which was about to undergo transubstantiation, with a sort of eyeball to eyeball fixity. The words Michelle had spoken returned: '. . . Reach for what you want . . .' It was like the old ask-and-you-shall-receive routine, Polly thought. She had tested this when she was a child by asking for a banana. But no banana had materialised. Right, God, she said silently. You'd better get on Your bike. I think I've had this conversation with You before! I didn't really expect You to send me an angel, You know. But I want some action. If You don't shape up with something pretty interesting You can say goodbye to me – and the kids. The only thing bringing that pair within howling distance of You is me . . .

She half expected the thunderclap, the bolt of lightning striking her down. But there was nothing except the murmur of the priest's voice and the shuffle as people got up to take Communion. Well, she thought, that's one piece of silly waffle which has fallen on deaf ears. Ask and you shall be rigorously ignored . . . Ah well . . . I'm only being selfish anyway. There are lots of people more important than I am.

But a strange thought came into her head, more a voice than a thought, clear and powerful: 'No one is *more* important than you are, Polly.'

She got off her knees and sat down in panic. I'm losing my marbles. Christ, I'm hearing things! She glanced around to see if anyone else had heard, but no one was taking any notice.

She gave a sigh of relief. Think about the bloody dinner and hold on to your wits, she enjoined herself.

After a few moments she found her attention reverting to the sermon. Father Brennan had, predictably, waxed wroth on the subject of divorce. With the referendum on the subject in prospect this was to have been expected. He spoke of what God had joined together and of children and of spousal duty and how divorce would leave the unwilling party adrift and unhappy and would not be for that party's benefit.

Polly listened and agreed. It would be terrible to leave one spouse unhappy through divorce. But then, came the thought, there were two spouses . . . was one spouse's happiness more important than the other's? Was a marriage which continued simply to serve the contentment of one spouse a good place for the other spouse . . . ? If someone poured their life into making sure the boat was not rocked for someone else was that a moral exercise? Or could it be described as . . . well, slavery?

* * *

42

When she was leaving the church Polly bumped into Laura Flanagan.

'Oh hell-o, Polly,' Laura said in a very bright and cheerful voice, showing a lot of teeth. 'What did you think of the sermon?'

'Not much, to tell you the truth,' Polly said and Laura Flanagan looked taken aback at her unwonted sharpness. Polly could generally be relied upon to approve of sermons.

'But of course . . . you couldn't be expected to endorse it, dear . . . although you are the shining example in the estate of domestic rectitude, despite,' and here she dropped her voice, '. . . your special circumstances . . .'

'Excuse me!' Polly said. 'I must get back.' She tried to summon a smile.

Not far away, in her splendid home, Muriel Reeves tuned in to the Protestant service on the television.

Sometimes she went to church, but mostly she didn't. She was always afraid that she would meet Alan Barrington there, as she had met him once, some two years ago, with his wife in tow. It wasn't his parish church but, when Muriel had been coming out after the service, there he had been, chatting to the rector. His urbane laugh had announced him. Their eyes had met, in his sudden recollection and then cautious politeness, in which there lurked condescension on the one hand and a kind of alarm on the other. In her eyes she knew not what message lay; she tried to keep them impassive.

'Hello,' she had said in as casual a voice as she could muster, turning quickly away.

But the memory had followed her, down to the road, into her car, back to Willow House and into her kitchen. It seemed to her that he wore his conquests on his sleeve, like ribbons for successful combat. The years had not withered him; he had seemed expansive, self-satisfied, like a vampire who collected energy from a wide spectrum. It doesn't matter, she told herself. Why don't you simply laugh it off.

She even tried to laugh and Sable her small black cat looked up at her in surprise.

'What I want to know,' Muriel whispered to Sable, looking into her crystal green eyes, 'is why it had to happen in the first place! And, above all, why did it have to happen to someone who was simply not equipped to cope with it!'

Sable jumped into her lap and Muriel stroked her until she had stilled the spiritual and mental turmoil which perpetually lay in wait for her, and into the silencing of which so much of her energy was diverted.

'Are you hungry, darling?' she asked the cat, stroking the small, cool paws. But as Sable did not respond she did not bestir herself either and sat for a while, grateful for the warmth of her little cat, looking out of the kitchen window at nothing in particular.

# Chapter Three

When Polly came home from Mass she stopped off at Sue's to find out if she had any plans for the afternoon.

'Would you like to come out for a walk, or something, after lunch? Rory is stuck into his cybernetic love and I'm getting to the point where I hear voices!'

'What voices?'

'Oh nothing . . . just something at Mass . . . I heard a voice in my head!'

'Divine Revelation you mean?' Susie asked with twinkle.

Polly laughed a little self-consciously, ready and willing to discount the experience. 'Nothing so spectacular.'

Sue was getting lunch. There was a smell of roasting lamb. From somewhere upstairs came the sound of rock music. In the sitting room Fergus's legs could be seen among the Sunday papers. Wags, the pup, was outside in the garden and was yapping at Cat who was teasing him from the safety of the garden wall.

'That fucking dog is driving me crazy,' Susie said. 'I'd be only too delighted to get out for a bit. Where were you thinking of going?'

'Anywhere!'

'Sounds good to me!'

'Will you come over at two-thirty? We can clear off then.'

'OK.'

Polly parked the car near Joyce's tower in Sandycove and walked with her friend by the sea.

'Do you ever get fed up?'

Susie gave her a careful sideways look. 'Of course.'

Polly sighed. 'It's hit me recently. It's like waking from a long sleep! What the hell have I been doing for the past twenty years?'

'The same as everyone else . . . Having kids, loving a man, making a home . . .'

When Polly did not elaborate Susie added: 'What else would you have done that would have made you happy?'

'I don't know. I'd probably do it all over again. It's just that life doesn't stay the same; you're given one script, but the plot, the characters, the scenario all change and the script becomes a nonsense!' Sue did not know what to say.

'In your case,' Polly went on, 'things are different, because they have evolved; you have a besotted husband; you've kept pace with each other!'

'He's all right,' Susie conceded, frowning, but a small smile played in the corners of her mouth. 'Yeah . . . He's OK . . . my poor old Ferg. He's jealous and possessive and he'll be redundant in a fortnight. I can hardly bear to think of him at home all day!'

Both women looked out over the sea wall, watched the grey-green breakers, heard the scream of the swooping gulls, felt the sting of rain in the wind. Susie turned up the collar of her jacket and Polly wound her tartan scarf round her hair. Behind them rose Joyce's Martello tower, and to their left the path curved down to the Forty Foot. The sea was choppy, muddy grey-turquoise churning around the rocks. They stood in silence, gazing out at the lonely vista of the horizon, facing the cold bluster of the wind, tasting salt in the mist thrown up at them from the rocks below.

A few deliberate drops of rain fell.

'We'd better get back,' Polly said. 'It's going to pour!'

When they were in the car Susie asked, 'Tell me about Tom's new fiancée?'

Polly blew out her cheeks. 'Well, you should have seen her! A glamour puss of forty-one who looks about twenty-eight. I had tea in the Westbury with her yesterday . . .'

'So that's what has you so discontented! You've been making comparisons. But I bet you she's got her problems too; everyone has!'

46

Polly sighed. 'Oh, Susie, it's just that she made me realise that if anything happens to Rory I'll be without a roof over my head. I'm scared. And nothing seems to work out any more . . . He's been taken over, body and soul, by a machine. And the kids are growing up and away. I feel as though I'm the only person in the house who speaks my language!'

Susie looked at her friend's profile, at her plump person and thought of Polly, wafer slim, who had once rushed to tell her she was expecting a baby.

'She has reminded me of how much I miss Tom. She wouldn't even give me his phone number,' Polly added, in a dead-pan voice.

'You know what you need, Polly,' Susie said. 'You need a job. When you've nothing to think about but immediate domestic problems they assume gargantuan proportions. A real job would use your brains . . . would give you prospects . . .'

'And where would I get a job like that?' Sue shrugged and Polly gave a dismissive laugh. 'No . . . I've left it too late! I should have realised in time that life has no use for shrinking violets, that only soldiers need apply. And there's something else – by the time you cop on that Time is limited you've squandered it!'

'Fiddlesticks. You've never squandered anything.' Susie stared moodily through the windscreen at the rain-spattered street.

'I'm a good one to talk,' she added ruefully after a moment. 'Stuck with bloody old Penston in his one-horse outfit . . . I was going to set the world on fire and instead I've just sat on my fanny and taken dictation because I became comfortable. I could have done a degree at night; I might even have become a solicitor!'

'And spend the whole of your mortal days perusing one heap of old papers after another?' Polly enquired. 'There's not much excitement in that!'

'Maybe not. But there might be a bit of money! Perhaps then Fergus might not be so certain that I'm going to abscond with Willy Penston!' She glanced at Polly sideways and smiled to show she was joking.

When they got home, Polly accepted Susie's invitation to come in for some tea. They brought the tray into the sitting room, found Fergus was there asleep on the couch. The *Sunday Tribune*, the Sunday *Independent*, the *Sunday Times* were scattered on the floor at his feet.

She began to tidy the papers and picked up one of the supplements. 'Do you see this?' she said with a laugh, reading from the open page.

'Gentleman, accountant, seeks lady forty to fifty for companionship, romance, love. You are fun-loving, intelligent, loyal, and I will adore you.' Susie laughed. 'There you are, Poll! Now's your chance!' Polly looked at Fergus surreptitiously. He lay sprawled, his mouth open. A sudden staccato snore, a catch of breath, interrupted the rhythm of his breathing.

'Oh, shut up, Ferg,' Susie said equably.

Polly sipped her tea. She said hello to Fergus when he surfaced jerkily. 'Oh, hello, Poll . . .' he said, gathering himself up. 'I just dropped off for a bit.'

Polly said she had to be going. She helped carry the tea and biscuits back to the kitchen, which was pristine because Fergus and the children had tidied up in Susie's absence. From without came the supplicating whine of Wags who wanted in. Polly took her leave and Susie let the pup into the kitchen.

But Polly did not go straight home. Instead she directed her steps to Kinlan's the grocery cum newsagent in the village, which was always open on Sunday. There she bought some milk and a copy of the *Sunday Times*.

When she came home Rory was still at the computer. Notwithstanding her injunction to clean things up, the kitchen was still in the same state of post-prandial disarray as she had left it and she began to clear up. The boys were nowhere to be seen. She stuck her head around the dining-room door and asked, 'Where are Peter and Jason?'

'They went out!'

'Where?'

'I don't know. They didn't say!'

'You might have asked! And you could have made them clear up . . .'

Rory registered the displeasure in her voice. 'I've more to do than worry about their comings and goings. They won't do anything we tell them anyway. They know everything!'

The keyboard clicked as he said this and his complaint petered away as the computer reclaimed him.

Polly stood at the door for a moment, but knew she was invisible. She returned to the kitchen, shut the door and looked at the mess. Cat got out of her basket and began to mew, suggesting that she had been badly treated, had not been fed for three hours, and that it was high time something was done about it. Polly fed her. 'How many meals a day do you get?' she asked the cat. 'I feed you and the boys feed you and every time you go out someone else feeds you. Yet you always behave as though you had just escaped from a famine zone! And you're getting so fat you need a wheelbarrow!'

Cat ignored this and strolled to the door, giving a polite n'urp.

Polly opened the door and let her out. For some reason the kitchen, the house, seemed empty and forlorn, a kind of desert. But Polly did what she always did and patiently cleared away the table, washed the dishes, stacked them, got the mop and gave the floor a going-over. Then she put the paper on the table.

Rory came into the kitchen.

'I'm going out for some cigarettes,' he said. He looked at her and added in a slightly appeasing voice, 'Is there anything you'd like?'

'Not really!'

He glanced at the paper. 'Which paper did you get?'

'The *Sunday Times*.'

'Anything interesting?'

'I'll know when I've read it.'

'There's no need to bite!' Rory said acerbically, turning on his heel and heading for the door.

Polly heard the car door slam. She boiled the kettle, reached into the cake tin and cut herself a slice of chocolate cake. Then she turned carefully to the section of the paper marked 'Encounters'.

When Rory came back Polly had read through all the potential encounters. There was a Loveable Old Goat who wanted some bright and sexy young thing to take his mind off impending senescence (he hadn't put it like that but Polly could read between the lines); there was an Active Bachelor of forty, 'caring but cautious'; there was a Chivalrous Knight who was looking for a lovelorn maid. Polly giggled a bit. Then there was a warm and caring Professional Gentleman, who was looking for an educated, intelligent lady 40–50 for a lasting relationship. Hmmnn, Polly thought. What if he was really genuine? What if there was a man out there who really wanted intelligence in a woman, who longed, as she did, for conversation, warmth, love? I'm intelligent, she thought. I must be; I got a degree once. And I'm warm and caring; just look at this family. I have cocooned them all to the point where they take it for granted, the way you do climate, all done by the sun and the wind and the rotation of the earth on its axis.

She glanced at her expanding midriff: Christ, I'd better do something about that or I'll definitely look like the rotating earth. This thought depressed her and she had another slice of chocolate cake to cheer her up.

'Well,' Rory repeated when he came back, 'anything in the paper?'

He put a bar of Belgian chocolate down in front of her. Polly knew that this was a peace offering. She always told him he shouldn't and he always seemed well pleased with this response. He knew that his wife's will power was no match for Belgian chocolate.

Now she said, 'Oh Rory, I've just had some cake!'

'So what? A little bar won't do you any harm!' He glanced at the open paper. 'Any ads for computers, or software . . . Much better value in England!'

'No,' Polly said. 'I haven't seen any. I was reading the Encounters columns!'

'Oh . . . looking for Prince Charming? Ha ha!'

'Yes,' Polly said. 'Whom do you think I should go for . . . the Loveable Old Goat or the Matchless Male . . . ?'

Rory laughed. 'Why not try both? Can't get too much of a good thing after all!'

Polly was secretly hurt. 'Wouldn't you miss me if I ran off?'

'Of course I would; who would be here to find fault with me then? . . . Think of the cosy background buzz that would be missing . . .'

Polly felt a lump in her throat, but she let it stay there. Rory would think she was being female and irrational. Instead she said mildly, 'Well, if that's all you'd miss me for, I may as well reply to the ad!' But Rory was en route to the dining room and didn't answer.

'Rory,' Polly said loudly, 'did you hear me?'

The clicking of the computer keys signalled that Rory was back at his station.

'Hmnn?' he said.

Jason came home a few minutes later.

'Where's the Hobbit, Mum?'

'Your father is with his computer,' Polly said with a sigh. 'And you shouldn't call him the Hobbit!'

'Why not? I've got the most eccentric father in the estate. Everyone says so!' Jason hesitated and then his eyes lit up as he saw the crumbs on the plate.

'Oh good . . . cake . . . You've been pigging it again, Mum . . . Where have you hidden it, or have you gobbled it all up?'

Polly looked at him and wondered what had happened to the worshipping child he had once been.

'You should show more respect for your mother!' she said with an edge to her voice.

Jason bristled. 'I wasn't showing you disrespect!'

'Yes you were, Jason; don't argue. And there's no need to be aggressive!'

Jason's voice rose. 'I wasn't being aggressive; I was just looking for a bit of cake. You're the one who's always aggressive; always finding fault! Ask anyone in this family . . .' He stood there, firmly planted, six feet of him looking down at her.

Polly felt bewildered. Was this full frontal attack the natural outcome of what she had said? Yes, it must be her fault. One should make allowances for adolescents, be careful what one said in case they were upset. Knowing this she did not reply.

But Jason had experienced a mood swing and needed to give it vent. 'You're the one,' he went on. 'We inherited our traits from you, so whatever we are you can blame yourself!'

'I see! Your traits, as you call them, would have nothing whatsoever to do with you, I suppose?' But maternal dryness was lost on Jason.

'Even if it is me,' Jason added bitterly, 'I'm only a poor little illegit, so what do you expect!'

Polly felt as though she had been punched in the stomach.

'You're not illegitimate,' she said weakly. 'They did away with the status of illegitimacy a few years ago!'

'But you and Dad jumped the gun! And you never even got married . . . you're still living in sin!'

'Not in sin, Jason . . .'

'No, just bigamously!' Jason glanced at her and, satisfied that he had won, strode into the hall, leaving a trail of dirt on the carpet.

Polly restrained the impulse to follow him. But she went into the dining room and informed the back of Rory's head, 'Rory, it's time you started taking some responsibility for your sons! I've just had the most insufferable cheek from Jason; he thinks he can say what he likes!'

'Hmnn,' Rory said in an absent tone. 'What did he say?'

Polly lowered her voice. 'He said he was illegitimate!'

'Well he is,' Rory said mildly, without taking his eyes from the screen. 'Tough, but that's the way it is! He can't be legitimated unless we get legally married!'

'And we can't be married unless Martha dies!'

'Something like that,' Rory muttered with sudden irritation, glancing at her sideways. 'Christ, Poll, what a thing to say! Poor old Martha.'

'Well, it's true!'

'You can't spend your life wishing someone would die!'

'Can't I?'

Rory turned to look at her speculatively, guardedly.

'Polly?'

'Oh I wasn't thinking of Martha. I was thinking of me!'

Rory turned back to the computer and said in a chill voice, 'Polly, you should listen to yourself. You should carry a tape recorder around with you and listen to yourself. You're always bitching; if it's not me it's the boys! You're always on about something; always these subliminal complaints, these threats as to what you'll do if we don't shape up. Has it ever occurred to you that life is no cake-walk for me either, or for the boys. If you would stop being so self-centred for a moment you would see that!'

Polly tried to remember when she had last complained, realised that it was yesterday, and swallowed the retort. But it's unfair, she thought silently. Before yesterday I had never articulated a single word of complaint for years and years. So why does he accuse me of always complaining? She glanced at his righteous face and felt as though she was in a camp run by aliens.

'Well, will you tell him to hoover up the mess he has left, yet again, on the carpet?'

'What mess?'

'He brought mud in on his boots!'

Rory sighed and assumed a masterful voice. 'No. I won't, Poll. It's not the end of the world and I'm not going to harass him. You'll end up making a sissy out of him if you keep on at him like this!'

Polly left the room and went back to the kitchen. She stared at the paper for a moment, at the ad made by the Professional Gentleman. The temptation was strong, but if she replied she would have dropped anonymity, and the professional gentleman might turn out to be a psycho. So instead she found the scissors and cut out the form from the paper, filled in her name and her and Rory's joint Visa number and added her personal Encounters ad.

'A gentle lady, warm, intelligent and educated, would love to meet a similar man (45+).'

She printed this message out in capitals on a sheet from a jotter, put it in an envelope with the form cut from the paper, and walked straight out with it to the postbox.

Susie was in her sitting room when she saw Polly walk by with a letter in her hand, a floral umbrella held over her head.

'Poor old Poll,' she said to Fergus. 'Rory has turned into a computer junkie and the two boys are like something from a comedy. They never help her! She may as well be a slave! She spends her whole life cleaning that house and cooking! She's a typical example of the woman-who-gives-too-much. And now she's in the throes of what the smart asses call a mid-life crisis! Dissatisfaction has suddenly struck! The trouble is – she's far too good for the lot of them, and can't see it!'

Fergus surfaced from the paper.

'When you're talking to Rory next,' Susie continued, 'why don't you suggest that he buy her some flowers or something . . . Do it tactfully. She could do with some affirmation!'

'It's her own fault,' Fergus said. 'You get as much crap in this life as you are prepared to put up with!'

'Oh, Ferg, she's just innocent and she's really terribly shy . . . She wants everything to be good and perfect, and she thinks the responsibility for this happy nirvana rests entirely with her.'

'Well, she'll just have to wake up, won't she!'

Susie gave a snort of exasperation. 'No sympathy . . . Typical man!'

Fergus grinned at her, narrowing his eyes menacingly. 'Right now I'm feeling particularly typically male.' He raised lascivious eyebrows, shifting them up and down like the Marx brothers. Although his hair was now grey and thinning, his eyebrows had retained their dark brown colour, and made up in lushness for what his pate had lost.

Fergus had the face of a joker; the lines were ones of laughter, long years of humour. No one could have imagined from looking at him the disciplined software engineer who lived in him, or the driven eroticism in his soul.

'Seeing as the kids are out why don't you take that delectable, sensual body of yours to the upstairs *palais de joie*?'

'You make our matrimonial couch sound like a brothel!'

Fergus moved. Sue gave a screech as his teeth nipped her neck. But she felt the frisson of excitement travel down, down, to her toes. It had never left her, this chemistry; every time Fergus touched her it was there again, powerful as the first moment he had suddenly taken her face in his hands when she was twenty and kissed her.

'You're a sex maniac!'

'We haven't done it on the hearth rug for ages,' Fergus said, lying belly up on the floor, like a great dog.

'Well, we're not doing it on the hearth rug now! But, if you promise not to behave yourself, I'll see you upstairs in fifteen seconds . . .'

She laughed, ran for the stairs as Fergus came lumbering after her. Neither of them heard the back door open and their children return.

'I bet you that pair are bonking again!' Sharon said with an exasperated face to her brother, as they heard their parents' squeals from upstairs.

'Disgusting!' Mark replied. 'Wouldn't you think at their age, they'd have more sense! Where's that new chocolate spread? I know Mum hid it somewhere.'

'I wonder what it's like,' Sharon said meditatively after her sibling had discovered the spread behind the packets of spaghetti. 'Bonking, I mean. Dad is such a hippopotamus . . . think of poor Mum with that on top of her!'

Mark put a spoon into the chocolate spread, drew it forth and put the contents in his mouth.

'I suppose the old dears work something out,' he said, putting the spoon back for seconds, 'maybe they've a portable crane we haven't found yet!'

Sharon said, 'Hey, stop eating the spread with the spoon. You're supposed to eat it on bread! It'll be all contaminated and there won't be any left! It's not fair!'

'What are you complaining about? If you eat this stuff you'll end up as fat as Mrs Caine!'

Sharon clicked her tongue. 'Mrs Caine isn't that fat! She's just a bit plump!'

'OK, "plump" if you want to go in for euphemisms. But if you're plump how will you snare the bold Peter?' Mark looked at his sister triumphantly. 'I met him earlier in the village, by the way,' he added slyly.

Sharon shrugged, but she left the kitchen and went into the sitting room, stared out of the window. Inside her a storm was raging. How did Mark, her irritating twin, know how she felt about Peter Caine? She had never told him.

She contemplated Willow House for a moment, saw that the gates were open – saw that Miss Reeves' car was in the forecourt. She envied Miss Reeves, who had everything. Suddenly she caught sight of Peter Caine, who made her heart stand still every time she looked at him. He was sauntering along the wet pavement with his collar up, apparently oblivious to the drizzle. She loved the funny, serious expression he had; she thought his round glasses were cool; she dreamed of being his girlfriend. She thought of the chocolate spread Mark was scoffing in the kitchen, but she went softly upstairs to her room.

Sharon's room was the second largest bedroom. It overlooked the front garden and the road and Willow House. It was painted white, had a green carpet ('yuck green' her brother called it) and green and pink curtains. The curtains had a pelmet and tiebacks, and she was quite proud of them. The walls were decorated with various posters; there was one of Boyzone, whom she adored, and one of Batman. There was also one of Joan of Arc which someone had brought her back from France, sitting up very straight in her silver armour, holding her standard aloft and facing whatever was to come.

The wall by the window was taken up by a built-in pine wardrobe and dressing table; there was some strip lighting over the mirror. She had her cosmetics in a drawer, a selection of cheap lipsticks and eyeshadows. She experimented with them sometimes. 'You look as though you were in the last stages of decay,' Mark had informed her when he had interrupted a private make-up session. But Mark was her brother and a boy and knew nothing.

The small DIY desk on the other side of her bed was stacked with her school books. At the bottom of the heap, secreted away in a Geography book, she had a few photographs of Peter Caine. She took them out sometimes when she was sure she would not be interrupted, and stared at him with burning intensity. They had been taken at a barbecue in the garden the year before. Oh God, the way he held his head; sweet Jesus, the way he smiled, as though it was being dragged from him, his eyes giving him away. She saw the veins in the back of his hand, and his slight Adam's apple, as though they were the marks of divine approbation, as though no one else in creation had a vein or a small bump for a larynx.

Sharon desired Peter with a terrible fervour; but she would have been horrified if anyone had mentioned the word sex. She wanted him the way you want heaven when you die, the way you need to be where there is fascination and challenge, the way certain music sears and satisfies the spirit. He represented an absolute, a model of attraction and perfection. Of course, she was creating him, but she did not even suspect that she was. She heard some scuffling sounds from her parents' bedroom which she ignored. Whatever they were doing it couldn't be very romantic. It was all behind them, the agony and the ecstasy.

She sat at her desk, found her jotter and wrote in it, 'My

56

darling P . . . I love you for ever. Your ever devoted wife . . .'

And underneath that she drew in doodles big words . . . 'Mrs Peter Caine.' She scribbled this out, but added a soulful verse by Byron, which she had recently discovered, paraphrasing it to meet requirements.

She thought she heard Mark on the stairs and she stuffed the jotter under her school books, and turned towards the door. But Mark visited his own room and returned to the kitchen.

Susie drew back the curtains which Fergus had hastily pulled across in his eager transport as he tore off his clothes.

'Gestapo Gertie is staring in on us,' she said. 'She seems to spend her entire life at that window!' Susie was regarding the elegant Victorian mansion across the road. It had a lovely old front door with a big fan light and four stone steps. It was at a forty-five-degree angle to the cul-de-sac, and overlooked its own spacious front garden. Its architecture, its tall windows with their eighty panes each, were redolent of another time, and through them the looped-back curtains were visible and the pale face of the owner, Muriel Reeves, gazing out at the world from her bedroom.

'She's like the bloody lady of Shalott!'

'Ah, give her a break!' Fergus said sleepily. 'Try liking her!'

'That one gets her jollies by being able to compare her lot and ours!' his wife replied. 'Why else would she stay in a house like that surrounded by the kennels of the would-be middle class!'

'It's her old home!'

'If I had a house like that nothing would persuade me to sell the land for housing, and if I did I'd move out . . .'

'That's because you're a snob, Susie.'

'Of course I am, or would be if I had anything to be snobby about!' Susie conceded.

Fergus, lying on his side, did not immediately respond.

'Come back to bed,' he said after a moment or two.

'No, I heard the children come in. Anyway, speaking of Muriel, she could write a thesis about the frequency of sexual intercourse in this cul-de-sac on Sunday afternoons!'

There was silence.

'Don't dare go to sleep while I'm talking to you!'

57

Fergus opened one eye and smiled at his wife, and shut it again.

'It's a sociological statistic,' Susie said. 'It's bound to be of value to someone.'

'So what if she is writing a thesis!' Fergus suggested dreamily after a moment. 'If we asked her nicely she might let us have a copy . . . It would be interesting. I mean, does Laura Flanagan have a lover, and what about Eugene and Phil in number ten?'

'. . . What she needs is a few kids and then she'd have no time to show up the rest of us!' Susie continued with a sigh of exasperation. 'She's changed her car again. She has a bloody Aston Martin this time!'

Fergus heard the envy in his wife's voice and kept his eyes closed. He always wanted to be somewhere else when he heard that longing. He experienced it as an accusation. So he let sleep overtake him. Susie looked at him when he did not reply. A burbling sound suspended itself momentarily in his uvula and was then ejected.

'I hate men who snore,' Susie said crossly. But she covered him tenderly. 'By the way,' she added, 'I meant to tell you. I'm going out tomorrow evening . . . I'll be going straight from the office so will you see that the children eat properly?'

Fergus stopped snoring, opened both eyes and asked in a flat voice, 'Oh, where are you going?'

'So you weren't asleep!' Susie said. 'Valerie, Willy's secretary, has got herself engaged and we're celebrating!'

'Oh,' Fergus said. 'Will Willy Penston attend this illustrious get-together?'

'How should I know!' She opened the door and went downstairs.

'Hi, Mum,' Mark said.

'Hi, Mum,' Sharon said, coming downstairs behind her mother. Both of her children stared at her fixedly.

'Two parents would a-bonking go,' Mark hummed with an innocent expression on his face. 'Heigh ho . . .' Sharon turned her face away and giggled.

Her mother clicked her tongue. 'Your father and I were not "bonking" . . . And don't use that kind of language. We were just having . . . a rest . . . a lie down . . .'

Sharon's giggles escalated into a nervous shriek of laughter.

Christ, Susie thought, once I had a private life.

'Make the sandwiches for supper,' she said to Sharon.

'Why can't Mark make them?' Sharon replied. 'I always have to do it!'

'I don't know how,' her brother said. 'Anyway, it's women's work!'

Sharon directed a kick at him and he gave a yell, limped around the floor, holding his groin and groaning: 'Oh God, she got me in the nuts!'

'Good,' Sharon said. 'A few more jabs in the family jewels and you won't have any problems getting employment . . . as a choir boy!'

She fled through the back door as Mark recovered miraculously and sped after her. 'Come back, you little cow . . .'

Susie looked in the fridge at the remains of the lamb.

'Frig the little swine,' she muttered. 'I hope they kill each other.' She glanced out of the window and saw that Wags had entered into the spirit of things and was tearing around the garden after the twins yapping excitedly.

Susie went into the hall with the intention of phoning her sister. Fergus's snores, which had now gathered momentum, came drifting down the stairs through the open bedroom door. She dialled the number, got through at once.

'Hi, Jean. It's me. Do you still have the details of that job . . . the one in the Civil Service that you have to do the exam for. It's for a friend. Yes, I know, but there's always a chance . . . She's well up on current affairs. Christ, Jean, she's not too old . . . !'

'What is that sound?' Jean asked suddenly.

'It's Fergus bloody snoring. You mean you can hear him?'

'I thought it was your washing machine!'

'Very funny.'

'How do you get any sleep with that going on every night?'

'I give him a good beating. It's the only thing men understand. Now will you give me the details.'

She took them down. The Civil Service Commission was looking for high achievers to fill a few vacant posts as Executive Officers and Administrative Officers. An honours degree was required. Closing date for completed application forms was in a week's time.

'Poll has a degree,' Susie said, 'for all the good it's done her!'

'She hasn't a chance,' Jean said. 'But don't say I said so. It's a tough exam and the competition is fierce!'

'Nothing ventured nothing gained,' Susie answered. 'Or so they tell us.'

She went over to Polly's house with the details of the Civil Service job. She knocked on Polly's kitchen door and opened it.

Her friend was sitting at the kitchen table looking fixedly in front of her.

'Poll . . . If you were interested in a job in the Civil Service, they're looking for people. I phoned Jean for the gen . . . All you have to do is phone them for an application form.' She put the slip of paper on the table. 'Is something wrong?'

'Sue, I think I've lost my marbles!'

'Why?'

Susie saw that Polly's eyes were feverish and that her forehead was damp.

'Poll, has something happened? You look terrible!'

Polly began to laugh, an unnatural laugh which sounded brittle and slightly hysterical.

Sue stood staring at her and repeated in a lower and more anxious voice, 'What is it, Poll?'

'Nothing!' Polly said. She glanced at her friend, saw her consternation and sagged a little in the chair. 'I know it's very silly but I was just wondering how I would go about retrieving a letter I put in the postbox.'

'Who was it to?'

Polly giggled, put her hand over her mouth. 'You won't believe this, but I've just sent off an ad to the *Sunday Times* Encounters column . . . looking for a nice gentleman . . .'

Susie looked at her, tried to think of a fitting riposte, but saw that her friend was completely serious.

'Oh, Polly,' Susie said with a shriek of laughter. 'What on earth did you do that for?'

'Don't mention it, for God's sake. It was an impulse of the moment . . .'

'Oh, Polly,' Susie said with tears of laughter, 'I just love you!'

* * *

Rory felt the familiar gout-like pain in his index finger. It came from his incessant pressing of the mouse. He ignored it as best he could, concentrated on his data base. The dream of writing the definitive comparative reference work on global history in the first millennium was now a passion, and the sustained effort he put into it an obsession. He knew this; it was something which lured him on, this vision of his eventual success. He could almost hear the advice to future students of early history, 'Look up your Caine.'

Without a computer he could never hope to build a comparative data base, establishing the extent to which the Chinese, Indian, and Egyptian civilisations had influenced each other. He was particularly fascinated by Genghis Khan, and wanted to examine the theory that these three great early civilisations were inter-influenced despite the depredations of Genghis Khan, precisely because his empire linked all three.

He also wanted to straighten out the mess caused by the Catholic Church when it introduced the Gregorian calendar and, through it, lost eleven days to the world.

He wanted to show whether certain mythical kings and princes had existed. To do this he was preparing data bases for various countries in Europe in the first millennium and comparing their data against each other.

The Internet was fascinating. It was the first real genuine clearing-house of information, and was worth the expense of the escalating phone bill. After all, if he could bring this book off his financial worries might well be over.

He thought briefly of Polly, fondly because she was such a funny, innocent little thing, in exasperation because she was becoming so waspish. Then he wondered what she would dish up for supper.

Far away from Ashgrove Lawns, in the London suburb of Wimbledon, Bernard Whiston was by the fire. The Sunday papers reposed tidily on the coffee table; he hadn't opened them yet. He was thinking of a certain block of shares which he intended to purchase; a risk certainly, they might go either way rapidly, but if the merger came off . . . Yes, speculation was the answer to ennui and old-age blues.

61

He was dimly aware of the heat from the fire, of the sound of the radio in the kitchen, of the small, more distant, sounds of the spade being deployed in the garden.

He started when the phone rang, stumbled across the room to pick it up. 'Hello?'

'Grandad!' a young female voice said after a second or two.

'Miss Mo . . . my darling . . . how are you?'

'Terrible . . . I've had a row with Bob!'

'Who's Bob?'

'Oh God, I told you. Anyway it's all off . . . I told him never to darken the door again . . . How are you keeping? Are you minding yourself?'

'Dear child, I'm minding myself to the point where the boredom will get me before the decrepitude! But I have a trick or two up my sleeve yet . . .'

'I'm sure you have, Grandad! Get rid of them. You know what the doctor said . . . No booze and no fun and you're to behave yourself! Is Dad there?'

'He's in the garden; hold on . . .'

Bernard opened the French window and shouted, 'Keith . . . Sophie's on the phone.'

Keith stuck the spade into the loam and rushed indoors, kicking off his wellies on the patio.

Bernard returned to his chair by the fire and listened as his son-in-law spoke to Sophie, otherwise known as Mo. He needs more than this, Bernard thought after half an hour, during which time Keith had hung up by arrangement and called his daughter back. He's only fifty-something for God's sake, a mere stripling! It's not possible to live through one's children! But what can I do?

He picked up the *Sunday Times*, leafed through the various supplements. An idea occurred to him suddenly, making him chuckle, but he put it from him as possibly over the top.

# Chapter Four

Polly went to the village postbox at 9.55 a.m. next morning and waited for the postman to collect the mail. She had made her mind up to get her letter back, and the only way to do it was to beard the postman and make him hand it over.

It was very cold and she felt very foolish. She stood back against the railing of the National School and pretended to look for something in her handbag. Someone went by in a car and tooted a greeting. Polly looked up. It was Muriel in her new blue Aston Martin. The window opened and Muriel called to Polly in her semi-RP accent, the one she had inherited and which had been honed in school elocution lessons.

'Would you like a lift?'

Afraid of leaving the postbox, but unwilling to be impolite, Polly walked to where the car had pulled up a few yards away and looked in at her neighbour. Against the black leather bucket seats Muriel Reeves seemed like a visitor from the planet Perfection. It seemed to Polly that she eyed her curiously and Polly reddened, aware that she must have looked a bit silly standing there in the cold. 'No thanks, Muriel, I'm just waiting for someone.'

'You'll freeze to death,' Muriel said.

From the corner of her eye Polly saw the Bord Telecom van arrive, the postman alight, unlock the green postbox, take out the letters and put them in his canvas sack.

Polly excused herself to Muriel and ran to accost the postman. He was wearing a navy uniform with a blue shirt and straightened as she addressed him.

'I'm sorry . . . I put a letter in the postbox yesterday . . . I'd like to get it back!'

63

'Jaysus, missus,' the postman said, 'I can't go handing out letters to people who come askin' for them. Sure where would that leave us!'

'It's important,' Polly said. '. . . I need to get it back . . . It was something I did on the spur of the moment . . .'

The postman pursed his lips, shook his head. His body language was full of deliberation, for he was a man who knew his power.

'When you put a letter in the post it's not yours any more,' he said with the air of someone delivering a lecture on the facts of life. He glanced at Polly's stricken face. 'Sure I had a girl here one morning who had got her letters mixed up. The one she had written to her boyfriend she put in an envelope addressed to her mother, and the one she had written to the mother she sent to the boyfriend. She was in a right dander!' He glanced at Polly. His demeanour suggested that the story could be worse.

'Please,' Polly said. 'It's important!'

'You shouldn't have written to whoever it was, missus! You should think before you leap!'

He tied the neck of the sack, threw it into the van and left Polly behind on the pavement.

Polly turned back to see if Muriel's car were still there and realised that it was pulling away from the kerb. She crossed the road and went to Kinlan's. She bought the *Irish Times* and a brown loaf, had a few words with Peggy behind the till on how cold it was still keeping.

Peggy's pregnancy was beginning to show. The girl looked tired. Her hair was lank and her plump face had lost the buoyant expression it used to have. She had a boyfriend of twenty-two who worked in England. Peggy's mother was up the wall about her child's pregnancy, the interruption of her schooling (she had dropped out of school). They should fit vaginal rat-traps on teenagers, Polly thought. Intruders on the very young should have a few surprises.

On the way back she walked to the end of the road and entered the church. Mass was just ending. A handful of people were leaving. Polly knelt in the back pew.

'I did a stupid thing . . .' she told the unseen Presence on the altar. 'Go on, have a laugh . . . It's all You're good for! You must be vastly entertained watching the idiotic things we do. Now there'll be an ad in the *Sunday Times* and an inexplicable item on the credit card bill. How am I going to explain that to Rory? You could have stopped that letter, made that little poison postman give it to me!'

There was no response from the tabernacle with the golden door.

Polly got up, walked out, passed a poster which someone had put up in the vestibule saying, 'The Lord delighteth in Thee.'

'Huh,' Polly said under her breath.

She walked through the village, noted the newly opened restaurant called the Furnace with its brass rod and jazzy curtain, inspected the bill of fare which was mostly French, and wondered if she could interest Rory in taking her out for dinner.

In the offices of Penston and Company, Solicitors, Susie was at the word processor, checking out a draft Conveyance for her boss.

Mr Penston was at least ten years older than she was, and it always amazed Susie that he still took life seriously. That anyone over fifty should think work was a serious business, when the sands were so obviously trickling away in the hour glass!

'Now this fucking Indenture witnesseth,' she muttered, in a bad mood because Mondays had never agreed with her, 'that in pursuance of the said effing agreement and in consideration of the sum of one hundred and fifty thousand quid . . . Christ, he's paying that sort of money for a flat . . .'

She printed the deed on deed paper, a more sober document than the version she had hissed to herself between her teeth, prepared the Memorial, and presented the documents to Mr Penston with the rest of her work at the end of the morning. Her boss looked at them.

'Thank you, Susan.'

'When are you moving house?' Susie asked.

Mr Penston looked at her. 'Moving house?' he repeated.

Susie gestured at the documents. 'Yes . . . To the flat . . .'

'The flat is an investment,' Mr Penston said. 'I shall not be moving house!' His demeanour suggested that Susie was in serious breach of decorum, that she had, in effect, forgotten her place. Mr Penston lived a bachelor existence, and adhered, so far as could be ascertained, to old world values.

Pompous prick, Susie thought, muttering an explanation to the effect that a flat in Dalkey must be lovely, what with the view of the sea . . . a penthouse one too . . .

'Indeed,' Mr Penston said sternly, stressing each syllable. 'Thank you, Susan.'

'Ah, fuck off,' Susie said to him silently. But she lowered her eyes demurely in overt submission. After a moment her boss added in a tone which Susie could not interpret: 'Of course if you would like to see it sometime – the flat – some evening . . .'

When Polly got home she put the radio on and started into the housework. Her mind churned over the foolish envelope which was now finding its way to London, to the desk of the editor of the Encounters Page. There was nothing for it but to grin and bear it. No one would answer the ad anyway.

She turned on the radio. The presenter Gay Byrne was talking to some woman who said the school system was a disgrace, streaming children and forcing them to regard themselves as duds from an early age. Polly, Jason in mind, was very interested in this topic. She made a cup of coffee and listened. But first she turned off the kitchen light so that Cat, who had lumbered on to the windowsill outside and was anxiously scanning the interior, would not see her. This manoeuvre proved futile. Cat spotted her and started mewing, beginning with gentle reminders, progressing to threats, and then to a form of feline clucking, as though she wanted Polly to know that she was a cat who was not without resources, that she had a few atavistic chromosomes tucked away which could be mobilised in an emergency.

Polly leaned towards the window and the cat got agitated, opening her mouth and showing her array of small, razor teeth.

'You'll just have to wait, Cat,' Polly said. 'You will be fed in the fullness of time.'

Gay Byrne was nice. He called his caller 'love'. She made her point well. Her son had been placed in the bottom of the C stream, and thought he was useless, she said. She had had to teach him herself, to force self-esteem on him.

I can't teach Jason, Polly thought. He won't let me; I've tried to do some French with him, but he knows everything. If he has to repeat the Leaving he'll want to go to the Institute and that will cost an arm and a leg. I wish we had some money. There's no use talking about the virtue to be found in poverty: all poverty does is leave you powerless, pouring your life force into the miserable business of making do. I don't want to make do any more.

The phone rang. Polly hurried to the halfmoon table in the hall where the phone sat and picked up the receiver.

'Hello?'

'Hi . . . Polly? This is Michelle!'

'Oh hello, Michelle . . . I thought you had gone back to London!'

'I have. I'm phoning you from there. Look, Polly, I thought I'd give you a call . . . What are you doing for Easter?'

'Nothing special.'

'Why don't you come and spend it here with me! Tom will be away for most of Easter week and I thought you might like the break! Just the two of us in our flat in Eaton Square . . .'

'Thanks, Michelle, but I can't . . .'

'Why not?'

I can't afford it, Polly thought. Why does she have to be so obtuse? I haven't got the money to go gadding to London at a moment's notice. Rich people never realise how poor other people really are, especially people who pretend they aren't, the genteel poor, the workers and underpaid intelligentsia who prop up the tax system! People who work so hard to stay in the same place, people so busy pretending that they are much better off than they are that they have no energy left for revolution.

'Pity,' Michelle said in a disappointed voice. 'I'll cancel your ticket. I know I took a liberty, but as Easter is such a busy time I booked it provisionally, thinking you might be free!'

There was silence. Then Michelle added in a coaxing voice, 'Polly, won't you reconsider. I'd be really grateful; I'll be on my poor little ownio . . . and I know hardly anyone in London . . . and I simply loathe my own company!'

Polly realised that if Michelle was going to pay for her ticket this put a completely different complexion on the matter.

'I don't know . . .'

'Look, I'll pick you up at Heathrow: we'll have a bit of fun. Surely Rory and the boys can look after themselves for a few days?'

'I suppose they could. The effort wouldn't do them any harm anyway!'

Michelle laughed. 'Good. The ticket will be waiting for you at the Aer Lingus desk on Easter Saturday . . .'

'Well, if it's just for the weekend . . .'

'You can decide that when you arrive. It's an open return ticket. Why not give yourself a real break!'

Why not indeed, Polly thought with sudden excitement. She hadn't been to London for years.

'You're very kind to think of me, Michelle. The truth is I'd love to go!'

'Good girl. Have you got a pencil handy and I'll give you the flight details . . .'

Life is about variety and movement, Polly thought when she returned to the kitchen. If there is no variety, no dynamic, you might as well be dead. The trouble with the way we live is that we are snared by circumstances and perception. We dig burrows for ourselves, and they get tighter and smaller, but, rabbitlike, we are afraid to move, because the open plain is dangerous and the burrow seems to be safe. But something evil happens in the absence of courage; the safe burrow becomes a grave.

The escalating caterwauling from the windowsill interrupted the flow of her thought. She let Cat in, lifted her up and stroked her cunning, domed skull.

'I'm going to London, Cat,' she said with a laugh. 'Rather like Dick Whittington. Do you want to come?' The cat looked at her suspiciously for a moment, then squeezed both eyes shut and began to purr. 'You'll wear your leather jerkin, of course, and your suede boots . . .' Cat seemed happy to go along with any arrangement. I'd better do the bloody brasso-ing, she thought with a sudden return to normality. And then the bathroom needs a scrubbing . . . In her mind's eye she already saw how perfect she could make the bathroom, shining bright, and the door knocker and letter box and doorknob too by the time she had finished with them. Then she could attack the ironing and give the kitchen a thorough going-over. She could see how perfect and shining the floor would be and the units and the sink and the fridge, all shining bright. Her mind scanned the possibilities for the evening meal. Lasagne, perhaps; everyone liked it. She'd have to check the pasta situation; she could always nip down to the village.

When Polly met Muriel that afternoon she was struck by her pallor.

'Hello, Polly. You're looking very cheerful!'

Muriel addressed her through the open window of her car. She was wearing a beautiful pure wool suit, under an elegant wool coat. She was expertly made up and a sweet fragrance wafted from her. She was putting her car away, waiting for the gates to her spacious forecourt to open in response to the remote control.

'I hope you got the postman to give you back your letter this morning!' she said.

Polly flushed and cursed silently. She hated Muriel knowing what she clearly knew, and she hated the amused condescension with which she mentioned it.

'I couldn't help overhearing you!'

'Oh, it was just something I posted for Rory . . . he put it in the wrong envelope!'

Muriel studied her with appraising eyes. 'I see. And he sent poor old you down to intercept it! Men! I'll have to talk to him!'

'Don't!' Polly said before she could stop herself. She flushed and said that she had better be going.

'Polly,' Muriel said with a light laugh, 'you're blushing. Anyone would think you had a lover!'

I wish that woman wouldn't needle herself into everyone's business, Polly whispered through clenched teeth as she walked to the village. Hasn't she anything better to think of than other people's affairs? It's no wonder her fiancé ran off!

When she was at the village she saw Rory's car approaching. For a moment she experienced a surge of joy and she stood and waved. But he did not see her. He kept his eyes on the road and did not notice the waving woman on the pavement. He was concentrating. He was pondering whether the program he had been trying to use should be run on base memory or expanded memory, and, more seriously, whether he would have to delete the ANSI SYS driver, because that would break his heart.

# Chapter Five

In the next few days the weather improved. Sunday was fine, even warm, and the light air was full of burgeoning spring. The daffs were past their prime, but those in chill sheltered places still blazed in full glory.

Polly felt the joy in the air, heard the birds, sensed the hope that the spring brought. And then she remembered that today was the day. But maybe the stupid ad would not yet have made the paper. Thank God it would be anonymous. Thank God at least for that.

She tried to drag Jason with her to Mass. 'I don't want to go!'

'Well, you're going. I'm not having this family growing up like pagans!'

'What's wrong with being a pagan? At least it's intelligent!'

'How could it possibly be intelligent?'

'Because, Mother dear, none of the tripe that they throw at us is even remotely likely. Pigeons simply do not impregnate virgins, and dead men stay down!'

Polly did not argue. She gave an order. 'Come to Mass!'

'No!'

Polly went herself. The church was full of people in cheerful clothes. The sunlight streamed through the stained glass. The organ music swelled and retreated. Except to mouth the responses, Polly did not pray.

'I'm tired,' she whispered half aloud when a reproach strayed through the door of her mind. 'I'm foolish and I'm tired.'

In Kinlan's she bought the *Sunday Times* and scuttled home. Laura Flanagan was out walking her dog and she stopped to

71

have a chat. Wasn't it a lovely day, a perfect day for a drive in the country, she said in her loud, cheerful voice. Laura's condescension was of a different order to Muriel's. In Muriel's case it was really self-projected because the woman herself didn't give a damn. She had reached the point where money, and all its ramifications, was meaningless.

With Laura, on the other hand, condescension was part of the support system of her soul. After all, she had been an accountant's wife and a doctor's daughter. Her father had had a big practice and a house in Upper Mount Street, in the days when being a professional was regarded with some awe.

'We had a cottage in the mountains, you know . . . It was burnt to the ground one September evening after we had left. The flue was defective, and the hot ash escaped to burn the rafters!'

Polly said how nice it must have been to have a place out of town, how lucky she had been, and Laura was gratified.

Once home Polly opened the paper, found the Encounters column, searched and located an ad in bold print which announced: 'A gentle lady, warm, intelligent and educated, would love to meet a similar man (45+). Photo appreciated. Please reply to Box 1287.'

Polly stared at it. Then she started to laugh, putting her hand over her mouth.

God, she thought, here I am looking for a man in the paper. This happened because I got fed up and put an envelope into the local postbox. That gesture was minuscule; the result disproportionately bizarre.

Peter came into the kitchen. He had just got up and was in his bathrobe.

'What are you giggling about, Mum?'

'Nothing,' Polly said, closing the supplement.

The phone rang. As Peter showed no inclination to leave his Wheat Bisks Polly went into the hall to take the call.

'Could I speak to Jason please?' the peremptory female voice said.

'Hold on.'

'Jason,' Polly called, but there was no reply. 'Jason!' she called again, louder.

'The zit-bag went out,' Peter's laconic voice announced from the kitchen, from a full mouth.

'He's out, I'm afraid,' Polly said into the receiver.

'When will he be back?' the voice demanded in a no-nonsense tone.

'I don't know. Can I take a message?'

'Tell him that Veronica phoned.'

'All right.'

When she went back to the kitchen she said irritably to Peter, 'Why can you never bestir yourself? You never answer the phone, you just sit there like some kind of oriental potentate!'

'Sorry, Mum; it's just that my old war injury keeps acting up!'

Polly made a gesture of exasperation.

Rory was in the dining room at the computer. Polly didn't have to look in, because she could hear the keys clicking. She went back to the kitchen. Peter had let the cat in and was feeding her.

'I fed that animal before I went to Mass,' Polly said. 'She's getting so fat she'll burst!'

'That would be interesting,' Peter conceded. 'Fur and hair really flying; Cat plastered across the kitchen . . .'

He tickled his pet under her chin. 'You won't do that, will you, Puddy?'

He turned to his mother. 'And how are we today, Mother mine?'

Polly knew that this was the precursor to a request for an advance on his allowance. She calculated that he was so far on now with advances that he was paid up to sometime near the turn of the millennium.

'Can I borrow ten quid?'

'When do you envisage repaying it?'

Peter smiled. Once he would have responded to the edge he heard in her voice with a churlish answer. But that was before he had learnt about the power of charm.

'I will be your slave!'

'Oh, get away with you!' Polly said. 'Just try to remember that I'm not a money tree!'

Peter hung his head. 'I know . . . Now you're going to tell me that money is tight . . . But I promise to pay it all back!'

'I don't want it back,' Polly said. 'I just want you up and running, and off the books!'

'You've got it!' Peter replied. 'Soon . . . very soon!'

'Good,' Polly said. I won't hold my breath, she added unkindly to herself.

'Don't go asking your father for money as well,' she added aloud. Peter often did this. The poor mouth worked as well with both parents as with one, and it doubled his takings.

'Hacking hobbits are best left undisturbed,' Peter said mildly, taking a large spoonful of Wheat Bisk. 'Besides, he wouldn't know who I was!'

Jason arrived in the back door. He looked at his mother carefully, wondering if she was angry with him, wondering at the extent to which he was in the dog house because of his refusal to accompany her to Mass.

Polly was cool with him. 'Where were you?'

'Out.'

'I surmised as much. Would you care to be more specific?'

'I went next door to talk to Sharon and Mark. They're in an awful state . . . Wags is missing!'

'That's very sad,' Polly said. 'Are you sure that Cat hasn't eaten him!'

Jason laughed in spite of himself. He looked at the cat curled up in her basket. She seemed suspiciously enormous.

'She's eaten everything else she can find. I don't think mere aesthetic considerations would deter her . . .'

'You're in a very funny mood this morning, Mum,' Peter said with his mouth full. 'What's got into you?'

'Spring!' Polly said. 'Once I was young and foolish and now I'm old and foolish!'

'Ah well,' Peter said. 'That's what time does to you!'

Jason, realising that no one was paying much heed to him and feeling cheated of the contretemps he had anticipated, put his oar in.

'It's the twins' birthday tomorrow!'

'It's mine in three weeks,' Peter said. 'I mention this lest ye forget!'

He leant his long form back in the chair and wiped his mouth with a man-sized tissue. 'Do you still remember the day I was born, Mum?'

'Ah,' said Polly, 'I remember that morning well. The sunlight was streaming into the ward; I asked the nurse whether it put her off having children – seeing what women had to go through to get them. But she said, "Not at all – it'll be all over soon and look what you'll have!"' She gazed fixedly at Peter. 'I'm looking!'

'Mum,' Peter said. 'Although I say so myself, you have a lovely son. He's six foot three, has a forty-five inch chest, can bench press eighteen stone . . .'

'And is able to bore everyone to death in three sentences . . .' Jason finished, turning on his heel.

'Wait, Jason,' Polly called after him, 'someone phoned for you, a girl called Veronica!'

Jason paused at the foot of the stairs, then nodded as though this intelligence was of scant interest to him.

When her younger son had disappeared upstairs Polly turned to Peter.

'Who is this Veronica anyway?'

'She's some babe he met at that nightclub he went to a few weeks ago.'

'Did you see her?'

'Yeah.'

'Is she nice?'

Peter shrugged. 'She's all right.'

'What does that mean?'

'It means he's fine so long as she doesn't sit on him!'

'You mean she's heavy?'

'Depends what you call "heavy". She's about fifteen stone.'

'Poor kid,' Polly murmured. 'Puppy fat can be such a problem!'

'This is no puppy, Mum. This is a fully grown female.'

'What age is she?'

'Dunno . . . around thirty!'

Polly looked at him aghast. 'Christ. My baby!'

The phone rang again. This time Peter went into the hall to answer it.

'. . . Oh, hello, Veronica,' he said. 'I'll just see if he's in!'

Polly saw Jason's head appear above the banisters. He was

shaking his head vigorously at his brother and his demeanour suggested someone on the run.

'Oh I'm sorry . . . he seems to have popped out,' Peter said urbanely into the receiver. 'Yes, I'll tell him you phoned. I don't know if he got the earlier message. OK, give me your number and I'll see he gets it.' He wrote something down on the pad and put down the receiver.

'Jason, you little zit-bag, you should think before you chat people up!' he hissed at his younger sibling who was standing on the top step of the stairs.

Jason scowled and moved his head in wrath. The light from the landing window caught his pimples. 'It's not my fault if women find me irresistible!'

Polly came into the hall and looked up at her younger son.

'Is this Veronica person being a nuisance?' she demanded. 'I'll warn her off next time she phones.'

Jason bristled. 'NO, Mum. I'll deal with this my way!'

Polly did not allow dismay to register. She already knew that where every evil chance may fail, your children can still defeat you.

'Jason, you're a spotty, pimply git,' his brother informed him.

'But at least I've a few more years left in me, Old Stuff . . . !'

Peter puffed out his chest. 'I can see I'll have to give you a good thrashing!'

'Stop it,' Polly said. She went back to the kitchen, took up the *Sunday Times* supplement and found again the advertisement inserted by the gentle lady, warm and intelligent, who was basically looking for one other human being who would talk to her on the level where she lived.

Muriel phoned Claire, her old friend who lived in England.

But Claire had gone to Scotland with her husband for a break. The phone was answered by their eldest daughter, Annabelle.

'Mummy and Daddy are away,' the girl's voice said. 'They'll be home tomorrow.'

'How are you, Annabelle? Do you remember me?' There was a hesitancy. 'Of course you don't,' Muriel added. 'You were quite a little girl when I saw you last. What age are you now?'

'Twelve,' Annabelle said shyly.

Muriel made a few more polite noises, asked Annabelle to

give her love to her parents and put down the phone. Twelve, she thought. Almost a teenager. Almost a woman. She didn't know who I was. Why should she, after all? She looked out the window at the cul-de-sac. She saw some of the young people who had been babies a few years ago saunter down the footpath, laughing.

Before you know where you are, she mused, the world you thought was yours belongs to other people, the hungry new generation. And then she thought in sudden fear: have I already outlived my life?

# Chapter Six

The replies to Polly's ad in the *Sunday Times* began to come in at the end of the following week. The big brown envelope marked 'Private and Confidential' fell on to her mat with the rest of the post at eleven o'clock on Friday morning. She looked at it for a moment, wondering what it could be, and it was only when she had it opened that she realised, with a start and a sense of the ridiculous, what she had. There were four letters, all addressed to her box number. She reached for a knife and slit open the first one that came to hand and with something like disbelief took out the letter.

> Hi,
>     You sound just the kind of woman I like. Gentle! Women should be gentle. I'm enclosing a picture of me (I'm the guy in the middle) with some of my pals. If you'd like to phone me you can get me at the number given below. Just ask for Fred.

A phone number followed.

Polly looked at the photo. Fred was plump. He was grinning, wore a short-sleeved shirt and had a tattoo on his forearm. His pals were holding pint glasses, and looked like the kind of guys who would get in first with the retaliation.

The second letter was written in an educated hand. A photo was appended. The face which looked out at her was clean shaven, earnest, bespectacled. The writer said that he was divorced and that he loved violin music. Polly studied the face, the weak mouth, the undershot chin, the large, apprehensive eyes.

The third missive contained the picture of an old trout with spectacles. His letter was categorical.

'I want you here with me at once,' he said. 'You can share the house with my children. I know they'll love you.'

The handwriting was infirm. The address was wedged, by way of afterthought, into the bottom left-hand corner. Polly studied the face in the small photograph, the general air of bewilderment, as though events had overtaken him and he needed steering. She began to think that life with Rory wasn't so bad after all. A sense of dread bordering on panic subsumed her as she opened the final letter. The photograph was stapled to the stiff paper. A balding head stared out at her with protuberant eyes.

'The story is not as bleak as it looks,' the letter said. 'This was taken in poor light.'

In the days that followed the post brought Polly more and more replies. It was a bit like being under siege: all those men addressing themselves to her. She began to feel like some sort of courtesan-by-correspondence. But it was also borne in upon her that many men were neither so happy nor so self-sufficient as she had always thought men were. Many of them spoke of their loneliness; many of them seemed to long for a real relationship, genuine companionship. One of them even spoke of finding 'the elusive soulmate'. One of them said how he longed to find a 'loving honest woman'.

In the evenings when she saw the back of Rory's head while he was lost in cyberspace, she thought of these men who secretly longed for companionship and who did not know how to go about getting it.

'After twenty-five years I have forgotten how to chat people up,' one of them had said.

After twenty years, Polly thought, being chatted up would be the strangest thing in the world. The thought conjured up such a sense of impropriety that she was glad none of these people knew who she was or where she lived. It was a relief mentally to reassume the mantle of the good housewife and mother who is protected from the world.

\* \* \*

The only letter which gave her real pause arrived almost a week later.

Dear Gentle Lady,

I am fifty-six, a psychiatrist by profession, now more or less retired. I was widowed two years ago. It is with some diffidence that I answer an advertisement like this, but you sound like a genuine person. It would be a pleasure to come and see you wherever you are.

As you can see from the address I live in Wimbledon. My house is old and too big for my needs, but it has a large garden which I love.

I have a daughter, presently working for a law firm in New York, whom I see from time to time.

I play bridge, read a lot, do a bit of gardening, and try to keep fit by walking my dog on the Common!

Occasionally I do some jogging. But something is missing from my life – the most important ingredient of all!

I look forward to hearing from you.

With best wishes for your happiness,

Bernard Whiston.

Polly peered at the photo. It was small, and the figure in it was seated in a garden. She went into Rory's desk, found his magnifying glass which he kept in a drawer, studied the face which leapt into focus. The head was balding, but the face was refined, the expression kind. He looks nice, Polly thought. He looks very nice indeed. She studied what she could see of his garden – roses and lupins and behind them a French window to the house. She looked out at her own modest patch. The grass needed mowing and big, fat, selfish Cat was asleep in the spring sunshine. It was no use having aspirations for a lovely garden. The boys would still kick ball in it, and it would never sustain the lovely things she would sow.

Ah well, Polly thought: I can't answer these letters. I'm too much of a coward. I did a silly thing. But I'll send everything back, letters, photos, the lot. That's only fair.

She went into the dining room and switched on Rory's computer. She knew how to work the word processor – at least in its most basic form – put a letter on screen and get the printer to do the needful. It would be the perfect way of answering her mail.

So she began:

> Dear . . . (and here she put in the appropriate name) thank you for your letter. However, the ad was a silly impulse and I'm sending back your photograph. I'm sure you're a very nice person.

She looked at the little heap of letters and thought about whether she should sign a name. It seemed a bit mean to get people to write to you and then not even sign your name. But I can't give my real name, she thought. So she tried to think of one which would do, and in a fit of sudden levity signed the letters Concepta.

She had had a schoolfriend of that name. When the friend had gone to work in England she had changed it to Carmel. It seemed that the English didn't know much about the doctrine of the Immaculate Conception and she had run into the occasional misunderstanding.

But Polly lingered a little over the letter from the nice man in Wimbledon with the garden. She sighed a little as she put his photograph into an envelope with her letter. For some reason she did not understand she delayed sealing it. She found the box of stamps and stamped each letter, putting it into her bag for the post. But as she was about to affix the stamp to the letter for Bernard Whiston it suddenly occurred to her that she would be in London the following weekend and that she could post it over there.

'What does it matter where it's posted?' the little sardonic voice in her head asked her. She answered it humbly. It simply meant that she didn't have to send off her categorical refusal to Bernard Whiston just yet. This left her room for a little fantasy.

I suspect I have become half witted, Polly thought as she walked to the village. Is this what happens when you lack stimulus? You become a little strange in order to create diversity.

The voice which she recognised as her private alter ego, which of late seemed to watch over her and occasionally interrupt with comment, whispered: How can anyone deny you anything?

You're an adult! Seize what is yours. Don't be cracked, Polly rejoined. What do you want me to do?

She went into the church, more out of habit than anything else. The stained glass rose in symmetry above the altar; the white marble altar had statues of Our Lady and St Joseph on either end of the centre piece. She thought of Jason and his comments. 'Pigeons do not impregnate virgins, and dead men stay down.' What do You say to that? she said silently to the unseen Presence on the altar. You can't fault the logic!

When there was no reply she added, I suspect, God, that when You are routed in the logic stakes You become boring.

As she was coming out of the church she met Father Brennan, the parish priest. He was a thin, friendly man, dressed all in black except for his white dog-collar. He was avuncular to women; he particularly approved of Polly. Polly was aware of this, knew whenever he spoke to her that he saw her as a shining example of the good woman. His approval always wrapped her around like some sort of strait-jacket. Part of her wanted to go on deserving it; part of her chafed at the narrow base from which this sanction emanated. Those who live in caves, she thought in a sudden unbidden flash of insight, will inevitably approve of those who do the same.

Behind them there was a sudden sound of altercation. Turning they saw, just outside the church gates, the person of Sam Riley, handing out some abuse to a passer-by. The passer-by moved on, and Sam sank against the low wall and eventually disappeared below it on the other side.

Father Brennan sighed; said, 'Poor Sam! A tragedy! But what can you do?' He shook his head and went into the church.

As Polly made her way through the church gate Sam hailed her from the pavement. He was sitting, leaning drunkenly against the wall. 'Would you have a few pence, ma'am . . . for a cup o' tea?'

Polly opened her bag and searched for some change. She felt sorry for this man; he must have been handsome once, before his raddled face and matted hair had marked him out as one of life's failures. They said he was only thirty, that his family had thrown him out. He lived in a derelict cottage behind the village, with sheets of newspapers sellotaped to the windows. His coat was closed with the assistance of a boot lace; his face was grimy and his eyes staring.

'Do you know the paper they use to wrap fish?' he demanded, as Polly handed him some money. Polly nodded. There was no point in asking Sam to clarify his parameters.

'Well, I had two lovely fillets of cod wrapped up and I put them in a biscuit tin to keep the fucking birds away . . .'

'Oh,' Polly said, 'I see.'

'I put the tin in the dustbin for safe keeping . . . but when I came out this morning the fish was gone!'

'Oh,' Polly repeated. 'What a pity!'

'The paper was all torn!'

'I see,' Polly said again.

'It was them cats,' Sam explained, hitting the pavement angrily with his fist, '. . . them bastard cats!'

She went into Kinlan's for the paper. There was no sign of Peggy. Only her mother, Madge, was in the shop.

'Cold enough today,' Madge said as she opened the till and gave out the change. '. . . You'd never think that Easter was upon us! Are you doing anything nice?' Madge asked.

'Yes, actually. I'm going to London, to stay with my prospective sister-in-law!'

'Lucky you! That'll be a nice break!'

'Doing anything yourself, Madge?'

'Are you joking? With grandparenthood looming?' Madge looked a little grim as she said this.

'How is Peggy?' Polly asked sympathetically, remembering all too well her own first pregnancy as it approached full term.

'Dead beat.' She lowered her voice, into a confiding woman-to-woman tone, 'It's always tough for the last month – if you remember!'

'Yes . . . I remember,' Polly said. 'I was so fed up I went for a short run – I mean a kind of sprint – on the day before Peter was born. It did the trick! As soon as I got home the pains started!'

'God,' Madge said. 'That must have been something – running when you're nine months pregnant!'

'Well it wasn't recognisable as running . . . more a sort of trundle . . .'

'Poor kid,' Madge said, lowering her voice. 'She doesn't have a bull's notion what's ahead of her!'

'It's not so bad these days,' Polly murmured. 'They have all sorts of new-fangled methods and epidurals.'

'It's the hell of the damned!' Madge insisted. 'One way or another, new-fangled methods or old-fangled methods! For all the thanks any of us ever get!' She broke off as a male customer came to the counter with his basket of groceries. 'Hello, Mr Cassidy,' she said, changing the subject to make it fit the male ears, 'how are you at all. 'Tis fresh and well you're looking!'

'Ah get away with you, Madge . . .'

Polly wandered into the street. It was quiet, except for a few cars down near the junction which led to the bypass.

Once the village had been on the main road. In those days it had been choked with traffic, smothered in fumes. But now it could have belonged again to the last century when most of it was built, so quiet it was, at least during the day, before the homeward commuters from the city descended on it en route to the housing estate.

'I need some new clothes for London,' Polly thought with pleasure, imagining the forthcoming weekend, the trip to the airport, the descent into London, the new world of the weekend, with sophisticated Michelle. I can't look like the country cousin.

Mentally she vetted her bank balance and realised with an inward sigh that things were not rosy; she was overdrawn.

At least there was the credit card, but she was terrified of paying interest on that and she had already made an incursion by her ad in the *Sunday Times*.

Oh ye legislators, she thought; if ye would only ease up a bit on tax, ordinary people like Rory and I could live. She knew they missed out taxwise because they were not legally married. Married people got the marriage allowance. Single people got two single allowances, but that didn't amount to the same thing unless both of them had incomes.

She dumped the shopping in the kitchen, checked in her wallet for the credit card.

She looked at herself in the mirror in the downstairs loo, at the slightly flustered air. I'll improve, she thought. I have to. I can't spend the rest of my life looking like something out of Winnie the Pooh. I'm forty-four, and now is the time for metamorphosis.

\* \* \*

She got the bus into town. Halfway there it filled up completely because the bus ahead of them had broken down. An elderly woman got on. There was no immediate place for her to sit and Polly, seated on the bench seat at the front of the bus, moved up against the glass partition to create some room between her and her male neighbour. But the room was inadequate.

'Excuse me,' she said to her neighbour, seeing that he still had room to move in the opposite direction, 'will you let this lady sit down!'

'You're very ignorant,' he replied in an undulating Cork accent, 'but I'm not going to be shuffled around.' He compressed his mouth and lowered his chin on to his chest to show that he was a man who would not be taken advantage of.

Polly squeezed herself tighter into the corner, and gestured to the elderly woman to sit. The latter did, perched precariously, and then more comfortably as Polly, to make room, hitched her bottom half off the seat. Across the aisle a woman in a blue anorak glowered at the man who didn't want to be shuffled, and kept on glowering at him.

When the bus arrived in the city centre the woman in the anorak got off. She paused at the top step, fixed the disgruntled Corkonian with her eyes and shouted: 'May God forgive your mother for giving you such a fat arse!' Ill-suppressed laughter followed her out of the bus. The man reddened. Polly stifled her mirth. No need to go to the theatre in Dublin, she thought. Just hop on the bus!

But Polly found in her shopping expedition that she could find little that fitted her. Have I got bigger and older and more and more awful? she asked herself. Or what? I don't eat much. Just bits and pieces. The odd slice of cake. It shouldn't matter so much.

'Buy a bloody calorie counter,' the new voice inside her head suggested.

What do I need a calorie counter for? Polly wondered.

'So you can get yourself a life!'

I need to be free from home-brewed voices in my head. Maybe I'm mad.

'You're not mad,' the voice said. 'Not yet . . .'

Polly was passing through the glass palace of the Stephen's

Green shopping centre when she decided, on impulse, to buy a Lotto ticket. There was a ticket stand in the middle of the hall and a small queue had formed. That's a pound wasted, she thought, as she filled in the numbers; but nothing ventured and so forth . . .

She put down two numbers randomly, chose 21 as the number of years she had been married, and then 14 and 15, being the numbers of her own and Susie's houses, lingering over the selection of the final number. Should she choose twenty or thirty. Neither, Polly decided. I'll go for one. It is, after all, the only singular number.

She brought her form to the counter.

When Polly alighted from the bus that evening she met Muriel in the village and accepted a lift home in the pale blue Aston Martin with the black leather seats.

'Did you buy anything nice?' Muriel asked, from a cloud of perfume.

'Oh nothing much . . . a pair of trousers and a top in Dunnes Stores.'

Muriel did not reply and Polly thought she was pitying her.

'Not a bad day after all,' Muriel said. 'Looks like we're going to have a nice Easter!'

Polly glanced at Muriel's blood-red nails, at her lacquered coiffure. Her face looked very pale. She shouldn't wear such a pale foundation, Polly thought, liking her neighbour in the moment of sympathy. It makes her look like death warmed up.

'Are you feeling all right, Muriel? You look very pale.'

Muriel turned to her, and her eyes seemed strange, the pupils wide and full of pain. Suddenly, Polly felt that she looked through those eyes into vistas she had not suspected.

'Of course I'm all right, Polly. What a thing to say!'

Polly fell silent. When the car stopped she got out of it and thanked her neighbour. She felt a bit uncertain, like someone who has received a glimpse into a private space, into the world beyond illusion, the storeroom of the vulnerabilities.

Susie came around later that evening. She had Wags with her. He had returned unscathed from his foray into private experience and sat obediently in the hall. Cat was in the kitchen and spat when she saw him, but Polly shut the door.

Sue looked at Polly's beige trousers, but did not compliment her.

'Black ones would have been more slimming,' Peter opined, 'but they're . . . very nice, Mum; you fill them very well!'

Oh God. Polly said; 'From the expression on your face anyone would think I resembled a whale.'

'Well, not a whale exactly, Mum . . . I was thinking more of a well-rounded porpoise . . .'

Peter waited for a maternal swipe with the teatowel, or some other indication that the joke had been taken in good part. But Polly made no move to touch him. She just turned away, struggling with the sudden sense of desolation.

She went into the sitting room and Susie followed, looking at her friend's tense face sympathetically.

'Look, why don't you go on a diet, Poll? You're not fat or anything; it's just that you'd feel so much better if you lost a few pounds. I've got this stuff at home that Fergus is using – Svelte, it's called and it fills you up and suppresses appetite.'

'It's not a real appetite I've got; it's a bored stiff appetite!'

'Did you apply for that job in the Civil Service?'

'Yeah . . . *Fat* chance!'

'Don't be negative. You need something to occupy you!'

In the ensuing silence Rory's clicking at the computer keys could be heard.

'Is he always at that thing?' Susie demanded irritably.

''Fraid so . . .' Polly sighed. 'It's much more interesting than I am!'

'I saw you get out of Muriel's car earlier. Did she give you a lift from town?'

'No. Just from the village.'

'I suppose she was sober?'

'I think so . . . Why? Is she hitting the bottle?'

'I don't know. It's just that I could swear I saw her staggering the other day.'

'I feel sorry for her,' Polly said. 'I think she's lonely. It's a pity about her broken engagement . . . I know it's a long time ago but . . .'

'Lonely! With all her money! You must be joking! She doesn't have to be lonely!'

Polly sighed. 'I don't know. I just had a feeling that things are not going well for her.'

'What she needs is a brood of teenagers. It'd give her something to think about other than her blood-red talons and her cashmere coats and that new car!'

'Ah, don't be so hard on her,' Polly said. 'After all we should rejoice for her. It's good to see someone in this life get something out of it!'

Susie shrugged again. 'I know I'm a cow. But I'm dying of jealousy. I see that supercilious woman, who never has to do a day's work, with everything that money can buy, and she has the gall to condescend all around her . . .'

'I don't think she's condescending! Maybe it's just her manner!'

Susie's brown eyes clouded. 'Nope. She's sitting back luxuriating and watching the rest of us squirm on the slings and arrows of this life!'

'Oh, Susie . . .'

'Don't mind me! I'm fed up this evening! I've had words with Ferg—'

'Oh . . . !'

'He thinks I'm seeing Willy Penston!'

'Are you?'

'Well, not really. I just went with him to see his new flat . . . out in Dalkey! It was curiosity, Polly!' she added dangerously. 'I just wanted to see what it was like . . .'

Polly walked Susie to the gate, stood for a further minute with her and went back into the house. She met Peter in the hall.

'I didn't mean you looked like Pam the Porpoise, Mum,' he said contritely. 'You look great . . .'

Polly ignored this. 'Where's your brother gone?'

'The zit-bag is meeting Veronica!'

'Stop calling him that! It's not right! Who's Veronica?'

'The girl who keeps phoning him, of course. He said to tell you he'd be back late.'

'I see.'

Polly had an image of the fifteen-stone woman and her teenage Jason. It smote her suddenly how life changed, assumed different coats, explored different chapters and that you were doomed, left behind, if you became fixated in any one of them. Her baby was now a young man. Well, not quite, but almost.

She went into the dining room and said to the back of Rory's head: 'Jason is out with some girl. Did he say when he'd be back?'

'Hmnn?' Rory said, and moved his fingers over the computer keys.

Polly repeated the question. Rory replied that he hadn't a clue when Jason would be home. 'He's grown up, Polly, for God's sake!' he said irritably.

Polly stood behind him and watched the monitor for a moment. 'He's not grown up yet . . . but he's trying his wings,' she said more to herself than to him. Then she added almost sotto voce, 'Everything has changed; I should change too, but I'm afraid!'

She did not expect an answer, but Rory said in a very quiet voice without turning his head: 'The trouble with life is that if you do not face it with courage it will destroy you!'

Polly went to the kitchen, bemused as she always was when Rory delivered himself of some instantaneous profundity. Oh, Rory, she thought, how I would love you if you would let me, if you would give me room, an inch or two, a real toe-hold. But you challenge me to the point where I must either break or become someone else. And either alternative is certainly our swan-song.

Suddenly Rory called out, 'Poll, I've been meaning to ask you . . . there's something weird on the credit card bill, for seventy quid or thereabouts . . .'

'Oh, that's just one of these mail order things,' Polly said hastily.

Muriel let in Sable, her cat, and had her spartan supper in her spacious pine kitchen. The evening light filled this room, as it did the small kitchen garden outside the window, where she liked to sit in summer, reading, or knitting, dreaming sometimes of the past. I shouldn't think of the past, Muriel said to herself. There is only the future; it is the only thing to be concerned with. But no matter how often she enjoined this wisdom on herself, she was never able to practise it.

If I could even talk to someone about it, she whispered. What a merciful release that would be. But to whom? Claire was in England, up to her ears in children, still keeping in touch, but only just. She expected that she would phone her later, because Annabelle would have told her she had called. But otherwise she might not. There had been something from *Macbeth* which had surfaced during the day. Years ago she had done the play at school, had enjoyed its drama, its language; garnered some pearls from it. Now she tried to remember what had returned to her with such force in the mid afternoon.

She knew the *Complete Works of Shakespeare* were in the room that had been her father's study. It was the only room in the house which she had not decorated. It had not been used after his death. It was locked, shuttered.

She searched for the key, found it in a tin box in the dresser where she had put it long ago. It was substantial, a solid early Victorian key, touched with rust. She dipped a tissue in olive oil and rubbed the key, brought it to the study door, inserted it in the lock. For a moment it was unyielding, but when more force was applied the key turned with a sudden scraping. The door opened with a small reluctant sound when she turned the knob and pushed. In a moment she was standing in the room.

Yesterday smelt of must. There was a chink of light from the shutters. She lifted the iron latch which secured them, opened them back. The sudden brightness showed the dust floating, aerial plankton in the still, stale light. The room seemed frozen, changeless. The bookshelves, the leather armchair, the mahogany desk, the silver ink stand, the paperweight in the shape of a lizard, were all as he had left them. On one of the shelves behind the desk was the *Complete Shakespeare*. She walked towards it, a life-prisoner asserting autonomy, took it from the shelf.

'Come here, child.'

Her father's voice. She saw the marks her fingers made in the dust on the binding. She knew that whisper – honeyed, commanding, primed with her guilt.

'No, Daddy . . . Please . . . Please . . .'

She grasped the book. Her knuckles cracked. She stood immobile, aware of the rhythmic thunder of her heart, the conflict between obedience and flight, the weight of dimly felt female responsibility for everything.

'Come here, child!' Then softly, coaxingly, 'I have some acid drops . . .' She heard the drawer slide open, smelt the faint, male whiff of tobacco.

'No . . . I need to admire you, Daddy . . .'

She had never said it to him while he was alive. It was a need. To admire him. Greater than many others, as great as that of love.

From somewhere at the other side of her garden wall a dog barked. Muriel backed out of the study, shut and locked the door.

'You'll have to stay there, Daddy,' she whispered as she turned the key. 'I'm sorry, Daddy . . .'

Later, with the book dusted and open on the kitchen table, she found the place she had sought:

> '. . . Canst thou not minister to a mind diseas'd,
> Pluck from the memory a rooted sorrow,
> Raze out the hidden troubles of the brain,
> And with some sweet oblivious antidote
> Cleanse the stuff'd bosom of that perilous stuff
> Which weighs upon the heart?'

Shakespeare knew. Had he been there too, in the Gehenna of self-hatred, enslaved to the unforgiving self?

She felt the headache start, reached for her tablets, told Sable she was going to bed.

# Chapter Seven

Polly got little sleep that night; she lay awake waiting for Jason's return. The room was in darkness, except for the light from the landing, but she was far from dropping off. She was in that state of super-alertness where every sound in the house is magnified, and thought is a mill-race. She was searching the night for the sound of a key in the door and at the same time her mind dwelt in the past.

Ballyglen! Her aunt's home, a cut stone house in the Tipperary countryside. She had been seven, Tom four. She had wept that first night, alone in a big bed, surrounded by the unfamiliar camphor scents of the room. It was so dark you could see nothing, not like her home in Dublin where the street lights cast a glow. But she could hear Tom's shallow breathing. He was asleep in a bed by the window. She didn't want her sobs to waken him so she was careful to cry under the covers. Her throat was paining her from crying; her face was stiff with salt.

Tom didn't really understand that Dada and Mama were gone; he didn't know that if someone died they never came back. The car accident meant little to him; as far as he was concerned Mama and Dada were gone to Heaven; they were with God. They were somewhere; they had been places before and other people had minded him. They would be back soon.

I'll look after you, she had thought in a terrible rush of tenderness. No matter what, I'll be here. Oh Mama, oh Dada . . . don't leave me alone.

But life with Aunty Rita had eventually overtaken them both. Their cousins, Marie and Kate, both older, ten and eleven respectively, had tried initially to conceal their resentment and had then been won over by Tom.

He was beautiful, 'like an angel', she heard one of them describe him. It was true. He had the face of an angel and the aplomb of a natural diplomat; he was the child who rushed out to open the car door for Aunty Rita; he was the cherub who sang so beautifully in the Christmas school play; he was the thief who stole so skilfully that it was years before he was found out.

She could still remember the letter from her aunt. She was at college, in her final year. The missive had been waiting for her when she got back to the flat one evening; she had read it with gathering dread; nausea spread through her, fear and anger. His headmaster had contacted Aunt Rita; he wanted him removed from the school. He had been caught red-handed taking money from the Prior's office. They had been suspecting him for some time.

He had come back to Ballyglen. 'It was all a mistake,' he assured everyone. 'I got the rap for it! Father Andrew always had a down on me, ever since I came . . .'

They had all wanted to believe him, but the shadow had stayed in Aunty Rita's eyes. Polly was certain that he was innocent, had eventually convinced her aunt. All right, he had pilfered as a child, but what child did not go through some such phase? Aunt Rita began to wonder if she should consult a solicitor about the matter. Expulsion from school, when all was said and done, was a serious blot on one's character.

'I'll offer it up!' Tom said.

For a while it looked as though he would study privately for the Leaving, but suddenly he announced he was off. A job in Dublin had beckoned, in Handbury's, a big builders' providers; the manager had known their father.

Polly was glad to have Tom near her in Dublin. He would call on her at the flat, and she would give him a meal. Her flatmate Anne had said afterwards, 'Your brother looks like Clark Gable! And where did he get the charm for God's sake?'

There was a dinner dance run by his employers. He had asked a girl in the office. That night, after leaving her home, he had arrived on Polly's doorstep. She had got out of bed to let him in, had seen at once that he was strangely distraught. He looked like a film star in his hired dinner jacket and black tie and had sat on her couch in a strange mood, subdued yet feverish.

'How do I look, Poll?'

'Like a million bucks!'

'Oh, that's just the point. I want to live in dinner jackets and cashmere coats and have the doorman call me sir . . .'

'Is it that important?'

'Yes! I don't want to spend years and years inching my way up the ladder in bloody Handbury's . . .'

He had stood up, walked to the mirror above the mantelpiece, inspected himself, turned his face sideways to catch a glimpse of his profile. 'I love money, Poll. It is God. There's nothing else!'

'Don't be ridiculous!'

The next time she had seen him he had been buoyant. Then a few weeks later he told her he was leaving to work in England.

'Where?'

'London!'

'What will you be doing in London?'

'Initially the same slop! But watch this space!'

On one of his visits home she had told him about her engagement to Rory, had introduced them. He had erupted. Rory was a square, a bore, a creep, a little teacher without a future. He was already married. How could she even take him seriously? She was pretty, well educated. She could have anyone. He was beginning to make money; eventually he would be able to introduce her to interesting people.

'What are you doing exactly?'

'Oh . . . I've my fingers in various pies.'

'What kind of pies?'

'Business pies, Polly. Business pies . . . where the money is!'

'You think too much of money, Tom.'

'And you think too much of being the paragon, the goody two shoes, the one who always steps into the breach . . . You're marrying this cretin because you want a little niche. Why don't you throw your life to the winds a bit, see what comes when you take a risk!'

But Polly had told him to get lost.

'I'm going to spend my life with Rory and that's that! I love

95

him, you see, something you wouldn't understand . . . The only thing you understand is money!'

Now the same Rory stirred beside her and muttered something incoherent. There was still no indication of Jason's return. Then, when she was wondering should she phone the police (but she knew that if she did Rory would surface and raise the roof – 'What are you trying to do to the boys, wrap them in cotton wool?'), she heard the key in the front door. She jumped out of bed and came halfway down the stairs.

'Where were you, Jason, until this hour?'

'Out,' Jason said.

'Where?'

Jason's mouth tightened. His demeanour suggested that it was none of her business, that she was an overprotective and interfering old mother who was ruining his youth.

But he contented himself with an exasperated sigh and said, 'At the pictures with a friend. Then we had coffee and then she missed her bus and I had to walk her home!'

'Where does she live?'

'Drumcondra.'

'And you had to walk all the way back?'

'Yes, as a matter of fact. I had no money for a taxi.'

'You have school tomorrow!'

Jason shrugged, compressed his mouth and beetled his brows. School did not seem to feature at the top of his agenda at that moment. The impression given was that the whole system was a trespass on one's autonomy. But before he could articulate something along these lines his mother asked, 'Are you hungry? Did you have a supper?'

'No. I'm starving!'

'Do you want me to make you something?'

'It's all right, Mum. I'll do a pizza.'

Polly was about to utter some further remonstrance about the smell of the cooking pizza and the lateness of the hour and the looming morning and his French test, but knowing how churlish Jason could be, and being anxious to avoid unpleasantness, she turned and went back to her room. She opened the window wide to give some relief from the impending cooking smells. It's three o'clock in the bloody morning, she thought looking at the liquid crystal face of the alarm clock.

She got back into bed. Rory was snoring and was halfway across the bed. She put both her feet against his bottom and tried to push him over to his own side.

'But I can't use three E Zero . . . that's my mouse,' he said, speaking with strange precision from the Land of Nod.

'It's not your mouse, it's your arse,' Polly said in his ear, 'and it's taking up more than its fair share of the bed!'

'Eight chip ram; don't use nine chip,' he replied after a moment in a staccato, anxious voice before resuming his snoring.

'A real sex-pot I've got here!' Polly muttered.

Rory started. 'What did-ya say?' he demanded from the murky depths of a Stygian sleep; 'That's an MFN drive, you fool!'

'Should I make a few suggestions,' the unwelcome thought purred inside Polly's head, 'about what you might consider as your options . . . unless of course you want to continue these scintillating bedtime exchanges well into the next millennium?'

Why am I thinking like this? Polly thought in panic.

She turned off the bedroom light, listened for the sounds in the kitchen, and after a while the smell of cheese and yeast dough filled the air. She wanted to rush down and tell Jason to turn on the extractor, but her limbs felt leaden and her will tired, and she simply fell asleep.

She dreamed she was walking with Rory by the side of a lake. The water lapped quietly; it was evening and, in the manner of dreams, she suddenly found herself in the water. She knew that Rory was swimming out towards the centre of the lake, and she tried to follow him, but, being a poor swimmer, she got into difficulties. As she panicked and floundered she tried to call her husband, but was unable to make a sound. The water closed over her head and she knew that she was drowning.

It was then that her mysterious helper appeared. He emerged from the dark, still water, a man in a short black cloak, wearing a medieval helmet, the visor down so that she couldn't see his face. He took her to the safety of the rocks. His mystery surrounded her – his aura of care, interest, and unaccountable tenderness. Polly felt suddenly real, visible, recognised. The yearning of twenty years rose to meet this man; she was certain that she knew him and longed to raise his visor so that she might see his face.

But just then Rory called, his familiar voice, half anxious, reaching her where she leaned on the arm of the stranger who was still voiceless and faceless.

'Polly,' he called. 'Polly, where are you?'

Polly hesitated. The silent stranger was motionless as though awaiting her decision. But the voice of duty, of old loyalty and love, prevailed. She pulled away from her rescuer, emerged from the shelter of the rocks and called, 'I'm over here.'

But when she turned back her rescuer had merged into the element from which he had materialised. She saw, with dismay, the top of his helmet as it sank beneath the water.

The rocks bruised her feet as she stumbled ashore. Rory joined her. They walked away together along the lakeside path. She wondered if she should tell him about the strange man, but a glance told her that his mind was preoccupied. Now that he had her back by his side, she had reverted to invisibility. The old, well-worn loneliness engulfed her. She looked across the pleasant expanse of the lake, but, with a single violent frisson, the lovely, limpid vista turned into a functional tarmacadamed car park. She realised, too late, that the choice she had been called on to make was immutable.

She woke with a start. Rory was snoring and through the curtains came the first glimmering of the dawn.

'I don't know what's the matter with you at all,' Rory said next morning. 'What were you going on about last night?'

'I was merely trying to get you to move your bulk to your own connubial territory!' Polly said with what she thought of as fitting dryness. 'I too like a patch of the bed upon which to park my person!'

Rory smiled. 'But I seem to remember that you were waffling about something . . . making complaints!'

'No complaints,' Polly said smoothly. 'No point in railing. Action speaks louder than words and all that sort of thing . . . I merely pushed your bottom to where it belonged and when you assured me that I was interfering with your mouse I corrected you politely!'

Rory laughed out loud, then smiled a winning smile.

'Poll, is something biting you?'

'Not a bit of it!' Polly said. 'Why should it . . . ?'

Rory scrutinised her for disingenuousness.

'But I had an interesting dream,' she went on, 'one where a lake turned into a car park and a strange knight tried to rescue me.'

Rory sighed. His interest transferred itself to the whereabouts of his car keys which he could not find and which he announced that those blasted children must have moved, and as soon as that particular crisis had been resolved (the keys being in his pocket all the time) he left for work.

Polly cleared up the breakfast table. 'Faith, hope and a sense of humour is all very well,' came the new autonomous thought process in her head, 'but when are you going to get yourself a life?'

'Jesus!' Polly said. 'Am I going mad or what!'

'Everyone is mad,' her own mind answered. 'It's the secret of survival . . . But it is very important to keep the secret secret . . .'

Cat was now on the windowsill, furry head undulating as she tried to get a fix on Polly through the glass. Then she started mewling to summon her attendant.

'All right!' Polly said. 'Godammit, all right!'

'You should chop that cat's head off,' the whisper came in her brain.

But Polly shook her head, slapped her hand against her forehead. Then she let Cat in for her breakfast.

At lunch time the phone rang.

'Could I speak to Jason, please?' the young female voice demanded.

'I'm afraid not,' Polly said. 'He's at school!'

'I thought he might be home for lunch.'

'No.'

'Well, tell him to phone me tonight?'

Polly took a deep breath. The young voice was just a tad too peremptory. 'Who am I speaking to?'

'Veronica.'

'Well, Veronica, I'll tell him you called. If he wants to phone you he will, presumably, phone you! But if you think I'm going to order him to phone you, you don't know very much about Jason or about me or about how to manage a relationship! I think you should also know that Jason is seventeen years old!'

'Oh,' the voice said. This was followed by a short silence, then came the self-addressed whisper just as the caller hung up, 'The mother's a nut!'

Polly went back to the kitchen, took out some cheese and made a sandwich. There was some chocolate ice cream in the freezer compartment so she had some of that too. She found a half bottle of white wine which Rory had left at the back of the fridge. She had a glass. It made her feel a bit muzzy, so she sat in an armchair in the sitting room for a moment. She did not feel sleep stealing on her, but when she jerked with a sleep-spasm it was borne in upon her that she was snoozing. She realised that someone was tapping on the window. For a moment she thought it was Susie, but then saw her mistake. The person tapping at the glass of her sitting room was the real co-owner of the house, none other than Rory's legal wife.

'Hello, Martha!'

Polly held the door open. She did not want to see Martha and she did not want to talk to Martha, but she held the door open and let her in because she could not bear to be rude.

Martha was tall, thin, with black hair streaked with grey, but becomingly so. She had a kind of stalking gait to her, like some kind of long-limbed predator used to roaming across prairies looking for buffalo. She had the aura of one who was not to be trifled with.

'The preying mantis', Rory had called her, and in Polly's mind the name had struck a chord, conjuring up images of mandibles, and long stick limbs. In fact Martha was quite attractive, and had the kind of figure which, properly trained, might have sashayed down cat-walks.

'Would you like some tea or coffee?' Polly asked her politely.

'No thanks,' Martha said, but she walked into the kitchen, looked around, stalked into the sitting room and looked around. Polly was terrified of her, of her measuring glance, of her air which said, 'So this is how they are looking after my house!'

Martha was the kind of person who, if left alone in a room,

opened all the cupboards in secret reconnaissance. Her curiosity was vast, but earth-bound. She was made of pragmatic stuff. She had had a half interest in this particular house, and although she had been paid some of the instalments which Rory had undertaken to give her in reimbursement of her share, she had not been paid all of them. Now she was looking for the rest.

'This is not a social call,' she said to Polly. 'I wanted to let you know in advance that I will be suing Rory for the balance of the money he owes me on my share in the house. I wouldn't like to inflict that sort of surprise on you.'

She watched Polly's face as she said this. Polly struggled to keep the dismay from her eyes, knowing that this woman must hate her. Had she not stolen her perfectly good husband from her? (But I didn't steal him, Polly had often reminded herself; he ran after me until he caught me.)

'How much does he owe you?'

'Sixteen thousand, which includes interest. The rest of the debt is due as he failed to honour the agreement!'

'We haven't got that kind of money!'

Martha looked sad, shook her head.

'I need it, I'm afraid. I have my own plans . . . I've broken with Joe, you know . . .'

'What can we do?'

'I don't know . . . I suppose you'll have to sell the house! You could always get a smaller place . . .'

'I suppose so,' Polly said. 'But this isn't very big to begin with.'

Martha shrugged. 'Sorry, Polly . . . but you do see my position? I can't put my life on hold.'

Polly stared at her and to her own consternation her eyes filled with tears.

'I know it must be tough . . . but what can I do?' Martha added, suddenly sounding miserable.

'What about the children?' Polly demanded, wiping her eyes.

'Well, they'll adjust. Anyway, they must be quite grown up by now!'

'Jason is doing his Leaving this year!'

'Well, nothing will happen for several months . . . you know how the law grinds on.'

She studied Polly for a moment. 'Does he make you happy?'
Polly started. 'Who?'
'Who do you think? Romeo!'
Polly made a noise which was open to interpretation. Once
she would have hastened to reply in the affirmative. Now she
did not know what to say. It struck her suddenly that it was
not Rory's business to make her happy, that her happiness was
her own responsibility.
Martha's brow darkened. 'Well, in my case I could have had
a miscarriage on the floor in front of him and he wouldn't have
noticed. Too interested in electronics . . . it was his passion in
those days! But I'm glad it's worked out for you!'
She looked at Polly keenly, but when the latter did not
volunteer any confidence she added, 'I'll be off so. You needn't
tell him I called . . . unless you particularly want to!'
She stalked to the door and let herself out. Polly closed it
behind her.

'Martha was here today,' Polly informed Rory that evening.
'What did she want?'
'Nothing much. Just the house!'
Rory made a gesture of irritation. 'You don't want to listen to
her, Poll. I have everything under control!'
'She had a miscarriage on the floor!'
'What?'
'Bad joke.'
Rory's face was tight. 'Sometimes I worry about you, Poll!'
'No need to,' Polly said airily. 'I'm not as much of a nutcase
as I seem! But experience has taught me the galvanic power of
the outrageous comment . . . the gratifying manner in which it
can wake up even the most moribund conversation!'
Rory gave a whinny and shook his head. 'I hope you didn't
give Martha the notion that you were . . .'
'Unhinged? Not a bit of it! She knows I'm delirious with bliss.
Am I not living in her house? Anyway she wants sixteen
thousand pounds; she's going to sue you!'
'She can't get blood out of a stone!'
'She's going to make you sell the house! She said she has her
own plans. She's broken with Joe . . .'
Rory straightened. 'Is that so?' He seemed quietly pleased. 'I

never liked the fellow! Did she say what they were . . . her plans, I mean . . . is there someone else . . . Someone new?'

Polly considered her husband for a moment, saw the interest in his eyes. 'I hope so for her sake! You're not jealous, or anything, are you?'

Rory leaned his forehead against his hand. 'Of course not . . . Oh, Poll, let me worry about all this. I have the problem in hand. Why don't you just go off on your London trip and forget about things for a while!'

'How can I?'

'I insist that you do!' Rory said sternly. 'You've been behaving very peculiarly for the last while . . . It might help you straighten yourself out . . . And you'd be a fool to turn down an all-expenses paid holiday!'

That evening while Polly was rooting in her handbag for her new lipstick she found the letter she had addressed to the nice man in Wimbledon, the one she was going to post in London. It was wedged in the back pocket with the folded Lotto ticket she had bought in town during the week. The envelope was not sealed, so she took it out and had another look at his photograph. A psychiatrist, he had said he was. She needed a psychiatrist. Was she not carrying a newly assertive self inside her head, which was her, and not her at the same time?

She heard the phone ring in the hall, heard Peter answer it.

'He's not in,' he said. 'I'll tell him you called.' Polly went to the head of the stairs.

'Who was that?'

'Oh, just Jason's Jezebel!'

'You mean that girl Veronica?'

'Who else? She's got the hots for him!'

'You shouldn't be so crude! And, another thing, you should treat your brother with respect. He's the only one you've got! This constant putting him down is disgraceful!'

Peter looked taken aback. But before he could reply a particularly vociferous wailing was heard from outside the kitchen door.

'That Cat's in such a knacker!' Peter said with a half-laugh. 'Just listen to her!'

'Is she all right?' Polly asked, having detected a new note in Cat's repertoire.

Peter let the cat in, but she seemed uninterested in food, mewling disconsolately, finding her basket and continuing to wail like a small lost soul.

Muriel sat by the gracious drawing-room window and looked out at the cul-de-sac. She thought of each of the families she knew, especially of the O'Briens and the Caines because they were nearest and she knew them best. For years she had envied them their full lives, their children whom she had watched grow from babyhood. She thought of Susie and her spirit and her bad language, the way she was protective of Polly, whom Muriel especially liked, because there was something innocent and strangely terrified about her. Sometimes she watched her cleaning and shining the front door and wondered how someone with such passion for the beautiful managed to sublimate everything in the name of domesticity. Creativity subverted, channelled into dirt removal! What, she wondered, had domesticity ever done for her that she should serve it so faithfully? Was there something wonderful in the married state which brought peace? Or was this frenetic attention to domestic seemliness an escape? After all, if one considered it objectively, to expect people to live together all the years of their lives in a nuclear set-up, without parallel avenues of growth and development, without an escape hatch, was to expect something unnatural. Were Polly and Sue really caged birds compensating for their imprisonment? And if so, what would happen if they were set free?

Muriel thought she had become sensitive to the forces which shaped people's lives. Sometimes she tentatively traced the circumstances which had shaped her own, the life she once thought she was getting to grips with, not knowing then how it could turn and twist from you, slippery as an eel. Her thoughts returned for a moment to her gregarious and charismatic father, not the ghost in the study, but the father other people knew and admired. When he came to tuck her up at night she would lie still, keeping her eyes closed so that he might think she was asleep. She would smell the alcohol on his breath. She loved him. She wanted this love to be a strength; she did not want to despise him. She was more terrified of despising him than of the things he did.

'You mustn't tell anyone: it's our secret, Poppet.'

Only after his sudden death in a hunting accident when she was twelve were his debts discovered. Her mother had paid most of them off with her own money. It was the fifties and there was little income from the land. The subsequent deterioration of the house was gradual, a missing slate here and there, a broken eaveshoot, untended new potholes in the tree-lined avenue to the main road. In those days the main road was a relatively narrow and leafy byway, where in summer, wild flowers – buttercups, dandelions, foxgloves – grew in the 'long acre' in abundance. The trees had spread a canopy of overhanging branches, meeting each other in the middle, so that you felt you were walking in a green tunnel. The nearest dwellings were in the village and Dublin was a city somewhere in the dim distance.

At seventeen she had left school and got a job in the Anglo-Belgian Bank. Her salary helped the precarious budget, and relieved her mother of the dreaded prospect of selling Willow House and its accumulation of family treasures and memorabilia. Muriel had hated boarding school, had longed all term for the holidays when she would immure herself in the acres of her home, read romantic novels where the hero loved and recognised the heroine, and climb trees when she could escape from her mother. In this sanctum she had a refuge; she did not have to look in other people's eyes and wonder if they could read her secret. But her mother knew it. It was never mentioned, but it loomed between mother and daughter, something which must never be spoken of, something which grew larger with every passing year, becoming, because it must never be alluded to, a divide of mammoth proportions, like an impenetrable glass wall fixed between heaven and earth.

# Chapter Eight

The Boeing 737 emerged eventually from the clouds and swooped into Heathrow. Polly, relieved that they were no longer stacked blindly in the grey mist without view or prospect, like people who had died and been sent to Limbo, followed the crowd to the baggage carousel. From there, having collected her bag, she walked through the blue exit to where a small crowd waited, scanning the exiting passengers. It took her a moment to see Michelle, who had raised her hand to catch her attention. She saw her with fresh eyes, this new American addition to the family, saw that she stood as sharp and straight as an exclamation mark, with something of the Here-I-Am-and-Don't-You-Forget-It attitude of the same.

'Polly!' she said. 'Hi! Did you have a good flight?'

'OK . . .'

Both women exchanged pecks and then headed for the taxi rank, Michelle taking charge of the trolley – 'Here, let me wheel that thing!' – and in no time a black taxi was whisking them into central London.

Lounging back in the cab Polly studied Michelle covertly while she carried on a superficial conversation about home. Yes, Rory was fine. The boys were fine too. Cat had been to the Pets' Hospital again, but all that was wrong was a rubber band which some child had put on her tail and which had been cutting off the blood supply.

'You couldn't see it through the fur . . .' Yes, she was fine, except her tail was shaved, and she now looked as though she were half rat. Yes, they hoped to save the tail.

Michelle didn't seem too interested in this history.

'How is Tom?' Polly demanded shyly after a moment. How to shed it, this sense that his defection was her fault; that her crimes were enormous, away beyond anything she could understand? Otherwise why would he have left her to weather everything alone? All those years? OK, she had Rory, but that was more or less the same thing as being alone.

'Tom is abroad . . . I told him you were coming and he sent his love!'

Polly glowed. 'Did he really?' Then she asked, diffidently in case Michelle would think she was being tiresome, 'What did he say?'

'He said to give you his love!' Michelle repeated not unkindly. Polly beamed.

Michelle was smelling expensive. The scent of First by Van Cleefe and Arpels emanated subtly from her. Her hair was gathered back with a black velvet ribbon, and her smooth face and deep-set amber eyes seemed foreign somehow, almost oriental in their inscrutability. Polly envied this. It must be nice, she thought, to have a face which didn't show the whole world exactly what you were feeling at any particular moment.

'I'm delighted you could come,' Michelle said, smiling at Polly. 'I simply hate my own company! How are you, Polly? You look a little tired if you don't mind me saying so.'

Polly caught her reflection in the glass.

'Well, other than Cat, I've had a few alarms and excursions lately. Martha came around; she's threatening to sue Rory and make him sell the house!'

'What a cow!'

Polly frowned. 'I don't know that she is. I even felt sorry for her. But I don't know what we'll do if we have to sell the house.'

'What does Rory say?'

'He says he has everything under control!'

'Well, that's good anyway . . .'

Polly met Michelle's eyes and looked away. She felt ill at ease. The gulf between Michelle's life and her own seemed so wide and unbridgeable, a chasm of lost and unattainable possibilities. What was it like to be so successful, never to have to advert to economy, to scrimping and scraping, to know that the world was yours in whatever way you wanted it, when you wanted it?

But after a while she forgot these considerations in the delight of gazing around her. It was years since she had visited this great city, and the throb of it quickened her pulse, revitalised the young girl in her who had come here to work in her student days.

'Look,' she cried somewhere near Oxford Circus, 'there's The Gorgeous East where I was once taken to dine by a law student called Tony Maloney. He was from Donegal and was working for the summer with Wimpey. He missed his last tube back to his flat and had to spend the night on a park bench!'

'Were you on the park bench too?'

'God, no. I went back to the girls' hostel in Westminster where I was staying.'

'You sound like a very proper young woman.'

'That was the theory,' Polly conceded. 'Propriety was thumped into me at an early age . . . But I was very malleable, easily influenced . . .'

Polly flushed as she spoke, for she remembered Tony Maloney and his kisses in St James's Park, his wandering hands, his air of urgency as he explored under her blouse. 'Don't, Tony . . .'

'Why not, you gorgeous thing? Don't you like it?' Even now she remembered his rapid breathing, the way his voice thickened, the feel of his erection pressing against her.

Had she liked it? There had been no question of relaxing enough to find out. He had left her and wandered off to his bench. At least that was what he had told her afterwards.

The taxi stopped outside an imposing cream-porticoed building in Eaton Square. Michelle paid the taxi and led her guest through the front door to a spacious marble hallway where an elliptical stairwell wrapped itself around a lift.

'Flat's on the first floor,' she said as she pulled back the partition and pressed the button marked 1. The lift deposited them soundlessly at a landing thickly carpeted in crimson; Michelle conducted her guest to a panelled, white-painted door into which she inserted first a mortice key and then a Yale one.

'Number thirteen,' Polly said, looking at the black numbers on the top of the door. 'Aren't you superstitious?'

'You silly girl! Thirteen is a power number. Whether it is lucky or not depends on you! I suppose it's a matter of courage,' she added in a slightly surprised tone of voice, 'although I've never thought of it in that way before.'

The flat seemed immense, two decent bedrooms, a good-sized kitchen, a large drawing room with a dining alcove, a big bathroom with Grecian-style decor. The view over the square showed tended gardens, and all around them were stately houses in mellow brick or painted in uniform cream, their pillared fronts magnificent Regency.

'Tom must be making a bomb!' Polly said. 'I never thought he could afford something like this!'

'Oh, I make the odd contribution to the kitty myself,' Michelle said.

'You must have a very good job!'

'Well, good enough . . . But I have a few shekels put by from previous incarnations!'

Polly looked at her doubtfully. 'What do you mean?'

Michelle laughed. 'Nothing at all except that I do not come with empty hands!'

Polly looked at her prospective sister-in-law with only half-concealed envy and curiosity. 'You seem to have everything sewn up. How did you come to meet Tom anyway?'

'I heard him in a dream!' Michelle said flippantly and laughed. 'Rather like that idiot Saint Patrick who heard the voice of the Irish in his sleep!'

'Oh, Michelle,' Polly exclaimed in exasperation. 'I don't know what to make of you at all! You treat nothing seriously and it seems to have beguiled Fate.'

'I am a believer in upheaval,' Michelle said. 'You cannot beguile Fate except by challenging it! Have a drink,' she added. It was more a command than a question, and she filled a glass with gin and tonic. Polly was about to say she didn't drink spirits, but the glass was already in her hand.

'Sit down for God's sake,' Michelle said.

Polly sat. She looked around the room, at the pastel furnishings, the great splashes of colour in the painting above the mantelpiece, the way in which light and colour had been used to create the illusion of extensive space. The couch was very comfortable, the silk cushions supportive, the sudden strains of Bach, which had started when Michelle waved a remote control at the music centre in the corner, wafted softly.

She took a sip, and then another one and before she knew it she was feeling that the moment in which she found herself was perfect, and that she never wanted to move again.

'Are you hungry?' Michelle asked her a little later.

Polly had heard herself talking in spasmodic dream-like bursts of communication, and now she heard Michelle's voice as though it came from a great distance.

'No,' Polly said, wondering whether the gin had been unusually strong because she felt not just woozy, but a migrant from another dimension. 'I'm not hungry at all. I don't care if I never eat another bite . . .'

'What would you like to do, Polly?'

'What I would really like to do,' Polly said dreamily but honestly, from the depths of a languor which provided no scope for prevarication, 'is for a handsome, loving man to take me in his arms. No, on second thoughts, I don't care if he's handsome or not . . . just so long as he's loving. Why do I tell you these things?'

'Because you want to tell me. Is there anything else you would like?'

'I would like to be beautiful!'

'But you are!'

'I am overweight,' Polly said.

'Fat is a relative concept. You are generously endowed. You are very attractive.' She lowered her voice and added very silkily, 'If you would like a loving man one could be here tonight . . .'

'What are you?' Polly whispered. 'Some kind of witch?'

Michelle laughed. 'We are each of us in charge of our own witchcraft!'

Polly stirred luxuriously. 'I wouldn't mind being a witch, but I wouldn't know how! It assumes wide spectrums of understanding, things I would condemn without investigation. I think you need experience to be able to evaluate experience.' She laughed softly. 'I am rather lacking in that department. In marrying a married man I sowed all my wild oats in one fell swoop. After that I did what was expected of me . . . I had to prove how good I could be . . . how respectable!'

'And . . .'

'It has suddenly struck me that I cannot confine myself to the parameters set by others and say that I have lived!'

In the ensuing silence Polly added dreamily, 'I suppose I'm pissed!'

Michelle was silent. She looked at the telephone across the room like someone who had a decision to make.

'Experience is yours, my dear, for the asking!'

'You're so kind,' Polly continued in her dreamy voice. 'You're a really good, fine person!'

'Oh, Christ,' Michelle said to herself and threw her head back and closed her eyes.

When Polly woke up the next morning she found the flat empty. She assumed that Michelle had gone out for the paper until, with a sense of let-down, she saw the note on the fridge.

Dear Polly,
    I've been called away for the day . . . I'll tell you about it tonight. Sorry . . . Have a good day! Enjoy!
    Michelle.
P.S. Spare set of keys are hanging by the kitchen door.

It was Easter Sunday. The sun was shining; Eaton Square was green, quiet, august. Polly made some coffee, nibbled at some toast.

I'll go out for the Sunday papers, came the half-formed thought. That'll be something to do. At least there won't be any ads in them from me today, which is a considerable relief.

She looked around the flat, peeped into Michelle's (and presumably Tom's) bedroom. There was a splendid dressing table with a deeply flounced skirt, its glass surface home to an array of French perfumes and cosmetics. It struck her suddenly that there was no evidence of a male presence, neither in the sitting room, where you might have expected some photographs, nor in the bedroom, nor anywhere. She would have liked to open the wardrobes and see Tom's clothes, but could not bear to be so sneaky. But she did open the bathroom cabinet in the hopes of finding some evidence of his existence, shaving cream or something. There was no sign. The white cabinet contained a mouthwash, facial scrub, dental floss, Dettol, band aids, aspirin and the contraceptive pill.

She showered, dressed, reached for her bag to find her lipstick and came across the letter for the man in Wimbledon. The thought formed itself: why not deliver it? Instead of putting it in the post why not take the tube to Wimbledon and drop it through his letter box? Yes, she thought. That would be something to do with the day.

God damn it, Polly thought, I'm a grown woman, middle aged, and I have the uncertainty of an adolescent.

At approximately one o'clock Polly found her way to the underground station in Sloane Square. She spent some time scrutinising the journey planner on the wall, found Wimbledon on the District line, bought her return ticket from the dispenser, and trundled her person down the stone steps to the platform.

The nice thing about Sloane Square station was that it was open to daylight, not a burrow hidden in the bowels of the earth.

I am free, she thought. I am going on an adventure to Wimbledon. I have never been there but I shall find it. The limits of my world are such that this small escapade has taken on the character of romance. It is as though I am going into terra incognita to confront the dragon.

She felt in her handbag for the letter, thinking with amusement how strange it would be to drop it into Bernard Whiston's letter box; how strange to see the house where he lived, this unknown man who had answered her brazen advertisement in the *Sunday Times*.

Sometimes, Polly conceded, thinking of what Michelle had said to her the night before, it is pleasant to beguile Fate. If it has done nothing else, it will have shown me some of London, the route to Wimbledon, the dwelling of someone whose life I have touched by the most bizarre of circumstances. If I were not married, or half married, or whatever I am, I might even have answered it properly.

The *A to Z* of London came into its own when Polly alighted from the train. She stood for a moment to study this guide and ascertain the whereabouts of Marbonne Road. She found it on the map eventually; it was a road near the Common, off Parkside.

Polly climbed Wimbledon Hill, walked along High Street, found herself eventually in Parkside. On one side were fine houses behind high railings; on the other side was the green expanse of the Common, with its trees and open spaces.

She came, eventually, to Marbonne Road, a quiet patrician boulevard with a variety of house styles, some stucco, some brick, some Tudor-style, all set back from the road in their own grounds. No 17 was mock Tudor, with dark beams inset in the brick, and a glossy black door. A white Mercedes was parked in the gravel driveway behind tall closed gates. A yellow labrador lay across the granite doorstep in the afternoon sunlight. The front door itself was slightly ajar.

Polly hesitated at the iron gates. She suddenly felt utterly, and murderously, foolish. The labrador raised his head from his paws to stare at her, and then gave a short, almost conversational bark. Polly felt panic burgeon and the voice she had begun to dread said silkily inside her head, 'What the hell are you doing here, you silly bird?'

Somewhere out of sight came the rustle of vegetation, then a male voice. 'Hello . . . can I help you!'

A man emerged from the shrubbery, a pair of hedge clippers in his hand. He was middle aged, balding, slightly rotund, of medium height, with shrewd, kind eyes. Polly, remembering the photograph, realised that she was looking at none other than her erstwhile correspondent.

'Mr Whiston?' she said.

He started visibly, stared at her, knitting his brow, as though she had asked for a ghost.

'Who wants to see him?'

Polly blushed. She felt the fire of the hot blood flooding to her hairline, down her chest and upper arms. She had not blushed like this for a long time; it was something Rory used to joke about, this incandescence which was once so easily provoked.

'Oh . . . it's just that I have a letter to deliver . . .'

She opened her handbag, found the letter, handed it over.

He took it, frowning, and, turning a little to one side, slipped a finger underneath the flap to tear it open.

Polly moved away with as much speed as was decent. She willed her feet to carry her with maximum momentum, without running.

'Wait,' the man's voice called behind her. 'Hold on a minute!'

She glanced back, saw that Mr Whiston was walking towards her down the pavement.

Oh God, Polly thought, if the ground would open up and swallow me . . .

'Stand your ground, you idiot,' came the thought. 'Learn how to act . . . You got yourself into this! The least you can do is get yourself out of it with dignity! This man won't eat you!'

Polly turned, schooled her face, waited for him to catch up with her.

'Are you the writer of this letter?' he asked almost diffidently.

'Good heavens, no,' Polly said, while her colour deepened. 'I have a . . . sister who asked me to post it for her when I was in London. But as I was out for the afternoon, I thought I would just deliver it myself . . .'

'I see . . . So it's from your sister! Concepta McCann?'

'Er . . . yes . . .'

'Well, thank you for taking the trouble of delivering it . . . May I ask where you come from?'

'I live in Dublin. I'm here on a short holiday . . . staying with my sister-in-law . . .'

'Locally?'

'Not exactly. She lives in Eaton Square.'

'In Belgravia?'

'Yes.'

Polly relaxed a little. He seemed mild, half amused, half perplexed. 'I take it you are Mr Whiston?' she said.

'No, as a matter of fact. He was my father-in-law. He died suddenly last week!'

He studied her gravely, frowned. 'You see, I can't help wondering why a letter addressed to my deceased father-in-law should arrive from your sister,' he went on, glancing at the letter in his hand, 'indicating that he had written to her with some kind of . . . well, familiar intent! It's rather puzzling!'

'Yes it is!' Polly conceded. 'I don't know anything about it myself of course, but I could ask her about it . . . if you like!'

'That would be kind . . . Will you come back to the house for a moment, and we can talk about it. You see, I'm the old boy's executor and perhaps I should know if he has been up to something . . . I'd like to think I'll leave no loose ends outstanding . . .'

Polly did not know what to do. The panic seemed idiotic, but it was there.

'Go on!' her horrible private voice said. 'None of your nauseating hesitancies. Lie your way through. Do not imagine for one instant that you can beguile destiny by a childish adherence to veracity! Truth after all is just another name for laziness!'

Polly followed her host through his driveway and then across a parquet floor to a sitting room where two French windows overlooked a huge back garden. The sun flooded the tree-lined red brick wall facing the house. The green, newly mown sward, the stone sundial, the rustic bench, were as she had imagined things would be in this enchanted garden. There was a willow tree and shrubs and herbaceous borders.

'Won't you sit down,' her host said, moving to a drinks table in the corner.

Polly moved back from the window and perched on an antique armchair.

'What will you have to drink?'

'Oh . . . anything . . . lemonade, mineral water, whatever you've got!'

'How about a gin and tonic?'

'. . . Thank you.'

He handed her a glass. She inhaled the scent of the spirit and the quinine, shook the ice cubes, took a gulp, tried to appear collected. The labrador, who had followed them in, put his muzzle on her knee and looked at her speculatively, before wandering away to lie panting by a French window. Polly looked at the dog hairs on her trousers.

'That's Herbie. He seems to have taken a liking to you!'

Polly looked at the dog.

'Who are you?' her host asked suddenly and almost sternly.

Polly did not hasten to reply. She was unprepared for this and disliked very much the sense that she was a fraud and an interloper.

'My name is Pauline . . .' she said slowly.

'Pauline what?'

Polly gave her maiden name. 'McCann,' she said.

'And your sister is Concepta McCann who has written a strange letter to a dead man?'

'I was merely asked to post it,' Polly said, suddenly beset by her own absurdity and badly needing to laugh. 'I'm afraid I am not privy to its contents.'

He sat down opposite her in a matching armchair of faded damask and regarded her doubtfully.

'Is this some kind of joke . . . a prank?'

Polly looked at him, saw that an uncertain smile lurked in the corners of his mouth, and then looked swiftly away into the sunlit garden.

'No actually,' Polly said, forgetting that she knew nothing about the letter or its genesis, 'I don't think it's a prank at all. I think what happened was that my sister was very lonely and very unhappy and she put an ad in the paper. Your deceased father-in-law answered her. He seems to have sent your photograph . . . but that is not my sister's fault!'

'No. The old buck had a warped sense of humour! Would you like to see what he really looked like – so that you can tell your sister?'

Polly raised her hands to indicate non-involvement, but her host had already walked to a bookcase and abstracted a photograph album with a red cover. He flipped through a few of its pages, thick with the weight of many yesterdays, and then passed the book to her.

'That's him on the top of the right-hand page!'

The face that Bernard Whiston had often inspected in the mirror looked out at Polly. He resembled, she thought, a particularly aggressive salmon; there was the same kind of business-like chin, and the eyes were round and cold. But there was a sardonic twist to the mouth, as though their owner had taken a long look at life and had decided that he was going to get it before it got him.

'He looks like a funny old bird . . . wouldn't you say?'

'I think he looks like a cynic,' Polly said, putting the matter as tactfully as she could.

'Oh, Bernard was that all right!'

There was silence for a moment.

'My name is Keith Warrington,' her host said. 'But other than that the details given by Bernard are mine and not his. My wife died two years ago; I am semi-retired, and I do have a daughter working in New York. So there you are! We are all at the mercy of our eccentric elders!'

Polly put her glass down. 'Well, I'd better be going. Thank you for the drink.'

She was about to apologise for her intrusion into his Sunday afternoon, but thought better of it. After all, he had asked her in, and falling around the place with apologies only made things worse.

'Must you go?' he said. 'You've just whetted my curiosity. Why don't you tell me about your sister? Why is she so unhappy that she puts ads in the paper?'

He said this very gently. Polly felt the gin in her brain. She wished she could think of something light and witty. But instead she said, 'Well . . . she's sort of married . . .'

'Sort of married! What does that mean?'

'We don't have divorce in Ireland . . . at least not yet . . . so when marriages break down people try to get Church annulments and then they re-marry in church. These second marriages are bigamous in the eyes of the law . . .'

Keith waited, raised his eyebrows.

Polly shrugged. 'But the marriage, if such it may be called, was a mistake . . . She tried to make it work . . .'

'And now she wants out?'

'I don't know,' Polly said. 'But I think she was hoping to meet someone she could talk to. But she got cold feet and sent everyone's letters back. It seemed very improper, you know . . . having strange men write to her!'

She glanced at Keith Warrington, but his face was carefully expressionless. 'You see,' she went on, looking out at the garden, 'if you have no one to really talk to, you begin to go mad. It has something to do with a certain level of intimacy. If you are denied it, reality is only a word; you lose self-definition; you begin to choke on the plethora of all the feelings, the joys, the small things, the challenges that you could share. You could have so much to give and all of it is wasted . . .'

Keith did not reply. His listening was so unobtrusive that she hardly noticed its quality, or how his expression had altered to one of professional evaluation.

'But,' he said, 'your sister could leave. Why doesn't she?'

Polly raised her hands to distance herself from the vagaries of sisters. 'She doesn't know how. She has children . . .' She lowered her voice, looked down at her hands. 'I suppose she's trapped! She's anxious to keep up appearances . . .'

'Why?'

Polly shrugged. 'People do . . .'

'Because they allow themselves to be defined by others,' Keith said, adding after a moment, 'Are you married yourself?'

Polly started. 'Not really,' she said.

'And what do you do for a living?'

'Not much,' Polly said desperately, reaching for some image that would not portray her as housewife, that would distance her from the indigent, dependent servitor. 'I have funds. It's a very decadent way to live, but I find it quite restful!'

When he didn't respond she added hastily, 'But I know a lot about antiques and I help my sister with her business. It's what brings me to London, in fact.'

'I see! Pauline,' he added after a pause, 'I have the evening to myself and would be delighted if you would be my guest for supper . . . that is if you have nothing better to do. I find myself very intrigued by the whole case you have outlined and feel that both you and your sister are very interesting people.'

Polly flushed and stood up. 'I couldn't possibly. I really must be off! Thank you for being so kind . . .'

'There are many old things in this house you could give me some help with . . .' Keith persisted, 'seeing as you're in the business, I mean – valuations and so forth. My wife was a collector of sorts,' he went on. 'I've been meaning to get someone to have a look at them for insurance purposes. How, for example, would you value the chair you are sitting in?'

Polly was uncomfortably aware that her face must be very red. But she looked at her armchair and at its comrade, and around the room.

'This is a Louis XV *fauteuil* . . .' she said, 'as is the one you're sitting on. It's worth a great deal . . .'

'Indeed. What about the rest of the furniture? I'm a bit of an ignoramus!'

'Well, that's a Victorian tallboy,' Polly said, gesticulating to the alcove by the fireplace, and then to other pieces in the room, her face animated with interest. 'The halfmoon table seems to be a Georgian mahogany and satinwood card table and presumably opens into a circle. The round table by the French window is a Sheraton mahogany and boxwood inlaid work table . . .

Keith relaxed visibly. He already knew this.

'And that bookcase?' he asked.

Polly let her eyes rest on it, tried to read the titles through the glass.

'It's a Victorian mahogany cylinder bookcase. You seem to have some fine old books in it . . . perhaps some first editions?'

She looked back at him and her colour which had begun to abate in her absorption rose again.

She started to her feet. 'I must be off . . . Thank you very much for the drink!'

'It was a pleasure! Will you tell your sister that you met me . . . ?'

'I don't think so. The embarrassment would be too much for her! I had no mandate to intrude . . .'

In the hall Polly asked shyly, 'Would you mind if I used your loo?'

Keith motioned her to a door. 'Just in there.'

Polly stared at herself in the mirror. God, she thought, I look like a tomato that's been left too long in the sun. Oh God, why did I make up such a string of childish lies? What kind of a half wit am I?

She rooted in her bag for her small plastic phial of make-up, couldn't find it at first, delved deeper among the debris of bills and located it at the bottom, half wedged under the spine. She did a quick cover-up job on her face.

When she emerged the hall door was open and Keith was sitting on the front steps.

'And you're staying in Eaton Square while you're in London?' he enquired as he saw her to the gate.

'Yes . . . My brother's fiancée is on her own this week while he is away. She has a lovely flat, and very kindly invited me to share it with her for the week. It's number thirteen,' she added inconsequentially.

'Are you superstitious?'

'Good lord, no.' She laughed, and her laughter was full of real humour. 'Despite appearances I'm really quite . . . balanced. At least,' she added with an uncertain grin, 'I think I am, but

120

that of course is a purely subjective assessment!'

Keith Warrington smiled. His eyes crinkled; his face creased in ready-made lines, dry grooves where long years of tolerance and kindness had etched their hallmarks.

Polly touched the gate where she had stood so uncertainly an hour before. A word kept Herbie on the ground, where he thumped his tail.

'You have livened up my Sunday, Pauline McCann,' Keith said. 'I have a suspicion that we may meet again!'

Polly beamed. The prospect of parting for ever from her congenial companion had not been pleasant. But realisation came swiftly to dampen presumption.

'I don't think so . . . but it has been a pleasure!' She shook hands with him and walked away.

Keith Warrington stood at the gate and looked after her thoughtfully for a moment. Then he went back to his gardening.

At home in Willow House, Muriel was going through her papers, putting them in two heaps, one for burning, one for keeping. There were letters from Michael, but there was no point in keeping them any more. She found the drawing of the wedding dress she had once fantasised about. Wild silk. 'White,' her mother had said, with a twist to her mouth, 'I suppose it had better be white!'

'Of course, Mummy!'

'Of course . . .'

Muriel's mother had died from a heart attack, which felled her as she descended the stairs at precisely nine o'clock one rainy morning.

Muriel had her interred in the family crypt with the Reeveses who had gone before her.

'Life must go on,' Michael had said. He was looking into his finals and was as supportive as time allowed. Muriel had mourned in privacy, wept for the mother who had so irritated her, who had so judged her, and whom she now so terribly missed. There had been things she should have said to her, should have forced her to understand, should have opened the door and let the light in on. But it was too late.

\* \* \*

121

She picked up the envelope with the Saudi stamp, removed the letter, glanced at it, remembered how Michael had graduated with flying colours and almost immediately had been offered a year's contract at a hospital in Saudi Arabia.

He had been so excited, telling her of the great salary and fringe benefits. 'Riches,' he said, 'beyond the wildest dreams of avarice! We'll be married the minute I come back . . .'

Muriel decided she didn't mind staying behind. It was only for a year. Absence would make the heart grow fonder. She would sell her mother's jewellery for money to repair the roof of Willow House, do herself up, have a wonderful reunion.

So Michael had gone. And it was shortly after this that Alan Barrington, as though waiting in the wings for his cue, had entered her life.

She put the letter back in its envelope and consigned it to the heap for burning.

# Chapter Nine

Keith Warrington wrote to his daughter that evening:

Dearest Mo,

I assume you got back safely, darling. Funerals are always so depressing, and particularly so when it is someone we love. In a way I thought poor Bernard was indestructible, but when he decided to go he certainly didn't waste any time! But I've already told you the whole story . . . Although the stroke was so sudden I keep thinking he was trying to tell me something before he slipped away, but we'll never know now.

Today I imagined you like a mote in the Big Apple, smothered in the unhealthy air of your concrete gulches. This is because I spent the day in the garden, with only poor old Herbie for company, did some pruning and weeding and generally pottered about, which is always so pleasant.

At about three o'clock I had a visitor, an odd little person who delivered a letter. I won't bore you with the details, except that it had to do with someone who put an ad in the *Sunday Times* ('Nice Lady seeks Kind Caring Gentleman' sort of thing) and actually got a reply from that old reprobate, your grandfather! The old goat had the gall to send my picture (one of the snaps you took last summer on your birthday). Anyway, the advertiser got cold feet and returned both missive and photo, but being curious she decided to deliver it in person. She says her sister did the actual advertising and she was simply delivering the despatch as a favour; but I've been long enough in the business of lies and subterfuge to recognise them when they come to see me in the middle of my Sunday afternoons!

Not that there was anything sinister about this poor woman; she struck me as a bit quaint and unused to lying; fortyish, a Dubliner staying in London for a week with her sister-in-law in Belgravia.

Doesn't it all sound a bit rum?! Maybe she was out to case the joint and get her thugs to steal those French chairs your mother was so fond of . . . Now that you have deserted me anything can happen! Maybe she's a front woman for the IRA! Anyway she beguiled my afternoon (in my Carthesian mind-set I am always enchanted by the bizarre).

Don't mind me, darling! I miss you very much, but I'm thrilled for you that the job is going so well. Poor Jack called on Saturday looking a bit woebegone. You could reconsider him . . . if your romance with Bob is really over. He's living for the sight of you and is a really nice young fellow. But I shouldn't interfere.

Look after yourself and write when you can to your loving,

Dad

When he had finished the letter Keith put it in an envelope, found a stamp and placed the envelope on the hall table. Then he went to the kitchen, took a Budweiser from the fridge and brought it into the garden.

The evening sun had moved around to gladden the patio outside the kitchen door, lighting up the wall of the tool shed where the clematis climbed in delicate pink profusion. Young swallows, who had been born and bred in the nest under the eaves, came dive-bombing for fun in the warm evening air, swooped and then soared triumphantly skywards.

Keith had a volume of Tennyson and he read aloud to Herbie from 'The Princess' about the moan of doves in immemorial elms and the murmuring of innumerable bees. The dog lifted one ear, flattened it and began to whine.

'I can't make up my mind as to whether you're an aesthete or a philistine,' his master told him, regarding him over his spectacles. 'Is that appreciation I hear or denunciation?'

Herbie thumped his tail, and looked up interrogatively, his muzzle flat on the ground and his eyes limpid with adoration.

Keith thought of Marguerite, his dead wife. Herbie had been her dog, and she had loved him with the careful love she gave everything she possessed, whether the recipient was her husband or Sophie or Herbie or the French armchairs which she had bought at auction at horrendous expense.

Marguerite always reminded him of the ill-fated wife in Robert Browning's poem, 'My Last Duchess':

> . . . My favour at her breast,
> The dropping of the daylight in the West,
> The bough of cherries some officious fool
> Broke in the orchard for her, the white mule
> She rode with round the terrace – all and each
> Would draw from her alike the approving speech . . .

Except, of course, that unlike the duke, Keith wouldn't have given his wife the chop for loving everything equally, even if this equality had been a thorn in his soul.

But she had not loved poetry, saying that it made her uneasy, that she was sure that the poets were disingenuously striving to manipulate. There had been a suspicious streak in Marguerite, at odds with her general kindness. He missed her terribly; the sense of purpose she emanated was missing, as was her kindly nurturing. But despite this he had, of late, begun to find in his own company strange vistas, hidden nooks and crannies he had always ignored. Solitude has a way, he thought, of introducing you to yourself, not the comfortable, well-worn self, but the one lurking and dreaming; the stranger within.

He thought of the woman, Pauline, who had dropped in that afternoon like a scout from Candid Camera. He had found her oddly attractive, the attraction of the outrageous and the diffident, although she was plainly slightly off the wall. But then he was used to people who were off the wall. They were his bread and butter, his bane and his delight.

He found himself wondering what kind of a life she had; what had precipitated her action in advertising? Had it been loneliness, shyness, frustration, passion, hope? The human condition was endlessly variable in its hunt for fulfilment. But

125

she had turned away from the possibilities she had precipitated, except that she had not been able to suppress her curiosity. And, God help us, the excuse about the sister had been beguilingly transparent.

But she certainly knew a bit about old furniture. Maybe his joke to Mo was not far off the mark; maybe she was really casing the house. Would he wake up in the morning with his head coshed and his armchairs gone?

When dusk was sweeping down on the patio and the air began to chill he went indoors. There was nothing on the box he wanted to watch; he looked in his fridge and found the remains of the ham salad he had had for lunch. This seemed suddenly depressing, so he decided to dine in Chez Patrice, the French restaurant in the High Street. He visited the downstairs loo, and noticed a pink slip of paper on the floor. He picked it up, turned it over and recognised it as a Lotto ticket, and an Irish Lotto ticket to boot, with pink phantom forms wrestling with various options – ballet, music, sport, all the delights waiting for Lucky Winners with nothing to do and all day to do it.

He chuckled. His visitor of the afternoon seemed suddenly normal, possessed of the same outlandish aspirations as everyone else. He was about to screw the slip of paper up and throw it down the loo, when he thought of checking the date. It was dated the day before yesterday. Should he send it back to her? But then he remembered he didn't know where she lived. He put it on the glass shelf above the wash basin and combed the remains of his hair. Then he went into the hall, looked up the number of Chez Patrice in the phone book, booked a table, told a disappointed Herbie that life was tough and to mind the house, collected his letter for the post and closed the front door behind him.

When Polly got back to the flat Michelle was lying on the couch. She was smoking and the room was full of a harsh, pungent scent. She smiled her deliberate smile at Polly and asked her if she wanted a joint.

Polly started. No one had asked her this question for twenty years.

'No thank you!'

She went to her room, looked in the mirror and gave a silent sigh of relief. Her face seemed to have returned to something like normal; the incandescent embarrassment had receded. But her thoughts were in turmoil. She had been editing and storing her strange afternoon in her head and now she had returned to find Michelle smoking pot. This begged the question as to whether Tom smoked the stuff too. Did he now toy with drugs – even soft drugs? She remembered how he had fulminated when he had seen her smoke an experimental cigarette. Perhaps I never really knew him, came the sober thought; perhaps I have honed my own susceptibilities around nothing but projection. Then, half humorous, half incredulous, came the recollection of her afternoon. She had met him, the man in the photo, except that he hadn't written to her at all. It had been some kind of joke dreamed up by his father-in-law who had then keeled over and died! And you could go through life thinking things were rational!

When she emerged from her room Michelle was still supine.

'Darling girl,' she said flippantly from her recumbent position on the sofa, 'I'm sorry to have disappeared! But I got a phone call early today which I simply could not ignore!'

'Oh,' Polly said, waiting for a few more details of whatever precipitous rendezvous had dragged her prospective sister-in-law from her side, but when they didn't come she added, 'What are you smoking that junk for? It interferes with brain chemistry!'

'That's why I smoke it!' Michelle replied. 'My brain chemistry needs interfering with!'

'A lovely woman like you?'

'You think I'm lovely . . . ?' Michelle said after a moment in a small voice.

'Of course. You have beauty and grace and charm, and brains to beat the band! And you've money too. You've everything . . . You don't need that! And you've Tom!'

Michelle turned her face away, a bitter line to her mouth. 'And what did you do with yourself today, Polly?'

'Oh a bit of this and a bit of that!' Polly said airily.

Michelle fixed her amber eyes on her and smiled. 'Well – if the glow is anything to go by – you should do a bit more of it more often.'

127

\* \* \*

Polly was taciturn that evening, privately mulling over her extraordinary afternoon which she was determined she would not share. When Michelle suggested they go out she said she was tired and would like an early night. There was a cold chicken in the fridge, and the two women prepared a salad for supper and, as the conversation lagged, they went early to bed.

Polly lay in the half-dark listening to the sounds of London traffic from the street. Her thoughts kept reverting to Keith Warrington, thinking of his marvellous garden and his gentle dog, and his funny, acerbic commentary on his father-in-law. In some ways she felt enormously enriched by the encounter, as though it had dropped precious stones into her lap, which she could examine at her leisure, hold up to the light, admire the facets and the colours. She remembered his kind, amused voice asking her if she would join him for supper.

After a few minutes Polly switched on the bedside lamp, got up, took off her nightdress and studied her naked body in the long gilt mirror. She tried to see it with objective eyes, ran her palms over it. Her waist was still quite small, relatively speaking that is, and her skin was soft and silken. Her body, she decided, could be described as voluptuous, like one of those Rubens women, all flesh and passive femaleness. I could lose some of this, she thought, and still have plenty left. And then she wondered why she was doing this.

In the room next to hers Michelle lay staring at the ceiling. Her bedside light was on. She reached for her small black diary and wrote in tiny writing, 'Fucked all day; Pollyanna in the evening. She'll never suit, but I'll try again tomorrow . . . This bloody innocence is almost contagious!'

The next morning Polly phoned home. Peter answered. Yes, everything was fine; the strange hobbit-like creature was in cyberspace. When she asked about Jason he said that the spotty little faggot was feeding his face.

In the background Polly heard Jason's voice, 'Stop calling me names . . .'

'The little turd is getting uppity,' Peter said down the line.

'Let me talk to Jason,' Polly said.

There was the clatter of the receiver being dumped on the

hall table and then Jason came to the phone.

'Mum?'

'Hello, darling . . . everything all right?'

'Yeah . . . will you get me some tee-shirts in C&A's?'

'All right. Are you working hard?'

There was a sigh and then her son said, 'If Peter would leave me alone I might be able to get something done . . .'

'Can I talk to your father?'

The receiver crackled. 'Dad,' came the faint voice, 'Mum is on the phone!'

Polly had to wait for a few moments before the receiver was lifted again at the far end.

'Hello,' Rory said eventually. 'Sorry for holding you, but I was in the middle of something important. How's London?'

'Rory,' Polly said, 'will you make sure that Peter is not teasing Jason. How can he get any work done if his brother won't leave him alone! It's not good enough! And he has his own work to do!'

There was a moment's silence. 'Jason is your younger son,' Polly suddenly shouted down the phone. 'Stop your elder son from badgering him. I can't do it just now!'

'I'm perfectly aware which of my children is which,' Rory said after moment in a masterful, righteous voice, the one he reserved for Polly-put-downs.

'That's good,' Polly screamed, 'because the last time the matter arose you hadn't a clue!'

'How can I be expected to know who people are if they look different!' Rory demanded, remembering the incident to which Polly was alluding with some annoyance.

'True,' Polly conceded. 'Except that a change of clothing, the presence or absence of spectacles, does not of necessity result in mistaken identity!'

In the ensuing silence she felt the dread weight of Rory's anger. 'I'm not going to stand here and listen to this,' he said, breathing heavily. Then he hung up.

Polly turned to Michelle who had come out of the kitchen. Her fine eyebrows were raised.

'Are you all right, Polly?'

'No . . . Why did I do that? I don't know what got into me. Do you mind if I phone back . . . He hung up on me!'

She pushed the buttons, the phone rang in Dublin, Peter's voice came again on the line.

'Peter, can I talk to your father?'

'I fear the Hobbit has gone out.'

'Will you show your father some respect and will you stop calling people names,' Polly said irritably. 'Now listen to me. Leave your brother alone . . . Let him study . . . and do your own and don't be such a perpetual persecution!'

There was an intake of breath on the other end.

'It might interest you to know, Mum,' Peter said in a suddenly miffed voice, 'that this morning, while I was still asleep, your little cherub came into my room and squirted me with water . . .'

'Oh God . . .'

'Yes, Mum,' Peter said, in the aggrieved tone he used when he wanted to portray the wrongs under which he laboured. 'Goodbye, Mum!'

Polly put down the phone, looked across the room at Michelle. 'The whole bloody place falls to pieces if I'm not there,' she said with a moan. 'The two boys are at each other's throats and Rory does nothing to prevent it!'

'That's terrible,' her prospective sister-in-law murmured. 'But I suppose boys will be boys . . .'

'I think I should go home!' Polly said miserably, biting her thumbnail. Against her will, her eyes filled with tears.

Michelle, an expression of incredulity on her face, crossed the room and put a strong, slim arm around her shoulders.

'Polly Caine,' she said, 'if you dare to desert me in my hour of need for three grown men who badly need to take responsibility for their own lives, I promise that I will never forgive you . . .'

'But the boys should be studying . . . and they won't if I'm not there.'

'Well then, they should be allowed to fail!' Michelle said, half under her breath. 'What on earth gives you the impression that you have to orchestrate their lives for them?'

'But I'm their mother!'

'You can kick-start them, nurture them until reasonably self-winding, but you can't, you simply cannot, live their lives for them!'

130

Polly considered this. 'Hmnn,' she said, not sounding convinced.

'And Rory is a big boy now.'

'It's just that he . . . tends to be a bit obsessive with his computing . . .' She glanced at Michelle. 'He's wonderful, of course . . . he's very clever . . . you wouldn't believe the brilliant things he comes out with . . . but he really doesn't want the bother of the children . . .'

Michelle nodded. 'They'll be fine, Polly. You know you need this break!'

Under her breath she added softly, 'Fuck the lot of them!'

Polly went to the window. She gazed out across the square, at the gracious Regency terraces, at the black taxis cruising, at the peaceful railed gardens with their lawns and herbaceous borders which could be glimpsed through the trees.

'I love gardens, you know,' she said a little wistfully. 'I tried to do something with ours, but the boys kick a ball around in it. If I had money I would . . . I saw a nice garden yesterday . . .' She glanced at Michelle. 'All the same,' she said, 'I think I should go home tomorrow . . .'

Michelle said, 'Well, wait until Wednesday, at least. I have plans for you tomorrow!'

'What plans?'

'Oh . . . I thought of taking you to . . . the Botanic Gardens and to meet a few people . . . Oh come on, Polly,' she added sternly, 'buck your tormentors! Make a stand for little Poll!'

Polly laughed. 'You make my family sound like Vlad the Impaler!'

'Sorry . . . I know they're wonderful, fantastic, adorable, sensitive, loving . . . but you've got rights too . . .'

Polly smiled. 'You don't understand.' Then she added to change the subject and also because she desperately wanted the answer, 'When did you say Tom would be back? I'd love to see him before I go home!'

'Oh, he won't be back until sometime the week after next,' Michelle said smoothly.

'Where is he exactly?'

'Dubai . . . I think. He's a great one for travelling!'

'What's he doing in Dubai?'

131

Michelle shrugged. 'How should I know? Probably selling arms to the Arabs!'

'What?'

'Or women to the Arabs for that matter . . .'

'Michelle, what are you talking about?'

'I'm joking! No, he's got involved with one of the oil companies.'

'I see . . . I didn't know.'

'Oh, he's branched out into various successful endeavours.'

Michelle poured a measure of ruby aperitif, which Polly assumed was cherry brandy.

'Now tell me about your neighbours and about life in Ashgrove Lawns!'

Polly sighed, sipped and felt the same glow suffuse her as on Saturday. 'Oh there's nothing much to tell,' she said dreamily. 'I have a good friend Susie and the estate is full of people like ourselves, working hard and doing their best, and being snobby about trifles because trifles is all they've got to be snobby about . . . And of course, there's Muriel . . .'

'Tell me about her,' Michelle said.

'She's a rich, lonely woman who lives beside us in that big house.'

'Rich and lonely . . .' Michelle mused. 'Not a usual combination. Has she no boyfriend?'

'I don't think so. She doesn't seem to go out much. She was engaged once, but it came to grief.'

'How would you like to have a boyfriend, Polly?'

Polly stared at her. 'Me? Are you crazy? I'm married!'

'Oh, just someone to chat to, go places with . . . In fact I've invited a few friends around tonight to meet you . . .'

Alan was a director of the bank and the most forceful, energetic person Muriel had ever met. He was some twenty-five years her senior, married with two children, both of them grown up.

'My wife and I live our own lives, you know,' he assured her. 'Our marriage hasn't been alive since I don't know when!'

He looked at her wistfully, as though seeking her compassion and understanding, a lonely man appreciative of the company of a woman young enough to be his daughter. Muriel, flattered, compassionate, had rushed, at least in spirit, to answer his silent plea.

Muriel had known Alan by sight for some time. When they met informally at a cheese and wine party his gentle and humorous demeanour had allayed both her natural shyness and any unconscious warning to which she might otherwise have listened. It was only a month or so after Michael had left for Jedda; Muriel was lonely, and a sense of insecurity had come to dog her, rooted in doubts about her attractiveness and whether Michael would meet someone in Saudi Arabia.

Into this private scenario came Alan, breathing life and charm. His attention gave her a sense of visibility, even personal power. He besieged Muriel for a date, phoning her with charming and outrageous comments such as 'What is the most lovely woman in the world doing tonight? Does she know how much I miss her?'

Muriel, twenty-three, shy, inexperienced, vulnerable and possessed of an elfin attractiveness she was largely unaware of, had been almost overwhelmed. No man, including Michael, had ever spoken to her like that. It conjured up vistas found in fairy tales, where the lover is true and pines in good earnest and speaks from the heart.

It won't harm anyone, she told herself, if I go out with him. It seemed to her a sophisticated and glamorous thing to do, to dine with one of the directors. Michael wouldn't mind. He doesn't expect me to sit at home every evening while he is away, she thought. Besides, Alan was so much older that there couldn't possibly be any ulterior motive.

So she had accepted a dinner invitation and had gone with Alan Barrington to the Mirabeau.

He had brought her back to her isolated run-down house and had kissed her suddenly and thoroughly in the car before saying goodnight. He had then stared at her tenderly, radiating a loving concern, holding both her hands and saying how much he had enjoyed the evening.

'It's been wonderful, you know, Muriel. You make me feel so young; you make me forget the angst of middle life!'

Muriel felt a little superior at this speech. It was true that she was very young compared to him, and this youth, because coveted by him, she suddenly experienced as a kind of superiority. She felt both excited with him and safe. He reminded her of her father and seemed, at the same time, utterly different to him, and this made her think, in a hazy and unformed way, that she could reconcile the old conflict. As a father figure, a trustworthy and honourable father figure, he was, for her, an icon of redemption.

There was something genuine, she thought, about the way he took her hands, about the way his face crinkled with kindness, about the fun and laughter they had together. It was so much nicer going out with a man than with a boy. A man didn't try anything on; a man respected you. So there had been a second date and then a third, and on the fourth Muriel, trying to be as sophisticated as she dared, but thinking of nothing other than a quick drink and a chat, and wishing to show him that she trusted him, invited him in for a nightcap.

'Darling,' he said, gathering her to him on the couch, 'I've been longing to do this all evening!'

And then he had brought his mouth down on hers, and his hand had strayed to the chaste precincts of her breast.

Almost from the first touch, Muriel felt the answer in her body and knew, in some dim recess of her being, that if she did not stop this immediately she was lost.

Two foreign-looking men came round to the flat in Eaton Square that evening. From the Middle East presumably, Polly thought to herself, remembering that Tom was working in Dubai. They seemed to know Michelle very well. They were expensively dressed, not very tall and carried bottles of wine.

'This is Hussein and this is Abdullah,' Michelle said with a very bright smile. 'This is my friend Polly Caine!'

'So this is the lady you talked about,' Abdullah said in a middle-eastern accent, smiling at Polly with smouldering eyes and lots of teeth. 'She is very charming!'

Hussein said something sotto voce to Michelle, at which she laughed, and his hand brushed her buttock as though by accident.

Polly flushed and wondered why anyone should speak of her as though she wasn't present, or why Hussein should be so familiar with Michelle. Then she decided that Michelle mustn't have noticed; perhaps they meant no offence, not being European.

They accepted drinks and sat around, talking to Michelle, turning to Polly with a familiarity she found increasingly astonishing. Occasionally they spoke among themselves in a language Polly did not understand. She wondered how Michelle could be so obtuse as to miss the clearly suggestive and impertinent glances thrown at both of them.

Michelle served some canapés – smoked salmon, prawns on little nests of noodles and little cheese delights on water biscuits which she and Polly had spent some time preparing.

Polly refused a gin and tonic, but she drank wine and tried to make urbane conversation, while all the time the mercury of her private outrage rose higher and higher.

Abdullah was particularly attentive. He sat beside Polly on the sofa and gazed at her with eyes like Omar Sharif's.

'My dear lady,' he said, 'you are so pretty. We so admire ladies who are a little . . .' and here his hands described the female form in voluptuous mode.

'I beg your pardon?' Polly said.

Michelle and Hussein were in the kitchen and Polly was left alone with her new admirer.

'I saw your face and your body when I came in and I fell in love with you,' he continued into her ear. A plump hand suddenly stroked her knee, and moved with calm assurance on to her thigh. 'You seem different . . . very fresh . . .'

Polly had a cloying sense of something very foreign, of an extremely distasteful intimacy and of a regard for womanhood very akin to the hunger of a pig at a trough. She flushed scarlet, stood up and confronted her would-be lover.

'I wonder if you are in the wrong place, Abdullah. I don't want to be rude, but I'm sure your wife would be shocked at this carry-on. There is no point in disgracing yourself just because you're homesick, or whatever you are! I don't want to be pawed any more than your wife would want to be, or you would want her to be!' Abdullah sat back as though he had been struck. Michelle and Hussein came out of the kitchen. They heard Polly continue without raising her voice.

'If you'll excuse me now I'm going out for a walk . . .'

She went into her bedroom to get her coat. Michelle followed her in and shut the door. She looked like someone on the verge of laughter.

'Oh Polly, what am I going to do with you,' she said cajolingly. 'Poor Abdullah didn't mean anything. He didn't intend to offend you!'

'I suspect he didn't care whether he did or not,' Polly said. 'And I also suspect that there is nothing poor about him, except his manners. I think he is a very over-indulged and spoilt little creep, and I, for one, want nothing to do with him. While Tom is away I wonder you would be bothered with such creatures . . . even if they are his business acquaintances . . . Do you put up with that kind of familiarity to bolster business?'

Michelle seemed flummoxed. 'You're much too lovely and clever to demean yourself by having to deal with men like that!' Polly went on in a fury. 'Business or no business, it's soul-destroying to be anywhere near them! It's a contamination. If Tom expects it of you it's really too bad; you should stand up for your dignity!'

Polly had her coat on now. She heard the two men speaking together in the sitting room. Michelle stood against the closed bedroom door.

'Oh Christ!' she said, with a jocose groan. 'Oh Polly . . .'

She opened the door, went into the hall.

'There seems to have been a small misunderstanding,' she announced with plastic laughter. 'I think you should both leave now as the ladies of this particular kasbah are no longer at home to visitors!'

Polly heard male tones remonstrating, heard Michelle's response in a voice that suddenly left no room for argument, 'Sorree, fellas . . . change of plan . . .' and, with considerable relief, heard the visitors departing.

Michelle returned to Polly's bedroom.

'You can take your coat off. They're gone!'

'I didn't mean to frighten your friends away,' Polly said, 'but they seemed such impertinent opportunists!'

Michelle didn't answer, but she looked at Polly as though something very funny had happened, as though she was vetting the events of the last few minutes against some private agenda and found the contrast amusing.

'My advice to you,' Polly continued, 'is to refuse to have

anything to do with their likes, Tom or no Tom, business interest or no business interests; there's more at stake here than a few shekels!'

Michelle left the room, but when Polly followed her she found her in the sitting room, tears of hysterical laughter on her face.

'Not another word, please, Polly,' she said, raising her head, and drying her eyes. 'But why don't you go up for Secretaryship of the United Nations . . .'

'Is there anything on the box?' Polly asked after a moment, feeling deflated and a little foolish as the anger left her. 'Why don't you relax, put your feet up, and I'll make you a nice little supper! What would you say to a nice cheese omelette?'

# Chapter Ten

Polly went home on Wednesday evening. In her case were two dresses which Michelle had insisted on buying for her. One was a black dinner dress and one an informal summer dress with a belt. Both were slimming. They had also been expensive, but Michelle had made light of the cost. 'Oh, Polly, do let me . . . It's a privilege to buy something for one's friends. Besides, you've saved me from myself over the weekend. How can you put a price on that?'

'How did I save you from yourself?'

Michelle smiled. '. . . In ways you wot not of . . .'

It was seven thirty when Polly got home. She was tired and looking forward to a cup of tea. The house seemed silent as she let herself in and for a moment she assumed she had the place to herself.

'Anyone at home?' she called.

Then she heard the reassuring clicks from behind the closed dining-room door and knew that her husband was at his usual post.

'Who's that?' he called.

'It's me!' Polly put her head around the dining-room door.

'You're supposed to be in London!' Rory said.

'I decided to come home. Where are the boys?'

'Out . . .'

Polly went into the kitchen which closely resembled the aftermath of an earthquake. Dirty dishes were piled on the table, in the sink; jars of chocolate spread and peanut butter stood open on the work surface beside the sink. Cat was in her basket and looked up, her face a mask of lightning calculation, a cat vetting her conscience.

'The mess!' Polly said in dismay, struck by it in a way she had not expected. For some reason the contrast between it and Michelle's pristine blue and white kitchen rose up before her like an affront. She had expected a bit of a mess, accepted it was her lot in life. She hated to make too much of a fuss about it, spoil the harmony she tried to maintain. What was a bit of housework after all, compared to a harmonious house?

'The mess!' she said again. 'I left this kitchen like a new pin!'

'Well, we didn't know you were coming back,' Rory said apologetically, coming into the kitchen behind her. 'I told those children of yours to clean it up . . . but as usual all they're good for is tearing spots off each other!'

'Were they quarrelling?'

'Do they ever do anything else?'

'I told Peter not to tease Jason . . . I rang back on Sunday.'

'Yes. He told me. But Jason is not such a lily-white drake, you know. He provokes his brother!'

'I know.'

Polly sighed. 'I wasn't trying to blame you for anything, Rory, when I was talking to you. I'm sorry for having shouted.' She smiled at him a bit ruefully. 'And I do know you can actually tell your children apart!'

Rory looked a little sheepish. 'They've both got so big and they look alike and when I'm not looking at them straight I get a bit confused. But they don't take any heed of me anyway. They had a slanging match today and then Jason went off in high dudgeon and hasn't come home since . . .'

Rory filled the kettle and plugged it in. Polly began to clear the kitchen table.

'Did you miss me?' she said.

'Of course I missed you!'

Polly shot her husband a penetrating look, but he was not looking at her. He was looking at the contents of a packet of frozen cannelloni he had fished out of the ice box.

'Would you like some of this?' he demanded. 'One million calories per bite . . . Ha ha . . . By the way, you've lost weight!'

'Have I?'

'I think so!'

Polly began to clear off the table and Rory set about heating the cannelloni. For a few minutes there was a conjugal atmosphere, one that Polly loved and had not known for some considerable time.

'Well, tell me about London . . . What did you do?'

'Other than scurry home because of those children?'

Rory looked annoyed. A frown gathered on his forehead; his face expressed exasperation.

'Was that why you came back early? What did you do that for?'

'Because,' Polly said, 'I was afraid the boys would do nothing except cut out one another's throats. Both of them have to work at their studies or I don't know what will become of them!' She put a pile of dirty plates into the sink, ran in hot water and added a squirt of washing-up liquid.

'Well, you must have done something in London!' Rory said.

'I went shopping with Michelle and I met a man called Keith and a dog called Herbie and I went on the tube and to the Botanic Gardens.'

'That was all?'

'Well, there wasn't that much time.'

'Who was Keith?'

Polly scrubbed dried tomato ketchup from a plate.

'Oh, just someone I met. He lives in Wimbledon.'

'Did you meet him in the Gardens?'

'Something like that!' Polly said after a moment.

'Well, I'll say this for you . . . You're a mine of information!'

'There's not much to relate. Michelle and Tom have a lovely flat. It must cost them a bomb! It seems Tom is away on business a great deal; he seems to have become quite international.'

'Tom? International? Pull the other one!'

'There's no need to be rude about my brother! He was always a go-getter!'

'Sure. But where did he go and what did he get? We don't really know, do we?'

Polly stopped what she was doing and stared at Rory.

'What do you mean?'

'Sorry, Poll. It was just a piece of smart-assery!'

Polly went on to describe the flat and its environs.

'Maybe they were the mystery winners of last Saturday's Lotto!' Rory offered, putting away the plates.

Polly's mind was on her sons, but she knew better than to harp on them. 'Oh,' she said absently. 'Was it won? What sort of a prize was it?'

'Only one of the biggest Lottery prizes we've ever had in this country. Four million!'

'Hmnn . . .' Polly said, scouring a dirty saucepan. 'Nice for someone!'

'The holder of the winning ticket has not come forward yet,' Rory said. 'It's probably some dozy hen who doesn't know she's got a fortune in her pocket!'

Polly scrubbed at the dried-in detritus of yesterday's dinner. 'I wish we could afford a dishwasher,' she muttered. 'Maybe you could get one second hand . . .'

'Not this year,' Rory said hurriedly. 'Not with the Preying Mantis on my back . . .'

Polly looked at Rory, but was afraid to ask any questions. The moment for knowing the worst would come, but not now, not tonight. If they were going to lose the house she didn't want to know tonight.

Polly and Rory dined on the cannelloni. When Rory was finished he said he had to check on something and in a moment the predictable clicking of the keyboard could be heard. Polly finished cleaning the kitchen. She threw Cat out, on the basis that the kitchen was not a cats' retirement home. She wanted, rather unkindly, to laugh at the shaven rat-like tail, a tail still devoid of feline appeal. 'Get some exercise, you fat heap!' she advised the family pet, ignoring the narrowed, menacing gaze directed back at her over a furry shoulder. 'Why not go and confuse some mice . . . Now's your chance . . . with your new tail and everything . . .'

Polly brought her case upstairs and unpacked, lost herself for a while with the pleasure of her two new dresses, put them on, paraded in front of the mirror, sucked in her stomach, fantasised that she would lose loads of weight.

When she had hung up her new apparel in the wardrobe and put her case away, her eyes strayed to the clock on Rory's bedside table. It was eleven. She wondered where the boys were, particularly Jason; why was he so late? She went downstairs and asked Rory if he had said he would be out until this hour.

142

'No,' Rory said. 'But then he never does!'
'He usually tells me!'
'You weren't here.'

Peter came home at midnight, evinced pleasure in the sight of
his mother before he remembered that he was annoyed with
her for ticking him off over the phone two days ago. Then his
demeanour became suitably cool and laconic.
'Where's Jason?' Polly demanded.
'How should I know? I'm not the little turd's keeper!'
'It's twelve o'clock at night and he's still out!'
'He's seventeen, Mum!'
'Seventeen is very young!'
'Only to old people!'
'Didn't he say anything to you?'
'No!'
Peter vetted the contents of the fridge, found a litre of milk,
filled a pint glass and downed it. 'I'm going to hit the hay . . .
Goodnight.'
'Goodnight,' Polly said. 'Are you sure Jason didn't say
anything about where he would be?'
'Oh God, here we go again,' Peter said. 'The answer is still
no. I don't know, and frankly don't care, what the little fart is
up to!'
'That's no way to talk about your brother!' But Peter had
moved into the hall and was taking the stairs two at a time.
Polly turned to Rory. 'He might have had an accident!'
Rory made a sound like a groan. He did not turn around
from the computer, and Polly knew from the set of his head
that any further discussion of this subject was useless. So she
went upstairs, undressed and got into bed, leaving her bedroom
door open. She picked up a book and tried to read, but she was
straining all the time for the sound of the key in the front door,
the sound of Jason's voice; even for the horrible aroma of cooking
pizza.
Polly was awake when Rory came to bed. She was awake
long after he was asleep, and awake when the dawn glimmered
through the chink in the curtains and awake when the first
birds gave exploratory rejoicing cheeps. But still Jason had
not returned.

\* \* \*

At nine o'clock she began phoning Jason's friends. They were still on holiday, so she had no difficulty in contacting them.

Her first call was to Conor who was still in bed. She explained to his mother who murmured in maternal sympathy and got her son up. Conor said he hadn't seen Jason since Sunday. Then she phoned John and got the same story. Then she phoned Declan who said that he had seen Jason the day before. Was there anything unusual about him, Polly asked, explaining that he hadn't come home all night.

Declan didn't seem to think there was anything unusual. But Jason did have a rucksack with him.

Polly thanked him and put down the phone. A rucksack! She raced into Jason's bedroom, opened his drawers, saw that several pairs of jeans were missing, ditto shirts and tee-shirts.

His books were cluttered on his table, and as she tidied them automatically she found the empty Marlboro cigarette box. Christ, so he was smoking! The little brat! After everything she had told him!

He's gone to stay with someone, she told herself; but who?

It was only as she left his room that she found the note stuck to the back of the door with Blu-tack.

Dear Family,
    There's no point in looking for me! I've gone away for ever and I will never come back again.
        Jason.

Polly pulled the piece of paper from its moorings and cantered down the stairs to where Rory was munching a bit of brown bread and butter in the kitchen.

'Rory . . . Rory . . .' she cried, pushing the note at him, 'Jason has run away!'

Rory paused to examine the note and then resumed his munching. He sighed, poured himself another cup of tea.

'Yeah.'

'Is that all you can say?'

'He'll be back, Poll.'

'He says he won't,' Polly said in a small voice. 'He says he's never coming back! We don't even know where he is! His friends don't know. He's taken his clothes. He's seventeen. He's due to do the Leaving in eight weeks . . .'

Peter, looking sleepy, appeared in the kitchen doorway.

Rory thrust the note at him. 'Is this your doing?' he demanded of his elder son.

Peter read the note. His mouth tightened in an expression halfway between fury and uncertainty.

'No, it's not. I'm blamed for everything in this house . . .' He turned on his father; 'You, for example, don't even know who I am!'

'None of your lip, young man!' Rory shouted.

The tears started in Polly's eyes. She sat down and put her head in her hands and wept. 'I should never have gone to London!'

'Oh Christ,' Rory said, patting her shoulder awkwardly. 'Don't be so silly, Poll . . . Kids are always carrying on like this!'

'No, they're not,' Polly sobbed.

'No, they're not,' Peter echoed.

Rory glared at his son, gave his wife a few more pats, got up and went into the dining room, switched on his computer and shut the door.

When Polly dried her eyes she saw that Cat was weaving around on the windowsill trying to attract her attention. When eye-contact was established the cat started to mew, at first gentle reminders, then warning notes.

'Oh shut up, Cat!' Peter said.

'Where's Jason? Where is my poor, silly baby?' Polly whispered.

'I don't know, Mum . . .'

He's not a baby! came the thought. He has probably absconded to London and is living in a cardboard box. Polly had a sudden vision of her adolescent son living rough, rubbing shoulders with all sorts of depraved people, being exposed to drink and drugs and everything that went with them; spending his nights sleeping under newspapers.

She went into the hall and phoned the police.

'Can you come to the station, ma'am, and make a statement,' the tired voice of the Law asked her.

\* \* \*

145

When Garda Scanlon took the details of Jason's disappearance he seemed unfazed by the catastrophe. This made Polly feel very much on her own. Neither Rory nor Peter had evinced much anxiety, saying that the missing family member would be back in due course.

'Who do you think he is with?' she had demanded again of Peter before she had left with a reluctant Rory for the Garda station. 'You must know something!'

'I don't!' Peter shouted. 'And I'm sick to death of being regarded as the zit-bag's superintendent. He's in a sulk, that's all!'

But Polly detected anxiety.

Garda Scanlon examined the farewell note, heard how Jason's rucksack was missing, noted the name of the boy who had seen him the day before, listed all of Jason's friends.

'Anyone else?' he said, before he closed his notebook.

'I can't think of anyone else . . .'

'Don't worry,' the garda said kindly to Polly, 'he'll probably turn up. Sometimes they're not far away and just trying to teach parents a lesson. But we'll ask the English police to look out for him in case he took the boat. Did he have much money?'

'No . . . Unless he cashed his savings certificates.'

'How much did he have in them?'

'About two hundred pounds . . . He was going on the other day about how they had matured. It was money he got for his Confirmation.'

'When will he be eighteen?' the garda asked then, as though he had forgotten an obvious question.

'In a couple of months . . . the fourteenth of June!'

'Oh . . . well, you know once they're eighteen they're of full age. He can't be forced to come home . . .'

'If I even knew that he was safe,' Polly wailed.

'Well, we'll try to find out where he is anyway, Mrs Caine. You should go home now and make yourself a nice cup of tea and get some rest. There's nothing more you can do. We'll contact you if we have anything for you!'

He looked at Rory as he said this, and Rory took Polly's arm and steered her out on to the pavement.

'He'll be all right, Poll,' he said for the umpteenth time.

Polly rounded on him. 'You don't know whether he will or not! If you had prevented Peter from constantly teasing him this might not have happened. Why can't I turn my back for a few days without the whole family falling apart?'

'For God's sake, Polly! What's wrong with you?'

'What's wrong with me is that you all just sit there like so many great, selfish cats and take everything I do for you all as your due. Where, in God's name, did you learn so much presumption?'

Rory looked stunned. Polly had not raised her voice but the edge to it was something he had never heard before.

She turned on her heel and walked away.

When Polly got home she found Susie at the door.

'. . . I'm sorry, Poll. I heard the news. Are you all right?'

'How did you hear?'

'Rory phoned me at work . . . I took the morning off.'

Polly brought her friend into the kitchen. Peter had left a note on the table to say he had gone into the college library and would not be back until the evening. She sat down and leaned her forehead against the table. Susie made some tea, put a steaming mug down in front of Polly, popped some bread into the toaster.

'I don't want anything to eat!'

'Polly, you must eat something. Anxiety like this will wear you down!'

'I can't eat. I feel as though my throat is about to close. It's just not knowing, wondering if I will ever see him again! You know, Sue, there are hundreds of disappearances every year. Sometimes the people concerned never show up again!'

Susie put a comforting hand on her shoulder. 'Jason wouldn't do that to you!'

'I wish I had some money . . . we could hire a private investigator. I'll do it anyway if I can get anything for my rings!'

'Oh, Polly . . .'

At one o'clock they turned on the radio news. There was nothing on it about Jason, although Polly had half expected that they would mention him as a missing person. At the end of the bulletin they mentioned that the Lotto prize of the preceding

Saturday had still not been claimed, and suggested that people re-examine their tickets, reminding the listeners that after ninety days the prize would lapse.

'The winning ticket was bought in the St Stephen's Green Shopping Centre on Wednesday of last week, at four fifteen p.m.'

'Maybe the person who bought it died,' Susie said. 'Or lost the ticket! Christ, imagine losing the bonanza of a lifetime!'

Polly wasn't interested. 'Oh, where is my baby?' she moaned as the news ended, and Marian Finucan's programme started and no mention at all had been made of the missing Jason.

When the doorbell rang Susie went to open it. It was Muriel. She had a bottle of Remy Martin under her arm in a smart box.

'I heard about Jason,' she confided to Susie. 'I thought . . . Is there anything I can do?'

'Not really, Muriel.'

'Peter told me . . . Wasn't Jason terrible to do a thing like that. He must have known how upsetting it would be!'

'I think we should avoid making judgements,' Susie said crisply.

Muriel looked taken aback. 'I'm sorry . . . I didn't mean to judge anyone,' she said in an uncertain voice.

'Polly is gone to bed,' Susie said in a gentler tone, to forestall the necessity of having Muriel come in.

'Oh . . . well in that case will you give her this,' she said, proffering the bottle of brandy. 'Sometimes a stiff nip is just the thing!'

Susie took the bottle, thanked Muriel and shut the door. She went back to the kitchen.

'I know it was Muriel,' Polly said. 'I was about to follow you to the door and I heard the voice!'

'Nosy cow!' Susie said. 'But she brought you this!'

'How kind of her!' Polly said. 'I should go and thank her.'

'Not now. I told her you were in bed. She said a stiff nip is what you need!' She raised her eyebrows, gave a half laugh. 'She should know . . .'

She fetched two glasses, opened the bottle.

The next time the doorbell rang it was the postman with a

registered letter for Rory. Polly signed for it and left it on the hall table.

'You need to get some rest,' Susie opined. 'Have you any sleeping tablets?'

'No.'

'I've got some Valium at home. I'll get you a few.' Susie disappeared and came back with the medication.

Polly swallowed a tablet and then drank some brandy, just as Susie tried to tell her that she shouldn't mix it with drink. Then she sat on the couch and, after a while, fell asleep.

Susie fetched a blanket, covered her friend, studied her with concern and cursed Jason under her breath. Then she rang the office and spoke to Mr Penston, telling him about what had happened, asking him if he knew a good private detective.

'They cost!' Mr Penston said.

'I know . . .'

Susie took down the details. Focus Private Investigators. She was thinking that the money she had saved would have to be called on. She thought of Fergus and his incipient redundancy. She wouldn't tell him. What husbands didn't know wouldn't hurt them. She chewed her little finger while she did some calculations. She would have to find out from Focus exactly what they cost.

Through the window she saw the sunlight glinting on the windows of Willow House. This gave her an idea. After all, Muriel had offered earlier to do what she could.

Muriel went home and said to Sable:

'I suppose they think I'm an interfering old hen. I don't blame them really. I wish I had an easy manner, but I'm always so stiff. The only time in my life I wasn't shy was with Alan. It was as though he knew me, as though I knew him in some strange way: I wasn't afraid with him; I suppose I thought he was a haven, the place where I could enact my own reality, distil conflict into some kind of peace.' She glanced at her purring pet. 'Or something like that . . .'

Sex with Alan had been akin to revelation. Muriel was completely unprepared for the power of it and the range of it, and the confident sexual experience of her lover. He did things

149

that Michael would not have done in a hundred years, nor would she have wanted him to.

But this man's sexuality was contagious; it fired the very air around him, was charged like an energy field. After a short period of uncertainty and shimmering guilt, Muriel, trusting in his declarations of love, trusting in the future he outlined for them both, gave him not only her body but also her soul. In the euphoria of her new-found freedom she was effusive:

'I love you so much, Alan,' she said happily, 'I could die with it.'

She dreamed of the wonderful future they would have together; they discussed it, where they would live, where they would travel. Even life with Michael seemed pedestrian compared to the dizzy prospects of life with Alan.

Alan kept the relationship going at an intense pace until he had plumbed the depths of Muriel's sensuality, had touched the core in her, and been gratified by what he found, and what he had awakened.

Muriel felt the headache coming on. She would have to take painkillers, go to bed, pull the curtains, get what relief she could.

She did not want to remember that when he began to distance himself she became desperate, like an investor who is already so severely compromised that he invests more and more to stave off disaster.

'It would only do terrible devastation,' he said apologetically, when Muriel finally tried to call in the fervent promises he had made her. He was referring to his wife, the woman whom, in the course of his affairs, he always kept in the background – an unimportant pawn until he needed her on the board as Queen. And then she was his right hand; the source of his inviolability. Was he not plighted to her after all? Was he not a married man?

'Yes,' Muriel echoed, 'devastation . . . !'

'I was brought up to take marriage seriously,' he added with a lugubrious smile, which sought her good-natured sanction of her own plunder. The tone of his voice suggested that she was being unreasonable.

\* \* \*

As she made her way up the stairs she heard the doorbell. It was Susie.

'Muriel, I have an idea . . . I thought you might . . .'

'Come in!'

Susie followed Muriel into her pastel drawing room. She thought Muriel looked as pale as her ivory walls.

'Are you all right, Muriel?'

'Fine . . . I have a bit of a headache. I was going to lie down.'

Muriel waited. Susie shuffled uncomfortably.

'The thing is,' Susie said, 'about Jason I mean . . . what do you think of us getting a private investigator?'

'What a wonderful idea! Do you know anyone?'

'Yes. A crowd called Focus. They come highly recommended. But they're expensive!'

'Oh . . . leave that end of things to me . . . !'

Susie's face cleared. 'Are you sure, Muriel? I have a bit saved . . .'

'Of course I'm sure. It would be a pleasure. I should have thought of it myself!'

# Chapter Eleven

Muriel thought of the first day she had brought Michael home, shown him around, brought him through the stable yard where the dandelions pushed their bright yellow heads between the cobbles, then back to the house. It had rained, a steady downpour which gushed and spurted from the broken eaveshoots. Inside the house the water had dripped, with steady, staccato precision, from the rusting skylight in the upper landing, into the old basin below.

'Aren't you going to repair that?'

'We really need a new roof. Mummy's money is all gone and I haven't enough!'

'You could sell the land!'

'That wouldn't fetch what we need to restore the house.'

'Oh, I don't mean sell it as land, you silly girl . . .' Kiss on the nose, smell of damp jumper, sense of sudden acumen, sharp young mind vetting possibilities, sense of togetherness, complicity. 'I mean sell it as building sites. The suburbs are already swallowing up the villages around here – the area has been re-zoned – and some day soon your mother will probably receive a query or two asking her if she is interested. You should get outline planning permission . . . be prepared to negotiate for a fortune . . .'

Muriel had laughed. 'You've a great imagination . . . anyway, Mummy wouldn't consider it.'

But, as though Michael had been clairvoyant, such a letter had arrived within three months.

Dear Madam,
    A corporate client is very interested in acquiring

property in your area. If you are interested in selling you will find the terms extremely attractive.

Please do not hesitate to contact us if we may be of service.

Yours faithfully,
Joe Murphy
Partridge & Ross Ltd.,
Estate Agents, Auctioneers and Valuers.

As Muriel had predicted, her mother had been dismissive, holding up the letter by a corner, as though it contained some contamination.

'What would be the point . . . we might get a lot of money, but we'd be surrounded by all sorts of dreadful people . . . How can you even think of it, Muriel . . . the avenue would be gone, the fields, the peace; they'd cut down the beeches . . . It would be hideous!' Her mother made three precise syllables out of hideous for added emphasis, her mouth widening into a thin, sharp line. 'I want to end my days here in peace and quiet,' she said.

Muriel knew her mother was right. She felt very foolish for mentioning any other possibility.

'Yes, Mummy,' she said.

Muriel lay on her bed and glanced around her. She knew this room well; it had been hers for long as she could remember. The walnut wardrobe had once been home to her teenage clothes; sensible stuff and two miniskirts she had bought in Dunnes Stores and hidden. In those days there had been trees outside and a long avenue, and nothing else except the gateposts. Inside, the house had been full of shadows, brown paintwork, faded wallpaper, a downstairs door locked against all intruders and a mother increasingly distracted by an increasingly puissant past, as though, with the future narrowing before her, the past had reached out to claim her as its own.

But Mother and gateposts were long gone. Rows of identical semis now filled the fields fronting what had been the old road to the village. Muriel didn't really mind; she welcomed it. There were people she knew, people she could watch. Sometimes she sat at her window for long periods, gazing out at the comings and goings of the inhabitants of the cul-de-sac.

Today she had taken an afternoon nap, had woken feeling desperate, trying unsuccessfully to recall the dream that had precipitated her return to the waking world – something to do with her parents. The light of early evening filled the room. She lay still. Her father's face rose before her, a forceful ghost at the core of memory; then her mother's.

'I'd like to go to the university, Mummy . . .'

'There's no point in over-educating a woman. You should get a good job and meet the right kind of young men! There's no money, Muriel . . . Your father saw to that!'

In her mother's perspective men were some kind of prize, awarded for good behaviour. Muriel had absorbed this mind-set, did not question it. It was not that she felt herself to be in any way inferior to men; it was just that very early in her life she had interiorised the knowledge as to who had the power. She did not question this custodianship; it had the same currency as the other immutable facts of existence, like the positioning of the sun and the moon within the solar system.

But to share in the system, to be a part of it, to be protected from the abuse of it, you had to marry. To be outside it was to exist in limbo, in the arctic cold. To achieve it you were circumscribed with so many strictures, the correct way of behaving, of thinking, that you dared not put a foot wrong. It went without saying that you could never, ever, free the individual fire in you, which slumbered like the Kraken, and which if it rose would herald the demise of the existing order.

She accepted without any question that a woman's truth was something to be suppressed, her identity disguised. First came survival. Only if that were secured, and it existed on so many levels, was there scope for anything else.

Her mother had seemed pleased with her engagement to Michael. Michael had let it be known that he was not a practising Catholic. 'I'm not really anything,' he had told her, raising quizzical eyebrows at his own foibles.

'A pity he's not of our faith,' Mrs Reeves said afterwards, adding that Protestants were thin on the ground these days. But he was a presentable young man, she said, and he had a very acceptable future, if he played his cards right. Anyway, she hinted, Muriel might have difficulty in finding another man.

'I'm not plain, Mummy, am I?' she had asked her mother on one occasion, pricked into audacity by her secret terror of the lonely life yawning before the plain woman.

Her mother's expression had frozen her. 'No . . . you're not plain!'

This statement carried such unspoken comment as to what else she might be, that Muriel retreated. She dared not ask what was being insinuated because she knew.

At all costs it must be kept from Michael. His face now swam into her consciousness, blue eyes, black lashes, curled like a girl's, black hair romantically streaked with grey at twenty-five.

Michael had been ardent but respectful. He was happy to wait until they were married, he said, if that was what she wanted.

Despite these protestations, however, he had been a bit carried away one night when she had gone back to his basement flat for coffee after the pictures. His flat mate was out. He had kissed her, fondled her, and one thing had led to another. But Muriel found that her reserve was not something she could jettison. She had lain stiffly, and awkwardly, waiting for him to do whatever it was he wanted, but he had looked at her, at her half-gritted teeth, and had, on an exclamation of wounded frustration, suddenly walked out, stark naked, into the wet garden, only to return to cajole her and stroke her hair as she wept in his arms.

'It's all right. It's just that it's new . . .' he said.

Muriel was not so sure. But she did know that the only thing she wanted out of life was love – for no matter how hard she scanned every possibility that life had to offer, she could not find in it anything else worth a damn. Sex was not love, had nothing to do with love; it was just something you had to give in order to get it.

Keith Warrington let his cleaning lady, Mrs Dencher, in on Wednesday morning and then took Herbie for a walk on the Common. It was a sunny morning, with the freshness of spring and the promise of a warm day. He brought along Herbie's toy, a sponge rubber ball that had once been multi-coloured, but was now so well chewed that only the drab, spongy interior was visible. Keith threw the ball; it bounced drunkenly in among the brambles and Herbie raced after it, ears up, tail down, tongue lolling. He found it triumphantly, brought it back to his master and waited, panting, for another throw.

Herbie was very happy. Since his master's retirement he had had a good life, plenty of walks and games, and all the things he liked. He growled purely out of form when Mrs Jopling came along with Fluffsy, her poodle. The poodle was blue-grey and had been turned into something of a comedy. Today she was wearing a particularly hideous tartan coat. Herbie sniffed her rear end but Fluffsy had learnt dignity through many trials, and did not stoop to show that she had noticed.

Keith exchanged a few words with Mrs Jopling. She was a widow and they had got to know each other from their walks on the Common. She lived a bit nearer the village than he did, and he had sometimes toyed with the idea of asking her around for a drink. She could usually be relied on to be fairly jolly, although her eyes had a haunted, famished look to them, and if her laugh was a bit like a neigh, what harm; it jostled him out of his introspection.

"Morning,' Mrs Jopling neighed. 'Isn't it simply lovely to see summer coming back!'

'First rate,' Keith agreed.

They walked along in silence for a moment. Then Mrs Jopling began to talk of how clever Fluffsy was, how she had almost spoken to her the day before.

'She put her two front paws up on the table . . . and she looked at me with such understanding, as though she understood how I was feeling . . .'

Keith avoided being drawn into any enquiry as to how Mrs Jopling had been feeling. He knew from experience that she would tell him, at considerable length, and then wait with bated breath for professional assessment.

'Did you know that poodles were originally gun dogs?' he said. 'They're highly intelligent!'

Mrs Jopling was delighted. 'Do you hear that, darling?' she demanded of Fluffsy who was straining at the leash. 'You're officially clever . . . but I always knew you were.'

Fluffsy turned pained eyes on her.

'Look at that lovely face!' Mrs Jopling cried. 'Look at that lovely face!'

Keith began to feel a sinus coming on.

'Did you hear from your daughter?' Mrs Jopling then asked and Keith said he had and that she was getting on well in her job and had got a salary hike.

'Isn't that wonderful . . . So nice for young people to be able to see the world. I was in New York myself ten years ago with my late husband. Frank was very fond of America. He used to say he'd like to retire there . . . he was joking, of course.' She sighed. 'Well, events overtook him . . . He's in St Swithin's Cemetery now! He was a lot older than me, of course,' she added hurriedly, in order to distance herself from macabre possibilities.

Keith made sympathetic noises. From somewhere above their heads a grey squirrel fluttered with cheeky, weightless ease from branch to branch. Herbie looked up and barked, but the squirrel laughed, darted out to catch another thin branch and disappeared into the foliage.

After about an hour on the Common Keith and Herbie wandered home. Keith raised his tweed cap to Mrs Jopling and bade her good day. He had changed his mind about asking her round for a drink. He was resentful of the incipient sinus and needed peace and quiet. For some reason his mind kept returning to the strange little body who had beguiled his Sunday afternoon and who had then disappeared as though she had been a trick of the light. His house had not been broken into so far, nor his head coshed while he slept, so he began to assume she was not a front woman for the IRA, although this could not, of course, be taken for granted.

When he got home Mrs Dencher was putting the finishing touches to the kitchen, shining up the old Wedgwood plates on the dresser. She flashed a toothy smile at her employer, then resumed her humming. She was airing a tune from *Oliver*. Keith remembered the musical; he had gone to see it with Marguerite thirty years before. He wandered into the sitting room where his dead wife's portrait looked down at him from the wall. She was wearing that lovely off-the-shoulder dress they had bought together, and was smiling, the small secret smile which he had once thought was reserved for him and indicated hidden profundities, until he had seen her give it to a succession of her dogs.

He suddenly felt the silence of his house, of his life, the way in which time had rushed him into middle age and widowhood, without as much as a by-your-leave. What on earth had he been doing that he could not remember growing older, did not know precisely when the momentum of his life had faltered? It wasn't even a physical thing particularly; it was more a change in perspective; not weariness, but inexorable, reluctant wisdom.

He picked up the post which had been left on the hall table, began to open the letters. One of them was from the solicitors dealing with his father-in-law's estate.

'Dear Keith,' the letter said, 'I would be glad if you would come to see me. It seems that all is not straightforward with the estate of the late Mr Whiston. I'll go into details when I see you, but there has been an unexpected development.' It was signed by his solicitor Jonathan Wheatley.

Keith whistled under his breath. 'Old goat probably left a string of bastards,' he muttered; 'I suppose it was too much to hope that the thing would be plain sailing . . .'

He thought immediately of his recent visitor and wondered whether there could possibly have been some shenanigans which she had not divulged . . . maybe there *was* a sister . . . maybe Bernard had been up to some of his old tricks . . .

Mrs Dencher rattled a bit more in the kitchen, then her sturdy form came into the drawing room. 'I'm all done now, Dr Warrington.'

Keith had her money ready and handed it over.

'Why don't you stay for a spot of lunch,' he said on an impulse. He had a sudden yen to talk about the world of thirty years before.

Mrs Dencher seemed taken aback; 'Well now,' she said, with a hint of reproof, 'but there's my 'Arry's lunch to do . . .'

'Of course.'

Keith thought his charlady was looking tired, and the medic in him spoke.

'You need a holiday, Mrs D,' he said. 'You could do with a rest!'

'A holiday!' she echoed. 'Bless you . . . I haven't 'ad a holiday for five years! Not since my 'Arry was made redundant.' She gave a small reproving laugh. 'No holidays is on the cards for the moment, Dr Warrington, not for me leastways!'

She disappeared and there was a soft clap as the front door closed behind her.

Keith wandered into the kitchen, took some fish fingers from the ice box and shook them on to the grill pan. He turned the grill on full and then opened a tin of Woof and filled Herbie's bowl. The labrador wolfed his meal, delivered himself of a malodorous fart and went to his basket by the door, licking his chops with a long pink tongue. Keith unfolded *The Times* and took in the contents of the front page, forgetting all about his lunch.

A smell of burning heralded the immolation of the fish fingers. Keith rushed to the kitchen, pulled out the grill pan, exclaimed in disgust at the smoking offerings, threw them out, searched for the tin of tuna he knew he had somewhere and made a sandwich instead. He had several things to do that afternoon, the principal one being to finish an article he was writing on schizophrenia. But first he tried to phone Jonathan Wheatley.

'He's still at lunch,' Jonathan's secretary informed him. 'But I'll tell him you called.'

Keith started up his word processor, but almost before he realised what he was doing he found himself tapping out a letter to the strange woman who had arrived at the gate on the preceding Sunday. He had in front of him the letter which Bernard had written her.

Dear Pauline,

I don't know where you live, so I'm sending this to the box number mentioned in the letter which my father-in-law sent your sister (does that sound convoluted?). I do hope everything has worked out all right for her, and that you were able to tell her you had effected delivery of her missive, and that she wasn't too annoyed that it was all a practical joke on the part of the deceased (whose affairs were never straightforward and seem to be still in a mess).

If you are in London again perhaps you would care to phone. I have a collection of silver snuff boxes I would value an expert appraisal of and several other antique items you might give me some advice on. My late wife was a great collector, and now that she is gone I find that I have no idea at all about the things she treasured.

Anyway, it was nice meeting you.

Sincerely, Keith Warrington.

P.S. Herbie sends his best regards.

In Ashgrove Lawns Polly answered the phone.

'Are you sitting down?'

'Oh God . . . Susie . . . What is it?'

'Good news. I'm phoning you from work. It would appear that your missing baby is living in sin in a bed-sit in Drumcondra.'

'What?'

Polly sat on the small stool which was usually left beneath the hall table.

'It's true. His partner in crime is a young woman called Veronica Settle. Does the name mean anything?'

'Jason's Jezebel!' Polly whispered. 'I never thought of her . . .'

'Well . . .' Susie said, recalling the glimpse she had had of the young woman in question, 'I wouldn't have thought her a Jezebel – more the camp commandant type.'

'I know . . . I mean I've spoken to her on the phone . . .'

'Oh . . . ?'

'Peter says she's thirty, and fifteen stone!'

'More like twenty-one and thirteen stone! But she's had quite a calming effect on Jason! I spoke to him. Got the impression life had softened his cough, if you follow me!'

'I'll break the little blighter's head!' Polly said, relief being followed by a sudden surge of fury. 'Where is he?'

'Well, I'll tell you . . . but on one condition . . . he doesn't want to come home, Poll. I've talked to him.'

'Doesn't want to come home! What does he do all day for God's sake? Does he even have a proper bed of his own to sleep in? Is he warm enough?'

There was a moment's silence and then Susie said, 'Polly, there was a time when some things were more obvious to you than they seem to be now!'

'Oh no . . .' Polly whispered. 'You don't mean . . .'

'I do . . . and I gather he's hoping to get a job in some local late-night café or other,' Susie went on, 'and is, generally speaking, ecstatic with his new lot. He never dreamed that life could be so fulfilling!'

'Did he tell you that?'

'He didn't. But you could see it – the shaky ecstasy of freedom . . . a cold, cruel family given the slip . . . etcetera . . .'

'We're not a cold, cruel family,' Polly cried. 'I love him! We all love him. And how can he possibly be fulfilled living in a bed-sit? And what about his Leaving? Does he want to throw his life away? And anyway the whole thing . . . living with a woman without being married . . . is immoral! Give me the address. I'm going to take him home at once!'

'My advice to you, Poll, is to let him be. He'll discover the real joys of sharing a bed-sit with Queen Maeve fairly quickly . . . but only if you leave him alone!'

'I can't just sit here and let my son run wild!'

'Don't just sit there,' Susie said. 'Join the health club in the Pyramid. You can work out all that angst and get into shape at the same time . . . It's not expensive. They've a special offer at the moment . . . for women . . . during the daytime. A free trial offer!'

Polly had a sudden image of herself in a leotard.

'Don't be ridiculous!'

Susie said goodbye then because Mr Penston was looking for her to take dictation, and Polly went back to her kitchen, made a cup of tea, sat on the chair, frowned and laughed intermittently despite herself at the thought of her baby Jason sharing a double bed with Queen Maeve.

'Laughing to oneself is one of the signs . . .' said the unwelcome mentor in her head.

Suddenly she asked aloud: 'How did Susie find out? She didn't say and I forgot to ask her!'

When she heard the post drop on to the mat she found the letter with the London postmark. There was also another letter, one addressed to Rory, and she left it by his computer. For a moment she was afraid to open her letter with the English stamp, dreading that it was another missive from a lovelorn respondent to her ad, but when she glanced at the signature

162

she was surprised by the sense of delight.

She read and re-read the letter from Keith Warrington. She was sorry she no longer had his photograph (she had returned it with the reply to Bernard Whiston), but his face was clear in her mind anyway. She remembered with pleasure their funny, quaint conversation of that Sunday afternoon. He had obviously swallowed her story about her sister. This made Polly feel a bit better about the whole thing.

She took a few sheets of paper from Rory's desk and wrote before she changed her mind:

Dear Keith Warrington,

Thank you for your letter. Yes, I told my sister about our meeting and it made her feel very embarrassed. I really can't say when I'll next be in your locality . . . I have so many things on my plate here – what with business concerns and everything – that it's hard to get away. But I do sympathise with you about your late father-in-law.

The next time my business brings me to London I'll be glad to look at your snuff boxes.

Polly crossed this last sentence out and re-wrote the letter without it.

It was sometime in the middle of that night, for no reason at all, that she woke up with a start, sat up in bed and thought, 'Jesus Christ, didn't I buy a Lotto ticket that week . . . ?'

She lay back again. Rory grunted in his sleep, and she pushed his elbow away from the small of her back, where it was hurting her. 'What?' he said. 'Wha . . . t?' A snore travelled down his nose, turned into a whistle, was ejected.

'Oh shut up,' Polly said.

I bought a ticket that week, she told herself again, that Wednesday before I went to London. At the Lotto stand in the Stephen's Green shopping centre. Wasn't that where they said the missing ticket was bought . . . Where did I put it? It's probably in my bag . . .

She slipped out of bed, went down to the kitchen to look for her handbag.

It can't be significant, she thought; there must have been

hundreds of tickets sold there that day.

Her handbag was hanging behind the door. She opened it, searched the three compartments, removed her wallet, searched it. There was no sign of the Lotto ticket. She emptied the bag on to the table, sorted through the shopping lists, the lipsticks, the hair clips, the credit card receipts, the bill from the dentist, but there was no lottery ticket.

'I know I had it in my bag,' she said aloud. 'Didn't I put it in there? It must have fallen out! But where could it have fallen out?'

The answer, she realised, was more or less anywhere. She sat at the table for a moment and then went back to bed.

It was in the morning that Rory finally told her that he had received a Circuit Court summons for the money he owed his wife.

'How are we going to pay it?'

'I'll have to sell the house, I suppose, Poll . . . We can get somewhere smaller. It won't be so bad!'

He looked at her, raised his shoulders in apology.

Polly stared at him. 'What you mean is it won't be so bad for you because you'll be doing your usual thing . . . and I'll be stuck in some little dump, miles from Susie, with no hope of anything!'

Polly's eyes filled and Rory turned away in exasperation as he always did at the sight of tears.

'There's no need to be so snide, Polly! You might show some sympathy! Now that that little troublemaker Jason has been found I thought you might have more time for the rest of your family!'

Polly stifled her sobs, but did not answer for a moment.

'You didn't find a Lotto ticket wandering about the house, I suppose?' she asked after a moment.

'No. Why . . . have you won something?'

'How the hell should I know if I can't find it?'

Rory compressed his lips and shook his head.

'You should have your head looked at, Poll,' he muttered. 'You're getting very aggressive, a bit strange in yourself!' Rory shook his head again. 'Now where did I put those hex conversion tables?' he muttered.

Polly looked at him for a moment, but Rory had located the missing conversion tables, and had reverted to absorbed contentment.

Polly, for some reason, thought of the gym that Susie attended, of the weights, of the bench press, of the way you could work out utter fury without breaking anyone's head.

Goddammit, she thought, I have an old track suit. Wouldn't that do to start with . . . ?

When Peter came home from college Polly told him the good news about Jason. Peter had been at first defensive over the matter of his brother's disappearance, and latterly rather withdrawn.

She saw the relief that swept his face, lit up his eyes. He turned aside, his body language suddenly vulnerable.

'I knew that little faggot would turn up. What he needs is a good beating!'

'He needs nothing of the kind. And he's not coming home for the moment!' Polly said. 'I had thought of going to get him, but your father and Susie both think he should be allowed to return of his own accord!'

'Yeah . . . Let him stew in his own juice! He'll come back with his tail between his legs.'

Polly clicked her tongue. 'But I can't help worrying! I mean is he eating properly?'

Peter looked at his mother with a great deal of love.

'Mothers are amazing!' he said. 'They really do care.' He looked at her teasingly. 'But I suppose it's all instinct!'

Polly swiped at him, glided her palm over the bent back of his head, felt his close-cropped hair like the pile of a carpet. He gave a purr of pleasure. 'Ah don't be hittin' me, Ma!' he said in a woebegone tone.

'Give me a hug,' Polly ordered. 'I need one.'

Peter obliged. When he let her go he said, his voice very low and uncharacteristically unsteady, 'It wasn't my fault, you know, Mum . . . I didn't drive him away!'

'Oh, Peter, did you think we blamed you?'

She saw at once that her elder son was close to tears.

'Well, the Hobbit did,' he whispered miserably. 'He told me it was all my fault! You heard him!'

165

'You shouldn't refer to your father as the Hobbit,' Polly said sternly. 'It's not respectful . . . And did you see a Lotto ticket kicking around the house?' she asked to change the subject, terrified that her huge son, who towered over her so easily, would give vent to tears.

'No . . . are we in the money or something?'

'No . . . it's just I bought one which I never checked!'

'Don't hold your breath, Mum,' Peter said, recovering his poise. 'The chances are only one in nine million . . .'

When Polly found herself alone she phoned the National Lottery and asked if the winner of the Easter weekend draw had come forward as yet. No, she was told. Then she asked for the winning combination. 1, 14, 15, 21, 32 and 41.

She took them down on a piece of paper and examined them for a while, trying to recall what numbers she had chosen. She had chosen 1, she remembered that. And she thought she remembered choosing 21 and also 14 and 15.

She phoned the Lottery again.

'I think I may have won the Easter prize,' she said.

'Have you the winning ticket?' the pleasant young voice asked.

'Well, no . . . Unfortunately I've lost it!'

'I see . . .'

'You mean you don't believe me?' Polly said, aware of the nuance.

'Well we do, actually, need the hard evidence!'

Polly put the phone down, muttered, 'I know you need the bloody evidence . . . Do you take me for an eejit?'

But where had she put the ticket?

Muriel appeared that evening to say how delighted she was that Jason had been found.

Polly, relaxing for the first time since Jason's disappearance, had been perusing one of her History of Art books, a tome on Egyptology. She left it open on the coffee table and answered the door, invited her neighbour in and offered her some tea. Muriel said she'd love a cup. Then she proceeded to tell Polly that she had lost a lot of weight; 'become so svelte' was how she put it.

'Have I?' Polly said, angling a glance at herself in the mirror. It was true. She had noticed her waist band being loose, but she saw how her face had narrowed, how her double chin had receded.

'You look very pretty,' Muriel said.

Polly flushed. 'I was when I was young!' she said.

'You still are! Nothing like anxiety to trim one down, I suppose . . .' Muriel continued.

'I suppose not,' Polly said, knowing that this was true, knowing that while Jason had been missing she had had difficulty getting any food down her constricted throat.

But as she turned back to her guest it occurred to her that the face before her was unnaturally pale and the eyes seemed large and lacklustre.

'Are *you* all right? Muriel, you look a bit under the weather if you don't mind me saying so!'

'Oh, I'm fine, thank you. Although sometimes I get a bit dizzy! Silly isn't it!' Muriel spoke in her usual precise voice, but the covert need for reassurance lingered on the last syllables, hung in the air. 'I suppose it's old age creeping up!' she ended on a note of forced jollity.

'Well, it's not old age,' Polly said. 'You're young yet!' and then she thought of Susie and her comments on Muriel's drinking and suddenly wondered if there was any truth in them. But she was saved by the ring of the doorbell. It was none other than Susie herself.

'Muriel's here!' Polly said sotto voce.

'Oh God . . . look, I'll come back later . . . I just wanted to tell you that little Peggy Kinlan has had a baby girl and both are fine . . .'

'Was that Susie?' Muriel asked when Polly returned to the sitting room.

'Yes. She couldn't stay . . . she just wanted to tell me that Peggy Kinlan has had her baby . . . a girl. Mother and baby are both fine!'

'That will be such a relief to poor Madge!' Muriel murmured. 'She's been so worried! Susie is so dynamic,' she added, 'so full of beans! And it can't be an easy time for her . . . I gather her husband will be redundant at the end of the month . . .'

Polly tried to keep the smile tacked on to her face. She thought that Fergus's redundancy was none of Muriel's business.

'Who told you that?'

'Laura Flanagan.'

'She's an awful gossip!'

Muriel looked taken aback. 'I didn't mean to say anything out of turn, Polly . . .'

'Oh, it's not you, Muriel . . .'

Muriel toyed with a biscuit. 'Polly,' she said, glancing around the room, noting her statuette of the Young Lady on the mantelpiece, her gaze lingering on the book entitled *The Wonders of Ancient Egypt*, 'did you never think of making a career for yourself . . . with your background in History of Art it's a bit of a waste isn't it, just being here all the time . . . ?' She paused. 'But perhaps I'm speaking out of turn again! I just thought that maybe you get bored sometimes!'

'Bored is an understatement!' Polly said with a grim laugh. 'I've applied for a job in the Civil Service recently, but I'll have to sit an exam.'

'Good for you!'

Muriel was silent as she turned a page in the book on Egyptology. Then she said, 'This looks so interesting. I've never been to Egypt, have you?'

'No.' Polly's eyes followed the turning of the pages, lingered on the face of the lovely Nefertiti, on the strange countenance of her husband, the Pharaoh Akhnaton. 'I'll go sometime, before I die . . . I'll do it, even if I have to walk! You see, the extraordinary thing about Egyptian art . . . at least to me . . . is its utterly seamless spiritual power, its serenity. When you compare it against Greek art – where you have so much aggressive hedonism, so much individual assertion – you realise what millennia of peaceful theocracy does for the mind-set and perceptions of a people . . .'

Polly stopped, looked dubiously at Muriel, afraid she was boring her. She was used to her occasional outpourings on matters artistic meeting with glazed uninterest. But her visitor was regarding her with grave attention.

'You have great passion in you, Polly . . . I understand that!' She lowered her voice. 'Passion brings belief, which is why it is so important that it should be well directed! Tell me . . . what would you do if you had a lot of money . . . would you visit all these places, see the things you so love?'

'Oh yes,' Polly said with a smile. 'But if I could even re-visit the Louvre – I was there once when I was a student – I remember the Egyptian section, the mummy in the sarcophagus, bound in linen cere-cloths, her little hands wrapped so securely, her small blindfolded head tilted back with such grace . . . ah . . . it was as though she spoke . . . down through the reaches of several thousand years . . .'

Polly did not realise how her eyes changed colour and how the warmth came and went in her face.

'Do any of your family share your love of Art?' Muriel asked in a half-whisper, touched to the heart.

Polly shrugged, sat back and said with a sigh, 'Not really . . . They find modernity adequately fills their cup with wonder . . .'

When Muriel had gone Polly went upstairs, looked at herself in the mirror, saw that she was indeed much slimmer, just as Muriel had said. She hunted in a drawer of old clothes and took out a skirt she had not been able to squeeze herself into for years. It glided on.

She gazed at herself in the mirror, brushed the hair back off her face. 'A few highlights in that hair, another pound or two off . . . Perhaps all is not lost . . .'

She left the straight black skirt on, put on a white blouse which had been a favourite before the buttons had begun to open across the bust every time she moved. It fitted. She flexed her arms. The buttons stayed closed.

She took off the blouse, sat on the end of her bed. Oh God, she thought, thank you for finding Jason. Now all I need is to make sure we can keep the house. Should I try to talk to Martha, ask her to call her hounds off, tell her I'm going to get a job and that I'll get a loan and pay her off? Who'd give me a job? History of Art is not a prime subject, especially not in Ireland. Fine Art here is a closed shop. But there must be someone who'll give me a job, somewhere. And if Jason is not at home and Peter is finishing at college and Rory lives in cyberspace, why shouldn't I . . . try for a job in London? Why shouldn't I do the bloody impossible?

She searched for and found her old navy Nike tracksuit. It was on Death Row – the landing chest of drawers where she had put things that might be still of some use. She put it on. The trousers were baggy. 'But it's serviceable ... it's serviceable ...'

Peter met his mother on the stairs.

'Haven't seen you in that old thing for yonks, Mum! What are you up to?'

'I'm off to re-make my person, young man. And no, you can't have any extra money this weekend,' she added as Peter looked at her with the woebegone expression that was the usual precursor to requests for beer money. 'Being still of relatively sane mind I'm going to spend my money on me!'

# Chapter Twelve

'You are dynamic, highly motivated, with a good degree
and an ability to deal with people. You have a knowledge
of antiques and fine art. We are an established auction
gallery, specialising in Georgian, Regency and Victorian
furniture, sculpture, miniatures, silver, longcase clocks,
bronzes and *objets d'art*, sold on the instructions of
Executors, Trustees, and Notable Collectors. You could be
the person we're looking for as assistant to the managing
director. Please send full c.v., starting salary, to Shetly and
Sons, New Bond Street, London . . .'

It took up a relatively small space in the Appointments
supplement of the *Sunday Times*.

Polly looked at it for a while, wistfully, an exile looking back,
a voyeur on a world forsaken. Shetly and Sons. She knew of
them. They were not in the same league as Sothebys, but were
a serious outfit. She turned the page, ran her eyes over the
other job-offers – for managing directors, company executives,
business analysts and project managers, over the half-page
advertisement which promised 'Tomorrow's Communications
Today'.

I already have tomorrow's communication today, she thought
sourly, and look where it's got me.

But even though she folded and put down the paper and
directed herself to washing up the egg-stained breakfast plates,
her thoughts returned to Shetly and Sons. It was as though
the small advertisement had brought with it the breath of the
world she loved, the mystique, the atmosphere, the smell of
old things, polished rosewood and mahogany, the soft sheen of

171

bronze, the mellow gleam of silver, and whispers of an elegance long gone.

When she had finished washing up and had put everything away Polly muttered aloud: 'Nothing ventured nothing gained. But I have about as much hope of getting this job as I have of flying to the moon! How can someone undertake a job which is pivoted on the world of the sophisticated and wealthy, who has hardly a good skirt to wear and has not engaged in decent conversation since 1970?'

Rory was chez O'Brien, working over something with Fergus on the latter's computer. Sue had gone out and Ferg did not know where. 'She's gone off for a dander,' he said when Polly went over to talk to her. 'She said she needed to be alone! Where do you think she might have gone? What on earth does she want to be alone for?'

'I don't know!'

'She didn't ask you to go?' he demanded half suspiciously.

'No, Fergus. Despite appearances, we are not Siamese twins!'

Polly went home and drafted a c.v. She put her heart into it; she didn't have much to offer in the way of experience, but the c.v. detailed her career as an antiquarian, short though it had been, before she married Rory. She had been with Adams in Dublin, and had followed antiques ever since. She had a first-class honours degree in the History of Art; she had written a couple of pieces in a collector magazine called *Times Past*. She was particularly knowledgeable about silver. She had married and had two children, but she was now free to pursue a career as her children were grown up. She was prepared to start at a low salary and would be in London in the near future and available for interview. When she had perfected the letter and c.v. she went downstairs, turned on the computer, tapped out the c.v. and printed it out. Then she put on a jacket and slipped out to the postbox in the village.

As she returned up the main estate road she heard a voice hail her and, turning, saw Muriel pulling up in her car.

'Hello, Polly,' the latter called, leaning through the open window. 'Hop in! I'll give you a lift!'

'I need the walk, but thanks all the same.'

But Muriel showed little inclination to drive away. 'You're

looking a lot better since Jason was found,' she said.

'I suspect that Susie must have put a private investigator on his tail!' Polly said ruefully. 'She's evasive about it . . . but I don't see how else she could have found out where he was!'

Muriel turned expressionless eyes on her. 'Did she really? . . . I've a favour to ask of you, Polly,' she added, 'if you don't mind!'

Polly said politely that she didn't in the least. In fact she did mind, not because whatever small service Muriel would ask of her would be in any way burdensome, but because there was something about Muriel which always made her feel that she had been rounded up, commandeered, herded into the glow of a rich woman's approval. It was a bit like the feeling she got in school when she was briefly teacher's pet, and too delighted by the attention to dodge it.

'I may be going away for a while soon . . .' Muriel went on. 'And I was wondering if you would keep an eye on the house . . . I'll leave the keys and the burglar alarm number with you . . .'

'Of course. Are you going somewhere nice?' Polly added, containing the envy which suddenly snaked through her, a tide of involuntary begrudgery. Muriel was probably off to the Seychelles or somewhere glorious, and the cost would make the same dent in her private exchequer as tea and a bun in Bewleys would make in Polly's coffers.

But her neighbour did not answer immediately. Then she gave Polly a small smile and said she wasn't too sure just yet, but she'd let Polly know.

Watching her neighbour's car glide away with a twenty-four carat purr, Polly permitted herself an envious whisper, 'Oh, Muriel . . . you are blest and don't know it . . .'

Laura Flanagan passed her on the pavement with her collie, Scrumpy, straining on a leash. Laura heard the private exclamation and gave Polly a queer look.

'Talking to myself . . .' Polly explained hastily, 'first sign of madness!'

'Was that Muriel Reeves?' Laura enquired, looking down the road after the departing Aston Martin.

Laura always had such an unsettling effect that Polly was on the point of divulging that Muriel would be going away and had asked her to mind the house, but she held her tongue.

Laura's question, however, had been rhetorical, and without waiting for an answer she added that, of course, her father used to be the Reeveses' GP. She had even seen Muriel coming for her appointments during the school holidays. 'She had a brace in those days . . . She was very quiet . . . but a lovely girl, of course . . . a real lady. When I reminded her about the old times she remembered me well, you know . . .'

Polly noticed how small dry gulches had formed in Laura's upper-lip, and wondered why her parents had not done something to straighten her teeth.

Laura looked at Polly's clothes, priced them swiftly, and permitted herself be dragged along by Scrumpy.

'Oops, sometimes I wonder who is taking whom out for a walk!'

When Polly got home, Rory was still out. Peter was in his room, ostensibly studying, and Jason had not come home, something she always hoped would miraculously occur. But at least, she comforted herself, she knew he was safe. She went into the front garden to pick the few remaining daffs and brought them indoors. As she was putting them in water the phone rang.

'Hello, Mum,' the sheepish voice said.

For a moment she didn't recognise it; the voice of her younger son was half tentative, half defiant. But there was a tinge to it of something she had never heard with him, a gravity associated with reluctant responsibility.

'Jason! Are you all right?'

'I'm fine . . .'

Polly was about to launch into a full-scale lament about what he had done by running away from home, but she thought of all the warnings Susie and Rory and Peter had handed out. Besides, a tide of an anger she had been trying to contain rose unbidden.

'Well, that's good anyway!'

'Aren't you going to ask me where I am?'

There was a faintly surprised tone to this query, but Polly thought she detected underneath it a certain smugness.

'No.'

'Why not?'

'Because I know where you are . . . and I think it's time you

174

stopped that nonsense and came home!'

Jason's voice lost its complacency and became hard and querulous. He was on firm ground now; he had been challenged.

'Mrs O'Brien shouldn't have told you where I am. She promised she wouldn't. I'm my own master, Mum. I'll do what I want with my life . . . Whether people like it or not is their problem . . .'

'Is that what you phoned to tell me?'

'No . . .' The voice became quieter, 'I just wanted to see if you were all right . . .'

'I'm fine.'

'Is everything OK otherwise . . . ?'

'If you want to know whether we're still at fourteen Ashgrove Lawns the answer is in the affirmative. But if you want to know whether we will continue at fourteen Ashgrove Lawns while you languish between return and desertion, the answer is maybe . . . depending of course on when you decide to put in your next appearance!'

There was silence. Then Jason's voice became smaller, lost its masterful tenor.

'You're not thinking of moving, Mum, are you?'

'Of course. Your father's wife wants money and there are no children here any more, only big, masterful types. But if you want me to save any of your things – old teddy bears, Action Force dolls, army Jeeps, Asterix books, spent chewing gum stuck to your headboard, rolled-up poster of young woman with no clothes – you can send me an inventory.'

'I don't believe you, Mum! And that poster . . . it's not mine . . . it belongs to—'

'I know, I know, it has nothing to do with you. You're just minding it for a deserving friend . . . And I'm getting a job in London!'

'London!' Jason yelped. 'But . . . you can't go to live in London?'

'Why not?'

After a pause a small voice said, 'But . . . what will we do?'

'Frankly, my dear,' Polly said, dripping the famous cliché slowly into the mouthpiece, 'I don't give a damn!'

'Mum!'

'Yes?'

'Are you sure you're all right?'

'Never better.'

'Could you lend me twenty quid? I'll pay you back next week!'

And thus we come to the nub of things, Polly thought.

'I'll send you ten pounds. That's the best I can do. People who embark on the seas of freedom should examine their coffers first!'

'But, Mum . . .'

When she put down the phone Polly began to dissect the conversation. I should have been nicer to him, came the habitual thought. Why the hell should you, demanded her new interior self. He runs away, he doesn't care what it does to you; then he has the neck to come looking for money. For the first time in her life Polly experienced anger as an authentic force, something to which she was entitled, a galvanic energy on course towards redemption. The sound of reproachful mewling came from outside the kitchen door. Cat had been fed earlier, but now felt her repast had been inadequate.

That cat, Polly thought, is driving me crazy! She suddenly wanted to go out and kick the cat's bottom, but as soon as this thought was formed the anger died, as though frightened by itself.

Polly put her head in her hands. I'm going crazy, she told her knuckles. I'm strained to the limit, pretending, pretending that I can cope. I don't think I can cope any more, not unless I change everything. And that will take more resources, especially emotional resources, than I may have.

She let Cat in, picked her up, stroked her funny tail on which the fur was making a come-back.

'You're a survivor, you poor old thing,' she informed her. 'There are lessons to be learnt from you, and all of them are about persistence!'

Cat began to purr.

Polly thought of her application for the London job which would be on its way tomorrow, wondered if she stood the slightest chance. If I had some money, I would have some freedom. This reminded her again of the lost Lotto ticket.

Upstairs she went through all her drawers, looking out for a distinctive small form with numbers, but there was none. No pink ticket appeared in any of the recesses she searched. When there was no sign of it she thought, I've obviously lost it. And then the weight of the what-if descended on her; *what if* the bloody thing had really been THE ticket? She could be a multi-millionaire and not know it. The more she thought about it, the more certain she became that it was hers. She could now remember clearly putting 1 and 21 on the form and also 14 and 15, because they were the numbers of her own and Susie's houses. That was four numbers. If she had the other two as well she was the winner. All the indications were in her favour. The ticket had been bought around the time stated by the Lotto people; it had been bought in the same outlet as the winning ticket; no one had as yet come forward, although four weeks had now elapsed. What did that look like?

Oh God . . . I should ask Michelle if she found it. Maybe I left it in the flat. She tried to relive what she had done on her arrival in London. She retraced her steps to Sloane Street underground station on the Sunday; had anything fallen out of her bag when she rooted for change? No, she could not remember. What about on the tube? But she hadn't opened her bag on the tube; there would have been no reason to do so. The same held true for getting off at Wimbledon and walking to Keith Warrington's house. And then she remembered, suddenly and clearly, hunting in the bottom of her bag for her foundation cream while she was in his loo. She had been in a bit of a tizz. The kitchen sink could have fallen out and she wouldn't have noticed. She could have left the stupid thing behind in his house.

What was the best thing to do? Write and say, 'Dear Keith . . . did you find my Lotto ticket in your loo?'

No. It was bad enough turning up with her idiotic letter, without subsequently writing ridiculous notes seeking lost Lotto tickets. Polly reddened, thinking of how foolish she had been, and how fatuous she would seem to the nicest man she had ever met.

I can't go writing to him looking for the bloody ticket, she thought after a moment. He's probably thrown it out and will have to go rooting in the bin. Or, by now, it's gone to the rubbish tip and been eaten by a seagull. It's too much. It's more than four million quid's worth of embarrassment. I just can't do it. I just can't.

* * *

She began to clear out her old clothes, making a heap of rejects, emptying on to the landing the stuff which had been on Death Row for years, and been constantly reprieved. Methodically and ruthlessly she threw out things that had been eyeing her apprehensively for a decade. Some of her more recent clothes were now too big, so she threw these out too. She found her old shoes and fired them into a plastic sack.

Peter came out of his room. 'What are you doing, Mum? Anyone would think you were preparing for an evacuation!'

'I am!'

He stood looking at her with an uncertain smile, but his eyes seemed anxious.

'It might interest you to know that I spoke to Jason earlier this morning,' Polly said.

Peter's eyes lit up. 'So the little snot phoned?'

'Don't call your brother a little snot!' Polly said angrily. 'I won't stand for any more of that!'

'Sorree . . . Is he coming home?'

Polly permitted herself a small, grim smile; 'I gather he's not ready for the Prodigal's return just yet . . . but I can't help feeling that the gilt is beginning to wear off the gingerbread!'

'You're a bit of a Machiavelli, Mum,' Peter said after a moment while he regarded her quizzically. 'I thought you would be so shocked with him running away, living with Veronica, that you would be prostrate! Instead you're actually sardonic!'

'I was sardonic before I met either of my children! I didn't spring into existence the day you two laid gummy eyes on me. And to tell you the truth I feel a bit sorry for that girl!'

'Why?'

'She's looking for something she won't get in that adolescent quarter. But she'll find out the hard way!'

'Mum!' Peter said, pretending to be shocked, his voice full of double entendre. 'The hard way!'

'Oh, go off and do your study!'

'Where's Dad?'

'Where is he ever? If it's not his own computer you can be sure it will be the one next nearest him!'

'So he's next door?'

'I believe so.'

Peter stood uncertainly for another moment while more items were hurled on to the reject heap.

'I'm going out for a while . . .'

Polly was preparing lunch when Rory returned with Fergus in tow. Peter, who had stooped to chat up the cat, came in behind them.

'Hello, Polly.'

'Hi, Ferg. How's everything?'

Rory produced a bunch of flowers from behind his back and deposited them sheepishly on the table.

'What's this for?' Polly asked, touched in spite of herself. For some reason she could not identify she wanted to burst into tears.

'Do I have to have a reason?'

Fergus looked a little self-conscious. Peter smiled. Polly suddenly knew that he had put his father up to the gesture.

'Thanks, Rory.' She took the flowers to the sink and scouted for the big glass vase.

'We've been having a chat about Ferg's future,' Rory said, as though he had to explain himself.

'You'll find something,' Polly assured her neighbour. 'Good software engineers must be at a premium!'

'Well, there are a lot of whizz-kids coming on the market now . . . and they don't cost as much. But I have a trick or two in reserve yet,' Fergus said without conviction.

Rory looked at him meaningfully and the two men went into the dining room.

'Poll,' Rory's voice came, 'did you turn on the computer?'

'Yes.'

'What did you want it for?'

Rory was now framed in the doorway.

'I wanted to use the word processor . . . I had to write a letter.'

'What letter was that?'

Polly put the chicken in the roasting tin, with a bit of butter paper on its breast. She popped it in the oven.

'Just a letter looking for a job!'

'A job . . . What kind of a job could you get . . . ?'

His voice tended to the incredulous. He was amused.

For a moment Polly almost told him. Instead she shrugged.

'Can you imagine our Poll with a job!' he asked Fergus.

'Of course,' came the hearty response from the dining room.

'Thank you, Ferg! All votes of confidence are appreciated!' Polly called.

Rory went back into the dining room and shut the door. Polly could hear the clicking of the computer keys, the two men's voices, hushed and reverential as though they were in church.

'Is Fergus here?' Susie demanded, coming round about an hour later.

'Yes, he was wondering where you had got to.'

'Oh, I just needed to get out for a bit!'

Polly regarded her friend for a moment. 'Is something wrong, Sue?'

'No, and yes. I'm scared Willy Penston is going to give me the sack.'

'What on earth makes you think that? I thought you two got on very well!'

'Just because he showed me his new flat? Don't read anything into that. I was a model of decorum and so was he! It's a lovely flat incidentally . . .'

'So what is it?'

'Well, Muriel has been around to see him a couple of times lately. And he's been a bit strange since, looks at me as though I'd done something weird.'

'Did you meet her?'

'No. She came on my afternoons off. And I don't know what she wanted to see him about. It's top secret. I don't think there was even an attendance note for anyone to type! And now Willy has become cagey about the work he gives me . . . She couldn't have said anything bad about me, could she, Poll? She knows him quite well, you know . . . his father was her dad's solicitor! I know I haven't always been nice to her, but . . .'

She sat on the edge of her chair and gnawed her thumb.

'You're good at your work,' Polly said. 'You get on very well with him. Why should he want to get rid of you?'

'I'm paranoid. It's just that if I lose this job . . . I don't know what we'll do. There's still the mortgage to pay, and there's no sign of Ferg landing a new job . . . He's like a cat on a hot plate.

I don't know what to do with him. His pride can't take the scrap heap! He's irritable and . . . changed! We go around trying not to walk on each other's toes. Why do things change, Polly? Why can't they stay the way they were? We used to be so good together!'

Polly looked at her friend. 'Because we cannot stay still. Momentum, for better or worse, is finally the name of the game!'

'You've changed too . . . become a bit formidable!'

'Have I? Someone once told me I should be seduced by life! I've decided to give it a chance!'

Sue indicated the dining-room door. 'What are our menfolk doing now?'

'All deliberations are top secret!'

'Do I detect a hint of sarcasm, Polly Caine?' She leaned back and sighed. 'I'm sorry – coming in here and moaning. And you're wearing away, Poll! How are you managing to lose so much weight?'

'I'm training myself to live without food!' Polly said with a mirthless laugh. 'It's the final solution! I mean – why bother with Zyklon B when starvation is free!'

She glanced at Susie, who was frowning. 'And I took your advice and enrolled in the gym . . . Special offer for the first three months and I'm going to make the most of it!'

Sue evinced astonishment. 'Good for you. I never thought you had it in you!'

Susie went to the dining room, opened the door and said, 'Fergus O'Brien, your lunch is ready!'

'Hi, Susie,' Rory said, in his slow, don't-bother-me-now computer voice.

'Do I have to sign the Official Secrets Act or can I just come in?' Susie demanded.

There was a small attempt at mirth. Both men were seated at Rory's computer, leaning forward to examine some graphics on the monitor.

'Where were you?' Fergus asked conversationally.

'I was out; I went for a drive to clear my head, meet my lover, have a quicky before lunch. Where do you think I was?'

But Fergus didn't answer and seemed to be excited by whatever was appearing on the screen.

'Goddammit,' Susie said on her way out. 'He's getting just

like Rory. The two of them should be tied into a sack with the latest offering from Silicon Valley and dumped into the Liffey at high tide!'

'Sue . . . did you retain a private detective to trace Jason?' Polly asked suddenly.

'Where did you get that idea from?'

'I just can't work out how else you came to know where he was! I met Muriel this morning . . . and she seemed to think you were behind all this.'

'Detective Muriel . . . !'

'So it's true!'

Susie hesitated. 'Look . . . don't worry about it!'

'I love you, Susie, and I'll pay you back. What did it cost?'

Sue looked uncomfortable. 'You mean she didn't tell you? She was actually able to keep her mouth shut?'

'We're very unkind about Muriel. She's not so bad. Incidentally, she's off on holiday. She's asked me to keep an eye on things for her!'

'There's nothing poor about that woman except her sensitivity! But have fun curating *le grand palais*!'

Polly felt ill at ease. She knew this constant criticism of Muriel was rooted in something much darker than mere justice.

'But what do I owe you, Susie? You must tell me!'

'Nothing. You can talk to me about it when you win the Lotto!'

This comment made Polly start. 'Sue . . .' she said, dropping her voice to a whisper.

Susie looked at her expectantly. 'Well, what is it? Go on . . .'

'You remember the Lotto prize that no one claimed?'

'. . . You mean the Easter prize?'

'Yes . . . I think I might have won the bloody thing, but I can't find the ticket!'

Susie's face assumed first an expression of amusement, as though this were a joke to be shared, then one of utter incredulity when she realised that Polly was serious.

'I bought it in Stephen's Green shopping centre about the time the winning ticket was purchased,' Polly went on doggedly. 'I know I had some of the numbers . . .' She glanced at her friend's uncertain face. 'I'm not joking . . .'

'What did you do with it?'

'Lost it!'

'The winner hasn't come forward yet . . . Oh God . . . just think . . . if you have won it . . . it's worth an utter fortune!'

'I think I might have lost it in London . . . perhaps in the house of someone I visited while I was there!'

'Michelle. . . ?'

'No . . . I don't think it was in her place . . . someone else's. It was a person I visited on the Sunday afternoon.'

'Who was that?'

'Just a bloke!'

Susie shot her a penetrating look. 'Have you asked this bloke?'

'No . . . I'm too embarrassed!'

Susie put her palms against the sides of her head.

'Get on that phone and find out, you eejit. With four million quid you can buy plenty of embarrassment balm.'

Before she went Susie added, 'And for God's sake don't talk to Muriel about this . . . if you don't want it all over the entire estate!'

When Sue was gone Polly phoned London. Michelle answered.

'Darling,' she said, 'here I was thinking of you and wondering how you were getting on!'

'Michelle, I know this will sound silly, but did I leave anything behind me in your place . . . Anything like a piece of paper . . . ?'

'A piece of paper?'

'Well, a Lotto ticket actually,' Polly said with some diffidence.

'A Lotto ticket? Did you win something?'

'I don't know . . . I feel so foolish about it, but I suppose I'd better check everywhere just in case!'

'I'm sorry, Polly. You left nothing here!' She paused; 'When are you coming for another visit? Tom and I would love to have you.'

'Oh, is he there now?' Polly asked eagerly.

'"Fraid not. He's a workaholic you know . . . Now you can see why I was so delighted you stayed with me at Easter. I'm not cut out for solitude!' She paused and added, 'So when am I going to have the pleasure of your company again? You'd better come soon, because I'll be going away for a while!'

Polly thought she detected a hint of mockery in Michelle's voice. She was about to decline politely, and then she thought

183

of her application for the job. Well, I might be invited for interview, she thought. You never know.

'I might just take you up on that . . . I don't know yet! I may be coming to London in the near future!'

'Well, let me know . . . You can use the flat anyway even if I'm not here . . .'

Then Polly added that nothing definite was decided, it was just that she had applied for a job in the fine arts business.

'That would suit you exactly, Polly! Oh, do it . . . don't spend your life looking back and kicking yourself . . .'

When she put the phone down Polly went to find Keith Warrington's letter. His phone number was on it. Oh courage, courage, you fool, she told herself. Phone the man. Ask him.

When Muriel got home she shut the front door behind her and looked around her spacious hall, up the curving staircase with crimson carpet to where the stained-glass window shed a kaleidoscope of colour on to the walls.

Her pleasure in this elegant fastness was muted; she saw it for a moment as a mirage, something which had promised but had not delivered.

She put her shoulder bag on the hall table, went up to her bedroom, took off her shoes and put on slippers, stood by the window and watched for a moment the Sunday morning saunter of the cul-de-sac.

Polly could be dimly seen in her sitting room arranging some flowers.

Someone was talking to a neighbour over the garden wall. The two O'Brien children, Mark and Sharon, were among a knot of teenagers heading down the lane behind Muriel's house to have a smoke. Muriel had often watched them from one of the back bedrooms, had seen how they adroitly hid the offending cigarettes if a parent appeared, losing them swiftly in the ivy.

It touched her, this dance between the generations, parents so absorbed in their young that they had no time for themselves; their young absorbed in doing what they wanted despite all parental strictures, because their imperatives were to find themselves and make their own mistakes. She was glad she had been able to help find Jason. It would never do for Polly to find out; she might think it was interfering. Better to let her think Susie had done it.

When the phone rang, she jumped. The pleasure of hearing Claire's voice at the other end of the line was almost sensual.

'Hello, Claire. How lovely to hear you . . .'

'Hello, Muriel; how are you keeping?'

'Fine . . . you've become quite a stranger!'

Muriel was sorry she had said this. It sounded like a complaint and was followed by a momentary silence at the other end of the line.

'Well . . . you know, what with the children and the house. I'm always dashing around like a lunatic . . . no time for anything. But I rang to tell you we're moving to Frankfurt.'

'When?'

'In July. It's just for three years! Nigel has been made European manager!'

'Congratulations! But what are you going to do about the children?'

'Well, Ellen and Gavin will go to boarding school. We're taking the younger ones with us!'

'It sounds exciting . . .'

'I'd prefer to stay put. But it'll be a change of scene.'

Claire then proceeded to tell Muriel about the restaurant in the West End where she and Nigel had recently dined. 'And you won't believe who was there, Muriel. A blast from the past . . .'

'Who?'

'A certain Alan Barrington!'

'Oh,' Muriel said. In her stomach was the cold void, familiar, hated, the weight of yesteryear's baggage, unresolved.

'And he had a dolly bird with him! But I don't think he recognised me,' Claire went on. 'He hasn't changed very much; he must have discovered the elixir of eternal youth, Dorian Gray in person! Oh, there's a certain jaded dissipation around the eyes, of course, and he's older, but wearing it well . . . I felt sorry for the girl, so obviously flattered . . . innocent as a rabbit . . .'

Muriel could find nothing to say. What the name Alan Barrington conjured was more than she could understand,

185

or could impart, or would pretend.

But suddenly, as she pictured Alan sitting across the table from his dinner date, from a girl young enough to be his daughter, she saw him as though for the first time. She saw his terrible need, his insecurity; she saw his assumption of his right to plunder; above all she saw his hate. He was not a man full of life, of fire, as she had once thought. No, his agendas were something else altogether, rooted in fear and predation.

'Muriel?'

'Yes?'

'Have I stuck my foot in it? You're not still carrying a candle for that fellow?'

'Oh no,' Muriel said in a strange, thoughtful voice which left no room for doubt. 'Not any more. Look, Claire,' she added, 'why don't you come over for a break before you leave for Frankfurt! We could have a laugh, take off for the west!'

'Thanks for the thought, darling. It would be lovely. But I don't know where I'd get the time. You'll have to come and visit us in Frankfurt.'

Muriel knew with sudden certainty that she would never set foot in Germany.

'Thanks, Claire,' she said. 'I would love to, sometime! I keep getting these headaches . . . Maybe when they begin to ease up . . .'

'Have you seen a doctor? If you're getting persistent headaches you should see someone.'

'Yes, I know . . .'

When she put down the phone Muriel opened the doors of both her wardrobes, examined for a moment her copious designer outfits.

'These are the badges of despair!' she thought. 'Not in themselves, but simply in my personal context. I tried to buy meaning and it cannot be purchased. When I come back, if I come back, I will give them away!'

She thought of Alan Barrington with a pity that astonished her. She had dressed him in borrowed robes. The sudden glimpse which had been vouchsafed her, had been as though she had seen him naked, stripped of lies and pretensions. In that instant the anguish which had blighted years of her life was gone. It was broken like a glass icon, shattered into small pitiful shards. She saw that he possessed nothing except what he stole; that he was, in reality, a man of no importance. The clarity of this perception left no room for error, made her wonder why she should have had to wait so long to access the truth.

She could recall now, without blocking it, the sequel to her affair.

When Michael had returned from Saudi Arabia, Muriel, half mad with pain, had confessed to him.

'A filthy old roué like that!' he said in a voice she had never heard him use before. 'You let a philandering ape who has been up every skirt in the county into your bed!'

'I thought he loved me! He said he did . . . I trusted him. I'm sorry . . . I'm sorry! Oh, Michael, I'm sorry! I don't know why I did it . . .'

But Michael could not forgive, was not old enough to forgive.

Muriel had swallowed a bottle of her mother's sleeping tablets. Claire, her friend and colleague, had called and found her, had made Muriel vomit by shoving her fingers down her throat.

When she was discharged from hospital Muriel resigned from the bank and sold the land around the house to a developer for more money than she had ever dreamed of. The proceeds – three million pounds – had allowed her to immerse herself in completely restoring her old home, in changing it to accord with her vision of what a home should be, bright, beautiful, benign. There had been pleasure in seeing it refurbished, although there was one door which was never opened, one room which lay in perpetual shadow, like a corpse lying for ever in state – the room that had once been her father's study.

But she had pleasure in the sense of the new era, in going through the chest of exquisite antique linen, of having paintings cleaned and restored, in knowing that she did not have to run to the landing with a basin when it lashed rain. True, the stables were gone, as were the avenue and fields, and all that was left was a garden which the builders landscaped for her. Around her sprang up the new semi-detached houses. She watched as couples moved in, as curtains appeared on the windows and prams on the newly laid pavement. Then she threw a party and asked everyone in the cul-de-sac outside her new front gates.

The housing estate grew around her; she lived in its midst, belonging without belonging. Claire married an English bank executive, Nigel Denton, and went to live in England.

For a long time Muriel had hoped that Michael would come back. She had dreams where she found him at the door in the middle of the night, forgiving and forgiven. They would be married – she saw them in Westland Row register office, a quick civil wedding. And then the house would change and mellow, would resound with the laughter of children.

But the dawn always revealed her folly; the big house around her, despite everything that she had done to lift its atmosphere, became forlorn and brooding. It had kept her here, like Miss Havisham, until she was no longer fit for the world. The love she had for it seemed increasingly demonic, a force of possession like a comely devil, familiar but intractable and a great, bloodless, substitute for life.

# Chapter Thirteen

Keith Warrington was composing his thoughts on the subject of paranoid schizophrenia when the phone rang.

Its bleep was inopportune; it disturbed a nicely rounded turn of phrase that was on the tip of his fingers. He liked rounding out his sentences, honing his phrases so that they flowed. He saw no reason why medical treatises should suffer from constipation. What was written should be readable; he had waded through enough turgid and self-conscious obscuration to be sensitised to it.

His hypothesis was that schizophrenic hallucinations were jointly generated by the cerebral structures regulating thinking and emotions, and by the regions that processed sights and sounds. In tandem these gave hallucinations a reality comparable to any tangible experience. If the brain circuits responsible could be precisely located, the medications could be fine-tuned . . .

It was another Sunday evening, another glorious day. Through the French windows he could see that the garden was at its zenith of seduction, hybrid tea and musk roses competing in pink profusion, the lovely Queen of Denmark pouring forth her fragrance in the sunlight. Herbie slept in the soft shade, too torpid to snap at butterflies or even bark at the briefly trespassing Jocasta, the neighbour's Siamese cat who wore a black suede collar and examined him with eyes of lapiz lazuli from her hiding place by the garden wall.

Keith picked up the phone.

'Hello?'

'Is that Keith Warrington?' a hesitant female voice enquired, and in a moment Keith, hearing the accent, the way the r's were embraced, knew who was at the other end of the line.

'Pauline! How nice to hear from you!'

Polly laughed, something she had not expected of herself.

'I shouldn't be phoning you . . . You'll think I'm crazy . . .'

'Try me!'

'Well, there are two reasons prompting this call: the first is that I may be in London in the near future . . .'

'Good. Will you have a look at those old things I told you about?'

'Yes . . . of course, if you like.'

There was silence for a moment, but before it could become awkward Keith said, 'And the second thing?'

'Well, I'm afraid it's too stupid for words . . .' Polly said, adding hurriedly, 'I can't possibly mention it . . . I'm terribly sorry!'

'It's too late for that,' Keith said drily. 'You already have mentioned it: all you have to do now is be specific!'

Polly made a strangled sound. 'OK. Well, I think I may have dropped a . . . Lotto ticket in your loo!'

'I see.'

'I don't mean into your loo . . . I mean I may have let it fall on the floor. The thing is . . . it may be worth a few pounds!'

'I see.'

Polly knew from the tone of his voice that Keith didn't see at all. She hated the way his voice had become careful.

'I know you must think I'm cracked,' she said with sudden acerbity. 'But I've actually lost a stupid Lotto ticket and the indications are that it may be worth something. The winner for that particular prize has not come forward and I bought it around the time and at the place where the winning combination of numbers was sold!'

Keith ran his fingers through what was left of his hair. They were soft and somehow reassuring, those few strands. 'Why didn't you tell me this before . . . ?'

'I didn't realise for ages . . . and then I couldn't bear to ring you with something so absurd!'

'How much is the prize worth?'

'Ah . . . around four million.'

'I see.'

When the silence deepened Polly said, 'Look, it's all right.

I'm terribly sorry for bothering you. You must think I'm nuts!'

This sounded so healthy that Keith began to wonder if there really was something in the story.

'I'm sorry, Pauline. I hope you're wrong . . . I mean I hope that the ticket you lost is not the one. I'm afraid I haven't got it!'

'Oh, that's all right,' Polly said, sounding quite relieved. 'I just felt I had to make the effort. Thank you very much.'

And then she was gone.

It was only then that he remembered finding a pink Lotto ticket in the hall loo, on the evening of the day when the odd little person had first presented herself.

Keith was unable to proceed with his treatise on schizophrenia. He sat back in his chair and pondered the extraordinary. The little Pauline person, who had dropped into his life out of nowhere, had lost a Lotto ticket. He knew enough about statistics to realise that the chances of the thing being worth anything were so remote as to be nil. But she had lost it and she was worried about it, and there just might be something in the story. He knew too well the dangers of clinging to one's own perspective as the only true window on experience. He had been disabused of that often enough in his career.

But what had he done with the ticket? He cudgelled his brains. He remembered picking it up from the floor and putting it somewhere. Where? He couldn't remember. He got up, went to the downstairs loo, looked around. It was devoid of Lottery tickets. Mrs Dencher had probably found it and thrown it in the bin. And that would mean that it was already orphaned in some godforsaken land-infill where its small decaying pinkness would be indecipherable from all the other hues of decay.

Interesting thought, he conceded – four million pounds languishing incognito among the bits of old newspaper, the broken glass, and the potato peelings.

He studied himself for a moment in the mirror, straightened under his gaze, assumed a quasi-military stance, sucked in his stomach and pushed out his chest. Not bad, he assured himself. The race isn't over yet! Assuming of course that I haven't begun to listen to the beat of that other insidious drummer, the rhythm-maker of alternative reality. Assuming, that is to say, that I haven't begun to imagine things.

He looked at his reflected eyes. He did not detect in them the glazed, misfocused expression he associated with certain of his patients. But that did not mean that all was definitely well. Something was playing games with him. Strange women materialised out of nowhere with queer letters; the same women phoned him looking for four-million-pound Lotto tickets which they had left behind in his loo. That deceased old goat, Bernard, was probably orchestrating things from wherever old goats went. The dirtiest trick he had played, in fact, was to do with the house. It had been Bernard's house, although Keith had lived there since his marriage, and Bernard had bequeathed it to him. But he was not to have it. Bernard had incurred an interesting debt to meet commitments made on the stock exchange not long before his demise. His solicitor Jonathan Wheatley had been apologetic when he had last spoken to him. The estate was solvent, but only provided the house was sold to meet the debts.

Tough, Keith thought, but you either rolled with life's punches or let it gobble you up. There was always the cottage in the Cotswolds; Marguerite had fallen in love with it and they had bought it, done it up, spent one or two weeks in it and then let it on a yearly tenancy to a pair of enthusiastic Dutch artists. He had been thinking of getting out of London anyway; there was the fresh air and a stress-free environment.

But he knew these cogitations were spurious. He loved this house and the garden in which he had invested so much of his soul. He loved the Common, its bridle paths and open vistas, the family of bold grey squirrels who teased Herbie, the Windmill and the café, the walk down Windmill Road, the short bus ride on the 93 to Putney.

And poor little Mo would miss the house when she came home from New York. He didn't really want to live in the Cotswolds. But, since he had helped Mo purchase her New York apartment, he didn't have the kind of money which would permit him to buy the house from Bernard's estate; it had been valued for Probate purposes at just over three hundred thousand pounds.

He sighed, wandered to the sitting room, through the French windows on to the patio and into the sheltered corner where the evening sun was still tenderly mellow.

Herbie looked up expectantly. He had been thinking of a nice tin of Woof, but the lassitude of the hour was such that he was content to wait. Later there would be a ramble on the Common before the light went, and so happily to bed.

'How will you feel about relocating to the Cotswolds, old chap?' Keith asked.

Herbie thumped his tail; his gesture said that life was wonderful and that he knew Keith would manage everything beautifully.

When he went back into the house Keith realised with a pang that most of the furniture would have to be sold. It wouldn't fit in the cottage. And again he thought of Pauline, and how funny she had been sitting there in the French armchair, flushed with a curious innocence, her dark eyes dilated with embarrassment and vulnerability. He knew there were people who gave the impression of being newcomers to the game of life, but she was the first he had met for a long time. Most of those encountered by him during the course of his career had spent years in institutions, remote from the rough and tumble of the everyday.

But what had prompted him to ask her in, and having asked her in, to invite her to supper? This was an un-English thing to do, given the circumstances of their meeting, his ignorance about her motives, and all the imponderables dictated by caution and propriety.

Difference, an unconscious femininity, ingenuousness? Perhaps. Mostly it had to do with his sense of what was original, in a world depressingly short of it. He had often lamented that the price paid for the information age was increasing homogeneity.

He sat down in the chair where she had sat, and began to wonder seriously about her life. He knew little about her; but she was almost certainly the advertiser, and not the mythical sister of the unfortunate name.

She apparently had some kind of antiques business; she certainly gave the impression of knowing a great deal about her subject. She was, or had been, married, because she wore a ring.

Suddenly it occurred to him that maybe she was a novelist,

carrying out some piece of provocative research to see what came out of the woodwork. You could never be up to novelists!

I should be one myself, he thought. The things I could write about! Someday I may surprise the world! It can't be that difficult. When I think of the idiots who write fiction . . . and the real-life stuff psychiatrists come across . . .

No, he had found her tone too level, her embarrassment too real for ulterior motives. But there had been something else, something he recognised at an intuitive level and which sparked the professional in him. He had felt it again strongly as she spoke to him on the phone.

She was almost certainly in the grip of some kind of serious stress. Not that he doubted her story about the lottery ticket. He knew she had had it; he doubted its value, but that was a personal evaluation. He could always find out whether there was a huge unclaimed prize in the Irish lottery. She might even have real reasons for thinking she was the winner.

Quite apart from that altogether, he sensed with the antennae which had developed in him over the years, that this woman was somehow at odds with herself, with life as it was, as opposed to life as her minimum requirements for living dictated it should be. He also sensed that she did not regard her requirements as respectable, and that this carried with it the possibility of her being fundamentally divided against herself. She was terribly alive in some way, and terribly denied, like a poor foot crushed in the restraining bands of the old Chinese custom.

The innocent and the beautiful, he thought, paraphrasing Yeats, have no enemies but themselves.

Keith found aberrant people interesting because they yielded up the complex secrets of the heart. In his book, the only difference between them and the rest of humanity was their disagreement as to the parameters of authenticity.

Well, he thought, I'm the strange one, inventing an emotional landscape for this person. I wonder if she will bother to contact me when her business brings her next to London, especially when I tell her, as I must, that I had found her ticket and that it is now gone. But first enquiries will have to be made from the redoubtable Mrs Dencher.

\* \* \*

194

Muriel packed a bag. She knew she wouldn't need too many things. But she remembered her favourite French perfume, and her white lawn nightdresses with the pin-tucks. They were Victorian, and very pretty.

She had been over to see Polly earlier, but she had been out and she had left her spare set of keys and the burglar alarm number with Rory.

'When will you be back?' he had said when Muriel had not been forthcoming as to where she was going.

'I really don't know, Rory. I'll play it by ear. I'll let you know.'

When she was finished packing Muriel walked around her house. She did this quite systematically, beginning in the landing, opening each door and entering each of the five bedrooms, lingering for a moment in the room she had once intended as a nursery. The pleasure that she had experienced for a long time in the pristine leakless ceiling, in the beauty of the interior decor, in the sheen of the old bedroom furniture, deserted her today.

She opened a drawer in her dressing table and took out the small music box her father had given her. It was painted cream with a spray of pink roses, and had a fine covering of dust. She wound it automatically. When she opened the lid a small ballerina in a small net tutu spun round and round to the strains of the *Carnival of Animals*.

The melody released memory, like a scent. She could remember the day he gave it to her; could remember every detail, how his hands had trembled, how he smelt of cigars, how his love was conditional. 'How pretty your skin is . . .'

In the same drawer she found a photograph of a smiling Alan, looked at it for a moment before tearing it across the middle.

She put away the music box, wandered into what had been her parents' room. There was her father's wardrobe, oval mahogany panels with the feather pattern; there was her mother's dressing table, tall Victorian, her silver hair brush still awaiting the touch of her hand. Muriel almost saw her, wrapped in her kimono, turning her head from the mirror, almost saw her own ten-year-old self, her tear-stained face.

'You are a very wicked little girl to say such things . . .'

195

She looked at the oil painting over the mantelpiece, an exquisite English country scene by an unknown artist of a hundred years before. Something Polly had recently said suddenly occurred to her. These things were but the wrappings of a tomb, like the impedimenta accompanying an Egyptian mummy to the hereafter, the little mummy wrapped in cerecloths gazing into the fathomless future with blind, dead eyes.

She walked down the stairs, pausing to look at each picture, the portraits of horses which her family had once owned, portraits of bewhiskered gents in frock coats, one of her great-grandmother in a satin gown, hair in coils, wistful eyes fixed on futurity. She went into the drawing room, looked up at the restored cornices, at the old marble fireplace, at the oriental rugs on the floor and the Georgian simplicity of the lady's desk, where her mother had written her letters.

In the hall was a French tapestry above a shining sofa table. There was an alabaster lamp on this table which had once possessed a pink silk shade. But the shade had flitted with the passage of years. The replacement was exactly the same shade of pink. She had had it specially made.

The dining room had a Hunt table and a Nelson sideboard, with the old silver resting on it. She saw her face distorted in a coffee pot as she stood for a moment looking at these heirlooms.

Why, she wondered, had she striven so hard to retain each vestige of her world as it had been, before her father had died, his debts been discovered, and the house fallen into disrepair? It was as though by so doing she could preserve him for ever, and in his preservation hold on to herself, or rather the self which he had moulded for her, and which was the only one she knew. It was only in holding on to him that she could resolve what had happened. Sometimes she did not know where he ended and Alan Barrington began.

Did she suspect even now the scale of her loss? She had been built for the future and she had fled it. Instead she was like the ballerina in the music box, revolving round and round the same point, to the same tune, dancing joylessly for ever. Something in her insisted that she must do this if she was to understand, to exorcise. It was like an insurmountable obstacle, which she must nevertheless surmount, or be left behind. But without a normal spectrum of experience, in what recesses of the imagination could she find enough strength and understanding simply to walk past the nightmare and get on with the race?

She did not open the drawer where she had put away the photographs of her father which used to sit on the mantelpiece in this room. She had broken them, mutilated her father's face. Childish? Perhaps.

Ah well, she thought . . . When I come back I will do things differently. I will get myself a life before it is too late.

# Chapter Fourteen

Polly decided to go ahead and sit the Civil Service exam. She felt a bit of an elder lemon because few of the candidates we out of their twenties, but she found her seat in the RDS in Ballsbridge and waited for the paper. The loudspeaker welcomed everyone, laid down the rules as to what was what, and wished them luck. Polly estimated that there were about one thousand people in the great exhibition hall. The successful ones would be further weeded out by interview. She herself had no illusions. She was not prepared for this exam; she hadn't a clue as to its content or format; but she would have a go, because it calmed her conscience and if she succeeded she would have a well-paid job in Dublin, and might even be sent to all sorts of interesting places abroad. Stranger things had happened.

The first paper consisted of one hundred multiple choice questions, all of them to be done in jig time. The first section of this had to do with the meaning of words.

What did the word diaspora mean? What did synthesis mean, and turbary, plectrum and plantain, catafalque and circumlocution?

After the word section came the general knowledge. Who discovered asepsis; what was the chemical formula for dry ice; who wrote 'Philadelphia Here I Come'; which Irish writer wrote *Good Behaviour*; what was a dendrochronologist; who was the American ambassador to Ireland; to which political party did Nelson Mandela belong. And so it went on.

Polly flew through all this. She was stumped by one or two of the questions, but in the main they presented no problem. When she handed her paper up she decided she had got herself a job. But when the second paper was delivered she knew the game was up. The whole thing revolved around economics and ratios and she could no more work out the problems in the allotted time or anything like it, than she could run a marathon in ten minutes.

I've tried, she told herself as she went home. I've entered the lists and returned on my shield. There it is.

When she got home Rory said that Muriel had dropped in the keys and that she had departed on holiday.

'Where is she going?'

'She didn't say,' Rory replied after a moment spent in racking his brain. He was afraid that Muriel had told him but that he hadn't been paying attention.

Susie dropped around that evening to find out how things had gone.

'Not too well,' Polly said. 'I think I got around ninety per cent in the first paper and what my kindergarten teacher used to call "a big fat zero" in the second . . . or something of that order! So there will be no job for the Pollys of this world in the Civil Service!'

'It's a stupid exam,' Susie said. 'They shouldn't base so much on maths . . .'

Polly made tea and the two friends sat together in the kitchen. Rory was out. He had gone back to the school to help out with some evening activity. And so the customary keyboard clicking was not to be heard.

Polly pulled a paper out of a kitchen drawer and presented it to Susie for her perusal. It was a Circuit Court Summons, citing one Martha Caine as Plaintiff and Rory Caine as Defendant, and was seeking the sum of sixteen thousand pounds due on foot of an agreement made between her and the said Rory Caine or in the alternative an order for the sale of 14 Ashgrove Lawns, Dundrum.

Susie read it in silence. 'God,' she said. 'What are you going to do?'

Polly shrugged. 'I don't know.'

'What about the Lotto ticket you lost? Did you phone that person where you think you might have lost it?'

'Yes . . . but he doesn't have it! And Michelle knows nothing about it. It's gone, Susie,' she said, and added a little sententiously, '. . . Things without all remedy should be without regard!'

'Which smart-ass said that?'

'Shakespeare!'

'I knew I'd heard it somewhere before.'

'I've applied for a job in London . . . fine arts . . . the love of my life. But I haven't a hope!'

'London! What on earth would you do on your own in London? But something will turn up,' Susie added without much conviction. 'I'll ask Willy Penston to think of you when Wendy leaves to have her baby. She's our filing clerk . . .' she added. 'You wouldn't mind a job as a filing clerk, would you?'

'God no . . . I'm at the stage where I'd take anything honest. I mentioned it to Rory and he said that no wife of his is going to work!' Polly gave a hollow laugh. 'I felt like reminding him that I'm not really his wife.'

Susie looked at her friend and scrunched up one corner of her mouth so that it rode up her face. 'God, this country,' she muttered. 'But if the divorce referendum is carried out . . . things will change! You and Rory will be able to get legally married!'

'Big deal!' Polly muttered, and Sue regarded her quizzically. The conversation turned to Jason.

'I'm heartbroken about that boy!' Polly said. 'I don't know where I went wrong. He's had the very best we could do for him. I think it's terrible that he should run away from home, live with a girl several years his senior, and waste his last year at school working in a late-night café. What's to become of him?'

'The trouble with Jason is that he is presently in command of all the knowledge known to man!' Susie said. 'When this monopoly slips, he'll be back. Wait and see!'

'Maybe it runs in the family,' Polly muttered. 'There was an old uncle of Rory's who went to the bad, ended up as a guest of her Britannic majesty. It's probably in the genes!' Her eyes filled with tears. 'I keep thinking of him when he was little, he was so gorgeous you'd eat him, and how I had all sorts of dreams for him . . . He used to remind me of Tom, so handsome and, at that point, so full of charm!'

'Did you have supper?' Susie demanded, reminded that Polly looked a bit starved.

'I made something for Peter . . . he's studying upstairs . . . but I can't eat any more.'

'You're getting terribly thin!'

'No harm in that. I'm taking vitamins.'

'Well, you wouldn't want to overdo it. You'll soon be as svelte as the Presence across the road, She Who Watches and Waits . . . Speaking of whom – I saw a taxi collecting her earlier today. I was coming back from the village and she waved at me. Off to her holiday destination with a smile. Pale as chalk, but she'll come back looking like Joan Collins with a tan. What that one needs is a brace of kids and a redundant husband . . . Give her something to think about!'

'She's rich,' Polly muttered. 'Such inconveniences wouldn't bother her!' Then she added, 'She left the keys in while I was at the exam.'

Sue went home, found the house empty. There was a note stuck to the fridge which said, 'Mum, Gone to Mary Lavelle's gaff. Be back at ten. Sharon.'

She called, 'Anyone upstairs?' but there was no reply. She wondered where Fergus and Mark were, and decided they must have gone out together, something they now did from time to time. Susie approved of this, because it meant there would be greater bonding between father and son, which, she thought, was no harm at all as Mark's adolescence moved into adulthood.

She went upstairs, glanced into her son's room. It was very tidy; his books were neatly stacked, his bed neatly made. Mark had a secret Jansenistic streak. He liked to pretend to his peers that he was as much of a 'lad' as any of them, but he had a covert contempt for self-indulgence and, behind the scenes, worked and schemed for his future.

Sharon, by comparison, was undisciplined. Her room was never immaculate. She was a dreamer, a romantic, and sometimes her mother worried that she would fall head over heels for the wrong kind of boy. She was good at French and English, liked essays, hated maths, wept silently at sad movies.

Sue stood in her daughter's room, in a mood of fond amusement, noting with nostalgia the once beloved cabbage-patch doll wedged in a corner of the bookcase, the poster of those boys in the rock band that Sharon so admired, the untidy way her books were cluttered on her desk. Sue went automatically to tidy the desk, and as she put one book on top of the other she uncovered a verse in Sharon's writing, surrounded by doodles of rudimentary daisies:

> When she who adores thee has left but the name,
> Of her faults and her sorrows behind,
> Oh say wilt thou weep when they darken the fame,
> Of a life that for thee was resigned . . .

Sue stared at this verse for a long time, caught between the desire to laugh and cry. Oh God, the poor child . . . It was no wonder she was off her food lately; she was in the grip of the old insidious blight, Love.

On Monday a letter on heavy bond paper arrived from London inviting Polly to attend for interview at the premises of Shetly's in New Bond Street on 23 June.

Keith did phone Mrs Dencher after hearing from Polly on that Sunday evening, with the intention of asking the former if she had found a Lottery ticket in the loo, but there was no reply. It was not until the following day when her daughter Chris phoned that he learnt that her parents had gone on holiday to the Bahamas and would be gone for a fortnight.

'Ye gods,' Keith muttered to himself. 'What should I do now? Write and tell Pauline that I found the lottery ticket, but mislaid it and that the only person who might be able to throw light on its whereabouts has gone to the Bahamas on a sudden holiday . . .'

He thought of Mrs Dencher and her robust housekeeping, and her honest face. 'She couldn't have,' he muttered. 'She couldn't have found it and . . . No. It's not possible! Not the redoubtable Mrs D . . .'

It was when he had recovered from the shock of this thought process that he sat at his desk and contacted Directory Enquiries seeking the phone number of the Irish Lottery.

* * *

Polly sat on the end of her bed in quasi-despair. She wanted very badly to go to London for the interview. She could scrape the fare; it was cheap if booked a reasonable time in advance. She even had a place to stay in London, thanks to Michelle. She had phoned her to tell her and Michelle had said she'd be away and told her who would have the key. But what she did not have was something decent to wear. She wanted to turn up at that interview looking the part, or not go at all.

She had gone through all her wardrobe and it was a bit like Mother Hubbard's cupboard. After the recent clear-out there were just a few serviceable things left, but they all bore the signs of honest wear; some of the skirts sported a shine, or were well and truly seated. Now that Michelle's gifts hung on her newly diminished figure, she had nothing glamorous, or classy, nothing shrieking of taste and discernment, which would express the elegance she wanted so desperately to portray, an elegance which, in fact, lived somewhere at the core of her identity and which had never left her through all the grinding years of making-do.

She thought of Susie who would lend her her last pair of shoes, but Susie, while slim, was petite, and none of her clothes would fit. There was really nobody she could ask; it was such a personal thing anyway.

She thought of getting a loan from the bank. But with the court case looming it seemed madness to ask Rory to guarantee a loan for her; without it she would probably be refused. What collateral did she have without a job, without property?

'You wouldn't get the London job anyway,' her interior self interjected. 'Who'd give a broken-down old bird like you a perfectly good job in a prestigious ambience?'

Polly said silently that she wasn't broken down; she said she was afraid of becoming so, but that it hadn't happened yet. It occurred to her suddenly that she could pawn, or sell, her engagement ring. She took it out to look at it, but it conjured such ecstatic memories that she put it away again.

The next morning Polly made the short walk to Muriel's house. She went because she had promised Muriel that she would check on the house every day and she was glad to do so, pleased at the prospect of simply moving within the precincts of so much space and beauty. Rory was not at his computer, for a change. He was marking scripts, which he hated, and he was, consequently, very irritable.

There was a high railing around Muriel's old Victorian house, enclosing a gravelled forecourt and garden. Polly opened the side gate, walked slowly across the gravel, enjoying the scents of the garden wafting around her, mounted the four granite steps to the front door. She unlocked it, slipped inside, disarmed the alarm, closed the door, and took a deep breath of pleasure.

Everything in the house was in perfect order, no sign of anything amiss. She sat for what seemed a long time in the drawing room, a room with a lofty ceiling, a delicate porcelain chandelier, a chaise longue in old gold, a painting of a lake scene, a portrait of a young lady, a few porcelain pieces on a mahogany tallboy, and an array of drinks on a Victorian sofa table. Outside was the garden with its roses, the quiet forecourt, the high railing, and beyond that the cul-de-sac. She could see part of her own house, although it looked funny from this vantage point, as though she were seeing it for the first time.

She imagined this house before the estate was built on its doorstep, imagined the avenue curving to the road. She wondered how the house felt about the change in circumstances, the encroachment of the hundreds of semis on every side, the armies of children, the cars, the cats and dogs, the strident waves of modernity breaking against its gentility.

But at least the house lived on, and with it the atmosphere of another time and another people, like a perfume hidden in the folds of an old gown.

It was only while she was in the kitchen looking for the tin of cat food to feed Sable, that she saw the note stuck to the fridge with her own name in underlined large letters.

Dearest Polly,

I'll be off in a minute. You weren't at home when I called, so I've left the spare keys with Rory. I just want to say thanks for being such a brick as to look after the place and feed my little Sable.

I wanted to tell you that I intend making a complete new start, begin a new chapter you might say, when I

205

come home. As I'm smothered in clothes, I'll be throwing out loads of things, so if there's anything you would like from the stuff in the walnut wardrobe in my room, please take it. Some of it is a bit too big for me now anyway. There are also a few shoulder bags you might be interested in on the floor of the wardrobe.

I hope you're not offended by me mentioning this, but you know me well enough to know that no offence is intended. I just thought you might have a use for some of my superfluous things and it would please me so much to think of them helping you to take on the world! I once hoped they would do as much for me, but my particular cracks needed more than papering!

Love, Muriel.

Polly, having fed Sable, and re-read the strange note several times, mounted the stairs and, with a great deal of diffidence, crossed the threshold of Muriel's bedroom.

The furniture was antique like that of the rest of the house; the bed was iron with brass knobs. There were two wardrobes, one was mahogany and the other walnut. The inlaid door of the latter wardrobe was open. There on a rail was an array of clothes, suits, dresses, coats, like a vestimentary version of Aladdin's cave.

Polly stood in front of this array for a moment, then put her hand upon a suit of jade green and black and drew it from the wardrobe. It was a blend of fine wool and silk.

She held it against her and looked in the mirror. Oh God, she thought, this is simply fabulous! The green showed up her eyes; the black made her skin glow, made her hair appear fair rather than mousy. She examined the designer label with awe. She took off her jeans and put on the suit. It had slim lines; it was cut like a dream; it took years off her. Suddenly Polly wanted to cry. The woman before her in the mirror bore little resemblance to the woman of but a moment before in the baggy jeans. Instead a sophisticate had appeared, albeit one who could do with a new hairstyle. She gathered her hair up and held it off her face.

Oh Muriel, she whispered after a moment, thank you, thank you. Because of you I am going to London. I am going to an interview. I am going to get my hair streaked and styled, and make up my face, and wear this lovely suit. I know that all of this is quite mad by all the safe criteria I have lived by, but I'm doing it all the same.

She tried on a black leather shoulder bag which was sitting on the wardrobe floor. Then she folded the suit neatly, found a polythene bag in the kitchen, set the burglar alarm, locked up the house and carried her treasures home.

When she met Susie later that morning she told her she would be going to London for an interview.

'I didn't believe you!' Susie said. 'But I can see you're serious! But what will you do if you were to land this job? Leave Rory? And the children?'

Polly looked at her friend's troubled face. 'I'd just take the job,' she said equably, 'and let everything accommodate itself to that reality. Rory needs a wife like he needs a domestic, so he won't miss me; Peter will be finishing college next year; and Jason,' here her face became suddenly vulnerable, 'is doing his own thing . . . But I'd preserve the status quo, come home when I can.' She gestured, 'But all this is romancing. The chances are slim!'

'I don't know,' Susie muttered. 'You've changed in some way . . . become a force to be reckoned with. As though you removed whatever lid has been holding you down! And you know bloody everything about antiques!'

'No I don't . . . but I'll be wearing a suit from Muriel's wardrobe to the interview!' Polly added with a twinkle. 'I must show it to you!'

Susie looked astonished, as though Polly had acted out of character.

'I didn't just swipe it,' Polly added, aghast. 'She told me to take anything I wanted! She's throwing out lots of clothes!'

Sue's face closed. 'That one tries to own everybody,' she muttered. 'I sometimes think that's why she really sold the land for building – so she could own the whole bloody lot of us! There she is, simpering under a mountain of designer outfits, and there you are, one of the nicest people in the world, broken with gratitude for one of her cast-offs. It's just not fair!'

'What on earth gave you the notion that life should be fair!'

Polly replied tartly. 'It never is! You're not going to blame Muriel because life isn't fair?'

Susie sniffed. 'Well, some of us have it a lot easier than others!'

Polly did not smile. 'I don't know,' she said. 'I rather suspect that the dice is loaded for us all!' When Susie didn't answer she added, 'How's your boss these days?'

'He's fine . . . He's just weird. I asked him the other day if anything was the matter, said I would resign if he wanted, and he looked thunderstruck! In fact he's asked me out on Friday . . . to advise him on the decor for the new flat, if you don't mind!'

'Are you going?'

'No. I'm not as dim as I look!'

'I don't think you're dim, Sue. On the contrary.'

'But you're going off to an interview which may take you away from me, from all of us! I'm afraid I'm going to lose you, Poll. And then I'll be left here with poor cross Ferg and madam across the road and the kids like the bewildered adolescents which they are . . .'

'No . . . Nothing lasts, not adolescence, not madams across the road. Everything is in flux. At least I hope it is . . .'

Sue chewed her finger. 'I thought I could rely on you staying the same, Polly Caine. But you have become challenging! You don't accept things at face value any more.'

Polly took her friend's hand. 'Will you have sense! I'm just trying the strength of my wings, to see whether or not they have atrophied.'

'Not true. You've got private agenda written all over you!'

'OK. I'm making an effort. If I have any choice in the matter, if Fate does anything to help me, I will not endure life as I have lived it any longer!'

Susie was silent. After a moment she said, 'Poll . . . it was Muriel . . . who paid for the private detective . . . not me. When Jason ran away . . . I should have told you . . . But I wanted to be the star!'

'You are the star!' Polly said after a moment. 'I will thank Muriel when I see her.'

Sue put her arms around her friend and hugged her in silence.

# Chapter Fifteen

Keith Warrington got through to the National Lottery in Dublin with some difficulty, the number being engaged for some time.

'The island must be heaving with gamblers,' he muttered under his breath, toying with the paper knife of Toledo steel with one hand, as he prodded out the phone number with the other.

He was eventually put through to someone who was able to assure him that yes, there had been a big prize of four million just before Easter.

'Has the winner come forward?' Keith asked. 'I lost a ticket . . .'

'Yes, the winner came forward last week,' the voice said cheerfully. 'It was won by an English lady who prefers to remain anonymous!'

'I see. Someone from London, perhaps?'

'Yes, actually, I believe she lives in London.'

'I suppose you couldn't tell me her address . . .'

'You suppose correctly!'

'Thank you very much,' Keith said.

'Not at all.'

Keith ran the tip of the paper knife against the palm of his left hand. 'She's been and gone and done it!' he whispered. 'The redoubtable Mrs D. Who would have believed it? A swindle the size of the great train robbery!'

He ran his thumb and index finger idly along the blade before contacting Directory Enquiries again and seeking the number of one Pauline McCann of 14 Ashgrove Lawns, Dundrum, County Dublin.

'That's in Ireland,' he told the man in directory enquiries who had an Indian accent.

'So I have heard it said, sir . . .'

'Jolly good . . .'

But this time he was unsuccessful.

'There is no number listed for that name and address,' he was informed.

'I see,' Keith said and put the phone down. What he really saw was that her name might not be Pauline and might not be McCann and she might not be living at 14 Ashgrove Lawns, Dundrum, or she might not have a phone, or might be ex-directory, and that he, who had been providing therapy all his life, might need professional help.

'Well, I did find that damn ticket and it is gone!' he reminded himself out loud, as though to prove that his parameters were solid.

He took a sheet of paper and wrote as follows:

Dear Pauline,

I tried to find your phone number, but they've never heard of you. The fact is, I'm afraid, that I did find your Lottery ticket. I remembered after I put the phone down, but could not ring you back because I had no number.

I'm sending this letter to the address on your letter and also a copy to your box number, just in case.

The Lottery ticket was in the loo, as you remembered, but has disappeared. The only person who could have removed it was my cleaning lady (now on holiday in foreign climes). I gather the prize has been collected, and I quail to think that she could be a criminal.

Please contact me so that we can sort this out. If my charwoman has collected the prize the police should (if necessary) be able to establish how she came by the means of doing do.

I'm very disturbed about all this.

Yours sincerely,
Keith.

Well, he thought, I've done all I can; at least for the moment. He ran his fingers through the short wisps of his hair as his mind raced into overdrive, imagining Mrs Dencher being taken into custody. But while Keith was worrying about all the unpleasant ways in which the plot might further thicken, Polly was already on a Ryanair flight to Stansted.

Polly, in fact, looked like a million dollars. She examined herself in the mirror in the ladies at Stansted. Streaked blonde hair, a fantastic understated suit with a silk blouse, a black Gucci shoulder bag, a hint of perfume. Learn how to act, she told herself, and you will pass for a high-powered female executive.

'You're losing it,' her self-deprecating voice said. 'Delusions of grandeur are a sign . . .'

The premises of Shetly and Sons were halfway down New Bond Street. It was a glorious day. The temperature was about 26 degrees, a bit warm for a suit, even a light one. Londoners, tourists, in cotton clothes, crowded the pavements, and the warm dusty air of the underground followed her into Oxford Street.

Polly walked at a measured pace down New Bond Street. She knew she was early; she took her time; some men turned to look at her. Mother Frances at school had always said that you should walk as though you were being pulled up to heaven by the crown of your head.

I will not shrink, she thought, remembering what Muriel had written. I am here to take on the world.

She expected the usual snort of derision from her unwelcome alter-ego, but it was silent.

The trouble with perpetual criticism, she reflected, is that you eventually come to believe it. But right now I am writing the scenario for my potential life. I will write it and reach for it and perhaps create it. At least I will have made the effort.

Shetly's occupied a good frontage in New Bond Street. Some nicely restored Victorian oils were in the window with a selection of old Coalport, which she estimated in a reflex way at about 1790. She tried unsuccessfully to still the sudden thumping of her heart, but she raised her head as she entered the showroom and smiled at the young man who came forward to greet her.

'May I help you, madam?'

'My name is Pauline McCann. I have an appointment with Mr Denniston-Figgs.'

She was shown into a small, windowless room and asked to wait for a few moments. There was a selection of magazines, mostly about antiques, and some catalogues. The air was redolent of beeswax, the scent of old hardwoods, and something else – the aura imported by fine historic things, as though the love and skill that had made and preserved them, had wrapped them in the fragrance of an immortal elegance.

The door opened and a man of middle years entered the room. Greying, well dressed, with shrewd close-set eyes, he gave the impression of English sangfroid stirred into a melting pot of Anglo-French ancestry. There was something Gallic in his body language, something English in his expression.

He measured her for hardly a split second, smiled, extended a cordial hand.

'Mrs McCann. How do you do? I'm Aubrey Denniston-Figgs.'

'How do you do?'

Polly took the outstretched hand. The handshake betokened a business-like character, but it was not so unyielding as to be merely schooled. It also betokened an immediate acceptance of the woman before him as a person. Polly felt this, experienced it as a gift, and was filled with gratitude.

'If you would like to come up to my office we can have a chat. Mrs Rollinson will be joining us.'

Polly followed him up the stairs and entered an office with a Victorian mahogany desk, and a view over the street. For some reason she felt perfectly calm. This milieu held no terrors for her. The tyrannies of domestic life might plague and diminish her, but the exigencies of these London offices required nothing from her that did not tap into the passionate aspirations of her heart.

She felt at ease, at ease in Muriel's lovely suit, at ease in her new slimness, which made her feel light and supple and graceful, at ease with the burgeoning power of her own individuality in a setting where it was not instantly construed as eccentricity. She caught a glimpse of herself in a mirror and knew that the woman she saw there was the real Polly.

She sat as invited, shook hands with Mrs Rollinson, a marvellous-looking woman of about fifty-five, answered questions, quipped in response to the occasional joke.

'What we were hoping to find,' Mrs Rollinson said, 'is someone who is absolutely au fait with this business. But you have very little real experience.'

'That's true. Experience, however, can be acquired. What cannot be acquired is the love and interest in the business which makes for truly committed work.' Polly looked about her. 'I could spend my life among these things, and count it well spent! What you will have in me, and perhaps it is not always available, is motivation!'

Mr Denniston-Figgs looked at her with a slight frown, as if this avowal was a little over-enthusiastic, and then reached into a drawer and withdrew a leather case. Inside was a collection of silver spoons. He pushed it across the desk.

'What do you make of these?'

Polly picked up one, then another, examined the hall-markings.

'These,' she said after a moment, selecting two spoons, 'are sterling silver, Edinburgh, around 1808. And these,' she went on, picking up two smaller spoons, 'are apostle spoons of around 1630, while the bigger ones are plate, about 1765, made by the firm of Joseph Hancock, if my memory serves me correctly.'

'And how would you value these?'

Polly felt dismayed. 'Frankly I'm out of touch. The apostle spoons are the most valuable, followed by the Edinburgh ones . . . But this is probably self-evident!'

'Only to the initiated,' Mrs Rollinson said with a smile.

'And you have a very good degree,' Mr Denniston-Figgs said, 'in the History of Art.'

'Yes.'

'But you didn't make a career for yourself . . . ?'

'For various reasons, husband, children, lack of real opportunity where I come from . . . a sense of beleaguered commitment. But my children are grown. I am free now and can offer dedication to the work I love.' She looked from one of them to the other. 'Quite candidly, I want to reclaim my life!'

She leaned back a little and let them study her. She did not want enthusiasm to be mistaken for angst. But she felt she had a right to her own honesty and earnestness, let it be construed as it would.

213

Mrs Rollinson smiled. 'Quite candidly,' she echoed, in what was an almost private aside, 'I think you are a woman after my own heart!'

Polly went into the sunlit street. She knew the interview had gone well. The sense of *joie de vivre* in having successfully asserted her own aspirations was so powerful that she felt almost light-headed. So this is how it feels to be in charge of your life, she thought, this surge of power.

More sober sentiments followed – maybe she wouldn't get the job. But whether she did or not she knew she had joined battle with the forces of tradition and entropy arraigned against her. She had taken hold of her own strength.

So what will I do with my time? she asked herself. There is a glorious day waiting to be lived.

She could go back to the flat in Eaton Square. She had arrived there that morning to find it empty, as expected. London was throbbing around her. She had no money for shopping, but there was one thing she could do, and the thought came on a sudden almost mischievous impulse. She could take the tube to Wimbledon and drop in on Keith Warrington!

Muriel thought for a while that she was a slug at the bottom of the sea. She hid under an overhang in the coral, knowing that predators were looking for her. Schools of fish, iridescent, swirled and turned in sudden knife-like shifts; the flora swirled in the underwater fairyland, but Muriel the sea-slug lay far down and waited.

Threads of conversation, dreamlike, disjointed, came to her from the world above:

'Well, she's still out . . . we'll have to wait and see . . .'

And again, '. . . rough treatment . . . but there's no alternative . . .'

She was glad the talk had nothing to do with her, that she could skulk in her fastness underneath the coral, where she felt safe. It was nice to be safe. Next to being loved, which only came to the elect of Heaven, it was the best thing in the world.

# Chapter Sixteen

Keith returned from his morning walk with Herbie on the Common. He had met Mrs Jopling who cheered him up a little, absolving him in her garrulity from the necessity of making conversation. 'Hmns?' and 'Reallys?' and 'Is that sos?' were the only conversational currency he needed. Fluffsy was the subject of an animated monologue for at least ten consecutive minutes. She really should enter her in the Dog Show; there weren't many poodles as intelligent and elegant ... didn't he think so?

'Quite!' Keith said and lapsed back into the brooding disposition which afflicted him today.

Nothing was going right. His second article on schizophrenia was overdue. Sophie would not be coming back from America until the autumn; the house was up for sale – they had come and put the sign up yesterday. And there was the lunatic element still hanging in there, the lottery-ticket foolishness which seemed to be rooted in hard cold fact, not to say hard cold cash. He hoped the whole thing was a mistake and that he would never have to talk to that Irish crackpot, Pauline, again.

And yet, when he thought of her, he could feel his nerve endings come alive, like river-beds after a drought. Why this was he did not know and did not waste time considering. She was a ship that had passed in the night, leaving only a bright wake behind her.

The trees were resplendent, chestnuts generously verdant, silver birches shining in the sunshine. The squirrels examined them from the branches overhead and then moved with sudden provocative and weightless grace. Herbie gave a couple of rhetorical barks; he knew the elegant little creatures and they knew him; they had sized each other up long ago.

Keith threw the sponge ball and Herbie retrieved it and returned for more, and after a reflex and quasi-proprietary fashion sniffed Fluffsy's behind. That animal put her nose in the air, directed a long-suffering glance at her mistress and looked over her shoulder at Herbie who, having found a suitable tree, was now anointing its bark, lifting his leg with a constipated expression as though suddenly conscious of impropriety.

'I wonder is that some kind of code?' Mrs Jopling said. 'You know . . . like the language of fans . . . in the old days I mean, of course. I mean a kind of dog code . . .'

'Hmnn?' Keith said. 'You could be right, Mrs Jopling!'

They went to the Windmill Café, sat outside at the wooden tables. The two dogs sat panting at their feet. Keith went inside to the counter.

'Two teas, please.'

'Large or small?'

'What? Oh yes . . . large. And two slices of apple pie.'

He carried the two mugs and the apple pie outside to a beaming Mrs Jopling.

'Thank you very much. It's nice to sit here, isn't it, and watch the world go by?'

Keith looked around. A solitary mounted policeman on patrol went by on the other side of the hedge. Beyond that was the stretch of common and the sun-kissed trees. Another couple sipped their tea at a nearby table and discussed some topic of apparently desultory interest. No one else was around.

Keith looked at Mrs Jopling. Her tired eyes dwelt lovingly on her poodle.

Hardly 'the world', Keith thought. He listened to the renewed account of the wonders of Fluffsy for a while.

I suppose I should shake up my days a bit, he mused. Bernard was probably right. But I'm not so sure how to go about it.

Mrs Jopling informed him that her name was Marcia and perhaps they should not be so formal. When Keith did not respond, she added that of course she did not want to be unduly familiar and was quite happy to go on calling him Dr Warrington if he did not want to be on first-name terms.

'Oh yes, yes of course,' Keith said, 'first names . . . mine's Keith . . . what's yours?'

'Marcia,' Mrs Jopling repeated.

'Jolly good,' Keith said.

And if Mo is not coming home until the autumn, he thought, she will never set foot in the house again because it will be gone! I will write and tell her. Pity to sadden her though . . . poor kid. Bloody Bernard had to drop us in it! I should have known he would!

'You must be lonely from time to time, Keith,' Mrs Jopling said, 'since your dear wife passed on.'

'Mmnn?' Keith said. He was thinking of Mo and how he could break the news to her.

When silence succeeded he surfaced with a perceptible start and added, 'My dear wife . . . oh of course . . . lonely? Well, sometimes I suppose. Yes, of course.'

Then he realised, with the insight that was his personal gift and, sometimes, his cross, that she was lonely too, more lonely than he had dreamed, an ageing woman who saw herself with the purblind vision of the prevailing social order, buried alive in the cellular structure called society. How we see ourselves dictates who we are, he thought. If we just define ourselves by the depredations wrought by Time we close the doors of the spirit. And the spirit is all we ever really had.

Something Yeats had said about the matter, about Soul clapping his hands and singing louder and louder for every token of mortality, recurred to him, but he couldn't remember the exact lines.

'You should come around for a drink!' he said. 'Been meaning to ask you!'

Mrs Jopling brightened. 'Oh, how nice of you. When did you have in mind?'

'Why not today?' Keith said expansively.

'How nice. What time?'

'About six? Would that be all right?'

'Thank you very much.'

When they parted Keith said, 'Eh . . . thank you for the chat . . . enjoyed it very much . . . eh . . . sorry, what did you say your first name was?'

'Marcia!'

'I do apologise. I'm a bit preoccupied today . . . things on my mind!'

Mrs Jopling said that she understood perfectly.

When he had fed Herbie, Keith looked in the fridge to see what delights were available to tease his own palate. He found a tired lettuce he had bought a day or two before and forgotten about, and two wrinkled tomatoes.

I'll make a salad, he thought. There should be an egg or two somewhere; wouldn't mind a bit of egg mayonnaise. He surveyed the flaccid lettuce doubtfully. 'How do you smarten it up?' he asked Herbie. 'Restore it to vibrant youth and so forth . . . If I steeped it in water would it do the trick?'

Herbie, who had gulped down his lunch, was biting his private parts which had been itching all morning, but he raised devotional and uninformative eyes to his master's voice.

'Not much of a chef, are we?' Keith said.

Herbie was all agreement. 'Well, we'll find out,' Keith muttered, and he threw the lettuce into a bowl and covered it with water.

Keith took his lunch out of doors and ate on the patio. The lettuce had been a disappointment. Instead of recovering any crispness it had more or less turned to slime, and so he had to make do with a hardboiled egg and what he could salvage from the tomatoes. It wasn't that he objected to their wrinkles, only to the small white spots which he had found on inspection. 'Nothing wrong with a touch of penicillin!' he told himself, but he cut the spots away all the same.

The garden was in full glory, and he blocked the burgeoning nostalgia that he would never have another summer in its bosom. Enjoy it now, came the thought; sufficient unto the day is the evil thereof. Why spend the present agonising over the future, or grieving for the past? That's a recipe for death in life. But all the same, the yesterdays came crowding; the summer teas on the lawn, Bernard in hale middle life playing with baby Sophie. 'Mo,' she had screamed when he finished feeding her ice cream, waving her little fat fists. 'Want mo!'

Marguerite smiling her reluctant smile, the one which said that it was all right to see the humour in the situation so long as one did not let it dictate policy; short summer dress, long legs over the deck chair; 'You'll spoil her, Daddy!'

'Spoil Miss Mo?' Bernard said, raising his eyebrows and regarding the ferocious baby with delight. 'Nonsense! Such passion for life should be rewarded! Isn't that right, Keith?'

Ghosts, all of them, except Sophie and himself. Two down and two to go.

When he had finished his small repast he knew he should go indoors and attack the word processor, but he lingered. The day was so nice, the soft breeze that rustled the leaves so redolent of summer and its blessings, that he could not, for the moment, bestir himself.

When the doorbell sounded he was half asleep. He stared when Herbie barked suddenly and lifted his head.

'Someone at the door, old chap?'

The thought of Mrs Jopling came to him with a surge of dismay. He knew he had invited her around, but was not too sure for when. He did not hurry to the door and consequently the visitor had regained the gate by the time the front door was opened.

No, it wasn't Mrs Jopling. Some kind of elegant blonde. She turned back when the door opened, approached smiling. Keith exclaimed under his breath and went to meet her. She was a dead ringer for that Pauline person. But this woman was slim, had poise and sex appeal, and was laughing.

'Hello,' Polly said. 'I thought I'd drop in . . .'

Keith was still half asleep.

'But . . . you're . . . Oh, of course . . . the sister . . . the strangely named one . . . Concepta!' he added on a note of triumph, delighted that he had remembered.

Polly looked at him severely. She could go along with this charade for the moment; it might be worth a laugh – if he had a sense of humour. Or she could come clean. But it suddenly seemed to her that anything other than candour was pointless, and undignified.

'Keith, I hate to tell you this, but Concepta doesn't really exist! There's only ever been me!'

Keith started to laugh. 'Who would have believed it!'

'For a moment I thought you had gone,' Polly said. 'What with the For Sale sign and everything.'

Keith followed her gaze to the square sign bearing the name of Spiffney and Co., Estate Agents, and their phone number.

'Oh yes,' he said, 'I don't want to sell, but my father-in-law's estate is in a bit of a mess. But do come in. You look a bit different; must be the hair-do.'

'I know,' Polly said with a sigh. 'I've lost some weight as well. Do you mind me dropping in like this? I thought as I was in London I'd darken your door . . . and look at those snuff boxes you've been going on about!' she added with a glint of mischief. 'If you still want me to?'

When Keith didn't answer she added, 'I know I should have phoned.'

'Actually,' Keith said, leading her into the patio and clearing away the remains of his lunch, 'I'm a bit dumbstruck. I've been trying to contact you! Did you get my letter?'

Polly picked up his coffee mug and followed him to the kitchen.

'Your letter? No . . .'

'I posted it yesterday.'

'I came to London this morning . . .'

Polly looked at the green sliminess languishing on the draining board.

'What's this?'

'I don't know,' Keith said. 'I thought it was a lettuce. But it had other ideas!' He picked up the offending vegetable and threw it in the bin.

Polly laughed. Keith reached into the fridge for a bottle of wine, found two glasses.

'Come and sit down like a good girl. I want to talk to you.'

When Polly was seated at the white Edwardian wrought-iron table that Marguerite had bought, and was gazing into the garden, Keith handed her a glass of wine.

'Thing is . . . here, drink this . . . you're going to need it!'

'Why am I going to need it?' Polly said amiably, accepting the glass. 'You sound as though you are the bearer of doleful tidings!'

Keith looked at her open face, into her dark eyes, and wondered how he would tell her. He experienced again the sense of her innocence, as though the person before him was not an inhabitant of the world. He felt in her a kind of quivering courage, the sort belonging to a shy woodland creature who had determined to venture on to the plain to take a look around. So far the venture had been a success, judging by the glow she emanated, the subtle pleasure of one who has, so far, survived on her own terms.

'Thing is, Pauline . . . I did find your Lottery ticket after your last visit. I forgot that when I spoke to you on the phone; that's why I was trying to contact you!'

Polly flushed. 'Oh God . . . I'm sorry for being such a scald as to bother you with all that! Where is it?'

'I'm afraid it's gone. I suspect the worst. My cleaning lady is on sudden holiday and I'm informed by the Irish Lottery that a big prize, dating back to Easter, was recently collected by a woman hailing from London!'

Polly did not move. 'What are you trying to tell me?' she said slowly. 'That you think your charwoman found my ticket and collected the prize?'

'Could be . . . I know the ticket was in the house . . . and now it's gone . . . and so's she and the prize.'

'It must be coincidence!' Polly said, badly needing to laugh at the incongruity of everything connected with this particular episode in her life. 'These kinds of things don't really happen!'

'Of course they don't,' Keith said doubtfully. 'But still . . .'

He studied her. He had expected her to become agitated, maybe even upset. He had been dreading imparting this news to her. But she seemed unruffled, almost resigned.

'Aren't you upset?'

'Things without all remedy should be without regard!' Polly said, trotting out her favourite bit of Shakespeare. But inside she was thinking, you can't be getting yourself knotted over this turn in the farce. Don't assume for a moment that such an unlikely set of circumstances could have real foundation.

'But it may not be without remedy. If this turns out to be a fraud, there are laws to deal with it!' Keith said sternly.

Polly looked at him for a moment with a slow smile. 'And what makes you think that a woman who has recently stolen four million quid is going to come back meekly from whatever idyll she is spending it in?'

221

'I hadn't thought of that!' Keith said. 'But the law has a long reach.'

'True. But there's generally a small precursor known as evidence! You know . . . tiresome complications such as proof.'

They stared at each other for a moment and then both of them laughed and turned to look at the garden.

'What would you do with it anyway?' Keith enquired after a moment. 'The money . . . if you had it?'

'Buy a house with a garden . . .'

He glanced at her. 'So you live in a flat?'

'No,' Polly said. 'I live in a house, but the garden is not very big. It's a very ordinary semi-detached house. I do not have any money of my own. I've come to London to look for a job. I'm a great one for concocting alternative worlds; I've even told you lies to cover up embarrassment!'

She did not meet his eyes. She thought of Cat and Wags and the shiny edge to the lawn where the boys had trampled the grass. She thought of Martha having a mythical miscarriage on the floor; she thought of a court order for sale; she thought of being trapped in some lamentable new dog-box away from her friends.

'Are you married?' He said this very gently.

'Not really,' Polly said after a moment. 'Although I used to think I was.'

'Would you care to clarify?'

'Certainly. I went through a marriage ceremony with a man called Rory Caine. He was already married, so the arrangement was bigamous!'

She looked at him, laughed at his expression. 'God, how you must think me cracked!'

'Not at all,' Keith said politely. 'I'm fascinated! Are you still with this Rory?'

'I live in the same house. I would like to leave him. And as for why I got myself into such a mess – it's a long story! It has to do with all the fictions which exist in Ireland . . . Look!' She pointed enthusiastically. 'Isn't that a gorgeous cat!'

Keith followed her gaze, saw Jocasta's smoky-blue coat and inscrutable eyes regarding them from a Hebe shrub, accepted the evasion.

'That's Jocasta,' he said. 'She belongs to my neighbours.'

Herbie sat up, growled menacingly.

'Down, boy,' Keith commanded and added laconically, 'Jocasta's very female. She likes to tease.'

Polly frowned. 'Do you think that typically female? Teasing?'

'Actually no. Men are the real teasers. They tease with all sorts of things, promises of love, tenderness, security, happiness, all the things women want. Many of them never deliver! In my profession you see a lot of the fall-out.'

Polly was silent for a while. Then she said, 'Keith, you're a psychiatrist . . . isn't that right?'

'Yes.'

'And you're retired?'

'Yes . . . perforce. I have something called angina pectoris. So I'm supposed to be a good boy and not overload the old cardiovascular system. But I keep myself busy writing the odd paper and so forth . . .'

'So you would know all about queer things which happen in people's minds?'

Keith was suddenly listening acutely. He did not move in his chair. He glanced at the woman beside him and saw that her eyes were fixed on the white wrought iron of the table. She seemed suddenly very young.

He asked almost tonelessly. 'What kind of "queer things"?'

Polly took a deep breath. 'I have this friend, you see . . . no, it's me . . . I'm going to stop inventing lives for myself. The truth is – I keep hearing voices!'

When Keith did not respond she added, 'I mean voices, or rather a voice, in my head!'

'Tell me!'

Polly looked into the heart of the garden. She saw the crazy-paving path which wound into a private corner by the mellow brick wall. In that secluded spot was a low screen of lavender, a strawberry tree, a pergola and a small rustic seat. She had a sudden longing to go and sit there.

'It's a kind of dialogue with myself. It started about a year ago . . .'

'Is it a voice or a thought?'

'Well a thought . . . really . . . I mean it's not a voice in the sense of being a real auditory experience . . .'

'What does it say?'

'Oh, this and that! Small chat, snippets of wisdom, surges of assertiveness and anger . . .'

'That's all?'

'Well, except that it told me to chop the cat's head off, it hasn't tried to foment violence, if that's what you mean!'

Keith nodded.

'I haven't chopped the cat's head off, incidentally!' Polly added quickly.

Keith relaxed. He watched her eyes as she turned to look at him.

'Do you experience this "voice" as emanating from someone else?' he asked.

'Oh no. It's me talking to me!'

'You're projecting, that's all.'

Polly stood up. 'I must go and sit on that rustic seat at the end of the garden. Do you mind?'

Keith followed her to the small wooden bench by the strawberry tree. And in this fragrant dell Polly told him the whole truth about her life. She told him everything, about Rory and cyberspace and Peter and Jason and Susie. She told him how she had stood by the postbox in the freezing cold and that the postman had refused to give back her letter. She told him about her loneliness, and how coming out to Wimbledon had been an adventure. She mentioned Muriel and the children and the village and Madge and daughter Peggy and poor alcoholic Sam. She also told him about Martha, the source of so much anxiety. And, finally, she told him that she came to London to be interviewed for a job and that she had the loan of a very posh flat in Eaton Square while her brother and his fiancée were abroad.

'But this "voice"!' she ended. 'I've been worried about it . . . It seems a kind of critical alter-ego . . . something of a dare.'

'Is it a constant presence?'

'No . . . just every now and then.'

'And do you see anything . . . is it manifested visually?'

'God, no! Visions are all I'd need.'

'I can't advise you professionally,' he said eventually. 'Not because I'm so retired that my wits have deserted me, but because I think I'm rather . . . fond of you. But I can arrange for you to see someone if you would like. Personally, I don't think your problem is very serious; it's recent and stress-related, is not accompanied by hallucinations and is not relentless. I suspect you have been suppressing your identity; it is now becoming assertive!'

'So I'm normal?'

'Very, I would imagine.'

'And you . . . what about your angina?' she said.

'Oh, all that's under control!' Keith said hastily. 'I've given up smoking and I've taken up pills. I've a reasonable life expectancy, and I can always go for a bypass if I have to. Does that sound like a letter of recommendation?'

He reached out and took her hand. 'I'm supposed to avoid stress, but right now there's a certain stress which seems entirely apposite . . .'

When Mrs Jopling arrived she received no answer at the front door so she came around to the back garden. And there she saw Keith Warrington and a blonde woman kissing each other on the rustic seat beneath the pergola. They were sitting up quite straight, were holding hands and were kissing each other tentatively like a pair of teenagers on their first tryst. A young Siamese cat was staring at them curiously, her head half out of a shrub. Dear me, she thought, backing away. And I used to think Dr Warrington was such a nice, quiet man . . .

In fact, the two subsequent days proved that neither Keith nor Polly were quite the kind of people they thought they were. Neither of them was quiet, although both found the other very nice indeed.

To begin with Keith showed Polly his collection of silver snuff boxes.

'Very nice,' she said eagerly, examining hallmarks and estimating dates. 'Think of all the sneezing this lot must have witnessed! That's what really fascinates me about old things . . . the human connection, the hands and bodies that once made contact, the lives they touched!'

She paused, afraid of being on her hobby-horse, picked up a hexagonal silver box, with a pierced and engraved grille. 'This is not a snuff box, by the way!'

'What is it?'

'It's a vinaigrette.'

'Oh?'

'It was used for holding an aromatic restorative,' Polly said primly, 'like smelling salts . . . in case ladies fainted.'

Keith laughed. 'Tell you what, let's have an aromatic restorative ourselves . . . in case we faint. Let me take you out to dinner!'

Later he escorted her back to the flat in Eaton Square.

'Would you like a nightcap?' Polly asked. 'There's a whole array of booze in my sumptuous quarters with which I have been invited to make free!'

'Thank you very much,' Keith said, and he was in the flat and sitting on the couch before she knew it. She found some ice, poured him a Dubonnet, had a gin and tonic herself, slipped off her shoes, sat in an armchair with her legs curled under her.

'So what do you think of the flat?' Polly asked, gesturing.

'Very nice! There's a hint of decadence in the air . . . What did you say your brother and his fiancée do for a living?'

Polly shrugged. 'I didn't! I thought it would be rude to seem too curious. They appear to have loads of money. Tom never qualified for anything . . . came to London when he was still very young, so he must have done something extraordinary. He hasn't spoken to me for twenty years because I disobeyed him by marrying Rory.'

'But I thought you weren't really married to Rory?'

'I'm not . . . I went through a church ceremony, I told you. But Tom was angry about that . . . He said I was throwing my life away!'

'So you don't know what he does to fund his lifestyle.'

'Not really. I asked Michelle . . . she has a strong sense of humour . . . she said he was selling arms to the Arabs and then she said he was selling women to the Arabs and then she said he was working for an oil company. I assume the last is correct.'

'And what does *she* do?'

'Oh, she's something or other in public relations.'

'I see.'

Keith watched the woman in the armchair, saw how her body curved, saw that she moved to settle herself with grace, saw her knees and the length of her bent legs. But mostly he saw the animated laughter in her face, and the way gravity would replace it suddenly, like a play of light and shade.

Why didn't I realise at the beginning how pretty she is? he thought. This must be the strangest thing that ever happened in my life, but it is real! She is real! He felt deliciously tormented by desire.

For her part Polly was considering how strange it was to feel such complicity, such natural sympathy, with someone she had only met for the first time a couple of months ago. Something in her kept waiting for him to rush off to a computer; something in her expected his demeanour to become wooden, his eyes to dart around looking for a keyboard, like an exile or a junkie longing for a fix. She was so used to this, that she thought it came with being male, a gender-specific attribute like beards and testicles.

That same something became warmer and warmer as she realised that he didn't give a damn about computers, that he was utterly absorbed in being with her and talking to her. What she saw in his eyes thrilled her; it was a long time since an urbane and attractive man had looked at her with dilated pupils.

After another drink, during which they had lapsed into a charged silence, smiling at each other, Keith got up, took Polly gently by the hand and led her to the couch.

'All this decadence is getting to me,' he said. 'What would you say to an old-fashioned snog?'

'The man should never ask,' Polly said. 'It compromises the woman's self-image!'

Keith pulled her towards him and kissed her. Polly kissed him back, at first slowly and then with a fervour she thought she had long forgotten.

'I'm acting completely out of character,' she whispered in a dazed voice when she found herself lying in his arms.

'Oh, I don't think you're acting,' he said into her ear. 'And in case it's of any interest to you, I'm not acting either!'

After a while the couch became a little shunted from its original position. This exposed a beige file, which someone had pushed under it.

When Polly, a bit flushed and breathless, went to the kitchen to make coffee, Keith noticed the file which was now sticking out from beneath the sofa. He picked it up and a stream of photographs fell into his lap.

'My, my,' he murmured, examining the studies of naked young women and what was being done to them, 'but doesn't her brother have exotic tastes! I wonder what the Vice boys would say to this!'

He heard Polly coming back from the kitchen and so he rammed the photos back into the file and restored it beneath the sofa whence it had come.

# Chapter Seventeen

Keith called into the police station to have a chat with Sergeant Marsden, whom he knew well, having met him from time to time while on perambulation with Herbie, and having had need of his services when his car had been stolen two years ago. The sergeant was six foot two, with a burly build and a pair of sharp blue eyes which now examined Keith quizzically.

'Hello, Dr Warrington,' he said. 'Something the matter?'

'No . . . Actually I was just hoping for a quick word, if you've time.'

'Would you like to come through . . . No murders or armed robberies today . . .'

'Jolly good.'

Keith was conducted into a small office overlooking the police parking lot. He sat in a plastic chair where many a distraught person had sat before him and asked the officer of the law what would happen to someone who had stolen a lottery ticket and cashed the prize.

'When did this happen?' the sergeant asked him.

'Oh, I don't know that it's actually happened! It's just that a friend of mine lost a ticket and I have reason to believe that it may have been found by someone else and cashed.'

'Was this a big prize?'

'Four million. It was an Irish Lottery ticket. An Irish friend of mine dropped it in my house.'

Sergeant Marsden raised his eyebrows and narrowed his eyes.

'Was the ticket signed?'

Keith thought frantically. He didn't like to seem vague when he had come into the police station with a serious matter to discuss.

'I don't think so.'

'These lottery tickets, if unsigned, are payable to the bearer. Very difficult to prove ownership if you don't sign them.'

'But surely the thief could be called upon to show how she came by the ticket. I mean you can't buy an Irish ticket just like that. Theft, after all,' he added, 'is theft!'

The sergeant was regarding him doubtfully. 'I suppose you're sure that the ticket your friend lost was the winning one?'

Keith felt a bit uncomfortable. 'Well, it looks that way. I was really wondering what the drill would be in case it really was and was really pinched . . .'

'Why don't you tell me the whole story?'

So Keith said that a friend had left a lottery ticket behind in his loo and that said ticket had been bought in Dublin at the same time and the same place as the wining ticket, and that he had found it, but had thought no more of it. That it was gone. His charlady must have found it, he explained, and what she had done with it thereafter he could not say, except that it was rather strange that a woman who had recently complained that she hadn't a bean was suddenly on holiday in the Bahamas.

'She might have had a recent windfall; it might have been a present from her family; she might have won it in a draw; she might have had savings . . . There are other possibilities. Can't you find out?'

'Yes,' Keith said. 'I can find out if she comes home. She might stay on, after all, to spend her ill-gotten gains!'

'Of course, if you've hard evidence . . . Have you?'

'None,' Keith said.

The sergeant made a few doodles on his notepad.

'What's her name?'

Keith told him that her name was Mrs Dencher.

'Does she have a first name?'

'I'm afraid I don't know it!'

'And the name of the putative winner?'

'Pauline McCann.'

Then Sergeant Marsden suggested that he get her to make a statement. '. . . I presume your friend is quite certain that she had the winning numbers . . . ?'

Keith muttered something which passed for an affirmative. He was beginning to feel a bit foolish, so he said he had to go.

'I'll drop by and see you one of these days,' the sergeant said, not unkindly.

When Polly got home from the airport she found Rory taciturn and morose. He was alone in the sitting room, and started when she came in. Polly found his presence there slightly shocking. It was so long since they had been in this room together that her first thought was that the computer had broken down. Then she wondered if he was unwell.

'What's wrong?' Polly asked. 'Is there any news of Jason?'

'Oh no . . . That would never do! He might put us out of our parental misery . . .'

'You sound in bad form?'

'I am. It's just hit me. Here I am, working every minute God sends for this family; and now I'm to be abandoned by my wife who goes off looking for a job – in London I ask you!'

When Polly did not reply he added, 'And don't worry about Jason – he phoned looking for money. It's all he's good for! I told him in no uncertain terms to earn his own!'

Polly studied the truculent face of the man she had once taken on for life. She sought for the old love, but found it had deserted her. In its place was compassion. She knew him so well, this other 'half' of hers, all his moods, all his obsessions, just as she recognised the fact that she was only half visible to him, if she was visible at all. She was slightly visible today, because he had identified a nagging possibility that she might disappear for ever.

Rory handed her a letter. 'This came for you while you were away.'

Polly opened it. It was from the Civil Service Commission, had as heading the names of the examination she had undergone and went as follows: 'A *Chara*, I regret to inform you that you have been unsuccessful in the above examination. *Mise le meas*.' There followed a signature.

She handed the letter to Rory who read it and said a little diffidently: 'Poor old Poll. You didn't expect to get this job anyway, did you?'

'No I didn't. My maths were terrible.'

'How did you get on at the London interview?'

Polly shrugged. The euphoria connected with that event had long since subsided. But the euphoria connected with events ancillary thereto had not subsided at all.

'Don't know yet. They said they'd write.'

Then Rory took a missive from his breast pocket and handed it to her. It was from his solicitor to say that Martha's case had been listed for 10 October.

'We'll be in the poor house after that!' Polly said in a toneless voice. 'I'll have to get some kind of a job. Maybe they'd give me something in Abrakababra! I'm a dab hand at hamburgers!'

'No wife of mine is going to wait at table!' Rory said.

'How do you propose we live?'

Rory replied that he still had his salary and that the worst that could happen would be that they would have to sell the house and buy a smaller one.

'But houses don't come that much smaller!' Polly said. 'And I don't want to live in a smaller one! And, what's more, I *won't* live in a smaller one!'

Rory looked at her. 'You mightn't have much choice!'

When Susie came around later she exclaimed on how slim Polly was looking.

'I hardly know you any more, you've become so gorgeous!' She turned to Rory, who could be seen through the open dining-room door, sitting at his computer, which had once again befriended him. 'Hasn't she got all gorgeous, Rory?' she demanded. 'You must be doing something right . . . ha ha!'

'What . . . oh yes, of course,' Rory said in a slow robotic voice.

The two women looked at each other. Polly shrugged, smiled and drew her friend into the kitchen, asked her about Fergus.

'Has he had any luck with the job hunting?'

'Not a sausage,' Susie said. 'He's driving me nuts, because he's anxious and irritated. He keeps hinting at some business he wants to set up, something to do with computer software. I'm just scared that he'll spend all his redundancy money on it!'

'But Fergus is very clever and if he's feeling entrepreneurial he'll probably make a go of it.'

Susie sniffed. 'Perhaps. There's loads of competition. You can't put your foot down in this country without standing on some computer hot-shot!' Susie sighed. 'And on top of everything there's my little madam.'

'Your little madam? Oh . . . you mean Sharon?'

'Yes. She won't eat!'

'Oh God! She's not getting anorexic, is she?'

'I hope not. She spends ages in her room, writing what I thought were essays, only now I find it's poetry and letters. The poetry is all about passion and the letters are addressed to someone called her "darling P". I found them in her drawer. OK, OK, maybe I was snooping, but I am her mother!'

'She must have a crush on someone,' Polly said. 'Can't you remember what it felt like . . . the agony and the ecstasy . . . the makebelieve?'

'That's why I'm so worried! It might be someone dreadful . . .'

'I'm sure it isn't! Did you keep an eye on Muriel's house while I was away?'

'Sure. I fed the cat. Couldn't bring myself to go in, though. All that wealth gives me a headache! She's probably in the Seychelles, hanging around a bar somewhere, desperately trying to pick up a fella . . .'

When the phone rang Polly rushed to answer it. There was a momentary pause and then the now-familiar voice said, 'Pauline, is that you?'

Polly's heart turned over a little and a small smile gathered in the corners of her mouth. She lowered her voice.

'How are you?'

'I've been to see the police about that bloody ticket!'

'Oh, Keith . . . there's no hard evidence. They can do nothing!'

'So it seems! And the intrepid criminal was due to clean my house today and has not arrived . . . so what does that look like?'

'She's decided to stay in the Bahamas!'

'Pauline?'

'Yes?'

'Something's just occurred to me. I should have asked you yesterday . . .'

'What?'

'Will you come over and see me again soon? There's something I forgot to mention.'

'What?'

'It's not for phones . . .'

'Oh?'

'So will you?'

'Are you serious?'

'Never more so!'

Polly laughed to indicate that she could take a joke. She looked around, saw Sue regarding her from the kitchen with interest. She could think of nothing banal to say, and dared not say anything else. She heard Keith's voice: 'Can you talk?'

Polly knew that Susie's ears were keen. 'Not really!'

She heard the chime of a doorbell in the earpiece.

'Someone's at the bloody door anyway,' Keith said. 'Talk to you soon!'

Susie pretended to be reading the evening paper. She had it open on the kitchen table.

'Who was that?' she asked conversationally when Polly put the phone down.

'Oh, just an old friend . . . from school,' Polly said. 'I haven't talked to her for ages!'

Sue gave her a queer look. 'Really! With a name like Keith I'm surprised you talk to her at all!' She pursed her lips; 'If I didn't know you better, Polly Caine, I'd swear you were up to something!'

'Ah, hello, hello . . . Mrs Dencher . . . come in, come in.'

'I'm sorry if I've disturbed you, Dr Warrington,' came the earnest voice. 'I couldn't come this morning. My 'Arry is poorly . . .'

'Not at all, not at all,' Keith said heartily. 'Did you . . . eh . . . have a good holiday?'

'Oh, it was lovely! You never saw anything so nice. Beautiful beaches. Just like from a postcard. Sunshine all the time! But to tell you the truth, Dr Warrington,' she added, dropping her voice to a confiding register, 'it was that foreign and that 'ot, and there were those mosquitoes whining and biting, that I'm ever so glad to be 'ome!'

'Something of a surprise, was it?' Keith asked. 'The holiday?'

'My 'Arry won it . . . you wouldn't believe it! . . . and we went for our anniversary! Forty years married!'

There was silence then, broken only by the sound of Mrs Dencher's footsteps heading towards the kitchen.

At that moment the doorbell rang again. Keith moved down the hall to open it and admitted a breezy Sergeant Marsden.

'Good morning, Dr Warrington. I was in the locality and thought I'd drop by . . . I was thinking about that business we discussed . . . time is running and so on and . . .'

He thought that Keith seemed a bit flummoxed and added in a loud and cheerful voice: 'Just wondering if that charlady of yours ever turned up. You know . . . the one who stole the lottery ticket!'

Sergeant Marsden was not his usual sensitive self that morning, otherwise he would have noticed how Keith gritted his teeth, and indicated with his hand that the officer of the law should keep his mouth shut.

'She's here,' he hissed, indicating the kitchen.

Mrs Dencher, who had clearly overheard in the kitchen, emerged looking very red and miffed.

'I'm Dr Warrington's charlady and I never stole nothing in my life!' she announced, squaring up to the policeman and staring him in the eye.

Sergeant Marsden looked abashed. But he had committed himself now, was used to his authority, and didn't realise he should back off.

'Did you or did you not find a lottery ticket in this gentleman's lavatory?' he demanded.

'I did not!'

'I see . . .' the sergeant said disappointedly, looking at Keith. 'Are you sure?'

'I am sure. Am I under some sort of suspicion?' she demanded, rounding on Keith.

'Certainly not,' Keith said.

But Mrs Dencher's blood was up. 'I'll just get my jacket,' she said, 'and I'll be off. I don't stay where I'm insulted! Though I wouldn't mind being paid for my trouble in coming here today!'

Keith attempted to say something. He gestured to Sergeant Marsden to stay where he was and followed the angry charlady into the kitchen.

'Please don't take offence, Mrs Dencher. The police officer was referring to someone who was . . . er . . . here while you were away . . . It was someone else altogether,' he repeated when the charlady remained grimly silent.

Mrs Dencher's face remained closed. 'Did this person steal something?'

'Well, not exactly,' Keith said. 'But I can tell you that as far as I'm concerned I wouldn't have anyone in to clean but yourself.'

Mrs Dencher brightened. She lowered her voice and confided, 'I knew the moment I came in the door there'd been another woman around. You have to be careful about the sort of people you let into the house!'

Keith returned to the hall.

'Not the culprit, eh?' the sergeant said in a musing tone. 'Either innocent or a good actor! We'll check her out . . .'

Polly inspected Muriel's house. There were a few items of post strewn on the tiles of the hall, and she picked the letters up and put them on the table. She went into the spacious drawing room and looked out of the window at the rows of semis and the cherry trees on the pavement. She wondered when Muriel would be back. It was strange that they had received no card, no letter, nothing from her in her holiday destination. She always wrote to say when she would be back and to give a few cheery lines about the weather and the food.

For some reason the big house felt forlorn, like a lovely ghost in a crinoline who had shown up at a modern disco, her beauty and grace incongruous in the cynical perspectives of modernity.

For the first time it occurred to Polly that the house was like Muriel herself, something from another era, too delicate and rarefied to attune to the modern world. She began to feel in it a strange sense of suffering, some crucifixion of the spirit borne in silence. 'Grace under pressure' was the thought which presented itself, and she dwelt on Muriel with a disturbed sense of having wronged her.

She fed Sable who came running in from the kitchen garden and then she went upstairs and returned the Gucci bag and suit to Muriel's bedroom. 'It's better to have borrowed them than take her at her word . . . I'll thank her when I see her. I owe her money anyway . . . over Jason . . .'

She glanced out of the window, saw her house, then saw her son Peter emerge and saunter down the pavement, saw little Sharon O'Brien approach from the direction of the village. She watched as Peter stopped to speak to her. Sharon seemed strangely embarrassed. She stared at her feet, so that all that Peter could see of her was the top of her head.

Such a shy girl! Polly thought and remembered what Sue had said about her being in love. She'll need to become more assertive if she's going to galvanise her inamorato – whoever he may be!

As she was leaving the room she picked up a piece of paper from the floor near Muriel's bedside table. When she turned it over she saw that it was a torn photograph; a man's head smiled at her from some sylvan setting. There were trees behind him, but he was lacking a body, for the picture had been torn across the middle. She examined him for a moment, thought he looked very handsome, put the torn photo down on the bedside table and went downstairs.

For some reason the beauty of the house no longer enthralled her; it was imbued with claustrophobic loneliness, as though the lovely antiques themselves had been clothed in the false camaraderie of desperate projections, as though they had been owned by someone who could not have life and therefore attempted to extract surrogate vitality from the inanimate.

For the first time she was glad to find the open air and escape back to 14 Ashgrove Lawns.

The following morning an unusually subdued Sue phoned from work. Her voice sounded low and shocked, as though the breath had been knocked out of her.

'Poll . . . have you seen the *Irish Times* this morning?'

'No. Can't afford it!'

But Sue did not laugh at the joke. 'Well, the obituary column has a death notice . . .' Susie's voice trailed away in evident distress.

'Of whom?' When there was no answer Polly repeated in alarm, 'Sue . . . of whom?'

'Oh, Poll . . . of Muriel.'

'*Our* Muriel?'

'Yes . . . Muriel Reeves of Willow House, Dundrum.'

'Oh God,' Polly said. 'What happened? Was it an accident? Was she killed in an accident?'

'No,' Susie's shocked voice continued, 'she died in Beaumont Hospital!' Her voice broke. 'They say it was after a cruel illness bravely borne.'

The implications bore in on Polly with a leaden sense of finality. 'But . . . I thought she was on holiday . . .'

'So did I,' Susie whispered shakily. 'I thought she was soaking up the sun and chatting up the Lotharios. But apparently not . . .'

'When is the funeral?'

'Removal of remains tomorrow, funeral following day. Oh, Poll . . .'

Everything ends, Polly told herself as she stood in the sitting room in tears and looked out at Willow House. The end doesn't always come heralded, with due notice, kindly warning. It just happens. The world flips upside down; the sun goes on shining. But it will never smile on Muriel again.

Now that her eccentric neighbour was gone for ever Polly felt the sense of loss, felt the reduction of Ashgrove Lawns to the ordinary. In five minutes it had become just another part of the estate, just an ordinary cul-de-sac with one incongruous house. The same house had become a stone monument, a thing.

'I'm going to miss you, Muriel,' she said aloud. 'I wish I'd been a better neighbour. I wish I'd known you better. But I'm going to miss you very much!'

The following day Polly and Susie attended the removal of Muriel's remains. People came whom they had never seen. Among them was a man of middle age, deeply tanned, who had an aloof and privileged aura. He reeked of the self-esteem of one who has spent years being worshipped.

'Hello,' Susie said, extending her hand. 'You won't know us, but we live just opposite Willow House. I'm Susan O'Brien and this is Polly Caine.'

'Ah yes,' he said, shaking hands politely. 'I'm Michael Connolly.'

'Terrible about poor Muriel!'

'Yes.'

Susie said fiercely, as they walked away, 'Isn't he the shit who dumped her?'

'Shsh . . .' Polly whispered.

A well-dressed woman detached herself from the back pew and joined Polly and Sue as they left the church.

'Hello. My name is Claire Denton. I'm an old friend of Muriel's. We used to work together.'

'Polly Caine, Sue O'Brien,' Susie said.

'So you're her neighbours! She often spoke of you. She envied you.'

'Envied us?' Susie intoned. 'She couldn't have! Compared to her, what did we have?'

Claire's eyes flickered. She regarded this small, brash woman with her greying red hair in distaste.

'I think she thought you had everything.'

Then Susie asked, 'Where did you work together?'

'In the bank, the Anglo-Belgian bank. It was taken over years ago.'

'What did you do?'

'We were clerks in those days,' Claire said tersely, as though she didn't care to be reminded.

While they stood in the sunshine a man in dark suit and glasses, a raincoat over his arm, came walking towards them from the church gate.

Polly regarded him automatically, but as he approached something in the set of his face reminded her of someone she had seen. He came towards the knot of women with an urbane stride, smiled at them. He had thick grey hair and smiled a conspiratorial smile, the sort which drew the recipient, willy-nilly, into a charmed familiarity. His was the charm which flattered, which said we're all friends and we all belong to the same order of importance and to the same understanding. He made eye-contact. He projected a knowledge and appreciation of the person he addressed, as though that person was known to him and valued.

'Excuse me – is the service over?' His voice was warm, cultured.

'Yes.'

He lingered for a second as though to assess the impression he made. In that moment his raincoat fell from his arm to the ground. He retrieved it. 'I'll just go in and pay my respects.'

Polly turned to Claire who was looking after the late-comer. She had suddenly remembered why she recognised him. His face was the one she had seen in Muriel's house, in a photograph which was torn across the middle, so that the head had been removed from the trunk. The man in the photo had been younger . . . but the resemblance was there.

'Do you know that man? Is he a relation?'

Claire was unsmiling. 'He's no relation.'

Polly's eye was caught by something on the ground. She was about to pick it up when Claire's foot descended on it and crunched it into the gravel.

'Oh,' Polly said, 'that man's lighter. You're standing on it! It must have fallen from his coat!'

Claire looked down. The lighter was lying well imbedded among the small stones.

'Oh dear! How silly of me.'

Polly picked it up. It was a Ronson. The initials AB were engraved on the front of it.

'What a pity it's scratched,' Claire said, but her voice was cold with venom.

She smiled at the two women as she moved away. Polly followed the man into the church, met him as he left and restored his lighter to him.

'Thank you,' he said.

Polly and Sue went home together in virtual silence.

'I get the feeling,' Polly said eventually, 'that there was more to Muriel's life than we ever knew. Do you think she could have had some kind of history?'

'Everyone has a history,' Sue said tartly. She added a little unkindly, 'Except you, of course, Poll!' As though struck by a sudden thought she turned to look at her friend. 'That is, as far as we know . . .'

The Caines and O'Briens attended the funeral the following day in the small Protestant cemetery. Muriel was buried in a new grave. The mourners could see the stark limestone crypt on the other side of the graveyard, where all the other Reeveses had been interred.

Everyone from the cul-de-sac came. Madge Kinlan from the village shop came. Sam Riley turned up, white as a sheet but miraculously sober.

'It was a brain tumour,' Madge said knowledgeably when the funeral was over and people had begun to disperse and were walking together in small groups along the yew-lined path towards the cemetery gate.

'Poor divil knew there was something wrong for some time and did nothing about it! Terrible headaches! A friend of my niece nursed her in Beaumont . . . Isn't it queer though, that she's not being buried with her family . . . A lonely new grave; she didn't want to go into the family crypt.'

Susie looked back at the cemetery, at the cold Romanesque-style crypt in the distance.

'Air's not so good there!' she quipped and when Madge looked at her reprovingly she added, 'Sorry, Madge!'

William Penston in gold-rimmed spectacles and pinstripe suit approached them at the gate.

'Hello, Susie,' he said.

Sue gestured at Polly. 'You know Mr Penston, my boss? This is my friend Polly Caine. You know Madge?'

'Of course!' He gave both women a smile and handshake.

Madge moved away and when she was gone William Penston added, 'I would like to see both of you, you, Susie, and you, Mrs Caine.'

'I'll be in at work tomorrow. You'll see me then.'

William Penston gave a small pained smile. His expression contained a silent comment on Susie's incorrigibility. It also contained a covert and reluctant delight in it.

'I know, Susie. But I would still like to talk to you both properly! There's lunch in the Furnace now and you're both invited of course . . . with your families. Everyone from Ashgrove Lawns is invited. Those were Muriel's wishes.'

'Are you her executor?' Susie asked.

'Yes.'

Polly and Sue exchanged glances.

'Why do you want to talk to us!' Susie asked almost suspiciously.

Willy Penston smiled. 'You may as well know – she has

mentioned you both in her Will.'

He allowed surprise to do its work and added, 'She was a very lonely woman you know . . . and very fond of you both!' He dropped his voice and added in a serious tone, 'In fact, she specifically charged me to tell you what a great comfort it was to her to have had two such wonderful friends.'

Susie watched the man's departing back. She looked as though she had been struck. She leant against the gatepost and put her head in her hands.

Polly held her. Sue's tears unleashed her own. When Fergus and Rory, who were discussing Windows while they waited for their wives, came to comfort them Sue only sobbed the harder.

'I am the greatest bitch who ever lived . . .' she kept repeating to her astonished husband, 'the most miserable old begrudger the world has known!'

Fergus patted his wife's shoulder. 'It's all right, love. It's all right!' He looked at Polly for enlightenment, but she was wiping her eyes.

'It's not all right! . . . I was so afraid I was a nonentity . . . !' But she let her husband take her arm.

Rory looked unhappily at Polly. He hated to see her cry; it undermined his usual defensiveness and it made him feel useless. His gesture of comfort was uncertain. The tears had upset him and he was struggling for his own composure. Sentiment was something he dreaded, because it was utterly contagious and it always unmanned him. He said, 'Come on now, Poll . . .'

Peter, who had suddenly appeared, whispered, 'It's OK, Dad, I'll look after her!'

He approached his mother and put an arm around her. 'Come on, Mum.'

As he led her away from the cemetery he added softly in her ear, 'Jason's back!'

Polly straightened, turned to her son. 'When?'

'Just this minute . . . he's been here and trundled off home on the grounds that he's hungry!'

Polly wiped her eyes. 'Thank you, God,' she murmured. 'Thank you, God!'

'Seems the little turd has had enough,' Peter went on

242

sardonically. 'He's all agog to sit the Leaving and make himself a life . . .'

'I don't believe you,' Polly said, searching in her bag for more tissues. 'What has brought this on?'

Peter smiled grimly. 'It seems he's discovered that there are worse things in life than home and study. The Jezebel, methinks, was a bit more than he bargained for. I don't know what she did to him, but there's a definite aura of relief in the air . . .'

'Peter,' Polly said after a moment, squeezing her son's arm, feeling the muscular strength, the iron biceps, the miraculous adult male tendons of yesterday's baby.

'What?'

'I love you!'

'Ah, don't be embarrassin' me, Ma!' Peter said lugubriously, but he smiled.

# Chapter Eighteen

The typewritten envelope with the English frank was carried around by Polly for some time before she could bear to open it. She knew it was from Shetly's and was sternly warning herself that of course there was no possibility that she could have got the job. If you knew the worst in advance there was no pain in rejection.

Eventually she got a kitchen knife and opened the envelope, scanned the letter quickly. A short one-sentence letter would have told her all she needed to know before she even read the words. But the letter was a bit longer than that. It said:

Dear Mrs Caine,

With reference to your recent interview we are pleased to offer you the position of assistant to the Managing Director at an initial salary of £15,000 per annum, to commence on the 25th inst. There will be a six-month probationary period and your salary will be reviewed at the end of it.

The hours will be as discussed at interview. You will be entitled to four weeks paid leave per annum.

If you wish to accept please let us know on or before the 17th inst. A telephone call will suffice.

I look forward to hearing from you.

Yours sincerely,
Jane Rollinson.

Polly showed the letter to Rory and he said, 'Well done,' in a preoccupied sort of way, and then followed her into the kitchen to ask in a worried tone of voice: 'You're not serious about any of this, Poll, are you? I mean it is all a bit of a joke . . . Isn't it?'

'Sure. I always get jobs for a joke!'

She saw Rory's chagrin with astonishment. He had never before evinced discomfiture at her plans. But he hadn't believed for a moment there was the slightest chance that this would happen.

'What harm can it do?' she asked sweetly. 'Of course I'll come back at weekends, stock the deep freeze, do a bit of baking, catch up on the cleaning, make sure the house runs like clockwork! I'll only be gone five days a week! You won't miss me . . .'

Polly wondered if she had offended Rory by so much dryness. But apparently not.

He thought for a moment. 'Well, when you put it like that . . . But it will be very expensive commuting at weekends.'

'I'll get special rates,' Polly said. 'It'll be quite cheap. And by Monday morning it will be the same as if I had been here all week; all systems will be going. I'll spend the whole weekend at the housework!'

'Hmnn,' Rory said. 'In that case . . .'

He went back to his computer. After a moment he called out, 'Poll?'

'What?' Polly said, fishing Jason's clothes out of the holdall he had left on the kitchen floor.

'You know with you working and everything . . . we could get a loan to pay off Martha. We won't have to sell the house after all!'

'That's true,' Polly said. 'On the other hand Sue and I were thinking of setting you and Fergus up in the computer software business you keep hinting at. He already has all the contacts you could hope for . . . and you both have years of expertise! That way you could pay off Martha yourself!'

The clicking at the keyboard ceased. Rory came into the kitchen.

'Polly . . . that's really nice of you.' He smiled a little indulgently. 'Now, I know you'll be earning good money, but if you're commuting at weekends and living the rest of the time in London . . . you won't have a spare penny left. What on earth made you think you could set us up in business . . . even with Susie's help. London is a terribly expensive place to live!'

'That's true,' Polly agreed. 'Well, we'll have to see! But, if we do, Susie and I . . . will want a stake in the business commensurate with our investment.'

Rory laughed. 'Poor old Poll. I wonder how long you'll last at the London job if you're going to go overboard like this!'

He caught the glint in Polly's eye and added hurriedly, 'I'm not being snide or anything . . . It's just that you don't know much about the real world. How could you . . . I mean you left it so long ago and it has moved on . . .'

'Watch this space!' Polly said.

But Rory didn't hear her. His thoughts were with higher things.

Polly and Susie went to see William Penston together.

'What do you think is involved?' Polly asked. 'Mentioning us in her Will, I mean . . . ?'

'If she had any sense of irony,' Susie said, 'she'll have left me her cat!'

'Sable has come to us,' Polly said. 'She cries at the front door and I bring her in and feed her. Cat is very nasty to her, so I have to keep them apart!' After a moment Polly added, 'Look, Sue, did you tell Fergus about this?'

'No!'

'Are you going to?'

'Depends. If she's actually left me some money the only person who is going to know about it is you! I think we should keep it to ourselves!'

Polly thought of what Rory would do with any money which might become available and nodded agreement.

'I thought solicitors' offices were all knee-deep in documents!' Polly said in a whisper, as she looked around her. The place was neat; good carpet, reception area with magazines and comfortable tweed settees, prints of Georgian Dublin; 'I had expected the dusty insulation of last century's left-over paper mountain . . .'

'When did you last darken the portals of a law firm?' Susie enquired tartly.

'About twenty-one years ago! I had an insurance policy and I wanted to make sure that if I died Rory would get the benefit! So I made a Will. But I didn't die,' she added. 'I only thought that I had!'

'What's got into you lately, Polly Caine?'

Behind his desk Willy Penston had the demeanour of a doctor. He had the same kind of hands joined together in apparent prayer, and, at least from the other side of his big Victorian desk, the same remote and slightly antiseptic aura. He flipped open the pages of a file and informed the two women that they were the principal beneficiaries of Muriel's Will. He handed each of them a copy of this document, which was typed in double spacing on paper with a wide margin. 'I, Muriel Reeves, of Willow House, Ashgrove Lawns, Dundrum, County Dublin, hereby revoking all Wills and Testamentary Disposition heretofore at any time made by me make this for my Last Will and Testament.'

The Will appointed William Penston to be executor, proceeded to give a few bequests to various charities, a thousand pounds to every family in Ashgrove Lawns, the gift of fifty thousand pounds and a particular painting to her friend Claire Denton. It then went on: 'All the rest, residue and remainder of my property of every kind and description I GIVE DEVISE AND BEQUEATH to my dear friends Pauline Caine and Susan O'Brien of 14 and 15 Ashgrove Lawns, Dundrum, respectively, in equal shares absolutely.'

There was a long silence. Susie did not speak. She bit her knuckle and looked hard at the desk. Polly had her hand over her mouth; her face was very pale.

'Our friends in the Revenue will take a terrible lump out of it,' the solicitor said uncomfortably, 'but Miss Reeves was adamant that she wanted it this way, even if it meant such a tax bill.'

'How much is in the estate?' Polly asked in a whisper.

'Not clear just yet. But it would appear that the total assets will exceed five million. Her money was very well invested; she had an excellent accountant. I don't think she knew herself how rich she was. Money, she once told me, was meaningless once you had enough and a bit to spare! She used to say that people were very silly to put such effort into making it. You could only be in one place at a time and could only eat so much and wear one outfit at a time . . .' He glanced at them; 'Well, that's what she used to say.'

'Jesus, Mary and holy Saint Joseph,' Susie said suddenly. 'I don't believe this!'

'Are you sure about . . . all this?' Polly asked, taking her hand away from her mouth. 'I mean, that this was her real Will and everything? She might have made another one after it! She might have changed her mind . . .'

William Penston smiled indulgently. He had made sure that the contents of this Will were unknown to Susie and was enjoying her surprise. It had been typed by a secretarial agency some ten miles away, and he had taken personal custody of it in his own safe. That way none of the staff had seen it.

'She made it at this very desk, just six weeks ago. After that she went into hospital where she died.'

The silence returned. The solicitor made embarrassed geometric doodles on his blotter, glanced at Sue. 'She knew she was unwell,' he said gently. 'It would have been improper for me to have told you, Susie, anything about it . . . you know that. Which was why I had a secretarial agency prepare the draft Will and the correspondence.'

The ticking of the clock sounded overloud in the silence. It was an old clock, with weights, a relic of William's grandfather's time. It was hung above the filing cabinets and lent a beguiling air of antiquity to the otherwise modern office. Its mechanism whirred suddenly and sounded a mellow half hour.

'I wonder is there some mistake?' Polly said after a moment. 'It seems almost indecent . . . I mean for us to inherit it. Had she no family?'

'Oh, I think she had some cousins somewhere, but she never saw them. No, she wanted you two to benefit . . . She was very taken with the idea of you as rich women. She even wondered, half laughing, what you'd do with it . . . that was if she died, of course. She was hoping she would pull through.'

When neither of the women responded to this he added with a slightly hang-dog smile, 'You'll be very well off, Susie. You both will. Have you any idea what you'd like to do with your inheritance?'

'I think I might give up my job?'

William Penston laughed. 'I thought you might. Although you're quite welcome to keep it on, if you want!'

'Actually,' Polly added, glancing at her friend, 'we might set up our husbands in a computer software venture . . . It's a possibility.'

William Penston seemed taken aback. 'You should be very careful,' he advised. 'You should make sure that such a venture is viable . . .'

'Oh, don't worry,' Susie said. 'They're both real hot-shots. And the shares in the new company would belong to the investors! The capital would be carefully allocated. I haven't been rubbing shoulders with the Law for all these years without some sense wearing off on me!'

She glanced at Polly before adding slowly and significantly, so that there could be no question of any misunderstanding, 'Our husbands and families know nothing about this . . . and we see no reason, for the moment at least, why they should!'

William Penston looked back at Susie across the desk. His eyes expressed respect. He turned to Polly: 'Naturally this is absolutely confidential. Of course, once the Will is proved, it becomes a document of public record. Any nosy-parker can find out who the beneficiaries are.' He paused. 'But I'll keep the file at home so no one here gets to see it yet.'

He leaned back expansively. 'Is there nothing you've in mind for yourselves, now that you know the extent of your good fortune?'

'Actually,' Polly said in a dreaming voice, 'there is a house I would like to buy. It came on the market recently . . .'

'Well, the money won't be available for some time yet, you know . . .' William Penston said hurriedly. 'The Will has to be proved and the assets realised, but if you're decided on a property a bridging loan could probably be arranged – once the Will is through Probate. Where is the house and how much is it?'

'Oh, it's in London,' Polly said. 'It's a house in Wimbledon . . . around three hundred thousand,' she added apologetically.

She glanced at Sue and saw that her mouth was open.

'What in God's name has you wanting to buy a house in London,' Susie demanded as they went home. Sue was driving her old banger, and thumped the gear lever with a trembling hand.

'I got that job I went for!'

There was silence for a moment. Susie did not like falling for jokes.

'Very funny,' she said. 'Pull the other one!'

'But I did,' Polly said. 'I told Rory and I'm off to London the week after next to begin work. And there *is* a house I want to buy. It's one of those Tudor-style places, has the most divine garden you ever saw . . . with a pergola and shrubs and roses and a sun-filled patio paved with real stone . . . none of your concrete slabs . . .'

'Wouldn't you be better off with a flat?' Sue said doubtfully. 'A big house and big garden sounds a bit much for just one person!'

Polly laughed and looked sideways at her friend. 'Who said it was for one person?'

There was silence for a moment. Sue glanced at her friend. 'Does that comment mean what I think it means?'

'Sure!' Polly said.

'It wouldn't have anything to do with someone called Keith you were talking to on the phone not so long ago?'

'It might.'

'So it's like that!' Susie said in a scandalised voice. 'Polly Caine, who would have believed it of you, pillar of the community, mother of two, devoted wife. Good practising Catholic! This is very shocking!'

'I know! To other people! But it isn't a bit shocking to me.'

She added, 'Rory won't miss me. He and Ferg will be too busy with their new business. And, quite candidly, Sue, I'm not going to spend the precious rest of my life as the unsung prop for a computer addict! If that's selfish, then I'm selfish!'

Susie looked at her sideways. 'What's brought all this on?'

Polly thought of something Michelle had said to her.

'I suppose you could say that I have finally been seduced by life!'

'Well, good for you,' Susie said in a matter-of-fact voice. 'It'll raise some eyebrows around here,' she added as they passed Laura Flanagan walking Scrumpy, 'but that's what eyebrows are for!' She glanced at her friend. 'Oh Polly, is he lovely? Tell me . . .'

'I'll have to do something myself,' she said with a laugh when Polly had assured her that he was indeed lovely.

251

'You'd never leave Ferg, would you?'

Sue thought for a moment. Then she smiled. 'No!'

When pressed with further enquiries Polly said hesitantly that she had met Keith more or less by accident.

'What kind of accident?'

Polly drew a deep breath. 'Do you remember that letter I wrote to the *Sunday Times*?'

Sue frowned, thought for a moment and then gave a shriek.

'Oh, you mean . . . THAT letter! Ooh, Polly, I don't, I simply do not, believe you!'

'It's true! Well, you're the one who put the idea into my head. So it's all your fault!'

She met her friend's eyes; they were smiling, then troubled. 'There's no point in looking at me as though I've lost my marbles. I have never, ever, been more sane in my life!'

'I'm going to lose you,' Sue said in a dead-pan voice.

'You can't. We're going to be business partners, remember . . .'

As they turned into the cul-de-sac past Willow House, Sue raised her left hand in a gesture of salute. 'Thank you, Muriel,' she said humbly. 'And God bless you!

'By the way,' she added, as she brought the car to a standstill in her driveway. 'Do you remember me telling you about Sharon?'

'Yes.'

'Well, I've found out who all the poems were written about!'

'Oh . . . who?'

Sue looked at Polly measuringly and smiled ruefully. 'I should have guessed it earlier, I suppose . . . Well, who do you think it was . . . ? The poems to her darling P?'

Polly thought of the glimpse she had had of Peter and Sharon from Muriel's window.

'Are you telling me it's my big baby?'

'Who else . . . I should have twigged it immediately. She's almost paralysed every time she sees him! But she's going to take her courage in her hands and ask him to her Debs. Do you think he'll want to go?'

'He'll be delighted,' Polly said firmly.

They sat for a few minutes more.

'What about the money?' Sue said eventually. 'What will we

do with it . . . It's not as though we deserve it? Do you feel OK about keeping it?'

When Polly got into the empty house she made a cup of tea, sat in the kitchen, talked to Cat who wondered what she had done to merit so much notice, wandered upstairs, opened her wardrobe, shut it, wandered back down again. On the hall table was a letter addressed to Jason. She picked it up, noticed it was very bulky. He was back at school, his first day of his repeat year. For herself, for this juncture in her life, she felt as though the end of term approached; she remembered the curious sense end of term had at school – that nothing could touch you any longer: Mother Josephine might growl, the awful Mother Frances might scowl, might threaten; but their claws were slowly being pulled. Each day, each hour that went by, was weakening their hold. Some day, she had promised herself, she would walk out of there and never look back. And she had. And now she was going to repeat the performance; she was graduating to another life.

When Jason came home Polly told him there was a letter for him. He looked at it, put it in his pocket, had a snack consisting of half a litre of milk, three peanut butter sandwiches, a slice of apple pie, a banana and a Twix bar he found in a kitchen drawer.

'Leave some room for your supper . . . I want to talk to you and Peter later.'

Jason looked at her closely. He put his head a little on one side. He had lost something of the challenging demeanour which had been his wont before he had strayed and returned. Small instances of what could be construed as maturity were now occasionally in evidence; small attempts were being made to harness the power known as charm.

'Why?'

'I just do. I want to talk to you on your own, so don't go out until I've had a chat with you.'

'You sound serious, Mum.'

'I *am* serious. I want to have a chat with my children. I want their blessing.'

Jason looked very taken aback. 'For what?'

'For a sea-change . . . Your father will be late home tonight. What would you say if you and Peter and I had an early dinner at the Furnace?'

'The Furnace! You bet!'

She indicated the letter sticking out of Jason's pocket. 'Are you going to read that or not?'

Jason took the letter out of his pocket. He looked at the envelope. 'I don't recognise the writing . . . But I'll read it upstairs if you don't mind, Mum.'

The Furnace was rich in lovely mouth-watering scents. Polly, dwarfed by her two sons, sat in a booth and ordered. Soup and chicken Kiev for the boys, salmon salad for her. She ordered a bottle of champagne.

'What are we celebrating, Mum?' Peter asked dubiously.

'Several things,' Polly said.

The boys exchanged glances and shifted uneasily. Their mother smiled. 'I've asked you here to tell you that I've got myself a job!'

'Oh . . .'

'In London!'

She had expected chagrin, or disapproval, but there was neither.

'When?' Peter asked.

'Soon. Two weeks. Do I have your blessing?'

'So you weren't joking!' Jason said conversationally.

Polly sat back and surveyed her children. They were eating with their usual gusto; her announcement might have been about the weather. It suddenly occurred to her that they were adult already in ways she had not guessed. They had moved beyond the point where they depended, in any radical emotional sense, on her or on her perspectives. Their horizons were filled already with their own dreams.

'So you don't mind?' she pressed.

'Go for it, Mum,' Peter said, looking at her over his spectacles. 'That's my advice!'

'Mine too,' Jason added. 'Why are you so worried about it? We can look after ourselves. We'll even look after the Hobbit. This job means a lot to you. You should take it. It would be stupid not to!'

'I'm thinking of buying a house over there, in London.'

'Good. Can we visit?'

'Of course. And I'll be back quite often. At the weekends and so forth . . .'

She felt a sudden absurd surge of grief. These young adults were autonomous intellectually and emotionally. They were able to sit there and tell her, albeit without spelling it out in so many words, that they didn't need her any more. They loved her, but they didn't need her. Where they were going she could not follow. They were the new ships sailing into unknown seas far beyond her reach.

It was the natural and proper order of things, and yet it came with a shocking realisation of mortality.

'I may separate from your father . . .' she said in a low voice.

The two young men stopped eating for a moment. Peter sighed. 'We know, Mum,' he said sadly. 'Jason and I have been saying for ages that it was only a matter of time.'

Jason's eyes filled with tears which he wiped angrily away.

When they returned Rory was at the computer.

'Where were you?' he called.

'Feeding our faces,' Peter replied. 'Mum took us to the Furnace for supper!'

'To celebrate my new job!' Polly added.

'Is there anything to eat in the house?'

'Sandwiches,' Polly said. 'I'll make you some.'

When the phone rang she picked it up.

'Could I speak to Peter, please,' a very tentative female voice enquired.

Polly went in search of her elder son.

'It's Sharon . . . and you're to say yes very nicely and tell her you're delighted she asked you.'

'What are you talking about, Mum?'

'Just pick up the phone and do what you're told.'

She heard him go downstairs, say 'Hello?', say 'Hi, Sharon', say 'Let me look in my engagements book . . . no, seriously, I'd be delighted . . .'

When she came downstairs he said with a bemused air,

'Sharon's just asked me to her Debs! . . . But how did you know, Mum, that she would?'

'Mothers are clairvoyant,' Polly said. 'I trust you accepted?'

'Of course!'

Polly tried several times to get through to the flat in Eaton Square. All she got was an answer phone. 'Hi . . . this is Michelle speaking. I'm afraid there is no one here to take your call at the moment . . .' Eventually Polly left a message.

'Michelle, this is Polly. I'm coming to London soon. I won't impose on you; you've already been far too hospitable. But I'd like to see you if you've time!'

Michelle did not ring back.

But a few days later Polly got a letter on stiff pale blue paper. The Eaton Square address was printed in Gothic lettering at the top of the page.

Dear Polly,

I got your message on the answer machine. I'm not at the flat any more, so don't mind the address on this note paper.

The fact is, Polly, that I'm going home, back to America. I've decided to do my Master's and get into teaching and leave the crap life I was trying so hard to make a mint in; trying, that is, until you came along!

Tom and I were all washed up by the time you first came to London. That particular paragon is undoubtedly very charming, but he is as unscrupulous a pimp as ever I've had to deal with. Oh, Polly, of course you hadn't a clue and I couldn't at the time disabuse you. It's so gorgeous to meet someone who believes in old values and who really is so family based. I thought people like that only existed in children's books!

But the truth about your brother is that he has been orchestrating a tidy little vice-ring for several years. It has made him a rich man. He contracts the services of women to various sex industries, not least to those in the Middle East, and has done very nicely through this particular form of exploitation.

He used to say that he wouldn't contact you until he

256

had made his pile and could rescue you from your awful little husband and your boring life. I told him, after I had met you, that you were happy as a pig in shit and to leave you alone!

Anyway, I was never a good girl, like you. I had a strict upbringing (lots of Americans do, Polly, despite what you see on TV) and I decided at an early age to rebel as a matter of principle. I didn't much care what I was rebelling against, so long as it was something. How did I get into prostitution? I glided into it quite easily, mostly out of spite. I knew it would really get to my folks, who were pissing me off at the time. The first trick was the hardest. After that the barriers don't operate so good.

But it is a shitty life; there's a corrosion in it that no amount of money makes up for; and the most awful guys, coarse, cruel, sometimes silly, think you're a thing and they're almighty God. If you begin to believe that yourself you're scooped. Some women do. There's a powerful momentum to this mind-set; it surrounds us, this imperative to please, the desperation that you might get old, and become nothing because men will cease to notice you or want you.

Crap! Men aren't gods; women in my business know that. But I've still had enough plastic surgery done to launch a Lego industry.

Funny thing is, I've rebelled again! Perhaps I have you to thank for the jolt. I never in my life met anyone so straight from the planet Jupiter. But you said a few things which made me feel sick to my stomach about myself. I began to think of what I could be. I began to feel tired. I began to think of peace.

I still don't have the kind of money I thought I would make, but money isn't everything and I'm getting out. And I've shopped that brother of yours because he is also running drugs! And because he deserves to be shopped. If you knew the full story there you might even approve, but I won't shock your innocence.

I once thought he really cared; we really were engaged, you know, but he was just messing me around. And I've had enough of being messed around. I had a bit of revenge lined up, which had you in the starring role – because he always painted you as such a paragon; I thought taking you down a whole row of pegs might stick in his shitty little craw. I won't go into details – I'd prefer if you didn't hate me – suffice to say there's a bunch who like older women, provided they're well endowed and inexperienced; those creeps who came in that evening were part of it; but you had the last laugh. They were sent away like naughty little boys.

I don't think you'll be hearing from your brother. He's too proud to write to you from jail. But you can always contact Her Majesty's Prison Service and find out where they are stashing him, if you really want to know, that is.

Anyway, stay real.

Michelle.

Polly was impatient on the flight to Heathrow. The plane was stacked over the airport for about ten minutes, which added to her frustration.

Keith was not there to meet her; she had not told him she was coming; not yet. She wanted to savour the pleasure of being able to surprise him.

Polly went to Wimbledon and visited the estate agents who had No 17 Marbonne Road on their books.

'I'm interested in this house,' she said. 'In fact I would like to buy it!'

'When would you like to view it, madam?'

'I already have,' Polly said.

'The asking price is £350,000,' the estate agent said, 'and we already have an offer of £300,000.'

'I'll give you the asking price!' Polly said. 'I can give you a deposit right now, in fact.'

'I see.' The agent opened a ledger and took her name and address. Polly gave her maiden name, McCann.

'What about a survey?'

'That's all right,' Polly said. 'I've had it surveyed. The house is in good order.'

'Who are your solicitors, madam?' the young man asked a little dubiously.

'Can you recommend a local firm?'

The estate agent was happy to oblige.

When all this had been attended to Polly wended her way to Marbonne Road. The trees on the Common were autumnal; the mild weather lingered with lovely russets and golds. She looked at the For Sale sign and wondered how long it would take them to remove it. The gate squeaked a little as she opened it. There was a short bark and a suspicious Herbie came trotting around the side of the house. He wagged his tail joyfully when he saw her.

Polly rang the doorbell, but there was no response.

'Is your master at home?' Polly asked Herbie.

Herbie was not informative. Polly looked at the car parked in the driveway, and at the drawn curtains in an upstairs window, and wondered if Keith were ill. Her heart, which had been so buoyant and hopeful, began to sink. It would be too much to expect, after all, for this happiness to last. Various vistas suddenly presented themselves: Keith was ill and would die and she would be left once more beached upon the sands of life with the interminable clicking of a computer keyboard for company.

No, she thought with a savagery which surprised her, not that, not ever again! And if Keith was ill what he needed was help and not some hen-witted creature imagining vain things.

She went around to the back of the house and gave one or two discreet throat clearings to indicate her advent. But all was quiet. The patio was deserted; the lawn was striped elegance.

And then she saw him. He was asleep under the pergola and a copy of the *Financial Times* was on the ground beside him.

Polly crept up on him very softly and knelt beside him while he still slept. He was wearing a sweater; his head was sunk on his breast.

Is he dead or alive? was Polly's first alarmed thought. But she was quickly disabused of anything dramatic because he stirred and sighed.

So she stayed by him and read the paper. Herbie lay beside her. A lonely bee came along, hovered around and went away again.

Keith started, looked up, straightened. 'Good Lord,' he said. 'Where did you come from?'

Polly put out her hand for his. 'I dropped from the sky, of course!'

'This time,' he said, 'I won't let you disappear!'

'This time,' Polly said, 'you couldn't get rid of me even if you tried!'

Jason re-read the extraordinary missive with dismay. It was anonymous; the writing was unknown to him; but he knew perfectly well where it had come from.

'I want to kill you, wedge-fuck. I've got your soul in a chalice and I'm going to put it through deadly anguish.'

Oh God, he thought, why did I think I had problems when I had none?

# Chapter Nineteen

'Dear Dad,' the letter with the American stamp said, 'I wonder if you're losing it! How can you possibly be thinking of getting married to a woman whom you met through the newspaper. I'm coming home at once to sort this out! Stay single till I get there. Love, Sophie.

When the phone rang on Saturday morning Polly dragged herself into alertness. She had slept after lovemaking, a long sweet sleep, and had woken to find she didn't know where she was, imagining for a moment that she was back in her room at Ballyglen, where the curtains also were pale yellow with a white stripe. The light coming through these curtains had a strange quality of peace. She felt as though she was where she belonged, here in this double bed belonging to a man she had met for the first time some six months earlier. Here was love and welcoming and the sense that he knew who she was, recognised her, the real Polly. This recognition was power.

She heard the phone. It was beside her on the bedside table and bleeped into her ear. She jumped. Keith put a hairy arm across her, lifted the receiver. She heard the male voice emanating from the earpiece, caught the words 'house' and 'buyer' and 'deposit'.

'What?' he said. 'Oh, all right . . . if she's stumping up the asking price then I suppose that's that! You can notify Jonathan Wheatley.' His voice sounded flat and dispirited and he withdrew his arm and lay back staring at the ceiling.

'Someone just bought the bloody house!' he announced gloomily. 'Soon won't have a roof to offer you. Only the cottage, but it's miles away from London and as you're about to become

261

a Londoner we need a shelter in the great metropolis . . .'

'Ah well,' Polly said, 'life never shuts one door but it opens another!'

'You sound very confident.'

'One of the things you have taught me is confidence,' Polly said. 'The other things you have taught me are not fit for polite discussion!'

Keith laughed and bent to nuzzle her neck. 'I'd better behave,' he said. 'I want years and years of this.'

'What did he say her name was . . . the person who's bought the house?'

'Forgot to ask him!' Keith said in an uninterested voice. He stroked her bare arm and down her back.

'You've lovely skin! It's like satin . . .' After a while he added in a languorous and satiated tone, 'Isn't this the way to spend Saturday morning?'

Keith went downstairs a little later to let Herbie out and put the kettle on. He had ordered Polly to stay in bed, said that he would bring up some breakfast to help her keep up her strength. As soon as he had booked the table for tonight's dinner with Sophie – who was arriving from New York at five – he was coming back to bed and Polly was to stay there until she had permission to do otherwise.

'I thought you were supposed to have angina,' Polly said, laughing.

'I haven't got it that bad. Anyway, what a way to go!'

But a few minutes later Polly heard Keith call her. She went to the landing, put her head over the banister. He was in the hall and looked up at her lugubriously. He had something in his hand.

'What is it?' Polly asked, coming down.

'My poor darling, but you've lumbered yourself with a total idiot!' He put a pink Lotto ticket into her hands.

Polly stared at it in momentary incomprehension.

Keith said, 'Your lottery ticket! I've just found it!'

Polly looked down at the ticket. It was crisp, like new. 'Where did you find it!'

Keith pointed to the hall table. 'It was in the phone book in the drawer . . . I was looking for the number of Chez Patrice, the restaurant I'm taking you to this evening!'

'Oh.'

He drew Polly into the drawing room and said, 'Can you remember what the winning combination was?'

'No . . . I haven't got the numbers on me!'

'Phone the lottery people . . . there's a good girl.'

Polly took the pink slip of paper from his hand, reached for the phone. When she got through to the National Lottery in Dublin it took the person on the other end only a few moments to locate the winning numbers for that fateful Easter draw: 1, 14, 15, 21, 32 and 41. Polly wrote the numbers down and then compared her own ticket.

'I have four of those numbers,' she told the lottery representative.

'Congratulations,' the voice said drily. 'You won ten pounds! But I'm afraid it's too late to collect it now! The ticket is only valid for ninety days!'

Polly put the receiver down and began to laugh. She threw the Lotto ticket on to Keith's desk, sank into one of the French chairs and shook with mirth.

Keith looked at her in anxiety. 'Well?' he demanded. 'Would you shut up that noise for a moment and tell me . . .'

'Ten quid,' Polly howled. 'I think you should buy Mrs Dencher a box of chocolates! You owe her a good, old-fashioned apology!'

Keith joined her in laughing until Herbie got alarmed and started to whine.

The following month, two days before they were due to be married in a quiet ceremony in a register office, Polly returned from work to find a puzzled fiancé.

'Is something wrong?'

'I was in to see Jonathan Wheatley . . . my solicitor . . . to sign the contract for the sale of the house . . .'

Polly waited. She suspected what was coming next.

'Would you believe,' Keith continued, 'that the woman who has bought this house – and it's a cash sale – is called Pauline McCann!'

'Really,' Polly said. 'What an amazing coincidence!'

Keith regarded her uncertainly for a moment. 'Are you some

kind of witch, Pauline, or am I being bedevilled by strange and inexplicable synchronicities?'

'I'm a witch,' Polly said with a laugh. 'I thought you would have found that out by now!'

'Someone with the same name as you has bought this bloody house!' Keith repeated.

Polly merely raised an eyebrow. 'You've just said that!'

Keith turned her face up to him. 'Don't play games with me. What's going on?'

Polly sat down and looked into her garden. She could see Sophie's fair head bent over Jocasta whom she was tickling under Herbie's supervision. She thought of Sable and Muriel. For a moment she felt she would burst into tears. Muriel and her pale face and the knowledge of her loneliness and of the trapped and warring factions of her life invaded her. For a moment she tasted fear.

Up to this point this episode of her own life had been a Cinderella story. Part of her had not believed, had been waiting for the coach to revert to a pumpkin, for the footmen to become mice once more.

But this wonderful man, whom she was due to marry in two days, had just gone and signed a legal contract to sell this house to her. The dream was impinging on binding, lasting, reality. Providence, for its own reasons, had poured gifts into her lap, for which someone else had paid.

She looked up at Keith who was watching her almost sternly.

'Pour me a drink, darling, and listen very carefully!' she said. 'I should have told you before, but it would almost certainly have got in the way . . .'

Polly had written to tell Rory that she was getting married. The letter came at the same time as one from his solicitor and, more importantly, an enhanced VL-IDE 4HD computer board from Bull Electronics. He was delighted with the latter, which he had been eagerly awaiting for some time; he read his solicitor's letter, but he forgot to open Polly's missive. It slipped down behind his computer and there it rested.

But when Polly did not come home for two weeks in a row Rory began to get restless. He thought of phoning her place of work in London, but decided against it on the basis that it would give the impression that he couldn't look after himself.

But he said to Susie one day, when she came in to find Fergus: 'I haven't seen Poll for a while; she didn't come home last weekend! When the boys were over in London four weeks ago she told them she'd be writing . . .'

'Well,' Susie agreed. 'She'll probably turn up next weekend, fill the deep freeze and so on . . . look after you . . .'

Rory relaxed. 'She's been in touch with you, has she? She hardly ever phones home, you know!'

Susie looked at him and said acerbically, 'Well, she's quite busy at present, you know. Between getting married last week, and the new job, she's got other fish to fry!'

Rory nodded, clicked a few keys and then the import of what Sue had said suddenly struck him.

He turned and stared at her. 'What do you mean – she got married last week! What kind of joke is that?'

Susie looked at Rory and lifted her shoulders. 'I thought you knew – surely she told you! She must have told the boys! She told me that she had written to you but had received no reply. When she tried to phone you the answer phone was on!'

Rory searched her face for disingenuousness, but all he found there was pity.

'She can't get married. She's married already – to me!'

Susie raised her hands.

'I know we weren't legally married,' Rory interjected. 'As though that mattered! Well, let me tell you something, Susie – there's more to life than legalities. Poll and I have been together for twenty-odd years; that has to count for something!'

'It counted for a lot,' Sue said drily. 'So much so that she was becoming ill . . . I'm sorry, Rory; but if it's any consolation she will pop back to keep an eye on things . . .'

Rory was very pale.

'She needn't think she can darken this door again!'

'Suit yourself,' Susie said. She looked at Fergus. 'Your supper is ready,' she announced, 'if you can tear yourself away.'

Fergus rather nervously said that he'd be home in a jiffy.

When Rory was alone he remembered that the boys had been a bit strange in themselves since they came back from their visit to London, like people who walked on eggshells.

Then he also remembered that he had received a letter with an English stamp about the same time as he had received the latest computer board, so he searched for it and after blistering the atmosphere with various expletives finally found it wedged between the computer and the wall. He tore it open and read:

Dear Rory,

I did mention in passing that I had met a new friend in London, but I'm not sure if you were really listening. For many years I have waited for you to notice the fact that I exist, but you did not. For a long time I thought this was a reflection on me; I thought there was something fundamentally wrong with me. I do not believe this any more. I think you were blinded by assumptions which were destructive of us both.

The fact is, Rory, that I have met someone else. His name is Keith; he is quite wonderful. He lives in London. He's a psychiatrist, a widower. He makes me feel stupefyingly alive. I love him much more than I ever loved anyone, even you. That is saying a great deal, because I adored you for a long time. Your originality bewitched me; your sharp perspectives on the world enthralled me; but your essential absence over every day I have lived with you has driven me away.

There is no point pretending I am sorry. I regret our marriage didn't work, because I invested so much in it. But I do not regret where I am now.

Keith and I will be married on Saturday week. I will come back from time to time to keep an eye on things until you become acclimatised to the change. Please don't worry about money. I will square everything with Martha, buy her interest in the house and give it to you. But I suspect that she would not be averse to looking in on you from time to time. She is your lawful wife after all, and if you have any sense you will invite her to dinner. Who knows what may come of that! And if you still care for her, which I think you do because we never really stop loving the people we have loved, you could re-make your life.

I have already told the boys about what is happening, and if you want to talk to them you will find them well

266

informed. When they came to London they got on well with Keith. I have their blessing, something for which I am extremely grateful.

Anyway, I hope everything works out for you. I hope that all the work and time you put into computers repays your efforts. I mean that! The things that fascinate us should have the decency to reward us for faithfulness.

Good luck, God bless. See you in six weeks, unless I hear from you to the contrary.

Polly.

For a while Rory thought that the world had come to an end. But then he remembered that Polly always stood by her word and that she would doubtless honour her promise to bail him out of the Martha mess and he decided he'd better not overreact. 'I mean, it's not as though we were teenagers,' he said aloud. 'One has to be adult about these things.'

He thought of himself and Polly on their wedding day and sighed and became quite sentimental and, for a moment, looked as though he might shed a few tears. But then he looked at his computer and remembered that he was in the middle of compressing a CD Rom on to a hard drive and was having trouble zipping the drive, and when Jason and Peter came home they found him immersed.

'Your mother's got herself married,' he announced to his sons in an aggrieved, dramatic tone when they told him to come to the kitchen while the hamburgers were still hot. 'The carry-on of the two of you drove her out of the house!'

Peter and Jason looked at each other with patent relief.

'We know she got married. She told us her plans when we were in London. We were waiting for *you* to mention it!'

'A nice how-do-you-do!' Rory said.

'Well, Dad, we may as well be civilised about the thing! She'll come back to visit and we'll be going over to see her and Keith after Christmas.'

'Will you indeed! Why does no one around here tell me what's going on?' Rory demanded in a truculent tone. 'Why do I have to find out that my own wife has got married after the event?'

'Oh Dad . . .' Peter said, but whatever he was about to add

died on his lips and he just looked at his brother and raised his eyebrows.

When Martha phoned later that evening Rory answered. She wanted to know if he was interested in settling the case; she didn't want to go the whole hog with it, not if they could come to some arrangement. There was no point in making lawyers any richer than they already were.

'Why don't we meet to discuss it?' Rory said. He remembered with sudden mouth-watering recollection the delicious stir-fries she used to dish up in the old days, lovely strips of sirloin, with onion, garlic, black bean sauce, a pinch of ginger and coriander. 'You could come around here, if you like,' he added. 'Polly's in England.'

'I know,' Martha said in a very even voice. 'She sent me a card to say she'd got married. I'll drop around later . . . Have you eaten, by the way? I could make us a little supper if you would like!'

Sophie had gone back to New York. 'He should have told me you were so nice!' she said reasonably before she left. 'I was afraid he had met someone awful . . . Are you going to have babies?'

'I don't think so,' Polly said. 'I've already been down that road. Are you going to marry Bob?'

'I might. I've got to really like him in the last week.'

'But you haven't seen him in the past week!'

Sophie shrugged. 'Well, you know how it is . . . when they're not there they're so wonderful!'

That evening as she sat on the hearthrug in his arms, staring at the fire, Keith suddenly said, 'Darling, did you get your letter? The one in the HMS envelope?'

Polly looked at him, ran her hands along his six o'clock shadow and smiled.

'I did . . .' Keith waited. 'I've been wondering how to tell you that you've married into a very dubious family,' Polly continued. 'You see, I have this brother, Tom, whom you know about . . .'

'The bloke with the flat whom you haven't seen for years?'

'The same. I'm afraid he's got himself adopted by the Crown

. . . I don't know if there's a delicate way of telling you . . .'

Keith looked at her, took a deep breath. 'What are you trying to say, Pauline McCann . . . that he's a serial killer who's got himself a jail sentence?'

'Oh no . . . He's not a serial killer. But he is in jail – I've just got confirmation.'

Keith thought of the folder which he had stuffed back beneath the sofa in Eaton Square, of the contents thereof.

'Well, well . . . what a surprise!'

He sat bolt upright and looked at Polly sternly. 'Are there any more surprises, any other skeletons in your particular closet?'

'I swear to God,' Polly said, 'that you are now, finally, truthfully, in full possession of all the facts! But I will have to visit a certain prison to see an old ghost.'

# Epilogue

In December Polly came back to Ashgrove Lawns for the last time. Everything was the same; the village had its usual coterie of evening life, well swathed against the cold; there were Christmas lights in Kinlan's window; a yellow radiance spilled from the church. The cul-de-sac was unchanged. But the atmosphere had altered. Willow House was in utter darkness; Muriel had always left a light on when she was out, but now the house loomed like a great hulk against the night sky. It had been sold to a developer and Polly knew it would be converted into luxury flats; the work was due to commence in the New Year.

She paid off the taxi, deliberately walked by Susie's house, although she knew it had been sold and that she and Fergus had moved away to a period house in Dun Laoghaire, near the office of the new company he had formed with Rory. There was a light on in the sitting room and a little girl, a stranger, could be seen watching television. Polly thought of Sharon, of the Debs dance which she had heard all about. Sharon and Peter had, apparently, kept in touch. 'I phone her sometimes, Mum, ask her out for a pint! She's now part of my harem!'

'Your harem? What a piece of old fantasy!'

'A man's entitled to his fantasies, Mum . . .'

'She doesn't drink pints, does she?'

'Well, she sometimes goes mad and has a shandy!' All of this had been retailed over the phone.

'Well, is there any other news? How's your father?'

'Oh he's . . . fine . . .'

Polly detected a hesitancy in her son's voice. 'Are you sure?

271

Is there something you're keeping from me?'

'He's fine, Mum, honestly!'

No 14 was in semi-darkness. There was a light burning in the hall. She stood at the gate for a moment, then walked slowly up the path and let herself in with her key, before remembering that they were not expecting her, and that she should really have rung the bell.

It struck her when she entered that the house already felt foreign, like someone else's home, as though it knew there had been a shift in allegiance and was putting up a kind of subliminal force-field to repel the intruder.

The hall struck her as smaller. There was a new vase on the table. Two ornamental Chinese porcelain plates, which she had never seen before, adorned the wall. The kitchen door was shut, but she heard the murmur of voices behind it, and assumed that Rory was there with the boys.

For a moment she felt like a ghost who had returned to the place where she had lived and who looks in for a moment on the life to which she had once belonged, but can no longer access. She knocked on the kitchen door, opened it.

Rory was sitting at one end of the table, peeling cooking apples. The scene was cosily domestic, but something in the way Rory wielded the knife indicated a lack of dedication to the task in hand.

Beside him a woman was sitting, engaged in slicing the newly peeled fruit. Her back was to the door and her head was bent; it was only when she moved and turned her head that Polly recognised Martha. So that was why Peter had been so hesitant on the phone! Martha had evidently come back to dwell in Ashgrove Lawns!

The radio was on. Mike Murphy was introducing the Arts Show.

Martha jumped in the chair. 'Christ!' she said. 'You gave me an awful fright!'

Rory looked at Polly with the expression of a prisoner who might be offered bail. 'Poll!' he echoed. But his face was uncertain, had the look of someone at a loss, someone in the throes of awakened sentiment, full of private reproach.

'I thought I heard the door!' Martha said when she had recovered. 'You have a nerve walking in just like that! I'm sitting here with my husband and another woman just walks in the door!'

'Sorry . . . It was reflex I'm afraid. Old habits and so forth . . .' Polly put the Yale key on the table. 'I didn't know you were here, Martha, and it won't happen again.'

She looked around the warm kitchen, saw how fresh everything was, how there were new curtains. For a moment she could not trust herself to speak. Here it was before her eyes, this place where she had invested so much of her will and hope, the place where she had swum with every ounce of her strength against the tide of whatever could be called her destiny. There was so much of herself in every tile, in every grain of the wood, in the sheen of the copper frying pan she had once been proud of, in the china coffee mugs she had bought in Clery's at their winter sale. For a moment there was panic that she could no longer belong to this world she had known so well.

But almost simultaneously came the sense of claustrophobia, the oppression of being in the wrong place, with the wrong person, the joyful knowledge of Keith waiting for her in Wimbledon with Herbie, the confidence of knowing that on Monday morning she would be back in the job she adored with the new people and the new world she had dared to find for herself.

'Where are the boys?'

Rory answered. 'Out . . . Peter is in the college library swotting. The first part of his finals are in January. And Jason is staying with a friend tonight. They're working on some school project.'

'Well, I won't intrude . . . I should have phoned to say I'd drop by. I'm staying in the Westbury . . . so maybe the boys would call me there tomorrow.'

There was silence. Rory was looking at the peel falling away from the apple, as though it held the answer to some eternal dilemma.

Martha got up and reached for the kettle. 'For God's sake, woman, sit down and have a cup of tea. We're not in that much of a hurry to get rid of you. We want to hear all about your exploits. You're famous in these parts as a species of delinquent!'

She moved with the sinuous purpose of a cobra, found the biscuit tin where Polly had kept whatever cakes and other goodies she had once baked in this kitchen. 'Father Brennan was around the other evening,' Martha went on, with a harsh laugh. 'He's completely scandalised, but he's going to pray for you! He's going to pray for me too, because I'm not canonically married to what he regards as your husband and therefore I'm living in sin! So we're both fallen women, you for deserting the man you weren't married to, me for returning to live with my legal husband from whom the Church divorced me! I suppose that makes Rory a fallen man as well . . . although I suspect that falling was really intended for the female of the species.'

She glanced at Rory and added drily: 'Women fall; men have the occasional little mishap. . .'

Rory grinned uncomfortably.

Polly turned to Rory. 'The trick is to get another canonical annulment – this time for *our* marriage – and then you and Martha can re-marry in Church! That should keep everyone happy!'

'It's too complicated,' Martha opined. 'You'd need a computer!'

'Speaking of computers,' Polly asked, 'how is the business going?'

'Grand,' Rory replied. 'Ferg and I are doing well. We're importing from Taiwan at a fraction of the European cost, and assembling our own. Ferg is in his element designing software . . . And I've been able to make some strides on my book . . .'

'Good.'

'We'll soon be able to buy your shares in the company,' Martha interjected.

'You can have them as a Christmas present,' Polly said. 'My going-away present, if you like . . . I meant to say it . . . but I've already instructed my solicitors.'

'Well, thank you!' Martha said. 'Of course you can afford it. But I'll have to watch Rory or he'll spend every moment at the office.'

She leaned fondly towards him, the dominant domestic goddess addressing her acolyte. 'Wouldn't you, love?'

She patted his hand. 'He used to have a computer in the dining room – of course you know that, Polly – but I made him get rid of it. No computing at home and no smoking indoors. Those are the rules!' She smiled at her own reasonableness. Rory picked up another apple and avoided Polly's eyes.

Oh Rory, she thought, how the wheel doth come full circle! Oh Rory, take heart. You can always put an ad in the paper!

She turned to Martha.

'I see no sign of Cat,' she said, indicating the empty basket by the bookshelf.

'You mean the dirty old tabby?' Martha said. 'I was going to have her put down – she was always getting sick! But she disappeared . . . must have heard me thinking!' She laughed. 'Now there's a little black cat which calls around. She's moved in, after a fashion. She used to belong to that woman across the road . . . the one who died.'

'How is Jason getting on?' Polly asked after a moment, in which she had privately congratulated Cat. 'He tells me he's working well.'

Martha nodded her head to emphasise the point. 'I told him, of course, that he either shaped up or shipped out! He got seventy-five per cent in his last French test, and is amazed at what happens when one does a bit of work! Oh, and we also had a bit of excitement recently; a bolshie little ten-ton tart came around looking for him, but I soon took care of her!'

Martha compressed her mouth and looked grim. Polly thought of Veronica, the camp commandant, and suppressed a smile. Veronica had met her match.

'How did you "take care of her"?'

'Well, she arrived at the door, wouldn't take no for an answer, raising her voice and demanding to see Jason. He was lurking upstairs and wouldn't come down. Rory was trying to be nice to her and getting nowhere . . . so I went out the back, broke a good strong stick from one of the trees. I brought it in and told her to clear off before I used it on her!' She added, raising an eyebrow, 'She seemed to understand that!'

Rory winced.

Ah Rory, I leave you in capable hands, Polly thought; your battles will be fought and your castle defended.

'Both boys, of course, are looking forward to spending Christmas in London . . .'

'Keith and I are looking forward to having them!'

Polly watched Martha, trying to assess to what extent she resented her return to Ashgrove Lawns being encumbered by someone else's adolescents. But she saw that despite her formidable air, she was pragmatic to the last, and would put up with short-term drawbacks in order to regain the long-term benefits of her husband and her house. She was not interested in personalities, either of Rory or his children. She was rooted in bread and butter issues; she was a survivor.

It was Rory who needed sympathy now. She saw how subdued he was; saw that his life was mapped for him now whether he knew it or not.

'Can I give you a lift, Poll?' he asked politely when she stood up to leave.

'No thanks, Rory. I'll get a taxi in the village. I want to walk around the cul-de-sac . . . say goodbye.' She smiled at him, seeking forgiveness. He did not smile back.

'It must be so nice for you to be wealthy . . .' Martha said a little sourly, as though the thought was corroding her and she had to vent it.

'It was a complete surprise. Anyway, who told you?'

'Oh, everyone knows about that!' Martha said. 'I was talking to Laura Flanagan the other day and she knew all about it . . . said it was indicative of a weak character for a woman to desert her family just because she had come into a fortune.' She glanced at Rory: 'Still, Rory and I are glad for you, and glad for us. Aren't we, Rory?'

Rory gave a feeble smile.

The door closing behind her she found strangely shocking. The lights were on in all the houses, the curtains drawn. She felt alien, shut out from the old world, like a child who had come back to her haunts, but finds she is grown and excluded. She crossed the road and walked by the wall of Willow House. The ivy was mantling it and brushed against her shoulder; she put a hand out to touch it; she could smell its pungency. She stood by the tall gates and looked in. The house seemed to watch her without being itself seen; for a moment Polly imagined a lonely face inside, looking from her window on to the cul-de-sac, on to the narrow parameters of her contracted world.

Everything was silent. A distant car swished by on the main estate road, but nothing broke the calm of Ashgrove Lawns, or the stillness of the old house in its abandoned garden. The shadows were deeper inside the walls and, looking through the gates, Polly could just make out the untidy flower beds.

'Is anyone there?' she whispered into the darkness, beset by a mélange of emotion and memory and vaguely remembering a poem called 'The Listener' which she had once learnt at school, about someone returning to an abandoned house. 'Do you ever keep watch from the window now, Muriel . . . ?' she continued. 'Or have you much better things to do? Do you have any idea what you have given me? I don't just mean the money . . .'

She paused, smiled at the image of herself standing alone on the footpath, talking to a ghost. 'And as far as that is concerned – Sue and I are giving most of it to cancer research. We have kept enough to make us free . . . which, I think, was what you wished . . .'

Something moved just inside the gate, making Polly jump. A mewing came from the gravel forecourt and a tabby cat, invisible until the lights of the cul-de-sac fell on her, manoeuvred herself through the bars of the gate and rubbed against Polly's legs. Polly picked up the warm creature, stroked her nose and scratched beneath her chin.

'How are you, Cat?' she said. 'It's very nice to see you again! Felicitations on escaping the chop!'

She looked once more at Willow House and at No 14 Ashgrove Lawns. Then she put Cat down, wrapped her scarf tighter against the cold, and walked away.